Prai...                                    ...*hts*

D0005507

"With her motley cast, Mendelson paints an accurate, often comical portrait of the Upper West Side."          —*The New York Times Book Review*

"An easy-to-read, tightly woven and touching piece of fiction."
                                        —*The Roanoke Times*

"Funny and wry . . . deeply satisfying."          —*Detroit Free Press*

"Ms. Mendelson's elegiac social commentary brings the neighborhood
and its residents to life."              —*The Dallas Morning News*

"This debut novel feels like a PBS melodrama from Britain: credibly pop-
ulated, determinedly middle-class and finely observed. But if its structure
and setting seem faintly retro, its sensibility is modern. Mendelson explores the intertwined family of second-tier classical musicians Charles
and Ann Braithwaite and their friends, academicians Merrit Roth and
Morris Malcolm and malapropism-prone psychotherapist Lily Freund.
The tale gains power through finely accreted detail. . . . This is a master-
ful novel."                              —Fort Worth *Star-Telegram*

"Readers will find it hard to resist Mendelson's radiant optimism, for she
creates a world in which people naturally find and follow the arc of their
true talents, lovers' defenses miraculously melt away, and decency and
compassion are richly rewarded. This is one seductive novel." —*Booklist*

"[A] marvelous, richly detailed, and engrossing first novel . . . Readers will
grow quite fond of Mendelson's full fleshed characters, so human in their
frailties and foibles; and even those unfamiliar with New York will prize
the unique neighborhood that is Morningside Heights. Highly recommended."                                 —*Library Journal*

"Thoroughly likable debut fiction."          —*Kirkus Reviews*

# MORNINGSIDE

## HEIGHTS

# MORNINGSIDE

# HEIGHTS

A NOVEL

Cheryl Mendelson

RANDOM HOUSE TRADE PAPERBACKS
New York

2005 Random House Trade Paperback Edition

Published in the United States by Random House Trade Paperbacks,
an imprint of The Random House Publishing Group,
a division of Random House, Inc., New York.

RANDOM HOUSE TRADE PAPERBACKS and colophon are trademarks
of Random House, Inc.

Originally published in hardcover in the United States by Random House,
an imprint of The Random House Publishing Group,
a division of Random House, Inc., in 2003.

Library of Congress Cataloging-in-Publication Data
Mendelson, Cheryl.
Morningside Heights : a novel / Cheryl Mendelson.
p. cm.
ISBN 0-375-76068-7
1. Morningside Heights (New York, N.Y.)—Fiction. 2. Social change—Fiction.
3. Intellectuals—Fiction. 4. Musicians—Fiction. I. Title.
PS3613.E48 M67 2003
813'.6—dc21
2002031760

Printed in the United States of America

www.readerscircle.com

246897531

*For James*

# PART

I

# 1

THIS NEIGHBORHOOD WAS always middle-class and urban. The advent of the subway at the start of the twentieth century transformed the countryside so rapidly that less than a decade after the stations opened, the fields were gone and the massive, sedate apartment buildings that you see today already lined the streets. They were grand places, designed to persuade prosperous New York families that their bourgeois dignities could be preserved as well in an apartment as in a brownstone row house with a stoop. The building at 635 West 117th Street was similar to scores of others built around the same time, and, like them, it filled with tenants as soon as it was completed, in 1906. It had twelve stories, with four ample apartments per floor, each divided into a living and dining room, several bedrooms, two bathrooms, all large and airy, plus a small library, and, behind the kitchen, a miniature bedroom and bathroom for the live-in maid. During the Depression, the landlords carved most of the apartments into two or three, creating the ten to twelve on a floor that you find now. The cut-up layouts made no architectural sense, but in those hard times the new tenants could not afford to be choosy. Only a few apartments in the building retain the original floor plan, with the cramped kitchen and tiny sleeping nook where a lonely girl spent her days and nights in service to the family living in comfort in the other rooms.

In the waning years of the twentieth century, prosperity returned to the neighborhood, if not to the cash-strapped middle-class and poor people who had lived there for many decades. Lobbies were spiffed up, exteriors scrubbed down. One rental building after another transformed itself into an ownership cooperative—"went co-op" in New York City parlance; and rents and prices began climbing out of reach. The elderly residents who had come during the Depression and World War Two barely managed to hang on to the dilapidated studios and one-bedrooms where they had hoped to live out the few years they had left. Except for the lucky ones who were protected by municipal rent-control laws, everyone, old and young, scrambled to meet the higher monthly payments, and when they failed and were forced to move, their apartments were immediately sold or rented for astonishing profits to high-paid business people and professionals. These mobile newcomers formed a growing group of the well-off: working single renters and couples investing in "starter homes" they planned to sell for a profit in order to finance bigger and better ones someplace else—moneyed transients who stayed only two or three years and disappeared, leaving behind not so much as a forwarding address and creating a stock of near-temporary housing that served them much as boardinghouses and residence hotels had served their impoverished counterparts a hundred years earlier. The residential buildings became home to ever more numerous strangers, people who worked long hours, dressed and dined out expensively, and whose names, faces, and circumstances no one knew, except, perhaps, the night doorman. They didn't say "good morning" or "good night" or hold the elevator for a straggler.

One day in April, apartment 9D came vacant for the first time since the building went up, when the last of its old-time residents died at the age of 103. Elizabeth Miller was the daughter of the original tenants, well-to-do people who had moved in when she was a child. Her father had owned a thriving lithography and printing business. Her mother, who had been left comfortable when he died, later received another substantial inheritance from her aunts. There were stories about Miss Miller: that she had run away to be something in show business—an actress or a dancer—or that her proper parents had thrown her out for leading a scandalous life. It was certain, in any event, that Miss Miller had lived elsewhere for a number of years before returning to care for her elderly widowed mother just after World War II. When her mother died in the late 1950s, Miss Miller inherited enough to support herself, and stayed on in her childhood home, living what seemed, to anyone who bothered to notice, a long, uneventful life in good health.

So gentle was her decline that even when she passed the century mark, no one thought her death was imminent. The only sign of her diminishing vitality in those last years was her difficulty in breathing. There were days when she could say no more than a word or two without pausing to take in air. Then she could do nothing but sit, and her home attendants would take her in a wheelchair down to the lobby or out for a bit of sun, moving her gently, because she might be left gasping by a sudden derangement of her position, or even a high wind. Yet she did not seem to suffer much, from this or anything else. She had a good appetite, smiled graciously at her neighbors, and attempted jokes with the children across the hall. Finally, one of the attendants said, she simply fell asleep at her normal time and never awoke. She had never married, had no children, no surviving relatives or friends, except, perhaps, her trustee, the son of a friend who had died years ago. It was he who paid her bills and hired the quartet of women who had stayed with her day and night on a complicated schedule of shifts.

These facts were familiar to many of her neighbors, who for months after her death missed the sight of her tiny figure, crowned with frizzy white curls, wrapped snugly in blankets, on the sidewalk at the front of the building, or being wheeled through the lobby, or riding in the elevator. But none knew her well enough to feel obliged to attend a funeral. The night attendant, who had been on duty when Miss Miller died, and the morning attendant, who had discovered her death, were shaken, however. After the urban death ritual of summoning ambulance and police, they had gone together to see the trustee, for reasons clear neither to them nor to him. He didn't want them in his office and quickly bundled them out with their final pay and their final instructions. The next morning, the two women returned to 9D and began cleaning and closing the apartment as he had directed. They gathered several bags of Miss Miller's things for thrift stores and threw out a great deal more. Then a truck arrived and carried off silver, china, rugs, paintings, furniture. Finally, they swept and scrubbed, and, before the week was out, they shut the door and left the apartment for good.

Anne Braithwaite, Miss Miller's longtime neighbor, who knew her well enough to call her Lizzie, observed this rapid disassembling of a century of life with uncomfortably mixed feelings. The Braithwaite family, in 9E, directly across the hall from Miss Miller, had been startled by urgent peals of their doorbell early on the morning that Miss Miller died. Charles was out of town, but Anne was at home with their three children, when Claire, the young morning attendant, came to the door, distraught, to say she couldn't rouse the old woman. Anne went to the bedside and saw for herself that Lizzie was dead. She called an ambulance, and told Claire what to do and say when the police came.

For a day or two, Anne suffered from the painful doublethinking that death induces, both believing in Lizzie's death and yet looking for her in the elevator or in the lobby. They had not been close, but she had been used to seeing her, with one or another of her attendants, several times a day for more than fifteen years. They had always said a few words, in exchanges that lasted a minute or two, or occasionally as many as five or ten, and Anne had been in Lizzie's apartment once or twice. These encounters were in the true New York style, full of goodwill that entailed no intimacy and promised no friendship. Nonetheless, they learned a good deal about one another over the years, as New York neighbors do, despite their standoffishness—enough, in fact, that even in the last couple of years, when Lizzie talked so little, Anne could manage a passable conversation with her, carrying the weight of chatter and filling in the blanks left by her sparse words and gestures. Yet almost before the tiny body had grown cold, Anne also found herself wondering guiltily whether the old lady's apartment would be put up for rent. It was not on her own account that she was interested but for the sake of a friend, who, she had learned only the night before Lizzie's death, had arranged to spend two years in New York—in fact right in the neighborhood, at Columbia University—and would need a place to live.

Later that week, Anne, returning home from a visit to a doctor with news that had crowded out any thoughts of Lizzie, saw the two attendants handing in their keys to the doorman on their way out of the building. After offering condolences, she got up courage enough to wonder aloud what would happen to the apartment.

"The trustee will try to sublet, I think," said the older one, Monique, a dignified Jamaican, who had been with Lizzie for many years. Now that her employment had ended, she felt a need to air her grievances. "Miss Miller wouldn't buy it when they were pushing her to. So now the building will want to sell it at last, but he'll hold on to it as long as he can, to make money charging ten times Miss Miller's rent. He's a cheap man. He grudged every mouthful that old lady ate, and she ate like a bird. He says not to burn so many lights, but that old lady she can't see. And he says no money for a new coat. He's so stingy so he can put the money in his own pocket."

"She was always trying to give us presents, and he kept warning us not to take anything," said Claire, who looked uneasy, "but I bet he took plenty." Still shaken by her first encounter with death, Anne thought. She had protective, maternal feelings toward Claire, who had been barely eighteen when the trustee hired her several years ago—deceived by her matronly air and figure, no doubt, into thinking her older. Anne knew her real age, just as she knew that money had been tight for Lizzie. These were the sort of domestic details about the household that she had gleaned in the years of hallway chats. The complaints about the trustee were new to her. She did not dismiss them, having confidence in both women after years of watching them care for Lizzie, but their suspicions amplified her queasy guilt about her own motives.

Monique and Claire looked pained and troubled after confiding these disturbing thoughts, and lingered aimlessly in the lobby. Anne saw that they disliked their roles as decent bystanders, awkwardly and unfeelingly ministering the intimate after-rites of death for this unmourned soul. Feeling officious yet unable to stop, she found herself offering them the speech proper to the occasion, which no one else seemed to be available to make. They had been good to Lizzie; Lizzie knew it; and Lizzie had died happy because, as she had told Anne a couple of years ago, "I just want to stay in my own apartment and keep my girls. That's all I want." They were kind and diligent even though, as Lizzie had declined and grown more and more silent, there was never anyone to thank them for all the little extra things they did, cooking up dishes she liked and taking her to see her favorite flowers on a spring day. But people here knew all this, Anne assured them, while wondering if anyone did but herself.

Now, Anne having said what a son or daughter should have said, they could behave the way they felt they should, and they replied with self-respecting modesty. Oh, she was no trouble, such a nice lady—to which Anne countered, graciously, that Lizzie's time was up and that we should all hope to be lucky enough to die painlessly in our sleep at 103. They nodded in vigorous agreement. Yes, yes, she had had a long life, not much trouble, no real want, and no suffering in her death.

And after a few more moments of good-hearted banalities, some tears, hands grasped, phone numbers scribbled on paper scraps, the two women went away, with sad but more peaceful faces. The doorman, Willie, who was putting the keys in an envelope and labeling it 9D—EUGENE BECKER, had listened carefully to the whole exchange.

"They were good to the old lady," he said, suppressed thoughts and emotions erupting in ephemeral twitches around his lips and eyes. "Lots of old people in this building have problems. But those ladies made a nice life for Miss Miller."

Charles Braithwaite got home from his out-of-town trip soon after this and heard the story of Lizzie, first the children's excited version and then Anne's, in which he quickly detected Anne's idea of getting Lizzie's apartment for his old friend Morris, a not entirely satisfactory plan from his point of view, although he could not bring himself to oppose it. And just as quickly he scented that Anne had a worrying secret that she could not tell in the presence of the children. As it happened, it was hours later before she found a chance to tell him in a questioning, apologetic voice that she was pregnant. And, as they were neither young nor rich and had three children already, this news was nearly as unwelcome as it was unexpected.

The Braithwaite family were among the middling people of the neighborhood. Middle-aged and middle-income, they had rented a portion of one of the original large apartments many years before, bought it when the building went co-op, and lived there for their entire married life. Over the years, as their three children came along, they began to feel squeezed in every way. Space and money got tighter and tighter until, now, they regularly exceeded their income by an alarming amount, falling deeper into debt each year. The children were still young. Besides Stuart, a three-year-old boy, who slept in the living room, there were Jane, almost thirteen, and Ellen, seven, who shared a bedroom. Anne believed that each child needed plenty of time as the youngest before the next one was born, and managed to produce her babies at intervals of at least four years. Charles thought this schedule was the product of sheer strength of will, as neither caution nor the lack of it seemed to affect the timing of her pregnancies.

Charles was a singer, a solidly second-rank baritone at the Met, who had accepted that he would never rise further. Still, he was well respected, with a modest international reputation, known for his versatility and scholarly knowledge and sought out by students as a master teacher; he had a broad operatic range and was also an accomplished recitalist and singer of art songs. What prevented his greater success was, in part, the lingering consequences of vocal inconsistencies that had plagued him at the start of his career. But friends who knew him well said that Charles's character had more to do with it. Unlike most people with courage enough to dare the uncertainties of a career in professional singing, Charles was modest, skilled at advancing his students' interests, but incapable of the ordinary tricks of self-promotion. The effects of this were amplified by stubbornness and by his inability to conceal his dislikes. For these reasons, he was incapable of navigating the star system and was fated forever to sing Leporello, never Don Giovanni. He didn't mind terribly, so long as the best students still begged him to take them on and he kept the respect of a small circle of admirers whose judgment he respected and so long as somewhere, if not at the Met, he found opportunities to sing what he wanted.

Charles's career had never brought in the kind of income needed to support a large family in the Braithwaites' habitual style. Nor could Anne, once regarded as a promising pianist, be relied on for more than occasional infusions of cash. As each of the children had come along, she had cut back on her practicing, performing, accompanying, and lesson-giving and now earned a small fraction of her income of ten or fifteen years ago — sometimes causing her husband to wonder, sullenly, why he alone in New York City, it seemed, was expected to support the luxury of a stay-at-home wife. She would go over the figures with him — the cost of baby-sitters, work clothes, transportation, housekeepers — and remind him of the strain that her working would impose on all of them. It was all more or less true, but he resented it, because he knew that the real reason she stayed home was that she wanted to. Yet he admitted to himself that he probably would not tolerate her going to work any better than she or the children would. All of them liked things as they were.

Not only did Anne fail as an earner, but because she thought nothing too good for her children and husband, she tended toward conscientious extravagance on their behalf. The children attended private schools and got carefully chosen outside lessons and classes. There were costly tickets, instruments, books, music, camps, and outings. Charles frequently consulted his throat doctor and his back doctor at Anne's urgent insistence — professional necessities that were usually uninsured. Anne liked to set a good table, and chose delicacies with no thought of their price, of which she was generally ignorant. She would have been horrified at the idea of planning menus around the cost of foods; the choice of whether to serve bean paste or Beluga caviar had nothing to do with money, only with questions of taste, variety, and nutrition. Their clothes were handed down, the furniture worn, the china chipped, and the paint on the walls peeling; Anne didn't care much about appearances. But their bodies and souls were nurtured with lavish indifference to cost, in accordance with Anne's assumption that this was their natural right. Once or twice each year they reached a crisis, when a tuition notice or bill arrived that couldn't be paid. Then there were scenes and oaths, and Charles would threaten to move them all to Cleveland, where he had once been offered a job. But these moments passed. The money, so far, had come from somewhere, and they had never changed their ways. Their friend Morris called them the Micawbers—but unlike that adaptable, wandering tribe, the Braithwaite family could not be imagined moving even from their present apartment, let alone quitting the neighborhood of Morningside Heights, where Anne was born and they had both lived for so many years. Their survival for more than two or three weeks in any environment outside Manhattan, their friends agreed, was inconceivable.

Charles and Anne argued for a while over the desirability of having Morris—a single man, like themselves on the threshold of middle age—living next door for as long as two years, the term of the grant that was bringing him to Columbia. Although Morris was his oldest and best friend, Charles, cautious and suspicious of domestic change, thought of many objections: the timing was wrong, as Morris would not arrive until the fall; the trustee, Becker, would charge more than Morris could pay; Morris—Morose, Jane called him—was too depressing to associate with, even if only in the elevator, on a daily basis; and so forth. But the discussion ended in a telephone call, and Morris was glad to let them contact Mr. Becker on his behalf. As for finding Becker, Mr. Morales, the superintendent, would be able to come up with a telephone number and address.

"Morris is a grouchy, gloomy, ugly old bachelor. No one will ever marry him," Jane pronounced, alluding to the news, imparted in the phone call, that his latest strange relationship (strange from the Braithwaite point of view) had ended more bitterly than usual.

"And you used to be so in love with him," said Anne, who still remembered a smiling, youthful Morris. "He'll get married." She had once had secret hopes of finding someone for him. She had given up matchmaking, but still believed that Morris would do fine if someone would only point him in the right direction.

"You don't know with Morris," said Charles.

"You'll see," Anne said, reading over a bit of Ellen's homework.

"You don't know, Mother," said Jane, with undertones of contempt. "Even if it actually happens someday, you don't know today at one in the afternoon whether it's going to."

Charles frowned at his daughter, who fled from the dining room table, where they were lingering after lunch. In a few moments they heard Chopin, mournful and violent, from the piano in the living room. Anne, stepping to the doorway, called to her over the sound, "No rubato in the sixth measure. *Why* do you insist on doing that?"

"Anne!" Charles objected.

"She's not going to make me handle her with kid gloves."

Stuart looked serious at this interchange and swiveled his head to examine Charles's expression. He had already overheard several tense, mystifying debates about managing Jane's new temper outbursts. This one, however, was cut short by the telephone's ringing. "That'll be your mother, Anne. Better tell her."

"Tell her what?" asked Ellen, who had detected an untold secret almost as quickly as her father had.

Anne's mother's laugh in hearing from Anne that she was "that way— you know, gestationally speaking" was audible across the room, and brought the first hint of a smile to Charles's face since he had heard the news.

# 2

MORNINGSIDE HEIGHTS WAS an enclave of respectable turn-of-the-century architecture, although little of it could be called distinguished. In a comfortable walk around its perimeters, a visitor could take in Grant's Tomb, Columbia University, one Jewish and one Christian theological seminary, a college of music, a hospital, a massive, brooding Episcopal cathedral, a skyscraper-Gothic church and a half-dozen ordinary ones, along with one tiny nunnery concealed in a pair of row houses—almost all of which went up in a thirty-year fever of institutional building that siphoned off some of the enormous supply of capital accumulated by New York businessmen and politicians in the late nineteenth century. These moguls, inspired by undeveloped acreage on a lofty plateau overlooking the Hudson River at the city's northern edge, aimed to create a modern Athens there, a center of scholarship, religion, music, and architectural marvels that would make New York City as much a world center of the mind and spirit as it was of commerce and finance.

The elevation on which Morningside Heights was built began its rise at 110th Street, on the southern edge of the neighborhood, and sloped sharply downward at 122nd Street, which formed its natural northern border. It was bounded on the east by the rocky cliffs of Morningside Park, a place of beauty so wild and threatening that a sense of ominous gloom hung over the venerable apartment houses on Morningside Drive, tucked between the institutional structures of the hospital, cathedral, and university. On the west of the neighborhood, bordering the Hudson, was Riverside Park, a long strip of pretty lawns and tree-covered hills along Riverside

Drive, the city's most gracious boulevard. Dignified apartment houses and a broad sidewalk promenade, with playgrounds and grassy plots deeply shaded by huge leafy American elms, ginkgoes, and maples, ran its entire length. Broadway, the spine of the neighborhood, divided the humbler buildings to the east from the taller, more pretentious buildings on the privileged riverside to the west.

This concentration of lofty institutions and natural beauties gave the neighborhood an improbably stable dual character. Morningside Heights did not simply decline from its middle- and upper-middle-class beginnings. Instead, it made room in its midst for poorer and rougher elements, preserving a civilized and grandiose aspect even while it became hard up for cash, marginal, and unfashionable, lacking even the student chic that grows up on the outskirts of large universities elsewhere. The privileged people from its colleges, churches, and seminaries mixed on Broadway with the poor residents of its single-room-occupancy hotels or, later, when the SROs had been forced out, with the lost souls invited by its soup lines and drug-treatment programs, and, always, with those who visited, uninvited, from Harlem and other tough areas to the east and north. Broadway never enjoyed the beauties and graces that had been planned for the avenue at the heart of the neighborhood. Instead, block after block, it had long been lined with dilapidated eateries, fly-by-night photo shops, understocked and dispirited drugstores, stationers', and bookstores, and a hundred other scruffy little businesses. Shabby and teeming, stinking of rotting garbage in the heat, Broadway was so littered in all seasons that when the wind blew, spilled trash rose off the sidewalks in funnel clouds.

The residents had uncomplainingly endured most of this. They wanted things to stay as they were and, until recently, had assumed that anything that attracted the moneyed and the upwardly mobile would surely be infected by the Broadway virus and die; but the new prosperity appeared to be resistant. Its changes were visible everywhere. Along Riverside Drive and in Riverside Park, the once menacingly half-empty sidewalks were crowded every morning with people strolling, jogging, walking dogs, and enjoying the fresher air blowing in off the Hudson and the spring buds, fall colors, or whatever the seasons offered. On Broadway, the drab, grungy student hangouts, local life-forms heretofore immune, suddenly succumbed. Grandma's, the College Inn, Salter's Books, Moon Palace, the Ta-Kome, the old Mill, the bad-tempered stationer with a half-dozen dusty college-ruled notebooks and a rack of stale candy bars—all were gone, replaced by trendy shops and bistros that were packed every evening. These developments created a general malaise and growing resentment among the less well-off. The old people were horrified by the prices in the new places. Two-fifty for a cup of coffee in the new café, an elderly socialist pointed out, was half the minimum hourly wage. Back in the sixties, local people had fought Columbia for trying to build a gymnasium in Morningside Park and for buying up half the neighborhood. But who was the enemy now? No one knew, exactly, whom they should go after this time.

Despite these worrisome trends, for the moment the neighborhood retained a core of middle-class residents who preserved what was in many respects a culture peculiar to the place. They didn't watch much TV, other than the news during national crises. Many of them played musical instruments or sang, alone or together in small groups, and were concert- and operagoers. They listened to CDs, records, and the radio, read books, and on Friday evenings and Saturday mornings spent an hour in the video rental store, consulting dog-eared copies of *Halliwell's Film Guide* while choosing a stack of films for the weekend with utmost care. They stretched their dollars, and were never ashamed of their worn-out clothes and furniture. Their threadbare Oriental carpets were tastefully arranged on bare wood floors in their two- or three-room high-ceilinged, ninety-year-old apartments, and their cracked and peeling walls were covered with books and cheap prints. They scouted out bargains, and, with their obsessive knowledge of their city, endlessly traded tips, in a competitive spirit, on where to find cheap sports coats, jeans, bookshelves, coffee, and wines. They yearned for comfort and stability but resisted worshiping the gods of wealth and practicing the arts of acquiring it. They wanted only enough money to pay for good food, the tolerable apartment, the books, CDs, tickets, and fare for an overseas trip or two each year, and felt it was outrageous that such reasonable and modest desires were becoming so expensive to satisfy.

Civic-minded, the residents of Morningside Heights cleaned up the playgrounds, attended neighborhood meetings, and signed petitions for local causes. In politics, they strained to understand the other's point of view and were contemptuous of people who were seduced or blinded by the rationalizations of power and interest. They strove for autonomy in judgment and in employment. A remarkable number were engaged in some kind of work that, they felt, connected them with the pursuit of beauty, truth, justice, virtue, even God, but they would have felt contempt for anyone who said so out loud. Thus the local population had always had a disproportionately large share of scholars, critics, musicians, scientists, editors, artists, poets, social workers, psychotherapists, librarians, theologians, would-be thespians, and all the artisans whose knowledge supported the arts and sciences. The doctors, lawyers, and business people who lived in Morningside Heights tended to be independent, idealistic members of their professions, or those with a strong interest in the arts or social welfare. The super-famous, the wealthy, and the powerful—with the exception of an eccentric or two with a mansion on Riverside Drive—lived elsewhere.

The natural consequence of so much idealistic striving was that many of the locals had large ambitions that were not met. In fact, such people, who were exquisitely sensitive to status and their own lack of it, comprised a group sizable enough that the neighborhood population of dented egos was noteworthy even in a city full of them. On the other hand, more typically, people in Morningside Heights were relieved of status concerns by their confidence that they lived in a social enclave that understood and valued their modest contributions to their chosen ideal. This enabled them to scorn wider fame and be contented with the recognition and honor of a group of fellow cognoscenti. Thus the neighborhood was inhabited, predominantly, by people so unaggressive, unpretentious, and civil that living here, in many respects, scarcely felt like living in New York City.

Although Morningside Heights had more than the normal share of the genuinely mad as well as the merely off-center and misshapen, it was not generally attractive to true bohemians, aging hippies, goths, punksters, or serious nonconformists. Nor was it home to many of the antisocial, with the exception of drunken frat boys from Columbia, who for generations had been prone to howl in the night. It had none of the hip sadness of Greenwich Village or the tight-lipped cool of Chelsea and Tribeca. Compared to other places, few in Morningside Heights succumbed to drugs or alcohol, and those few did so unobtrusively. Even the pair of addicts who some years ago had taken up residence in the deserted newspaper stand at 116th Street and Broadway were so quiet and considerate that they had managed to stay there for three or four years without inspiring complaints—in fact, until someone insisted on reopening the newsstand. This pair exemplified, as well, the stable nature of the average relationship in the neighborhood. It was not a comfortable place in which to split up, although, if it happened, your friends would cope, with artful diplomacy.

Only serious bad luck would let you discover that your former spouse had dinner with your neighbors or went out with someone's ex or with a graduate student in your best friend's department. A cad, of either sex, was shunned by those—about two thirds of the population—who knew one when they saw one, but the shunning was done so adroitly that its object rarely perceived it.

Charles and Anne Braithwaite had met at Juilliard, which by then had moved from Morningside Heights down to Lincoln Center. Except for a few years in their twenties, when they spent months at a time in Europe or on the West Coast, as a couple they had never lived anywhere else. They had the cloistered outlook typical of professional musicians, academicians, and poets. They were left-of-center liberals who never crossed a picket line, and were on the mailing list of every earnest, worthy cause. Neither knew how to drive a car. They walked whenever they could and otherwise relied on subways, buses, or, in a pinch, cabs or car services. They managed to visit Riverside Park almost every day. Like all true New Yorkers, they were masters of museum and zoo schedules and train and bus timetables. They lived much as their parents and grandparents had lived before them and as they hoped their children would after them. And they were doting parents.

They held once-progressive child-rearing ideas that were now adhered to only in a few social pockets, like Morningside Heights, that retained tribal memories of them. "Suddenly my ideas are conservative," Anne complained. "But they were radical enough for my socialist grandmother." She soothed herself to sleep with books about child psychology and development, and thought the present-day custom of sending small children to day care on a moral par with the nineteenth century's sending them to work in mines and textile mills. Elsewhere in Manhattan, who but the rich could afford to hand-rear children? But in Morningside Heights, rents were a little lower, idealism a little higher, apartments a little larger, and work schedules flexible enough to make Anne seem less of an oddity. Here the Braithwaites found other parents who understood parent-child triads and dyads, and—going one step further than their parents in psychological alertness—talked about pre-oedipal issues as knowingly as the older generation had talked about oedipal ones.

One morning in late April, a fortnight after Elizabeth Miller's death, Anne dropped Stuart at her mother's and Ellen at school and set out on a round of neighborhood errands. It was brilliant spring weather, and the enjoyment Anne regularly experienced strolling around Morningside

Heights was enhanced by the piquancy that the familiar and hopeful sensations of morning sickness endowed on ordinary things. As always, Anne's heightened mood in pregnancy made her impervious to money worries and, indeed, to any worries at all except those that might involve Charles. But as she felt sure this morning that by now he was reconciled to her pregnancy and would welcome the new child as he had the others, nothing interfered with her mild euphoria.

She picked up Charles's resoled shoes and petted the ancient dachshund chasing its ball in and out of the shop as fast as its tiny old legs could go. She bought freshly grated cheese at Mama Joy's, dried pasta at University Market, and a scarf for Ellen at Renell's. She saw one for Jane, too, but knew Jane would turn up her nose at anything Anne chose for her. At the Cathedral, she paused to let her good spirits merge with the soaring feelings aroused by the sight of its spires, and went in to visit the gift shop, where she failed to find the presents she needed for the next wave of children's birthday parties. She then walked to the Bank Street Children's Bookstore, where she succeeded. She considered hailing a taxi so that she would have time enough for a few errands on the East Side; but she feared being overcome with morning sickness if exposed to the lurching driving style and contortionist's seating of a New York yellow cab. So she walked to the bus stop at 112th Street, where, as she approached, she noticed a strikingly pretty girl, perhaps a student, standing there waiting. Anne observed with interest the wit of her clothes, and was discreetly cataloguing such details as the colors and clever buttoning of the tight knit top, when she was startled to perceive, close up, that the girl was Merrit Roth, a longtime friend her own age. The two gasped and hugged. Merrit had returned from London just the day before, and would have called this afternoon.

Even close up, Merrit looked thin, stylish, and fetching—easily fifteen years younger than her real age, which was in her late thirties. Merrit's hair fell in thick, dark clumps around her face and gleamed like a young girl's—like Jane's, Anne thought with satisfaction. Having ordinary looks herself, Anne had taken a vicarious pleasure in Merrit's since they were girls. "You look well for a woman in despair," Anne said, feeling it merciful to make a crude allusion to the worst right away. Merrit scowled in the same spirit, and the two abandoned the bus shelter for a reunion over coffee.

Settled in cozily, Anne beamed at Merrit and, as always, Merrit did not hold out for long before telling all.

"Amazing number of new stores in the neighborhood, aren't there? I was about to make a trek to the Forty-second Street library," Merrit began, looking around the coffee shop at the chain-store decor. "What an awful place this is. At least it smells better than my apartment. My tenant smoked and left burns everywhere. The place reeks. She was a nun no less. Can you believe it? Sexually frustrated, probably."

"Oh dear," said Anne.

"Anyway, it's just as well I didn't bring Brendan with me. He would have left as soon as he got a whiff of the place."

"What happened?"

"I pressured him to move in together. I wanted to have a baby."

"Oh dear."

"He said he wasn't interested in the marriage and family scenario, which I believed, because after all he's almost forty-nine. And I've never been sure I want to marry anyone, either, I mean instead of just living together, but I wanted a baby. So he left. But he was hardly out the door before I heard that he was seeing someone else, someone very young. And he's telling everyone he's going to marry her. All this in two months." And both of them teared up, not just because Merrit had suffered so greatly, but also because both of them perceived the end of this affair as the end of Merrit's hopes of ever having love, children, and all the rest. It's strange, thought Anne, that such a thing could happen so abruptly, yet she could not help feeling that it had. Suddenly, the desirably feminine Merrit was a spinster. Looking closely at her, Anne noticed that her face, while still pretty, no longer had its youthful softness; it seemed sharp, almost hard. Anne thought this, then resisted it, putting up a wall against whatever impulse tempted her to see Merrit in a pathetic light. Still, she thought, this is an emergency. Merrit's life is an emergency. There ought to be sirens, ambulances rushing to the scene, councils of worried friends and family. Why is she left alone to battle these dangers and endure these terrors?

"You're looking pale, Anne," Merrit said, when they had managed to move to another subject.

"Oh, I'm fine."

"Any news?"

"Well, no, not really." Here, however, Anne's face went dead white as her faint queasiness intensified and ceased to give pleasure.

"Is there a bathroom here?" Anne asked, taking deep breaths.

"There. Oh no. Out of order."

"There's got to be something."

"Let's go. You're only a couple of blocks from home."

"Can't make it," Anne gasped.

"Are you sick? Oh my God."

Anne begged to use the staff bathroom, but the cashier went stony-faced and said she wasn't allowed.

Anne turned to Merrit, "I'll get to the curb, I guess," and ran out, arriving just in time to lean over between two parked cars on Broadway. Merrit, meanwhile, paid, with a quick scold for the young cashier, and came out to pat Anne on the back, while the line of schizophrenics, addicts, alcoholics, impoverished elders, and mild-looking misfits, all waiting in demoralized silence for the soup kitchen to open at St. Ursula's Episcopal Church, stared in fascination at the lady retching into the street. "There's a quality-of-life crime," complained one man, with a week's growth of beard and rumpled clothes, who had been pulled from his drugged daze by the spectacle. "Now if you or I did that," he told a rheumy-eyed comrade, "they'd run us in." When Anne finally stood up again, the cashier from the café appeared at her side with a plastic cup of water and a paper towel and a cardboard tray holding their half-finished cups of coffee.

"Thank you," Anne said in the forgiving voice a mother uses to let a child know that a bad deed has been erased by a good one.

"Let's get you home," Merrit said, supporting her arm.

"No, I'm fine now," Anne said brightly. "I've got to get on the bus or I'll be late picking up Ellen."

Merrit understood. "Anne, you're pregnant."

"Yes."

"Good God. Was it on purpose?"

"No, a total surprise. Against all the odds." They walked toward the bus stop in silence, as Merrit struggled against an eruption of envy that kept her from speaking and Anne, who realized this, was tongue-tied. She felt genuine sorrow on Merrit's account, for in her mind the joys of husbands, pregnancies, and children were life's best, and Merrit was her closest friend. Knowing that her own excited anticipation of a new baby would deepen Merrit's sense of deprivation, Anne inwardly dodged and twisted, trying to evade the guilty sense that her delight injured her friend.

"Are you happy about it?" Merrit finally asked, in a neutral but lively voice.

"There are worries. I'm afraid Charles finds the idea hard to get used to, and I have no idea how we're going to put groceries on the table—let alone come up with school tuition for a fourth. Maybe we'll have to move to the suburbs, and Charles will hate me forever." Anne's worries were objectively real but subjectively unfelt, and she conveyed none of her elation in deference to Merrit's discontent.

Merrit was taken in by this half-deception. She fully credited the worries, indeed took them more seriously than Anne did. Charles might well be reaching some sort of breaking point. He was always complaining about the fact that Anne wouldn't get a job, and how he wrecked his voice and shortened his career by singing too much. She felt a small inner quake at the thought that Anne and Charles might fail to be her safe haven, might fall prey to the same instabilities that she lived with always.

"You know," Merrit began impulsively, "you wouldn't have to have this baby."

"I wouldn't? What do you mean?"

"If you don't want another child."

"You don't mean . . . do you mean have an abortion?" Anne asked. "What on earth for?" She tried to conceal it for the sake of an old friendship, but she was incredulous and offended.

"To keep life reasonable. If you want the child, that's different. But you've always insisted that an early abortion is perfectly all right, so I don't see why the idea should be shocking to you, or why you shouldn't do it if this is going to wreck all of you."

"It's not that there are never good reasons for abortion—it's that I don't have any. I'm a married woman in the business of rearing children. We'd be wrecked if I don't have the baby. Our marriage, our relation to the children, everything would be undone."

"I don't see that at all, but again, if you both want the child—that's all there is to it. But does Charles feel the same way? What if he wanted you to . . . ?"

"How can you even think that Charles would want me to abort his child?" Anne was too disconcerted to be able to call on her usual skill of changing dangerous subjects. What right did Merrit have to bring up such matters for discussion? It was a coarse invasion of the privacy of her marriage. Abortion could be debated abstractly, but her personal muddle of conscience, emotion, desire, and spousal compromise and demand could not be. Anne knew liberals who voted to support abortion rights but would never have an abortion, as well as conservatives who had had abortions yet voted against abortion rights. She blamed no one, except Merrit, who didn't know the difference between having a theoretical argument and wading in the moral swamps of motherhood and marriage. For a moment Anne was tempted to dislike her, then realized that Merrit, so good and thoughtful, simply could not understand marital intimacy. Anne instead tried to smooth things over the way a mother evades a quarrel with a child—by reassuming authority. This was not the first time she had had the thought that in certain respects, she and Merrit could no longer speak as equals. Merrit had had many fine successes in life, but in some ways seemed stunted, trapped in girlhood. In her inexperience, she made mistakes.

"Merrit, I think you've taken this on the wrong level. I complain about a sprained ankle and you suggest I get my leg amputated."

"It did sound more serious."

"It's not. Actually, Charles and I are both rather daunted but pleased."

"Well then—here's to the six of you," Merrit said, raising her paper cup. "What do the kids say?"

"We won't tell them for a while."

The conversation recovered to some degree, but an unpleasant undertone remained audible to both women, who now told each other that they "really must run." The two stood at the bus stop commenting on changes on the block since Merrit had left, almost three years earlier. "I see the bus coming," Anne said. "No. It's the 104."

"Oh, I'm taking the 104. And there's the M4 right behind it," Merrit said. As they parted, relieved to be spared a long bus ride together in their present mood, they exchanged promises to call and set a date for dinner, each intending to let a few days slip by first.

They all come back to New York sooner or later, Anne thought as the bus turned onto 110th Street. Her own brother, Paul, had come back from Berkeley last year, with his family, and was teaching at Columbia Law School. They had settled into Morningside Heights as though they'd never been gone. Morris, who hadn't lived in New York since his year at Juilliard, would be coming soon, and she had a feeling that he hoped to stay beyond the two years of grant support he could count on. And now here was Merrit. Morris and Merrit had met over the years through Charles and Anne. They had never gotten along, and now their differences would only be more pronounced. Morris, probably, had grown balder, plainer, and even less socially accommodating than he used to be. He was only three or four years older than Merrit, but he would look like her father. Anne herself had never had any problems with Morris, but he could be hard to get along with. She recalled a nightmare of a dinner party a dozen years ago at which Morris had picked a fight with Merrit.

Anne believed that something in Merrit was off-kilter where love matters were concerned. Over and over, she had love affairs, always with more or less prominent men whom she idealized; after a year or two, just when things should have fallen together, everything fell apart. Anne did not know just why or how, but she suspected that it would always be so. Years back, she had tried to encourage Merrit's seeing a shrink, but Merrit had walked out on two famous psychoanalysts without having gotten anywhere. The first time, after four months of thrice-weekly sessions, she had fallen in love and insisted she was fine; no one could convince her to stick through the analysis. That affair had lasted two years, and Anne had almost come to think Merrit was right, when things abruptly blew up in the familiar way. Merrit had tried again about three years ago, at Anne's urging, and this time she had been seeing the psychoanalyst for barely two months when she accepted an offer to go to London as a visiting scholar. The end result was yet another dramatic affair with a ghastly ending; and here was Merrit today, tenser and older, in the same precarious boat she had been floating in for a dozen years—since she was twenty-six and the first of her serious affairs had ended. Serial monogamy takes its toll, Anne thought. Merrit was beginning to have the weary, battered look that people get after they've had three or four bad breakups, and she had that air of withholding that they all have—like people who've been through wars or suffered life-threatening accidents or diseases and don't talk about it.

Merrit and Anne had grown up together a few blocks away from the bus stop where they had just parted. At sixteen, both of them thought that dazzling successes were what they wanted from life. Anne was obsessed with music, and spent all her time practicing and concertgoing. Merrit had equally intense literary ambitions, which gradually transformed into scholarly ones. Love, of course, was a desideratum too, but not necessarily married love. Anne and Merrit thought they might or might not marry. Living with someone without marrying was probably best. Why invoke the power of the state to sanctify a private state of affairs that two people ought to be free to establish and dissolve entirely on their own terms? They would have children when they were much older and trust their care to something like a kibbutz, which they would organize by themselves if they had to.

Then Anne had gone to Juilliard, where she was well enough appreciated to give her hopes of achieving great things and where, after a few weeks, she met Charles. Charles, too, had grown up in Manhattan, the child of a chilly marriage that ended in divorce when he was fourteen. After two years of spending alternate weeks on the East Side with his mother and on the West Side with his father, he quarreled so seriously with his mother, who was a dour, depriving, and disapproving woman, that he had rarely spoken to her since, and his relations with his withdrawn and inattentive father could be considered good only by comparison. When he met Anne, who was emotionally and physically the opposite of his mother, he was convinced that she was what life owed him. Anne's looks were nothing special, but she was all approval and smiles, blithe, generous, giggly, appealingly West-Sideish in everything from her humor, politics, and clothes to the way she played Bach. What really struck him was that you couldn't spend five minutes with Anne without her giving you something—a ticket or book or the loan of some remarkable recording or, her specialty, some off-the-wall comment about something you'd done or said which, hours later, you'd realize was actually true. Anne was delighted with herself, and with you; she was sure things would work out, confident that what she wanted she deserved and what she deserved she would have; and she seemed to think that Charles should feel the same way. Within a few hours of meeting her, Charles was in love.

Anne wasn't surprised at being sought by someone who was unusually good-looking and whose talent stood out even in a world of extraordinary talents. On the contrary, she seemed to feel that this was her due; it came naturally to Anne to be adored. What got her attention was the way Charles perceived goodness in everything that she had, did, said, and thought, conferring on her a fairy-godmother power to give pleasure. This, and the intensity of his reactions to whatever she offered, was a form of seduction that was hard to resist. Anne took only a day or two to decide she was interested.

From the beginning, however, Anne's interest in Charles undermined her investment in music. Her ambition flickered and went out, quite mysteriously. She hadn't particularly minded, and felt only mildly puzzled that it had happened. Friends, Merrit among them, were disturbed by this development and urged her to keep at it. For a few years she had done so—not out of the passion that had driven her before but because it was pleasant. "I was just more interested in you," she told Charles with a shrug, not in the least sheepishly. She began teaching children, especially very young ones, and did more accompanying, especially after she discovered that she and Charles performed together uncommonly well. Then Jane was born, and Anne practiced very little but still found time for a few favorite students. She had begun to practice more when Jane began nursery school, but soon Ellen came along, and then Stuart. Contented with her children, her husband, her small group of students, and a job as an accompanist now and then, Anne seemed to want only to continue to indulge her family as she had once been indulged. Until the past few years, she had been able to do exactly that. But lately the world seemed less willing than it once had been to cooperate with her wishes.

# 3

CHARLES USUALLY VOCALIZED and taught at home in a small studio
furnished with a dilapidated upright piano, a music stand, and a lumpy
sofa upholstered in balding brown velvet. The walls were lined by shelves
crammed with stacks of music and books on music theory and history, bi-
ographies of composers, texts on vocal pedagogy and diction, and old and
new books and treatises in English, Italian, German, and French on the
art of singing. More stacks of scores sat on the floor near the piano. Settling
to work here after Anne had gone out, Charles reflected, as he often had
before, on the room's transformation from the library of 1906—a place for
genteel leisure, or at least the pretense of it, for writing letters, reading
poems, novels, or newspapers—into the workroom of 1999, a place for
moneymaking, lesson-giving, and singing for pay. Anne's mother, Helen,
called it creeping proletarianization.

Charles had soundproofed and air-conditioned the studio, and the walls
and floors of the apartments in the building were so thick that even
Charles's thunders were almost muffled, unless he opened the window, as
he was tempted to do now and then, risking his neighbors' wrath. A pug-
nacious impulse led him to open it today, a beautiful spring day when he
was singing *Wozzeck*. "*Wir arme Leut!*" roared Charles into the soft air and
pastels and open windows of the April morning, remembering how much
pleasure it had given him to sing to the staid audiences of twenty years ago,
when he was still at Juilliard, that we poor people cannot afford morality.
But then, thought Charles, I didn't believe it and today I do.

Mozart might have been tolerated, but for Berg only ten minutes passed before the telephone rang. The superintendent, apologetically, said that he had received some requests. There had, in fact, been three enraged calls, but Mr. Morales's skillfully sympathetic response had already helped to calm tempers. Charles depended greatly on this man, and knew him to be better educated and more intelligent than his employers on the co-op board guessed. Had they known, in fact, that he was the son of a murdered Dominican politician and had pursued a humanities course for a time at the Instituto Tecnológico de Santo Domingo, they would certainly have held it against him. Overqualification was, in their minds, an intolerable employment sin.

Morales was a tranquil presence in the building, gentlemanly and always ready to listen. He spent fine mornings lounging outside in the sun at the entrance of the building and wet ones leaning against the doorman's station inside the lobby, chatting and greeting tenants with the manner of a genial, welcoming host. Morales knew everything that went on in and around his domain at 635 West 117th. In the small village where he had spent his boyhood, people had not learned to regard inactivity with suspicion, and a man could stand leaning against a doorway for an hour without losing respect or credibility. Charles approved of this behavior, and insisted that the low crime levels in the neighborhood were due to the watchful eyes of its loafing building superintendents. Charles understood Mr. Morales's conception of his own role: He should be wise, authoritative, paternal, knowledgeable—the sort of man others turned to for advice in emergencies, someone whose orders would be followed unhesitatingly. It would be base return indeed if, in addition to all this, Mr. Morales were expected to work. No, he was to be paid for his judgment and his respectability, for being the son of a mayor and the cousin of a magistrate, not for working.

To ensure that things operated this way, over the years Mr. Morales had caused to be hired for the building staff a crew of his own acquaintances, friends, and younger relatives, who took a similar view of his responsibilities. As years passed, the lobby increasingly acquired the ambience of the small village of his childhood. Each morning, men from the Dominican Republic and a half-dozen other Latin American countries arrived from up- and crosstown to staff 635 West 117th and all the neighboring buildings. There was a hum of Spanish indoors and out, the rise and fall of men's chuckles, calls, and shouts echoing down the block, doorman to doorman, super to super. Along with an assortment of plumbers, electricians, and contractors, they worked together in the style of their distant homes, in which intelligence and skill functioned as much socially as individually. When there was a problem they showed up in numbers, with smiles and bows, and, after a rising volume of talk and argument that always seemed to conclude that things were hopeless, swarmed all over the problem until it gave way. Then they departed, leaving the premises neat and clean—provided that the tenant was known to provide tips all around. Otherwise, the tenants learned, bathroom leaks and crumbling plaster might be tolerated for weeks before action would be taken.

Charles, a freehanded tipper with a pre-industrial sense of time and diligence, who resisted all schedules except the routines of his home and the opera house, was unlike the majority of tenants in his approval of this system. Some were so annoyed that they regularly called the board to complain. Charles only hoped that Mr. Morales would not push his luck too far. The capitalists who owned the building would tolerate feudalism only insofar as it paid; they certainly would be incapable of valuing properly its informal benefits of crime prevention and dispute resolution. Charles was, in any event, always glad to hear from Mr. Morales, and greeted him warmly.

"It was that paranoid Lyons woman again," said Charles.

"And the lady with the baby below, and the old man across the courtyard. I know how important your singing is, but could you, possibly, just . . ."

"Of course, of course. Don't worry." Had the objections come only from Ms. Lyons, Charles would have doubled his volume, but he respected both a baby's nap and shabby old Victor Marx, who had once written an admirably angry book about the exploitation of Appalachian mine workers.

Charles closed both the outer window and the inner one, which had been installed to increase sound insulation. He put *Wozzeck* aside, for he felt about it much as his neighbors did. In his twenties, he had interested himself in such music and pondered its social themes for the sake of getting on and because he wanted to love modern music and be at the cutting edge. Now, however, he admitted to himself that he could easily live without ever hearing *Wozzeck* again and that he found almost nothing to interest him in contemporary music. Charles had too much dignity to pretend otherwise, especially now, when he had so much less to gain. He hoped only to maintain his current status as long as possible, and to move gracefully into more and more teaching when performing opportunities—

or his voice—declined. So far, thank God, the voice promised to include longevity among its other virtues. Charles was singing better than he ever had sung, even if his quiet reputation had not translated into the kind of good fortune that pays bills. Anne was still convinced that Charles would be a star someday, even though he was forty-two, past the age at which stars are made. He took out a volume of Schubert, and, accompanying himself, sang, "*O du, wenn deine Lippen mich berühen . . .*" lost in the seductive pleasures of melancholia, until the telephone interrupted him again. He hoped it was Anne, but it was Eugene Becker, returning his call about Lizzie's apartment.

"Mr. Becker! Good of you to call," Charles said with the blend of authority and bonhomie that he used in all business negotiations. "Right— only two years, then he goes home . . . fifty-five hundred a month! Good God! Look, that place has a sixty-year-old kitchen and Elizabeth Miller probably paid around five hundred—that's what other renters pay. . . . Of course you're right to try to earn money for the heirs . . . who are the heirs, by the way? . . . Whether or not it's any of my business, I'm sure it's a matter of public record, but I don't want to butt in. I just want . . . that's right. I live directly across the hall. . . . For fifteen years. My friend is the ideal tenant—careful, undemanding, reliable, honest. I'll vouch for him. You can get the superintendent here to vouch for me. Really, you couldn't do better, but I'm sure no one will pay more than fifteen hundred for a place with no dishwasher. I mean, you have to light the stove in there with a match and the wiring's not good enough for a computer."

Despite his constant financial woes, Charles was clever at money dealings (if he hadn't been, they would have been bankrupt long ago) and perceived that Becker, contrary to expectation, was easily intimidated. Becker presumably inferred, as Charles intended, that if he asked an enormous rent, Charles would inform the board that he was setting up an illegal sublet. He wondered, privately, how Becker would get away with renting the place at all, but he had seen such things happen in the past. The conversation ended with Becker agreeing to rent to Morris for three thousand dollars a month—if Morris would sign a one-year lease beginning in May with no renewal option and pay two months' rent, nonrefundable, as a "finder's fee." This was outrageous, but given the scarcity of apartments, Charles decided that Morris might have to take a chance on it. He made a quick call to Morris, who was relieved to have his housing problem solved for him and decided to come to New York to firm up all the arrangements.

He shouldn't worry about renewing the lease, Charles told him. In New York, landlords always told you that you had only one year but you always got more time, because they couldn't avoid the temptation of collecting high rent as long as possible. Charles felt all but certain that the heirs, whoever they might be, would never see the $2,500-per-month premium that Becker would get. The thought annoyed him, and he filed it away with the others he intended to share later with Anne. In the meantime, it seemed, for the first time since Juilliard days, he and Morris were going to live in what would inevitably be near daily contact. This idea evoked memories of Morris calling him Micawber on a visit a couple of years ago, then a sigh, followed quickly by thoughts of tuition bills due this summer that he could not possibly pay.

Something will turn up, he thought, and wondered when Anne would return. How hard Anne worked, how much she gave up and did without, never suspecting, it seemed to him, that her petty domestic sacrifices had no tendency at all to produce cash or put food on the table—as though she thought that moral payment were coin of the realm. So she suffered her little deprivations, going without clothes, sleep, and vacations, wearing herself out over the children's homework and practicing and meals. Thereby, in her own mind, she earned the right to spread her table with lobster, caviar, and rare apples grown only in a small Civil War–era orchard somewhere south of Pittsburgh, and to spend thousands of dollars on tiny old violins for Ellen and Stuart. For all her orderly practicality, there were ways in which Anne's mind was really deranged.

But Charles, too, adored his children and begrudged them nothing. He had been taken unawares by the enchantments of paternity, not having known they existed. He had not yet ceased to be astonished that anything so good could be had without being sought. Each of his children, even Jane at her most difficult, was an exquisite soul with whom he enjoyed a kind of intimacy—simultaneously light, easy, fraught, and deep—that his own father had never known. Yet he could have been thoroughly happy with three fine children. They had been undone by Anne's urgent, unsuppressible wish for just one more. And how had she done it? Heaven knew. He couldn't really blame her, yet he knew, as well as he knew anything, that she *was* to blame. She had done it, somehow, with her hungry little womb. Her face as she left this morning had been glowing, although apologetic. She was far from indifferent to the troubles she made for him, but also irrationally confident that another baby would actually make him a happier man, no matter how much he worried about how it would all get paid for.

Charles wished that Anne would attend a little more to her husband and a little less to expanding her brood and taking on other people's problems. Anne wanted to help Morris, make a mensch of him, and that was why she wanted him to move in across the hall. But Morris could not be saved from his loneliness. He wasn't built for the kind of marriage Anne and Charles had, with its great sacrifices in individuality, freedom, ease, and even conscience. But perhaps he might make a different kind of marriage, in which his loneliness would be intact.

The way he went about things now, however, was bound to fail, in Charles's view. Charles perceived a coarseness in Morris's love life that was unaccountable, for he knew that Morris was a refined soul. Yet again and again Morris formed quasi-romantic connections that seemed to be based strictly on contract, quid pro quos in which the goods negotiated were job support, apartments, chores, sex, and leisure-time companionship. In these relations, Morris always had to give up something in exchange for tolerance of his occasional irritability, verbal meanness, and phlegmatic nature—traits that he exhibited exaggeratedly in his relations with women—and always seemed to end up with women who were sweet but dumb, or smart but ugly, or pretty but prone to paralyzing depressions. The deals fell apart sooner or later, when, after long mutual efforts at weighing the parties' merits and demerits, benefits and costs, down to fractions of an ounce, they discovered they were using incommensurate scales of values, as if Morris's were metric and the woman's were U.S. standard. Charles and Anne early on had reached the point where they rarely discussed or quarreled about finances or schedules, and they had never needed non-compete agreements. Of course, many things were unsatisfactory, but you settled for marriage problems as you settled for your own shortcomings and expected nothing in return.

Maybe Morris would get lucky and negotiate a stable arrangement with someone he could hold on to and grow old with. Yet Charles had an inkling that Morris deliberately resisted anything of the kind. Was it that Morris thought he would hold off marriage until he got tenure and a good salary? Then he'd just go find the right woman and do it up right? Things didn't work that way. Anyway, Morris had passed forty a couple of years ago, and tenure and the fine job were not around the corner—no matter how much he deserved them.

It was time to rest his voice and check the mail. Charles knew everyone in the elevator except for a besuited businessman with combed wet hair who paid no attention to the other riders and held his Palm Pilot in front of him like a divining rod. Charles nodded slightly to each of his fellow passengers and received in return, from all but this one, a grunt, a few raised fingers, or a twitch of the lips. The businessman, clearly one of the newer tenants, pecked notes into the device in his hand with astonishing speed, then deposited it into his left pocket and pulled a cell phone out of his breast pocket. Charles saw that he felt as though he were alone in the elevator. You couldn't say he's ignoring us, thought Charles, because people are aware of what they ignore, and he doesn't even register that we exist. With a stony expression, the man tapped numbers on the cell phone with perfect timing so that someone answered and he launched into conversation just as the elevator door opened at the lobby. Charles admired this trick but then wondered how the man could have been sure that no one would get on at the third and second floors and delay his arrival in the lobby. Would he then have begun his conversation in the elevator? Most likely he would have. Then Charles would have had to ask him to stop. Of course, the fellow would just sneer and ignore a polite request. You'd probably have to threaten to knock him down or something.

Dismayed to find himself slipping into satisfying fantasies of assault over an imagined offense, Charles sighed and took in the busy lobby scene. He slightly dreaded an encounter with Ms. Lyons, but she wasn't there. He saw Mr. Morales, who bowed gracefully despite his plumpness and, under his mustaches, smiled with a self-approving warmth. Willie, the doorman, wearing his navy-blue uniform jacket unbuttoned over street clothes, made his little military salute while listening to the building's handyman discussing jobs, in Spanish, with two outside repairmen. And then there was lonely old Albert Bernstein, whose wife had died six or eight months ago and who had begun to wander constantly down to the lobby to bend the ear of anyone he could corner. Today, however, he was silent, had a three days' growth of beard, and looked vacant and thin. He stood, mouth open, at the back of the lobby under a jagged crack in the marble wall that made it appear to Charles as though his stunned appearance was the result of having been struck by lightning. There, too, was septuagenarian Mary O'Reilly, retrieving her mail, in an elegant sixties-style suit incongruously paired with worn athletic shoes. Lately, Mary had tended to meander over to the soup line at St. Ursula's, leaning on her four-legged walker. There, she found lost and demented souls, whom she would bring home to help allay her loneliness and defray costs. Last week she had caused an uproar when it was learned she had given a set of keys to a strange man, obviously mentally unstable, who threw a temper tantrum in the lobby and screamed obscenities at Willie's cousin, Roberto.

Shuffling his mail, mostly bills and catalogues, Charles chatted with Willie. "What's with Al? He's gone quiet. I think I'd rather have him talking all day."

"Yeah. He stinks, he don't eat. I got him an account at Tom's Diner and they give him breakfast now. Every day, he goes over there, so that's something. But he's losing it, I tell you. Look, he's got on a sweater and big coat today, and it's hot. Mr. Bernstein," Willie commanded. "You go upstairs and take off your coat and sweater."

Al looked up dimly and stared at Willie.

"Yes, go upstairs and take off your coat and sweater. It's too hot for that." Al nodded and slowly shuffled toward the elevator.

"Sometimes I tell him to take a bath, but he don't listen. He's going down a little more every day. We gotta get him a social worker too. I'm gonna talk to Miz O'Reilly's social worker about that."

"Mary O'Reilly has a social worker?" This was stunning news. Fifteen years ago, when they had moved into the building, Mary, at sixty or so, was a fast-talking, cool-dressing woman, a live wire—quick, competent, informed, and aggressive. Then about five years ago she had fallen and was left half-crippled. She began to find buses and subways too much to cope with, went out less and less often with her girlfriends to dinner or Lincoln Center, and spent hours sitting on a bench in the median on Broadway down at 113th Street, which was already some sort of social fall—not at all like sitting on a bench on the promenade on Riverside Drive. That's where she should have been sitting, the way Lizzie used to. But she probably felt less secure there, because, unlike Lizzie, she had no one to take care of her. Then she began to be seen chatting on the bench with miscellaneous outré characters from the soup line. And the latest was this, that her soupline friends were moving into the building and getting keys.

"Oh sure. The social worker comes here, makes sure she goes to the doctor, takes her medicine. See, the firemen had to come two times because she left the stove on and started a little fire."

"A fire!"

"Just little ones—no big deal. This type of building don't burn, you know. Two times she did this. So a social worker started coming. And don't worry, I told her all about the crazy man Miz O'Reilly always bringing in here. He's gonna blow up one of these days. You tell your kids, stay out of the elevator if that crazy man's on, okay? If me or my cousin is here, don't worry, we'll make them stay with us."

Mary was now limping up to them, talking before they were in hearing range; she talked constantly, and was full of complaints.

"Yes, Miz O'Reilly."

"Why don't you carry up that box for me? I asked you to carry that up an hour ago. I need that carried up!"

"I told you, Miz O'Reilly. I can't leave my station, and that's not my job. The porter, he'll carry it up for you when he gets back. Any minute now. Don't worry. I'll tell him to carry it up."

"You can leave your station. You do it all the time. You just . . ."

"Miz O'Reilly, please. You just don't worry."

Charles was on the verge of offering to carry the box up when Anne walked in, laden with packages, smiling to see him.

"Hello, darling. You look pale. Let me carry those. You went to Zabar's?"

"Hello, sweetheart, thank you. Yes, oh, the mail. Mary, how are you doing?"

"Not so good! Not so good. You get old, and people don't treat you right anymore. That's the problem. Now if *you* wanted a box taken up, it would go up immediately. But, if you're poor and old, you wait, and maybe they never take it up."

"Mary," said Charles. "I personally guarantee they'll bring the box up." But he knew she was right. His boxes would be carried up immediately, and she was forced to wait. He must remember not to be poor when he was old. "What's in the box?" he asked.

"It's none of your business."

In the elevator, Anne told him there were clothes in the box.

"How do you know that?"

"I saw the box. It's from the Salvation Army Thrift Shop on Ninety-sixth. She always shops at the thrift stores. She's wild for clothes. That's her generation. All of them would rather starve than wear the wrong hat."

"So her entire social sense degenerates except that she remembers what hat to wear. Well, that's better than Al Bernstein."

"Guess who I ran into? Merrit is back—alone, of course. The breakup is permanent."

"Oh God. If Merrit isn't careful, someday she's going to end up like

Mary. No, like Lizzie, with Stuart for a trustee. She won't be poor like Mary."

"What can we do for her, Charles?"

"Nothing at all. There's nothing to be done. She's a free woman."

"Nonsense."

"Not at all. What would you do? Send her to another shrink?"

As this was an old argument, they soon let it go. Charles had once told Merrit that if she wanted to find a guy and have babies, she had to pick a mensch—a family man like himself, who loves his wife and his kids and his home and doesn't have affairs or leave. "But," he had warned, "the trouble with us mensches is, we're boring." Merrit had turned a look on him that suggested he was not boring at all, which was pleasant enough, but he was too wise to be deceived. If he were actually available, Merrit wouldn't have the slightest interest in him. She would be interested in Bryn Terfel, though. Anne, on the other hand, had always been interested in Charles, from the beginning, and vice versa for that matter. Yet he doubted that either he or Anne had ever been considered fascinating by the opposite sex. The kind of interest that sustained marriage was bestowed on its object, not created by it. Merrit, despite all her intellect, never got simple stuff like that straight. It was just like singing. He knew any number of brilliant singers who were continually bedeviled with terrifying vocal problems—as Charles himself had once been. They wandered from expert to expert, trying to find someone who could untangle the knots that formed when their minds attempted to make mere muscles do their complicated bidding. For every singer like that, he could point to a big, dumb one who could simply open his or her mouth and produce flawless tones, in any color or pitch you wanted. They never had any idea how they did it. Charles had finally learned to do it too, and even learned how he did it, but too late to do himself much good.

# 4

A FEW DAYS after her encounter with Anne, Merrit lay in bed, awake, too forlorn to get up and make the cup of coffee that seemed to be the only good thing in life within her power to attain just then. Last night her editor had left a message on her answering machine, praising her new proposal. There was a second message inviting her to speak at a conference at Berkeley in December and an e-mail from the *Times Literary Supplement* asking her to review a book about Margaret Mead. She was no longer excited about giving talks at big conferences or writing reviews of important books. Such things were just work now, obligations, not the successes and honors they used to be. But she would do all these things, because it would be irresponsible to waste the opportunity to say persuasive things about child rearing and the history of family life to those audiences.

Merrit had become so lonely that in her bed at night, when she closed her eyes and began to fall asleep, she had the sensation of flying off the earth into darkness, unmoored and lost. So she lay awake for hours, floating in vast, lonesome spaces, and slept later and later in the mornings. Yesterday, she had gotten out of bed at eleven, feeling dissolute. She had gone down to the lobby to pick up her mail, and meeting a cheerful young neighbor setting out for the park with her plump, rosy baby, she had had difficulty concealing tears.

This morning her mood was transformed when Jonathan Riesbeck called at ten to ask her to dinner that evening: sorry to call so early, and at the last minute too, but just heard she was back in town, some friends over, two or three of whom she knew. She very much would like to come, and, still holding the telephone, she got out of bed and began looking through her closet to see what she might wear. Jonathan was a kind man of indeterminate sexuality, neutral, chaste probably, but highly sociable and a gourmet; there were always people to meet at his dinners. Jonathan's intellectual persona was similar to his social one. He never showed his own hand, but he assembled and forwarded the ideas of others with skill and devotion.

Merrit decided that she must wear a winning dress, and here, fortunately, was one that no one in New York had seen, a cunningly understated, London-looking thing: perfect. This being settled, Merrit chose a different sort of costume, plain and dark, for an earlier engagement that day, and sat down to her e-mail until it should be time to leave. She was startled to find an enigmatic two-line message from Brendan, his first communication in months: "Saw you in Coliseum bookstore last week, but avoided you and then wished I hadn't. I'll be in New York for a couple of weeks. Shall we have lunch?" Agitated and undecided what to say to him, she noted down a possible date in her appointment book but sent no reply. She hadn't even known he was in the States.

Late that morning, Merrit boarded the M4 at the 116th Street stop. The M4 was known in the neighborhood as the "shrink bus," having for many decades served to transport scores of local residents cross- and downtown to their psychoanalysts and psychotherapists on the East Side. Years ago, in one of her brief periods of psychotherapy, Merrit would amuse herself trying to guess who else on the bus was en route to a session. Today, she recognized someone boarding the bus from her trips three years ago, a pretty woman in her late twenties, or perhaps thirty, with an hourglass shape, determinedly unfashionable and somehow unworldly, who radiated that psychoanalyzed combination of self-possession, goodwill, cheer, and the nuttiness that was only partly the result of knowing too many things that nature never intended to be known. The sight of this specimen of a familiar, highly cultured breed of New York woman—Anne had the same air as this one—comforted Merrit deeply.

Merrit nonetheless rejected the idea, pushed by people like Anne, that you could change the course of your love life by soul-searching. Psychotherapy was little more than a substitute for religious discipline, but it had a role to play. It offered comforts—sensitive, intimate attention was not the least of them—and it occasionally had some real usefulness in providing enough emotional support to enable you to go out and fall nicely in love.

That, she conceded, was not a small thing. Psychotherapy had served this function for Merrit at least twice.

Merrit had been an only child, and her father had died when she was small. Her mother was now a lively, still-youthful-looking woman in her seventies. Although Merrit had always been devoted to her, Mrs. Roth had been decidedly unmotherly. Growing up, Merrit had leaned instead on Anne and Anne's mother, a habit of reliance that had persisted all her life. When, late last year, she and Brendan had decided to return to the States together, they had planned to move into her tiny old apartment on 116th Street, a block and a half from Charles and Anne and four blocks from her mother. Anne wondered, in fact, why Merrit did not get a better place when she could certainly afford it. Perhaps her hold on her mother, the apartment her mother had bought for her, and the never changing Braithwaites, with their Edwardian mentality, enabled Merrit to venture on her travels and love affairs without feeling lost.

At twenty-five, Merrit had come into enough money from her father to live without working. She then abandoned graduate school, preferring to write and study independently, and took teaching posts and fellowships when it suited her, spending most of her time producing scholarly books on the history and structure of the family in different cultures. Her books, which were well researched and lucidly written, got noticed and argued about. Between books, she also made a name for herself in journalism, winning minor fame through a series of engaging social essays on women's lives. These had even earned her an occasional brief appearance on public television as a commentator. Scholarship, however, remained her passion, and she now was preparing to write something that she hoped would be a major contribution to the history of women's roles and the family, something that would still be read a century from now.

The day was drizzly and cool for the season, and the bus moved even more lethargically than usual, with rain-induced traffic jams and crowds of grim-faced, dripping passengers. The bus turned onto 110th Street and began its eastward journey along the northern rim of Central Park, where there were never many passengers to pick up, except, Merrit remembered, when it rained.

On Fifth Avenue she got off at Eighty-second Street and walked to the familiar building. There were the daffodils in the window box and tulips and irises in the miniature plot of ground at its front. The same doormen were holding the same umbrellas to shelter people getting in and out of cabs. Inside, the same prints of Renaissance architectural drawings hung on the wall in the waiting room, which had Oriental carpets and a masculine smell of something akin to tobacco smoke, even though ashtrays had been banished for years. Soon the door opened, and there was Dr. Freilich, with the barest momentary suggestion of a smile, unsurprised, neutral, unflappable, with something about him that suggested his eyes were looking in the wrong direction or didn't focus properly, although Merrit had looked carefully and knew this was not really so. Tall and stooped, light spring wool suit, hair shot with gray, horn-rimmed glasses, imperturbable—all the same. Time moved slowly here, because there was always enough time to understand, and yet every session ended too soon.

"All right, you told me so. Why not start with that?" Merrit began coolly, sitting in the armchair and glancing at the couch where she had spent her earlier sessions.

"I . . . what did I tell you?"

"Before we get into that cat-and-mouse sort of thing, can't we acknowledge a simple and obvious fact?"

"I'm sorry. But I just don't know what you mean."

Merrit realized that she had been assuming that they would continue their discussion precisely where it had ended one day in June almost three years ago. But of course, Dr. Freilich, with his many patients, would not remember their last words from so long ago. Merrit now feared he would recall nothing about her at all, but, recognizing this fear as equally irrational, forced herself to speak sensibly.

"You seemed to think when we spoke last," she went on in an altered voice, "that I would continue to have a troubled love life. You thought there was a pattern."

"Oh yes, and I recommended that you continue treatment in London. But you . . ."

"I did not continue. You didn't know that?"

"You didn't tell me. But I gather you think that developments have shown that my concern was justified. Of course, without knowing what's been happening for the past three years, I have no idea whether I agree. Why don't you fill me in, and then we can discuss it."

"Yes," Merrit murmured, struggling to extinguish the tiny spark of anxiety ignited by these words. She was relieved that, after all, he did remember, but she was dismayed, though she knew she ought not to have been, that he refused to give comfort by accepting her self-diagnosis, for this raised the horrible possibility that he would say, "Nope, doesn't sound neurotic to me. Terrible luck. Nothing you could have done." At this point, humiliating as it was to admit it, she would find more hope in being told she was neurotic—which she knew anyway—than in being told that the world was a hard place and had the power to thwart and defeat her. Of course, in their previous meetings, she had argued vociferously for the hard-world hypothesis. Now she wanted him to win the argument. But despite a sense of desperation, she was still not able to persuade herself that he could rescue her with her own insights. And why had he not sought to find out what happened to her while she was gone? He could have, easily enough. Did he have no concern at all, not even a little curiosity about her?

To say any of this, however, would have been humiliating. So she launched instead into an account of her life in London, at one point stifling tears only by keeping silent for what seemed a very long time, while feeling ridiculous. She had met Brendan on her second day in London. She had intended to phone the psychoanalysts Dr. Freilich had referred her to but had been so caught up in the affair that she kept putting it off, waiting for a contemplative lull that never came. Dr. Freilich, of course, recognized Brendan's name and asked how old he was and whether he had ever married. He was ten years older than Merrit, she said, and had had two live-in relationships that had each lasted for many years. The second had half-broken up about six months before Merrit met him. He had still been seeing that woman, but she wanted a child and he didn't.

"How soon did you know this story?"

She had been told it by others almost immediately, and by Brendan the first time they had dinner. "So you think I chose him because he was a bad bet?"

"I think you describe him as a bad bet."

She chose to ignore this and continued her brisk, increasingly frank narrative. She had had sexual pleasures with Brendan that she would not have believed possible before she met him.

"Why was that?"

"That question seems naïve coming from you. I mean, are you suggesting that it came down to bells and whistles? I can't believe . . ."

"Why do you think I meant that? I only asked if you know why it was that you had this response to this man. What was so exciting?"

"He was. Just him."

Dr. Freilich sighed in a way that expressed a gentle plea.

"You'll just say that I immaturely disregarded my own long-range interests for the sake of schoolgirl emotions."

"How does it help you to think of me as unempathic, judgmental, and not too bright?"

Merrit said nothing but reflected that it was undoubtedly bad psychoanalytic technique to engage in continuous jousting with your patients. This man always had to be right.

She continued sourly. "Well, he was extremely attractive—and intense and quiet. He was kind to me and, uh . . . he, he wanted me so desperately and passionately. That was a part of it. Actually, that was a major . . . actually maybe that was it. It was that he just couldn't live without me. He cried when I said I couldn't come home with him the first time he asked me to."

"Which was when . . ."

"About three weeks after I met him, and by this time we were talking all afternoon, and meeting for dinners, and, well, I was shocked to see tears on his cheeks when I said I wouldn't come home with him. He was a reserved man, very detached, and I had become fond of him. When this happened, I just went wild. Sexually, I mean. I was going through my classes and meetings in a daze. I couldn't eat or sleep. Everyone saw this, and there was a lot of gossip and . . . jokes."

Dr. Freilich, she could tell, was interested in this story. He sat thinking, a bright look of concentration on his face. He did seem to enjoy figuring out whatever it was he was always trying to figure out, and he took his time, unfazed by long, dead silences that made Merrit most uncomfortable. On this occasion, he took so long that she had to suppress an impulse to begin humming.

"You were in the market for a permanent relationship," Dr. Freilich declared at last. "Was he a real possibility?"

"Yes, actually. He was." Merrit's voice was cool and firm. She had no intention of wasting time discussing whether she had chosen Brendan despite his being, or just *because* he was, a dead end for her. That sort of thinking she could find reading *Cosmopolitan*.

"I don't mean, was he already in a relationship. I mean, was he husband material."

"Oh please! Husband material! I come here for a higher level of sophistication than that. First of all, I'm not sure if marriage is what I want. And anyway, he may not have been husband material for most women, but maybe he was for me."

"You're saying, really, that he wasn't."

"I'm remembering now how much I hated these debates with you. Either you say nothing or you're arguing."

"How did you feel about leaving me behind when you got to London?" Dr. Freilich asked, with innocent affability.

"Fine."

Dr. Freilich adopted a friendly, deliberative look and said nothing.

"Well, I did sometimes think about what we'd said here."

Silence. Merrit looked at the painting of a woman on the wall behind Dr. Freilich and felt sad.

"At times I thought a lot about it, things you said and what you would think about what was going on. In fact, I walked in here today with our last session as fresh in my mind as if it were yesterday."

"So you've been in treatment all these years, it seems."

"And a lot of good it did me."

"Maybe it did some."

"That fills me with despair."

"Why on earth . . . ?"

"This is why no one is willing to go through this anymore, you know," Merrit said, with some heat. "This is why psychoanalysis is dying. This horrible sense of time being wasted—hours go by, and nothing changes, and life's chances disappear, and we still sit and talk and quibble and split hairs and act as if reality doesn't matter, as if I have twenty years left to get pregnant, when I may have none."

"You're how old now?"

"I'm thirty-eight."

"All right. So you have a little time. Much less than you once did. But you feel the process here gets in your way, takes too long."

"You and I both know it's true. Why are we pretending we have this ridiculous neutrality when we both know we're weeping over a corpse, or at least I'm weeping over the death of my hopes. And you're thinking, Well, if she had only stuck to it three years ago, she could have avoided getting into this jam. She's made her bed . . ."

"Again you're attributing to me thoughts and ideas that aren't mine."

"They're mine, you mean. But that doesn't help me. It doesn't help me!"

"But it may help you at least temporarily to be clear that in fact I don't share the pessimism you feel about your life. Nor am I guilty of the sadism toward you that you are ascribing to me. To me, it is, and was, obvious that you could have everything you want. I don't understand—and here I'm speaking literally—I do not understand why you of all people think you can't have such ordinary things. I believe that it's extremely important that you find out, and I think you can."

"Sure. We'll just spend five or six or seven years chatting about it, until it's too late. The process is so much more valuable than my actual life— we won't care."

"I think it could be much faster than that. It's silly to set a time frame for such things, but I can't see why we might not understand some of these issues, say, 'sometime in the near future.' "

These words dissolved Merrit's angry cynicism. "Do you really think so?" she could not help asking, childishly, through tears. "We're not looking at years and years of wretched probing at my character deficiencies and . . ."

"Well, I won't try to predict how long we might think you're getting something out of coming—and I myself, by the way, don't think of it as probing at character deficiencies. But I'm quite sure that your fantasy of the treatment itself as forming the chief obstacle to your goals, and of me as sadistically overseeing your deprivation, slows things down."

"Oh," said Merrit, suddenly calm. "You're right." This unexpected lurch toward agreement left them both silent. Dr. Freilich, finally, proposed that they meet four hours each week, beginning Monday morning.

"Four hours!" she cried. "You mean four days a week?"

"We could do less, but I thought you were in a hurry," he said coolly.

"All right," she sighed. "I can't imagine what there will be to say for four hours."

At the end of the session, Merrit walked toward Madison Avenue feeling dazed and unexpectedly hopeful. The rain had stopped and the wind was not so chilly. She blessed the length of the bus ride home for giving her a chance to recover herself. By the time she reached the West Side, she had recovered so completely that her newfound hope was half extinguished by her habitual cynicism. It's brainwashing, she thought. The book-filled office, the couch, the psychological tricks that make you think he's got your number—it all softens your mind. I fall for it completely. I think he just told me he could get me hitched, and I believed it.

Back in Morningside Heights, Merrit resisted a temptation to call Anne
to rail against Dr. Freilich and hear Anne defend psychoanalysis. She sa-
vored the feeling of having somewhere pleasant to go that night and of
knowing that she would look good and that Jonathan would make just the
right sort of fuss about her. She even felt contented enough to try some
work, and sat down at her desk with something like enthusiasm for the first
time in months. Her latest project, a sociolegal history of sixteenth- and
seventeenth-century laws governing bastardy, adultery, fornication, and related matters, had gone awry from the beginning. Perhaps, she thought, it
had to do with the enormous success, in academic terms at any rate, of her
previous book. To some extent, she feared turning out to be a flash in the
pan, not being able to live up to her own reputation, but the problem appeared to be deeper than this. The material she was uncovering was, if
anything, more promising than what she had dealt with in her earlier
books, yet everything she began to write about it seemed either dull or only
half true. She would be interested in hearing what Dr. Freilich had to say
about all this—If he could be brought to say anything.

That was another problem with him: he tended to treat her work and
professional problems as though they were irrelevant. With him, everything was men, sex, and babies. But would he treat a man's career with the
same indifference? Certain that he would not, Merrit was so irked that she
took out her appointment book and on the date of her next session wrote a
note to bring this up. She saw there another note she had penciled in:
"Lunch with Brendan?" She had still not replied to his e-mail. Then she
felt a pang, recalling that she had thought of Brendan's message while she
was in Dr. Freilich's office but hadn't mentioned it, for fear that he would
disapprove or tell her not to see him.

# 5

ST. URSULA'S, OR, more precisely, the Protestant Episcopal Church of St. Ursula and Her Maidens, on 113th Street near Broadway, learned about Elizabeth Miller's death by chance a few weeks after it happened. The assistant priest in charge of fund-raising, Father Gregory Merriweather, noticed that she had not sent her annual gift, and, when he tried to call her, got a recording that stated that her number had been disconnected. The conscientious priest, seeing that this gift of a few thousand dollars had come every April in the forty years for which records were kept at St. Ursula's, felt conscience-stricken to think that a member of the congregation had perhaps fallen ill or died without any of them visiting, and tried in vain to recall Elizabeth Miller's face or to find some evidence that anyone at St. Ursula's had had any contact with her in the past decade or two. A few elderly parishioners remembered her and shook their heads sadly to think that no one from the church had kept in touch with her. She had given up regular attendance twenty years ago, they told Father Merriweather, although she had come occasionally for some years more. The church had abandoned her when she became an invalid, for at that time the church itself was sick.

Fifteen years ago, the congregation had been smaller than at any time in its history. St. Ursula's had been founded two centuries earlier, to serve genteel New Yorkers summering in what was then the countryside. Something about the place—perhaps its beauty—had inspired unusual loyalty, for many of the summer people had continued to make their way north to the old church long after the area was built up and urbanized. For a time, new residents of the neighborhood joined in great numbers as well, so that St. Ursula's thrived up through the middle decades of the twentieth century. But in the years when Lizzie grew old and declined, so, finally, did the church, and so did the last of the old-style rectors, Father Thornton, who died in 1982. After this, the congregation dwindled until they were so few and so aged that there was talk of giving up and making the church into a school. By the time the present rector, the Reverend Canon Richard S. Quincy, had taken over, contact with Lizzie and many other elderly or occasional parishioners had long been lost, and Father Quincy had so many other problems to worry about that he took little notice of a stranger's annual check while he labored to revive the church and congregation. Now, however, for the first time in thirty years, thanks to his energy and perseverance, there were assistant priests and pews full of young couples, singles, children, and babies—and these were of all races and ethnicities and persuasions. Father Quincy's innovations included a soup kitchen, which operated out of the back of the parish house regularly on Tuesday and Saturday mornings, under the direction of Father Merriweather, and a policy of hospitality toward dozens of community groups offering social services. Every evening the function rooms in the parish house were filled with meetings of AA and Narcotics Anonymous, cancer-survivor groups, gay-support groups, menopausal-women's groups, weight-loss groups, singles' groups, aging-parent support groups, Bible-study groups, and a half-dozen varieties of prayer groups. Add in all the vestry meetings, business meetings, choir rehearsals, theater groups, and many more groups who felt vaguely ennobled by St. Ursula's mission of benevolence and lovely stained-glass windows (depicting the history and ultimate fate of Ursula and her eleven thousand female followers), and you have the cheerful beehive of purpose that St. Ursula's had become.

In fact, the church had grown faster than its income. The loss of Miss Miller's few thousand, when the lines at the soup kitchen were increasing each month, was not to be overlooked even though Miss Miller herself had been. Father Merriweather pushed aside any suspicion that she might have died. Surely, in that case, there would have been a death notice or someone would have heard. He preferred to think that she was only ill, or had moved in with family or to a nursing home; or perhaps she had just forgotten to send the check. Maybe he could convince her to increase it this year. In any case, an elderly parishioner should not be ignored by her clergy, Father Merriweather decided. Miss Miller lived in the neighborhood; he would stop by to make inquiries or amends, as the case required. That very day he had his weekly Bible-study meeting—an informal inter-religious group composed of two rabbis, one Catholic priest, two people of indeterminate Protestant leanings from the Union Theological Seminary, and Father Merriweather himself, who was such a different sort of Protestant from the U.T.S. pair that three altogether did not create an imbalance. They met at the Jewish Theological Seminary, only a few blocks from 635 West 117th Street. He would perform his not entirely pleasant errand on the way home from the meeting.

The group was cordial and informal, but Father Merriweather was always disgruntled when he left. Of those present, only Father Merriweather and the Orthodox rabbi professed, unambiguously, to believe in God, although Father Merriweather knew that many Catholics were believers; the Protestants insisted on avoiding outright avowals of faith and preferred the word *spiritual* to *religious*. Father Merriweather complained each week to Father Quincy that the Protestants, relieved of the burden of making religious sense, seemed to feel free to make no sense at all, and indulged in what seemed to him a hideous, mawkish gush about the experience of God in the midst of forsakenness and the spirituality of hope. Father Merriweather claimed that he almost preferred the fundamentalists, who at least quoted the Bible.

At St. Ursula's, under the influence of the new rector, people really were quite unabashed about admitting that religion was what they were up to. Father Quincy led the way to faith with neither mawkishness nor mindlessness; he even managed to find an honorable way to deal with the annoying problem of the church's slightly embarrassing patron saint, whose very existence had always been in dispute. Even if there had been such a person as St. Ursula in fourth-century Germany, her eleven thousand virgin followers had more likely numbered eleven, or perhaps only two or three. With one raised eyebrow, Father Quincy suppressed any incipient snickering at the account of the heroism displayed by Ursula and by the maidens, which he blandly promulgated from the pulpit each year on St. Ursula's Day with all the pomp, music, and incense St. Ursula's could supply when it wanted to put on the dog. It was unseemly and disrespectful to inquire into the tale's moral or theological plausibility, in the rector's opinion. There were times when critical intelligence should be suspended out of respect.

As a general rule, however, the rector refused to indulge his congregation in fantasy or superstition, and insisted that faith did not require a belief in the occasional abrogation of the natural order. Any member of his congregation to whom God's voice was literally audible should see a good psychotherapist, snapped the rector. He had little patience for those who felt compelled to choose between irrationalism and irreligion. The church and the rector knew better than to read every verse of Scripture as literally true, and they mined the ancient texts for the treasures of their moral meaning. The rector preached strong sermons on the kind of social justice that good New York liberals supported, and he deplored efforts to replace evolution with creationism in school curricula out in the primitive wilds of the Midwest and South.

Father Merriweather found the rector's views congenial, although he worried that they tilted toward a mushy sort of deism, and he worried as much about the right way to approach fundamentalists on the one hand as non-believers on the other. He was careful not to hurt the feelings of the latter, and not to ask them what so interested them in the Bible, or, in the case of his study-group members, all of whom led churches and synagogues (or soon would), why they had sought ordination and paid employment in a house of worship. He felt that these were delicate subjects, to be tiptoed around considerately. He was a kindly soul, gentler than the rector, and a punctilious, careful man, who suffered much from the inhibitions, anxiety, and tension that went with an over-strict conscience. Merriweather had, in fact, trained to be a lawyer but, soon after entering practice, gave it up to go to seminary and be ordained—in large part because his inability to take the low road, or even the middle road, in legal matters had caused him excruciating anxiety. He was a backward, anomalous sort of character, with none of the self-affirming, self-confident egoism that was the prevailing ideal, tending always to believe more strongly in the other person's position and rights than his own. Even his own faith sometimes felt to him like a cruel, if unspoken, attack on the peace of perfectly nice people who lacked it.

At 635 West 117th Street, Father Merriweather asked the doorman if he could go up and see Miss Miller. Told that she had died a couple of weeks ago, he felt unsettled, as though something should be said or done, yet he did not know what. He stood awkwardly at Willie's desk and asked aimless questions about the old woman and her life and death. He had a dim sort of idea that the church should do something in memoriam. Willie eagerly told him about the events on the morning of her death, and, when the priest lingered, went on to insinuate that there were fishy things involved here. Willie, apparently, felt that a priest was the right person to whom to divulge, at last, his suspicions.

"Why, what do you mean?" asked Father Merriweather, although he felt of two minds about learning the answer. As a former lawyer, he felt an impulse to close his ears and avoid complications. As a priest of the old woman's parish, he felt an obligation to protect her interests, even after her death, even though he had never laid eyes on her.

"I mean," said Willie, "that there's people who might take advantage of a very old lady. You know, she was a hundred and three when she died."

"Good heavens. No children?"

"Nobody. She got nobody. Only people she ever talk to were her neighbors up there and her ladies that take care of her. You know, like a nurse."

"Yes. Well, who do you think . . ."

"You shoulda come before. That's your mistake."

"What do you mean?"

"I mean, it's too late now."

"Yes, I know *that*. But, I mean, who do you suspect of . . . of foul play?"

"Foul play! Yes, that's the word for it. Foul play."

"Well then, I take it that you don't want to say more, and so I won't press you, against your better judgment . . ."

Willie glanced quickly sideways and leaned confidentially toward Father Merriweather. "You talk to Monique, her nurse lady, and Claire—the other one. That's who."

"You think *they* . . ."

"No, no, no! They're nice ladies. Smart. They see what's going on, you know what I mean?"

"So who do you think did what?" Father Merriweather finally asked firmly, taking the plunge, and committing himself to learning whatever was to be learned.

"You talk to Monique and Claire."

Father Merriweather sighed and said, "Well, I have no way of finding these ladies, so I . . ."

"Miz Braithwaite knows. Miz Miller's neighbor. Nice lady in 9E. You ask her." And Willie buzzed the Braithwaite apartment as he spoke. "Miz Braithwaite, Willie the doorman. Look, there's a priest here about Miz Miller . . . yes, that's right. He just come to see about her, and didn't know she died. Okay." Turning to Father Merriweather, he smiled. "You can go up." He felt happy that he had divested himself of a problem, and Father Merriweather, who recognized that he had been outmaneuvered, felt unhappy that he had acquired it. He also was embarrassed about having to appear at a stranger's door as a priest, a role he had occupied for only about six months, to ask about an ancient woman whom he didn't know. Being a priest was embarrassing; he still wasn't sure how he should act. The clerical collar, he had learned to his dismay, opened a great distance between himself and other people. He felt a sense of loss in no longer being just like everyone else, and in the knowledge that it would be so forever.

He was blushing faintly when he rang the Braithwaites' doorbell, hoping it could be heard over the recording being played loudly inside. When the door opened, he faced a petite woman with untidy curls and a cheerful but slightly drawn face. A small boy hiding behind her and holding her skirt stared with big eyes at the priest. "Come in, come in," she said hospitably. "Wait, I'll ask my husband to close the door." This made him conscious that the singing was live; the door closing was remarkably effective in muffling the singer's extraordinary volume.

"Oh! Braithwaite! Your husband is at the Met, isn't he? I'm sure I've heard him . . . let's see . . ."

"Yes, that's Charles. What church are you from?"

"St. Ursula's."

Anne smirked slightly. "I'm Jewish," she confided, only half conscious of her satisfaction at saying this to a priest.

He had no idea what reply to make, so he smiled and nodded foolishly.

"St. Ursula's is . . . Anglican?"

"Episcopalian."

"The same thing, right?"

"Sort of."

"That's what Charles was raised as. But he gave it up."

"I'm an atheist now," said Charles jovially, coming in to see who the visitor was.

Father Merriweather once again could think of nothing to say, and attempted a knowing smile, which, he feared, came across as a foolish grimace. With lawyerly economy, he explained why he had come looking for Miss Miller and how he had arrived at their doorstep, omitting the details of his conversation with Willie. While Anne went to get the telephone numbers, Charles wondered who Lizzie's heirs were, as the trustee had more or less implied there were some, and whether they had shown up for a funeral; and he conveyed his suspicions about the trustee—pleased, like Willie, to be able to palm this off on someone else, who would now have to be responsible for deciding whether anything should be done about it. Anne, now that Charles had brought it up, added that Claire, too, had thought the trustee had been cheating Lizzie.

"Do you think," asked Merriweather, "she lacked anything necessary to her basic health or comfort—food, medicine, or such things?"

"Oh no," said Anne. "Not at all. She had no luxuries at the end, but she stayed in her own home and had plenty of help and enough to eat and a good bed and all the rest. Oh, I don't think, if there was a problem, it amounted to anything more than skimming the cream. And I wouldn't expect there was even much cream to skim. Certainly, she had tightened her belt, but no more than other old people around here."

Father Merriweather left the apartment believing that Willie's suspicions were probably baseless. Willie had heard some ordinary grousing and was inflating his own importance by bringing it up. Still, Father Merriweather had taken the telephone numbers, and he might give one of the caretaker women a call. It couldn't hurt, and he couldn't help worrying that the church had neglected Miss Miller, when she had never neglected the church.

# 6

JONATHAN RIESBECK EXPECTED nine people, counting himself, at his table that evening, for a total of three more than he thought ideal for a dinner party. Besides Merrit, he had invited one other single woman; two single men, making three single men altogether, which was good, as there should be no obvious attempt at pairing; one long-married couple; and a younger, unmarried pair, who were just beginning to circulate as a couple. He had invited two of the guests only that morning, against his better judgment, before he had much of a chance to turn over in his mind how the group might meld.

It was all beginning well enough, he thought. Merrit and the other single woman, Lily Freund, showed up simultaneously, having met in the elevator. Merrit recognized her as the young woman on the M4 that morning, and broke the ice by asking her if she too had been going to see her psychotherapist. Lily had laughed and said that it was even worse: she *was* a psychotherapist. Lily, a woman with no intellectual pretensions but a highly instinctual intelligence, was Jonathan's cousin and, except for that, would never have been invited to this gathering of scribblers and scholars. Good-natured, composed, and uninitiated, however, she would provide social lubrication in the event of friction. Besides, as his cousin, she was paired with him, for a total of three pairs, one married and two not; you always needed more than one or two pairs, or they would feel too paired. This balance, then, was perfect in the Riesbeckian social calculus—Lily was better than a wife, in fact, as she was someone who belonged to him, to whom he could expose panic if the lamb burned, while permitting him the freedom to romance someone if he felt like it, which he probably wouldn't.

Jonathan had few romantic aspirations. He only wished that in the ordinary cyclical course of things life would turn more Victorian, with the bachelorhood or spinsterhood of anyone over the age of thirty accepted as a permanent state unless or until the spinster or bachelor chose to surprise the world and take a mate. As things were, people who were unmated but middle-aged, or nearly so, were still in the game. There was no repose, no ease available to someone like him, who would always have ended up a bachelor. Women who had turned forty, as Jonathan himself had, were always looking him up and down as if he were some prime pig, trying to gauge his marital potential and hoping for an invitation to the movies, insisting that he carry the ball in some unduly prolonged version of the mating game. Dating and getting fixed up, dieting, people over fifty still sucking in their stomachs and wearing come-on clothes—it was all insanity. It had been far better when women past their twenties were simply not marriageable, and left men like him alone.

Neither Merrit nor Lily would be a problem that way. Merrit looked lovely and, thankfully, never had so much as glanced at Jonathan sideways. He had known her for years, and he liked to make a little fuss over her. He saw that Merrit's public persona of toughness and intellect was built on a receptive and sweet-natured temperament, and he had learned to admire her. Without the internal supports of rage or aggression, she would nonetheless persistently question eminences in their fields until they contradicted themselves, or would confound them with dazzling, unanswerable little briefs of her own views and critical positions. Snarls and power never intimidated her. Her books were characterized by the same dogged patience, enlivened by insight, in pursuit of unconventional truths, that she displayed in conversation. Lily and Merrit seemed to have hit it off, which would have surprised many people who knew them both, but not Jonathan. Merrit—so much older in years if not in looks, so apparently sharp-edged and able to hold her own with nasty poets and pundits—warmed to Lily and conversed guilelessly with her in a way that Jonathan had intuited was part of her social vocabulary but had not yet witnessed. Fond of both, Jonathan was pleased by this confirmation of his hypothesis about Merrit.

The three of them chatted in amiable innocence and sipped wine. They established that Merrit had grown up in Morningside Heights but that Lily and Jonathan had been there nine and seventeen years, respectively, and that both were from Chicago. Also that Merrit jogged on the promenade several mornings a week, Lily rode the M4 to the East Side every day, Jonathan liked to spend summers in the city, when he could get some work done, and it used to be, most summers, you wouldn't even need air-conditioning except in August. They felt warm toward each other, and were on the verge of outright affection when the Smith-Smythes, Teresa and Chalmers, arrived, followed minutes later by Howard Kappell, a journalist, and Pietro Bollo and Ani Singh, whose fields were political philosophy and logic. Teresa Smith and Chalmers Smythe were tall, gaunt, intimidating figures, whose extreme thinness was enunciated in black—in Teresa's case tight, stretchy, and shiny black. And neither of them as young as they want to be, thought Jonathan, who was of middling height, with fine, thinning hair, a slight, comfortable paunch, and, out of respect for his guests, dressed in tie and pressed shirt under a tweedy jacket, whose lining had worn through in spots. He didn't know the Smith-Smythes well, and had invited them in hopes of becoming better acquainted. Merrit had met them once, somewhere, sometime. The Smith-Smythes were always talked about. They had written democratic constitutions for nations emerging from political tyranny, modeling them on the United States Constitution with the bad bits omitted. They traveled fearlessly to dangerous places that locked their kind into dungeons and threw away the keys, or worse. They signed brazen petitions, wrote public letters that were signed by Nobel Prize winners, and held secret meetings with fugitives, the proceedings of which were reported verbatim the next day in the world's various *Timeses*—and still managed to hold to a punishing publishing schedule.

Jonathan had admired their courage and fecundity when he knew them mostly by reputation, but face-to-face he began to feel catty. Regretting this, he tried to find its roots in himself, for he was a man who sought to be benevolent, usually successfully. Was this a straightforward envy of people who were smarter, braver, more altruistic, and more famous than he was? It was easy to shake a finger at himself; not so easy to squelch his insidious hostility toward the Smith-Smythes. He hoped that over dinner he could get past their public personae and manage to like their real selves.

The Smith-Smythes tasted Lily for a fraction of a second before spitting her out. Merrit, they did not bother to conceal, they did not remember; and she too was initially suspect as being too girly and pretty to be properly smart and hard. In thinking so, Jonathan told himself, amused, they doubly mistook her; for they failed even to detect her sophisticated front of toughness and brains, so misled were they by her good looks, which, in their book, were ideologically iniquitous. Jonathan enjoyed watching people mistake each other as much as he enjoyed misleading them with his own harmlessly false front. He feasted inwardly on the Smith-Smythes' error while outwardly offering them an enticing conversation about a new book, *Margaret Mead and the Child,* which he knew Merrit was reviewing. The Smith-Smythes had already read an early review and praised the book for its critique of Mead's mistaken ideas on child rearing and distorted observations of child-rearing practices. "But," Lily interposed curiously, "I should have thought you'd favor all those progressive ideas about child rearing." Merrit, however, shook her head at this guess. She understood, as Lily did not, that Margaret Mead had offended the left. Merrit was not surprised, therefore, that the Smith-Smythes so liked this anti-Mead book. She herself, however, in many ways preferred Mead's views to those of her critics. The argument of this book in particular, she told them, was insupportable, and she offered some criticisms of it—quite cunning and well-informed ones, Jonathan thought happily—with such respectful grace, however, that once again Teresa and Chalmers were deceived. They could not recognize intellect when it was dressed in unfamiliar garb, and, in any event, they assumed that Merrit was too young and her academic status too low for her opinion to matter. They took her for one more graduate student destined for obscurity. At the end of her elegant little speech, therefore, they spoke past her and Lily to Jonathan and Howard Kappell, as though she had not spoken at all. Thus, Jonathan particularly relished telling them, in an aside, the essentials of Merrit's C.V.: Princeton, London School of Economics, public-television appearances, several books, and, the coup de grâce, a three-year affair with Brendan McGarry, the highest sociosexual qualification a woman could have. Teresa and Chalmers were properly chastened by this clarification, and began to see the force of Merrit's arguments. They sought her out to tell her that she did have a point, of course.

Howard Kappell had also enjoyed this comedy. Full of himself, warm, homely, and nosy behind thick eyeglasses, he settled into grilling Merrit for gossip. He asked, unabashed and full of grins, about Brendan—what had gone wrong, how it felt to return to New York, what she was up to, what she was writing, whom she was seeing now—to all of which Merrit gave devious and smiling responses. It was not easy to resist Howard, who, with the professional interviewing skills of the experienced reporter he was, punctuated his questions with intelligent compliments, squeezes, and affectionate and disarming non sequiturs; but Merrit was experienced. Lily stood by quietly and took it all in.

So far so good. Jonathan began to relax, except about culinary matters, for the lamb was in danger of over-cooking and one guest was still missing. He waited in the living room, propping up any conversations that threatened to flag, but the party had begun to slide from its peak, and the optimal moment for sitting down to dinner had already passed. "Well, I say to hell with Morris," he finally announced to the company. "Let's eat."

"Morris?" Merrit turned to Howard. "Not Morris Malcolm—the biologist Morris?"

"How should I know? Why?" smiled Howard, slightly eager, catching a scent of discomfort.

"Oh, it couldn't be," said Merrit, realizing that this was a great improbability. Why would Jonathan know Morris? Different fields, different universities, different cities. His name had come to mind only because Anne had mentioned just this morning that he planned to spend some time at Columbia and would be in town for a few days, sorting out arrangements for lab facilities and an apartment.

"Okay, it couldn't be, but things would probably be more interesting if it were." Howard laughed heartily.

Merrit knew enough to resist being flattered by Howard's sweet and warm attention into disclosing any intimate facts of her life to such a gossip. People found Howard amusing for about fifteen minutes; then boredom and, finally, a sense of oppression set in. Jonathan was aware that Howard could make or break a dinner party, as he tended to melt inhibitions more effectively than alcohol, but he had to be managed, moved along from guest to guest. The lateness of dinner had left Merrit prey to Howard for a dangerous twenty-five minutes, and she had to endure another five before Jonathan could call the guests to the table. There, fortunately, he was able to detach him from her side, announcing that he was prying them apart to prevent Howard's prying.

"Oh, but I've got to sit by Merrit in case Morris shows up after all."

"What are you talking about? Shut up, Howard, and sit where I tell you—there." He pointed to a seat between Teresa Smith and Ani Singh. Merrit he seated between himself and Chalmers Smythe. Even so, she was

out of sorts all through the soup and had only completely recovered when
the lamb appeared. At that very moment, so did Morris—Morris Malcolm,
the molecular biologist.

Oh God, thought Merrit, annoyed, but her face was a mask. Howard
was delighted.

The connection between Morris and Jonathan that Merrit hadn't
known about was one of those interuniversity, interdisciplinary committees for investigating the policy implications and ethics of genetic research.
Of course, Jonathan, a philosopher of science with an international reputation, being more widely read in a variety of disciplines than practically
anyone else, was a natural for such a committee. Morris, not well known
but passionate about the issues, got on because he had elbowed his way in.
Jonathan and Morris had known each other through the committee for almost three years, and Jonathan had learned to respect Morris, even to
the point of relying on his opinion—a privilege he granted few people.
Morris, in turn, liked Jonathan and trusted his thinking. They had the
easygoing camaraderie that Morris often achieved with men, never with
women. Neither knew much about the other's life away from the committee.

"How are you, Morris?" Merrit said, with Girl Scout decency and
friendliness.

Jonathan saw the stiff-upper-lip quality of this, and realized immediately
that he was faced with the great peril of dinner parties—unsuspected en-
mity between guests. Howard laughed again and said loudly, "She told us
all about you, Morris. You're in trouble."

Morris blinked and shook hands all around, barely acknowledging
Merrit. Brief explanations were made of their prior acquaintance and his
lateness—something about a notebook left behind at a health club.
"You're the same," he said to Merrit with something abrasive in his voice.
She wanted to tell him that she hadn't been talking about him, but didn't
because it would have sounded defensive.

"But you've changed," she said, adding, "You look good," to avoid the
implication that he had aged. It was true that Morris's appearance was im-
proved, but the compliment was nonetheless left-handed, and she immediately regretted it. Morris was slightly thicker, but that was better, as it left
him slender but not slight. In his twenties he had been so thin that, as
Merrit had remarked at the time, there was hardly enough of him to
count. His hairline was receding slightly now, which made his face look
longer and his forehead higher—both improvements, in his case. He no

longer fidgeted and jerked, and he was decently dressed for the time and place, as he never had been before in Merrit's experience. Altogether, he had more dignity. Even his horrid black eyeglass frames were gone, replaced by fashionably thin tortoiseshell.

Lily, the other single woman at the gathering, was disposed to take an interest in Morris despite his unprepossessing greetings. This she expressed by helping him to the courses he had missed, smiling at him unembarrassedly, and making a frank effort to connect. He seemed to return her interest in a shell-shocked way. While Howard chalked this up to his being disturbed by Merrit's presence, Merrit and Jonathan were both aware that Morris seemed shell-shocked most of the time, as though he had just escaped unscathed from a car accident. It was his general social demeanor, and it disappeared only when he was engaged in work or in intimacy. Lily guessed that this was how it worked, without articulating the thought.

When they regathered in the living room after dinner, Morris spent a half-hour in vigorous argument with Pietro and Ani about corporations and science: how it was a mistake for universities to have gotten so cozy with business, doing deals, sharing patents, and how science was undermined when researchers let business censor what they published. But Pietro and Ani both thought this was inevitable. Inevitability, thought Jonathan, listening, seemed to be the bedrock of the political thinking of so many young people, which was a strange reversal of the roles of generations. Pietro and Ani thought that the point was to develop appropriate rules and controls. Morris was beginning to talk about the inchoate factors involved, the pressure that the profit motive exerted on directions of research, when he spied an opportunity to re-engage Merrit. He excused himself, and let Jonathan take over the argument, as this was one of many issues on which he and Jonathan shared a well worked out position.

Morris pulled himself together and approached Merrit with a focused expression that she remembered. She looked for Jonathan, but he was still talking with Pietro and Ani, so she sidled over to Lily; not too obviously, she hoped. Morris was soon at her side.

"It's been all these years—and you don't even want to ask me what I've been up to?" he said. "I know what you've been up to. I heard . . ." And here Lily, seeing that some private contretemps was in the making, excused herself. Merrit, abandoned, roused herself now that she was faced with the inevitable.

"I'm remembering other dinners," she said.

"And sharing your memories with everyone here, it seems."

"I didn't. I didn't even know Morris was you until you walked in."

"That guy over there says you did. He says you were witty and entertaining, which . . ."

"Howard is pulling your leg."

". . . you always were, weren't you?"

"Morris, public squabbling is intolerable to me and unfair to anyone who is forced to witness it. We're going to make Jonathan unhappy. We used to upset Charles and Anne. Please stop this."

Merrit had not, at least not consciously, meant to make things worse, but this speech set Morris off.

"Imagine a nice person like you taking the trouble to set a Neanderthal like me straight about all that."

By now, Merrit was angry with Morris for involving her in such a childish interchange. She restrained herself, however. On another occasion, years ago, she had not, and had replied in an unbecomingly loud voice, making her humiliation more public than it need have been. This time their voices remained low, and they were standing far enough away that no one could be sure they were quarreling, let alone in such an infantile way, but Merrit was painfully certain that they were being watched. Morris observed her eyes darting sideways to check, and was irritated. Merrit was contemptibly interested in preserving appearances. It annoyed him that he did not have her full attention when he was needling her, that she would be distracted at such a moment by thinking about what other people were thinking; it made him want to escalate hostilities until she reached the point of not caring what anyone thought. But Merrit muttered something incomprehensible and walked away to sit on the sofa, opposite the Smith-Smythes, opening an awkward pause in their conversation, which she was too agitated to help smooth over.

"What were you two going on about over there with such long faces?" asked Howard, seating himself at her side.

Jonathan came to the rescue, not by changing the subject, which would have been too obvious, but by discussing Morris in a context that gracefully excluded Merrit. He launched into an account of Morris's conduct on the committee they both sat on, how Morris had sometimes defied the wishes of other scientists and of the politicos as well. Most people's positions could be predicted ideologically, but Morris's were too nuanced and commonsensical to fall consistently on one side or the other of any ideological divide. He was outspoken in favor of forwarding some research that the religious right wanted to stop, but had occasionally defended protective protocols and safety measures, and had flatly opposed research into human reproductive cloning and favored moratoria on other types of research. He made enemies among his colleagues, and his interests suffered for it. His own lab was forcing him out, first with stabs in the back and eventually by frontal assault, and that was why he was taking the shaky position at Columbia. But he had managed to bring a big grant with him, and he could look forward to two years of good work with reasonably good equipment. Matters could take care of themselves after that.

"So your friend Morris is a hero," Jonathan said in a confidential moment with Merrit a little later.

"I'm surprised to hear you say so," she replied.

"He'll say anything to anyone," said Jonathan, but immediately wished he had not, as he realized that the remark sounded double-edged.

"Oh, if that's all you mean. That I know," Merrit said, affecting indifference. "But his thinking is naïve. It's just teenage idealism. He's a typical half-educated scientist."

"Hm. I think I'll disagree with that," Jonathan replied mildly. "And it takes some idealism to be willing to argue with people who've made so many compromises that they don't know how to tell down from up anymore."

Merrit had always seen Anne and Charles's respect for Morris as a prejudice in favor of an old friend. Jonathan's was harder to account for, although she darkly suspected some repressed male bonding thing that had nothing to do with the issues or with the quality of Morris's thought. Jonathan was so placid; there was some attraction of opposites there. Still, she was surprised that he showed no more perception than this. Merrit had as little interest in Morris's scientific work as she had respect for his political and social thinking, and she took for granted that it would be impossible to have anything like an intelligent conversation with him. Furthermore, she had to admit to herself, part of her sense of being superior to Morris had to do with her belief that he was too socially inept to achieve any sort of recognition or be given opportunities to do the kind of work that would merit recognition. That sort of thing mattered in hard science as much as anywhere else. She, on the other hand, combined scholarly talent with worldly competence; Merrit had never found it difficult to win recognition or opportunities to pursue her work. She had known fifteen years ago that Morris disapproved of her because she sought out prominent, high-achieving men, and it was true that she did. Her looks, brains, and charm had always meant that, romantically, she could aim as high as she wanted. Morris, rube that he was, did not understand that this was how the world had to work. You couldn't make yourself fall in love with less intelligent, less successful, less attractive men just to be morally correct.

Merrit, however, also recalled that Morris had always objected to something artificial in her demeanor, reading it as evidence of a moral flaw, to which he reacted with a kind of teenage horror. Merrit was the more bothered by his judgment because lately she, too, had begun to perceive and dislike a hint of something like this in herself. She thought it possible that to some degree he brought it out in her. Maybe it was his Holden Caulfield integrity that did it, turned her into a Junior Leaguer or something. It was very strange, the whole dynamic. Whatever her flaws, what made him feel entitled to punish her for them publicly?

The Smith-Smythes had listened intently to Jonathan's report of Morris's exploits on the committee. They began describing another biologist, a good friend, who held many of the same views as Morris but who approached matters far more diplomatically and had managed to get a Nobel and now had a more visible platform to speak from. You had to be pragmatic.

"But after five years he hasn't actually bothered to mount it yet, has he?" said Jonathan.

"Then there are people who are always up there yammering, even though they never do or say anything that actually matters," said Morris, who, with Lily, had approached the group from behind the Smith-Smythes.

How crass and childish he is, thought Merrit, aghast.

Even tolerant Jonathan flinched. The Smith-Smythes, however, who were too self-approving to recognize themselves in this portrait, took no offense, and this—so Merrit hypothesized the following afternoon as she described the incident to Anne—is what really seems to have set Morris off. He had made the first nasty remark half out of dislike and half because Merrit had gone to sit with the Smith-Smythes for protection. But when that didn't work, he upped the ante.

"You know," he began again, smiling with a cheerful truculence, "as a newcomer to the city, I have a question for you, Chalmers. I've noticed that here in New York you see all these couples who not only dress alike but look exactly alike—gay, straight, whatever, it's the same. I mean, tall dark people are with tall dark people; short plump ones are with short plump ones. You always get two very good-looking people together or two people who both have big noses and receding chins. Just look at the pictures with the wedding announcements in the *Times*—all the couples look like brothers and sisters."

Chalmers's face was darkening, but Lily, oddly blind to any applicability to present company, was charmed by this observation, which she thought had a lot of truth in it. "Couple narcissism," she interjected happily.

"But you and Teresa really take the prize. You not only look alike and dress alike, you actually . . ."

Jonathan, however, did not give Morris the chance to say it. "Maybe this explains why you're still single, Morris," said Jonathan, cutting him off, but without annoyance, which irked Merrit. Morris had insulted guests in Jonathan's home. Jonathan should have been angry and come down hard on him. Merrit herself was red-faced in her fury.

Morris appeared to relax, satisfied now, as he observed that Merrit was outraged and the Smith-Smythes duly offended. "I'm no New Yorker," he replied. "Now, Merrit here is a true New Yorker—going on forty and still single because she can't find her double out there. That's the problem with being so superior to everyone else, and such a nice person to boot."

Here the entire group joined in silent moral denunciation of Morris by looking or walking away, except for Lily, who seemed to react with puzzlement. He'd gone so far over the top that everyone else's dignity was restored and his own lost, although neither he nor Merrit seemed to know it. Morris simply resumed his chatter with Lily, apparently cheerful and oblivious. Merrit once more tried to simulate indifference, but failed. She was mortified and her cheeks burned.

The Smith-Smythes said a crisp good-bye and left early. But, Jonathan thought, he'd had enough of them. Odd that Merrit had seemed to take to them after a while. You had to laugh at their pomposity, but you shouldn't call people hypocrites or tell them they're silly or try to humiliate them the way Morris had done. Why did he do things like that? Jonathan didn't know, but it worked out better in committee meetings.

"Don't worry, Merrit," Morris said, observing Merrit's funk. "I'm leaving soon, and you can fill in everyone on my personal flaws and unimportance behind my back, and then you'll feel much better."

Merrit's dignified silence did not abash him. Indeed, he seemed quite chipper and in no hurry to leave as he said a warm good-bye to Jonathan. He stopped on his way out and spoke to Lily, who scribbled something for him on a piece of paper and then, smiling but thoughtful, walked out with him. Lily glanced back at Jonathan, however, and let her eyebrows rise infinitesimally, knowing he would understand: she found his friend perplexing. Pietro and Ani followed them out a couple of minutes later. They made a point of warmly pressing Merrit's hand, saying with poise and feeling how they hoped to see her again. Jonathan registered this, and liked them for it.

Jonathan looked at Merrit and was too tired to think of the right thing to say.

"He's death to a dinner party," she said. But Jonathan was not entirely consoled, and came up with no consoling leave-taking remark for Merrit as she stood at the doorway in her coat, her face and shoulders sagging.

## 7

BY THE TIME he entered graduate school, Morris had long known that he wanted to work in genetics and that his goal was to prove that biological heredity did not work the way current genetic science said it did. Morris was by temperament a dissenter, and he was also the observant son of an Indiana farmer who bred and raised soy, corn, and pigs. "Any decent farmer," twenty-two-year-old Morris insisted to his fellow graduate students at Harvard in 1979, "*knows* that it doesn't really happen the way genetics says it's supposed to. Genetics draws you a pretty picture, with just enough reality to give a lot of egomaniacs room to run around saying they've got all the answers." His classmates tended to be put off by his argumentativeness and an embarrassing hint of Lamarckianism in his ideas, but by the time he turned forty, views like his were commonplace. He himself had carried out and published the results of dozens of closely reasoned, elegantly designed experiments that had in modest ways helped bring about the change.

Now it was obvious to everyone that epigenetic inheritance—biological inheritance that is not encoded in genes—occurred in several forms. Morris was one of the first researchers into a type of epigenetic inheritance called genetic imprinting, the phenomenon in which one and the same gene would either be expressed or silent in an offspring, depending solely on whether it came from the mother or the father, as though it bore the "imprint" of its parental origin. The field had been new when Morris was in his twenties, but scientists quickly realized that research into genetic imprinting would shed light on the origins of many diseases, cancers, and developmental disorders, and on healthy human development and other areas of genetic research as well.

Morris's early post-doctoral work at the Vandeventer Institute of Genetic Studies at Princeton, under his mentor, Nigel Duckworth, had helped support the Duckworth theory, an early explanation of how genetic imprinting worked. Morris had readily found funding to continue this work after he left the institute. It was a hot subject to which he appeared to take a conventionally promising approach, thus attracting support from leaders in the field who were anxious for independent confirmation of their own work. Morris had several good job offers to choose from; he moved first to the University of Chicago and in a few years was wooed away to Stanford's Leland Center for Genetics. There, however, Morris began to push his work in unexpected, deviant directions, and the trajectory of his career leveled and then turned downward.

Morris had begun experiments that cast doubt on the Duckworth theory; it became clear that he had, from the beginning, believed the Duckworth theory to be wrong and had been quietly following a long-range plan to disprove it. His results suggested at the very least that the phenomena Duckworth had investigated might well be nothing more than an unimportant part of a bigger, far more obscure picture than researchers had expected to see. These findings were sure to arouse interest, but Morris had not yet published them, as he hoped to expand on their significance through another, relatively short set of experiments, focusing on mechanisms by which genes were insulated from the effects of genetic imprinting. The hypothesis underlying this projected work was novel, startling even, to those accustomed to thinking in the Duckworth framework. Success was by no means guaranteed, but Morris felt sure not only that he alone among researchers in the field was on the right track, but also that he was three quarters of the way there. This remaining work, and a period of thought and analysis in which to write up his findings, was what Morris hoped to accomplish during his stay at Columbia. If things worked out as he expected, recognition—and a good tenured job—would follow quickly.

Morris's solid research for the past fifteen years should have seen him safely past the inherent skepticism of grant committees when it came time to apply for support for the final phase of this work. But because Morris's theory cut directly across the received views and the views of Duckworth, who was still the chief man in the field, it had been a struggle to find funding. Duckworth was just over sixty, with a prickly ego and brains enough to know that there was room to doubt his own approach. He had originally seen Morris's work as an intelligent but second-string reaffirmation of his own and therefore was prepared to support Morris's grant applications enthusiastically. But then Morris began complaining, publicly, that the deadheads had held up progress in this area for fifteen years. *Scientific American* phoned him for a quote on the subject, which they printed:

> Anyone who explains the evolution of genetic imprinting in terms of maternal-paternal genetic conflict or selfishness or any other concept that attributes wishes and intentions to biochemical processes is resorting to non-scientific metaphors. That's not science, it's emotion. You could just as easily describe the same facts as a courtly dance between the sexes, as a genetic minuet of cooperation. Sometimes, maybe it's psychologically useful to think about the processes of heredity as a sexual war or conflict, but scientifically it's nonsense, empty verbiage. It adds nothing to the verifiable content.

Everyone in the field knew that Morris was talking about Duckworth's latest research, which gave an evolutionary explanation of genetic imprinting in terms of competition between the sexes, with each trying to inactivate the other's genes. Morris won a few debating points but lost any further support from Duckworth in getting grants, and came dangerously close to being unable to work at all, for Duckworth's influence in the profession grew stronger each year. He was becoming more and more of a grand old man, hobnobbing with social biologists and economists, citing their theories in biological papers. It was this sort of thing, which impressed everyone else, that had annoyed Morris enough to give the quote to *Scientific American*.

Besides alienating Duckworth, Morris aggravated his problems by failing to publish most of his new work. Morris had held back because he knew that there were still holes in his own thinking, facts that he could not account for as neatly as the Duckworth theory did; and Morris hoped to be able to explain these anomalies before exposing his data to public scrutiny. Then, worst of all, his lab was tainted by scandal.

Morris's last set of experiments had been ruined by a mentally unstable young graduate student in his lab named Joey Delano, who, in order to make his own work appear more valuable, had fabricated data and spoiled the experiments of a postgrad working for Morris. Morris's work had been seriously delayed. The minor scandal was gossiped about in biology departments all over the country, and the credibility of Morris's work and the reputation of the Leland Center were tarnished. Morris wasted six months trying to salvage this data, on which depended much of his justification for the new grant. Although he undid the damage, his colleagues continued to complain, unjustly, that the whole fiasco was due to his lax supervision. In the end, the scandal, combined with the antagonism of colleagues whom Morris had offended over the years, and the fact that his latest theories were dismissed by his more hidebound colleagues, inspired efforts to squeeze him out. The breakup of Morris's five-year relationship with another biologist in his department got entangled in these machinations, as his former lover became convinced that Morris was, scientifically, off the deep end, and, romantically, not the marrying kind. She discreetly shared with colleagues her intimate feelings about both these convictions, along with speculations about ways he *might* have prevented the Joey Delano disaster. These confidences always ended with the thought, expressed with a sigh, that "God knows, if we were honest, we'd all admit something like this could have happened to any of us"—and had the effect of making her listeners feel more comfortable, not less, in blaming Morris and believing that their own virtues would have protected them from any similar fiasco.

It was at this time that Morris began negotiations with Columbia for a visiting position, in spite of its tentative and doubtful status. During this tormented period, telephone calls to the Braithwaites were frequent, and sometimes almost teary. Charles tried to understand the scientific business as well as he could. He took an enthusiastic pro-Morris stance, and believed that he was certain to win a major bioscience prize as a vindication—if only he could complete the last leg of his research. Anne and Charles had never liked the sound of Morris's ex-girlfriend Samantha, who called herself Sam, and they had urged him to cut her loose even before the full extent of the damage she had done became clear. They were face-to-face with Morris for the first time in two years the morning after Jonathan Riesbeck's dinner party. They had invited him to come to breakfast and look at his new apartment, which he insisted on doing as soon as they had exchanged welcomes. They had not expected him to look as well as he did, or to have so much spring in his step. When they last saw him, he had seemed older and slower. Perhaps the situation at Stanford had been worse than they had understood.

Anne and Charles gave Morris the keys that Lizzie's trustee, Eugene

Becker, had instructed the superintendent to give them and went with him across the hallway to point out the blandishments of apartment 9D. A wave of musty air greeted them when they opened the door. They wandered through the empty rooms, flinging windows open. The place was barren, and with the walls and floors denuded you could see how worn were the parquet floors and how faded, peeling, and dirty the paint and wallpaper. The kitchen's appliances, installed during a mid-century attempt at modernization when Lizzie had moved back in to nurse her mother, appeared to function well and had been left perfectly clean. The rickety kitchen cabinets and the large basin sink, with its exposed pipes, were of even older vintage. Lizzie's window-box flowers had feebly bloomed, despite their total neglect, and Morris found an old bottle in a cabinet and watered them. The footprints of Lizzie's bedstead marked its absence in her bedroom. The empty apartment, to Anne, seemed to insist that Lizzie's loveless end was sad, or even worse than sad. Wandering the rooms, she began to grieve not only for Lizzie but also for some hardness of heart in herself that had until now maintained there was nothing to mourn in the death of a very aged woman. Staring at the prints of the bedstead on the floor, Anne feared that this unwitnessed and unwept death, demanding recognition, might render the place uninhabitable. She gave a worried look to Morris.

"It's big," Morris said finally, and sighed, apparently displeased. But, he insisted, he was not disturbed by thoughts of the prior tenant, whom he had never heard of until Charles and Anne suggested he rent the place. Looking at things solely as a matter of real estate, Anne and Charles wondered whether Morris understood his good fortune in acquiring even a brief hold on such an enormous apartment.

"From the New York point of view, you're a little spoiled. See—you've even got a potato bin," Anne said, struggling unsuccessfully to open a small door in the wall under the kitchen window. Despite the lack of modern appliances, paint, and adequate wiring, the apartment was pleasingly designed. Its thick walls and floors reduced city noises to a faint baritone hum; light and air were ample; there were graceful moldings, high ceilings, built-in bookcases, and ceremonial French doors between the living and dining rooms.

"Oh it's fine, really. Actually, it's just a little too fine," Morris replied. "I'm used to one room for sleeping and another for working. This is a place that's trying to be serious, for raising six kids in."

"Mm—maybe four," said Anne. "Unless you divided that big bedroom."

"You're forgetting the maid's room," Morris said.

"That's your study, obviously." They told Morris the story of Lizzie Miller, the trustee, and the pleasant young priest who had come to call on her too late and regretted neglecting her.

"Imagine outliving everyone who'd ever known you," Morris said, "everyone who'd been alive when you were young. That would be impenetrable loneliness, unimaginable loneliness. I think I'd get loopy. I'll bet a lot of them do. And people say they're senile, as though they don't have human feelings anymore, whereas really they are breaking down under intolerable emotional strains. That's what happens if you don't have kids."

"I think he really wants six children," Anne muttered to Charles back in their own kitchen as they set out coffee, bagels, lox, cheeses, and fruits. Charles looked scornful. Jane, who missed nothing, heard this, and studied Morris intently when he walked in brushing a cobweb from a handsome, new-looking pullover.

"Why do you dress better now?" she demanded, aggressively and publicly, relying on the child's privilege of naïveté to ask embarrassing questions — unwisely, as it happened, for Morris, after considering for a moment, decided that she had outgrown any such privilege. He responded with full adult sharpness: "I don't care for that tone of voice, and I don't like rude personal questions."

Charles and Anne, shamed by her rudeness, nodded at each other. This was what she deserved. Jane was stung, and her cheeks flamed. When the conversation resumed, she tried to slip away from the table bearing a plate laden with food, but Anne refused to permit it. Jane often sought to engage in some forbidden act after she had been scolded, as though trying to establish the principle that scolding, being always unjust, earned her the right to further misdemeanors. Anne knew Jane thought this way, and refused to let it pass. "Eat it here or leave it. You know better than that." Charles realized that he had been too intimidated by the thought of a scene with Janie to say anything, but, strengthened by Anne's example, he responded quickly when the girl turned on Anne a look of frank hatred. It all ended, inevitably, with Jane sobbing in her room, Stuart sobbing out of sympathy in his mother's arms in the kitchen, and Ellen shrugging philosophically at her father and Morris while continuing her meal with a good appetite. She knew that Janie was often unreasonable lately — always pushing things as far as she could. She herself wasn't at all afraid of Janie's temper, and was glad to see her parents stand up to it.

"She's just at that age, that's all," said Anne, watching the sniffling Stuart furtively slip cherries into his pocket.

"Nonsense," Charles returned. "Something's eating her. I'd think you'd be more curious about what's on her mind."

"Nothing's *really* eating her," Anne told Stuart with a convincing smile. "That's just an expression. It means she has a worry. And, Charles, this all is in no way my fault and there's no need to worry about my maternal instincts."

"Of course it's your fault," Charles said. "My children would be perfect if their mother raised them right."

"He's just joking, Stuey," Anne said quickly.

"Yes, I am," said Charles, and winked at Stuart. Stuart soon slipped away to Jane's room, to comfort her with the cherries bulging in his pockets, followed by Ellen, who didn't want Jane to think she was enjoying her disgrace. Under the circumstances, neutrality was the decent attitude for a sibling.

"I'm going to stick to fighting with twelve-year-olds," reflected Morris. "I do much worse fighting with older women. Last night I dared to challenge Merrit Roth. It felt like mugging Mother Teresa."

"Merrit? What?" Charles and Anne were curious and dismayed. They were protective of Merrit and, since hearing about this latest breakup, felt more and more uneasy about the shape of her life.

"Morris!" Anne said reprovingly. "Where did you see Merrit?"

"Anyway, she looked great. She must be forty, right?"

"Thirty-eight. Morris, what did you do? I hope it wasn't like that horrible Christmas dinner when you were in graduate school. I really don't understand. Here's Merrit, with the best heart in the world, the best friend anyone could have—generous, loyal, kind, witty, lovely, intelligent—and you never meet her without trying to mortify her. It's unforgivable." Anne fell silent, dimly aware that this small tirade (out of character for her) was fueled partly by guilt about her own increasing disaffection from Merrit. Since their unpleasant conversation a few days ago, Anne had found herself thinking that Merrit became something akin to foolish . . . or rigid or . . . false as she grew older. Anne could not put it into words, because she found it unendurable to admit she had such thoughts. Now she was ashamed of bursting out at Morris; she had gone too far and didn't know how to backtrack. Charles was looking at her with a slight frown.

"Anne," Morris began in a patient, curiously unoffended voice. "I don't hate Merrit. I don't hurt or humiliate Merrit. I fight with her."

Anne could only emit a strained sound, conveying both scorn and remorse.

"I was nothing more than sarcastic—just teased her. Actually, I had reason to be a bit annoyed. You ask her. She'll tell you. I'm not going to say anything else. We were both at Jonathan Riesbeck's dinner last night. He's the guy I mentioned to you, on that committee. Not a bad sort at all, by the way. But he acts like her doting uncle or something. Is she going with anyone?"

"She recently broke up with someone in England, um, . . . Brendan McGarry," Charles told him, unwillingly, for he felt that the famous name would reconfirm Morris in some prejudice about Merrit, even though Charles was not able to discern what the prejudice was. The waters here were dark and murky.

"Brendan *McGarry*? Ha! The social-science-for-the-people guy? The one who's always deconstructing right-wing policy dreck with left-wing psychoanalytic dreck?"

"We haven't met him," Anne said primly.

"Well, I have. No—not met, was admitted to his presence, at a conference last year. He's on some committee for humane science or something like that. I had no idea he was Merrit's steady."

"I haven't seen you this upbeat in years," said Anne, feeling her way toward forgiveness. She let him kiss her cheek even though he was still enjoying his laugh.

"Sometime, you'll tell me why you think Brendan McGarry is so funny," she said, and left to seek reconciliation with Janie, too, feeling that enough time had elapsed to make this possible.

Charles looked inquiringly at Morris when Anne was gone.

Morris said simply, "A real ass, is all. I mean, a class-A jerk."

Charles nodded. Then it was so, because Morris, much as he misjudged women, understood men very well, and his judgments were never ideological. Charles didn't ask what had happened the night before, knowing that Merrit would tell Anne.

"So what's Merrit up to now?"

Charles explained that Merrit had returned permanently, on the heels of her breakup, that her last book had had an enthusiastic reception, and that she was supposedly at work on the next, but Anne and Charles thought her writing was stalled somehow. Although she had become such a hot item in the past few years, giving talks and appearing on panels, Merrit was lonely. Anne said that half the problem was that Merrit had always been over-involved with her somewhat indifferent mother. She came home to see her almost every weekend when she was in college, and as an adult moved into an apartment just down the street from her, visiting or calling almost every day.

"How did she manage to leave her mother to go to London?"

"She was e-mailing her constantly, and Anne too. We were hearing all about this great love affair, then out of the blue there's a big bust-up."

"So what's going to become of her?" Morris wondered. "This shouldn't be happening. If she weren't so annoying, it would be sad."

"We think it's sad. Anne has got her talked into seeing a shrink again." Charles thought that Morris's situation was sad, too, but said nothing.

"That's no good."

"We'll see."

"You and Anne don't understand Merrit."

Here Charles gave Morris a baleful look and said that perhaps Merrit was a subject on which they could not expect to agree. Morris, however, could not see why disagreeing about Merrit was so disagreeable to them. Morris could be obtuse.

They found a more neutral subject in the question of when Morris could plan to move his few furnishings and piano into 9D, and Morris went across the hall one more time, returning with a list of things he needed from the hardware store. He seemed more enthusiastic about the apartment, and exulted about the study he would have at home and all the friends he would be able to put up. Hearing Jane playing Chopin at the piano, he went to listen and was generous in his praise when she finished.

Jane blushed deeply, for she took her music seriously, and Morris, as she knew, had been a talented pianist, who, when Charles first met him at a music camp and later at Juilliard, had been torn between science and music. Her dignity re-established, she thanked him modestly. Before he left they played four hands, and he made her laugh with silly musical feints and jokes, winning forgiveness even from Stuart, who climbed into Morris's lap to be near the fun but refused to be shown the piano keys to play for "Yankee Doodle," insisting that he was a violinist. Charles and Anne came in just as Morris was standing and announcing that he had to go. Anne had been hoping to hear what he thought of Jane's playing. Charles, though, took his child's genius for granted and cared less about it, too. He wanted no children of his setting out on the long road to the concert hall, and hoped Jane would give up these dreams, but didn't say so, out of respect for her right to decide for herself. Jane understood her father's wishes, and knew that her mother refused to think about what striving for a concert career meant. The sense of endangerment that Jane felt as a result was one of the many things she was furious about.

# 8

ONE DAY EARLY in August, a week after he had moved into 635 West 117th Street, Morris walked the few blocks to Le Monde to meet Lily Freund for lunch. Columbia's summer-session final exams having ended, students had deserted the neighborhood and Le Monde was half empty. The restaurant was a new one, dark and woody, as it had to be to attract the local population. Lily was already there, sitting at a window and reading a newspaper folded vertically, New York subway–style, so as to take up minimal space.

"Wait," Morris said, by way of greeting. "This is Friday. Why aren't you working?"

"It's August—vacation."

"Imagine. August is when I get my work done. I never take vacations."

"Do you also work in the lab every night until midnight?"

"Of course. Am I late?"

"I'm early. I'm always early," said Lily.

"Good. I hate waiting for people. Now, are you going to New England for vacation?"

"To Maine, on Monday."

Morris laughed. He found humor in people acting true to type. Lily smiled, happy to have the joke be on her.

While Lily scrutinized the menu, Morris got his first daylight opportunity to study her face. In Jonathan's dining room, he had decided she was in her middle thirties, with a youthful appearance, like Merrit. Indeed, she and Merrit had struck him as age peers. But with the vigorous midday sun illuminating her features and Morris straining to evaluate her scientifically, rather than relying on misleading social cues, he began to think her much younger.

"How old are you anyway?" he demanded as soon as this thought took form in his mind.

"Twenty-seven," she replied.

"Jeez," said Morris. "Going on forty. I mean the way you act, not the way you look."

"Some women might think that's not very gallant of you," Lily said, "but I know it's true. They've said that about me since I was ten."

She didn't seem even slightly displeased. Something around her mouth suggested that she may even have been pleased with him, and with herself too. Morris did not know where to go with this, and sat without saying anything. After a comfortable pause, he began again, firing questions at Lily about herself, which resulted in Lily learning a great deal more about Morris than he learned about her. Morris was aware that she was reacting to him with psychoanalytical nerve tendrils that other people did not have and had ideas about him that he could not fathom. But, having little self-consciousness, he was not made uneasy by her acuteness—particularly as he felt that it lacked any critical edge. Lily had sparkling black eyes, creamy skin, and a graceful, rounded figure that stopped short of plumpness. Morris verged on being smitten already.

They ordered from an affectless young waitress, gauntly thin, who had short black hair of which a few tufts were bleached pale yellow. "This place doesn't really feel like Morningside Heights, does it?" Lily said, and Morris knew what she meant. When she inquired politely whether he liked the neighborhood and Columbia, he told her the entire story of his coming, not omitting the scientific aspects, because, as it turned out, Lily was an M.D., who both grasped the technical issues and understood why the stakes were so high. She leaned forward in her chair, interested as much in the science as in why he had come to Columbia.

"You really got backed into a hard place," she commented. "You might have a better shot at a tenured job if you'd stayed at Stanford, but the atmosphere there must have been intolerable."

"You mean," he said, after a moment, "backed into a corner? Or caught between a rock and a hard place?"

"Right."

"Did you hear what you said? You said 'backed into a hard place.' Hehheh."

"A slip of the tongue," she said. "A Freudian slip."

"What kind of slip of the tongue is that? Both things have the same meaning. That's no Freudian slip. Nothing's unintended."

"I do that sometimes." Lily tried to remember. "Once I said something was 'shut and dried.'"

"Like 'open and shut' and 'cut and dried'?" Morris laughed again.

"Why is that so funny to you?"

"A psychoanalyst who makes non-Freudian slips of the tongue. Cracks me up. I don't know why." And Morris did, here, slightly redden, and had to struggle to contain his amusement, for which he had no sensible explanation. Meanwhile, as Morris was not too distracted to notice, Lily was far more interested in understanding Morris's amusement than in being amusing. It was flattering, all that attention she gave him. Women didn't usually think there was anything puzzling about Morris; they liked him or didn't, but they assumed they understood him. It took a psychoanalyst, Morris thought, to be buffaloed by him—a thought that brought him again to the edge of laughter.

"You know, I'm not really very hard to understand, Lily," he remarked, out of the blue, in a patient and reassuring voice. "Or, as you might put it, I'm clear as a book. An open glass."

Lily smiled appreciatively.

The food came, but neither of them felt hungry. They began discussing her professional history, and Morris learned that the psychoanalytical institute did not require an M.D. but that Lily had gotten one because she thought it would be useful and because she had been so young when she finished college—only twenty. She was the youngest candidate at the institute by many years.

"And you're Jonathan's cousin. There's not much family resemblance."

"Actually, I'm his second cousin once removed—the grandchild of his mother's first cousin. Kissing cousins, so to speak."

"That's not really a cousin."

"Our family has tended to exaggerate the incest barriers," she said apologetically, "to the point that we feel related to almost everybody even when they're not really our relations."

Morris was astounded to hear such a thought voiced—and so conversationally, matter-of-factly. Even Anne would not say something as peculiar as that. Lily did not appear to notice his reaction, and went on to explain that she and Jonathan were all that was left of their family. Between them, they had no parents, no grandparents, aunts, uncles, siblings, or cousins.

Some had been lost to old age, others to disease or accident. But the real reason for the family's decline was the tendency of its members toward remaining single or marrying late and having at most one child. Morris, on the other hand, as he told Lily, was one of five children, and both his parents and three of his grandparents were living, as well as aunts, uncles, and cousins in numbers beyond the power of the most dutiful to visit.

"You're the oldest in your family, I'll bet," said Lily, and asked him how many boys and girls.

"After me, four girls," Morris told her.

She nodded, and Morris did not fail to detect the shadow of a conclusion pass briefly across her face and disappear, leaving it neutral and sociable again.

"You want to watch out with the secret shrink opinions," Morris warned.

"I never push my hand too far," she replied.

Morris was dumbfounded. "Did you hear what you said? I can't believe it! 'Push my hand too far'! Let's see, you've got there, 'overplay my hand' and 'push my luck' and 'go too far.' That's a triple. It's amazing how you do that."

"I guess I really meant it, that I really *never* overplay my hand." She smiled, but she was slightly unnerved. Morris wondered if she did tend to overplay her hand. She was really adorable.

Morris picked up the check the moment it came and insisted on paying. He wanted Lily to be in no doubt about the nature of his interest in her, and she did not object or offer to share it. When they left the restaurant, she invited him to visit her in the house she shared with friends in Maine, but he was not ready to accept such a major invitation. He was half-dazzled—but only half. Morris was a man of great self-control, who could decide whether or not to be dazzled, could even choose what degree of bedazzlement to experience. She was exotic; she had actually talked about "exaggerated incest barriers."

Morris wanted to get married, and seeing that he could not marry Anne, he had refrained from falling in love with her, and some years ago had even gone so far as to seek Charles's advice on finding a wife. After all, if you want to play the game well, you should get the advice of the best players. In Morris's eyes, Charles was the best-married man he knew. Charles had said to pick someone who smelled like home. This advice nettled Morris, who was socially liberal. It suggested that one should pick a person born to the same race, class, religion, or culture as one's own, whereas, he argued to Charles, they both knew people—including Charles and Anne—who had not done anything of the kind and were happily married. What smells like home, Charles had replied, is often as much a function of individual psychology and education as of external factors. "And what if home didn't smell so good?" Morris continued. Then, Charles had replied, people tended to marry badly or not to marry at all, until they had found a new sense of home, announcing yet another rule that his own case, apparently, contradicted. How smug Charles was.

In any event, Morris reflected, he was not sure that Lily smelled like home—or that she didn't, either. She hadn't really laughed yet, for instance. Smiles, but no laughing with her. And she was young—fourteen, fifteen years younger than he was. He didn't care for that. Younger, for the sake of babies, would be good, but not that young. When she was his age, he'd be sixtyish. No good. Was he, perhaps, being too particular, too mechanical? Like those people who wrote personal ads with lists of qualifications? Yet, in his mind, a woman in her late thirties had passed the point of marriageability. He felt uncomfortable about this, as it rendered women younger than himself unmarriageable, assuming that other men reasoned as Morris did. And a general social rule like this would be unjust. Yet Morris knew he would not marry someone who was past her mid-thirties. He did not intend to sacrifice his happiness to a principle. And maybe he had to consider someone under thirty. He was drawn into fantasies about Lily that began with her creamy skin. He decided that she was not the typical twenty-seven-year-old and would not be the typical forty-five-year-old. He liked her a lot; had not reacted so strongly to any woman for years. He wouldn't rule out going to Maine. He'd sit on it, and decide after getting his apartment in reasonable condition.

The following week, he discussed all this with Charles in the living room of 9D while waiting for the contractors, who were going to do some painting and repairing and put in new wiring so that Morris could set up his computer. The room held unpacked boxes of books, a few pieces of furniture scattered randomly about, and a large black grand piano. Charles was scornful of Morris's hesitation to accept Lily's invitation. "Why not just go up next weekend? Why do you have to make such a big deal out of it? You don't have to finish all this first."

"All the way to Maine for a weekend?"

"Fly to Portland and rent a car. Stay four days. Why not?" But Morris had settled on an order of events that suited him, and was not to be persuaded. Morris was really becoming fixed in his ways, Charles reflected; perhaps he really was a grumpy old bachelor. Kids kept you flexible. Without them, you got used to having everything just so, your own way. When Charles had gone, Morris, for his part, thought philosophically that Charles was under the impression that people on the wrong side of forty ran their love lives the same way Charles and his friends had done when they were twenty-year-olds—when Charles had met Anne and said good-bye to all that. Charles didn't know—how could he?—the way grown-ups went about these things.

Charles told Anne about Morris and Lily over dinner that evening. Ellen and Jane listened with their eyes fixed on their plates, in an unsuccessful attempt to conceal how keenly they were interested.

"I like the idea of a child psychotherapist," said Anne, "but twenty-seven is young. It speaks well of him that he hesitates over that."

"Yes, it's worth hesitating over. But oddballs like Morris and this woman—he says she's odd, anyway—often marry across gaps of age, culture, and so forth, because they find it so hard to meet anyone congenial. The number of potential mates the world offers people like them is very small. When they finally do run into one, they're lonely and they jump into each other's arms. And I have a feeling that Morris's rough edges might be a little smoother with someone younger, who might arouse a protective feeling in him."

"I totally agree," said Anne, nodding, and seeing that Jane had stopped eating, she asked the girl, "What do you think, sweetie?"

"I think it's nice. But I don't think Morris's rough edges would be any smoother with someone young."

"On second thought," Anne said, recollecting Morris's scolding of Jane a few months ago, "I have a feeling you're right. Don't you, Charles?"

"On second thought," he said, "I think she's absolutely right. In fact, I wonder if anything could soften up Morris. Maybe just falling in love."

"Has he ever been in love?" Anne asked.

"I'm not sure. I've seen him when he thought he was in love, but he was always so in control, I had my doubts."

Stuart smiled at his mother. "I'm falling in love with you." Then, climbing into her lap, he confided happily, "That's just an expression," and Ellen and Jane laughed, and Anne had to protect his dignity.

"Stuart is quite right that it's just an expression. You don't really fall, do you, sweetie? People say that because sometimes being in love happens very quickly and excitingly. But actually, sometimes it also happens quietly and slowly."

"Oedipus," muttered Charles, who, having raised only daughters until Stuart arrived, was surprised that he felt slightly disgruntled by Stuart's amorous declarations. He wondered whether they should ask to be told whether the amniocentesis showed a boy or girl on the way. With the others, they hadn't wanted to know.

# 9

WHEN FATHER MERRIWEATHER met Claire, one of Elizabeth Miller's caretakers, on Broadway in front of the bank, the August heat was already oppressive. They were glad to step into the sterile cool of its lobby. Claire was twenty-five, and although she was low-key and had the figure of a woman twenty years older, she had multiple piercings, anarchic curly red hair, a stretch top, tight jeans, and thick-soled clogs. Something open in her demeanor inclined Merriweather to trust her. He regretted having waited so long to call her.

"Claire, I'm just a little worried," he said. "I don't know what sort of man Becker is . . ."

"No good."

"It's possible. In any event, I'm worried about whether he could make trouble for you when he finds out about your access to this bank account and safety deposit box for so many years." And here Merriweather felt uneasy, since he couldn't justify to himself trusting Claire over Becker, whom he had never even met. Why should he be so sure it wasn't Claire who had cheated the old woman, assuming that anyone had? However, Anne, who had known both Lizzie and Claire for many years, seemed certain that Claire's word was reliable, and Claire herself conveyed an innocent faith that Merriweather would trust her. It was this that persuaded him of her integrity; crooked people—even many honest people—never had that faith. Claire did not want Becker to know that she had access to Lizzie's bank account and safety deposit box, however, and had not expected Merriweather to tell him. "Why do you have to do that?" she demanded.

"We could just leave now and forget the whole thing, I suppose, but that wouldn't be fair to Miss Miller, would it? Someone's got to make sure he knows about the money and the will, and when he knows, he'll go to the bank and find out you're the cosignatory. It would be better if I told him."

Claire nodded and walked toward the customer service desk. Her mind, Merriweather saw, was quick and efficient; she accepted the necessity of making these facts known as readily as she trusted Merriweather's good intentions, and relied on him to trust hers. Standing there in the lobby of the bank, Merriweather was struck that Claire took goodness for granted. She expected it—unlike lawyers, unlike most of the parishioners at St. Ursula's—and this gave him a tiny tremor of joy. Resisting a momentary impulse to hug her gratefully, he tried instead to imitate her matter-of-factness and take all this faith and trust for granted, but he failed. Against his will, he beamed at her for a moment, arousing a familiar sense of disappointment in himself as he sensed her subtle displeasure with this. Such little moments punctuated Merriweather's life, and were wrenching. Just when he loved his fellow human beings the most, he did something that put them off. The problem was, he thought, that he was a bit of a nerd.

Aloud, he told Claire, "But most likely nothing will be said, and if anyone does raise questions, Anne will back you up. We all will." Now Merriweather was pledged to faith in Claire, and why, he asked himself, had he volunteered to climb out on this particular limb? It was a good thing he was a priest and not a lawyer.

They stated their business to a young woman at the customer service desk, who escorted them down a winding flight of stairs and asked them to be seated in a cubicle that barely held the two of them. She soon brought them a small green metal contraption, which Claire unlocked. It held nothing but an envelope inscribed LAST WILL AND TESTAMENT OF ELIZA-BETH ANNE MILLER, JUNE 14, 1995. The envelope contained the original copy of a will executed with blue ink in Lizzie's hand, which was surprisingly firm. The will was short. "It says," Merriweather told Claire, "that you get fifty thousand dollars, Monique gets twenty-five thousand, and Anne Braithwaite inherits everything else she has, and if Anne feels like it, Miss Miller would be grateful if she makes gifts on her behalf, in Anne's discretion."

"That's real nice of her," said Claire, "but she didn't have no fifty thousand dollars."

"You'll get at least the fifteen in this bank."

"You mean ten for me and five for Monique, right?"

"Well, um, legally I don't know, actually. We'll have to see. And you never know. There might be more assets in the trustee's hands. I didn't realize Miss Miller knew Anne Braithwaite that well."

"She didn't really. But she was crazy about her, and her kids. So I'm not all that surprised, especially since she knew they were always hard up. I remember, one day it was cold and she noticed the little boy was wearing his sister's old coat, and she thought it was terrible that it wasn't really a little boy's coat. She talked to Anne all the time—she hardly talked to anyone else. Actually, Anne talked to her mostly. Anne told her everything— I don't know why, except maybe she just liked to entertain her, you know? And Anne was real good at figuring out what she meant, so she didn't have to talk too much on her bad days."

Merriweather told himself that proximity explained the whole thing, but the coincidental quality of his meeting with the Braithwaites and their turning out to be Elizabeth Miller's heirs—all this was slightly rattling. He himself, moreover, had a pang of disappointment on St. Ursula's behalf, for he had not been able to forget that Lizzie's parents had been generous to the church and that Lizzie had made a gift to the church every year until she died. What did this mean, this directive to Anne to make gifts on Lizzie's behalf "in her discretion"? Probably she was thinking about the building employees and her other caretakers.

Father Merriweather and Claire asked the clerk to make a copy of the will, replaced the original in its box, and returned to the heat of Broadway. They agreed to have the deposit box and checking account escrowed for the time being, so that Claire would be relieved of any responsibility or suspicion. But Merriweather's concern on that score was allayed. Bank records, the clerk had informed them, corroborated that there had been no withdrawals from the account since late winter and that no one had ever visited the safety deposit box after the initial visit, when the will was deposited. Merriweather promised Claire that he would call Monique, Becker, and the Braithwaites right after lunch. Then he would call her and let her know what steps she should take, but, he told her, things like this always move slowly. She shouldn't count on getting any money for months. Once more he smiled at her. She said, "Thanks, Father" sincerely, and he was touched—too touched, he noticed.

Merriweather walked immediately to St. Ursula's, thinking again that the entire affair was strange. Perhaps all these coincidences were providential. This was certainly not your average, expectable course of events.

That afternoon over lunch on the old mahogany table in the dining room of the rectory, Father Merriweather told the whole unsettling story to Father Quincy, who took it in at about the same leisurely speed as the lobster salad. "It's not so strange," the rector said finally. "An elderly woman who's outlived all her connections dies and leaves her money to a longtime neighbor and friend who needs money for her kids. Nothing strange at all."

"It's just so unlikely that everything gets found out in this haphazard manner," Merriweather said, "that I should decide to get involved, when the church essentially abandoned her for fifteen years, and then actually be present for the discovery of the will."

"Well, what I want to know is why hadn't this young woman, the caretaker, told anybody there was a will in a safety deposit box—if she's such a fine young woman? If she'd been more sensible, it wouldn't all have happened so haphazardly."

"I wonder if she simply didn't understand that it all rested on her. She probably thought Becker would have some other way to find out."

"It wouldn't have hurt just to ask her. That's one thing here that doesn't make sense. And another is why Elizabeth Miller didn't give this will to her trustee. I tell you what. This woman had no family except this church, so let's act a little like family. You call up that young nurse and the Braithwaites, and we'll all go visit this man Becker together and see what else he's got. There may be a substantial estate, and we'll just help make sure the right people get it. If Anne Braithwaite is requested to make gifts on Elizabeth Miller's behalf, that might be aimed at us. Now, don't just call her. Go see her."

"I'll go, but Miss Miller couldn't have had in mind anything for us. Don't forget, I knocked on the Braithwaites' door. They would never have known we had any connection to Miss Miller if I hadn't. I still can't help thinking it's all so strange that there has to be some significance in it."

"A coincidence or two is nothing to get all excited about, Greg. God speaks plainly, and he doesn't play magic tricks."

# 10

IN MID-AUGUST, the Braithwaites' precarious finances suffered three toppling blows. A lucrative series of concert engagements for Charles was canceled, reducing by a third the income they had counted on to see them to the end of the year. Charles ranted about lawsuits, but his contract unambiguously gave the sponsor an out. On the very morning on which his agent called to convey this disastrous news, they received a notice in the mail that the board of directors of 635 West 117th Street had voted a heavy assessment for repairs and renovations, along with a permanent and sizable increase in the monthly maintenance charges, and a letter informing them that the nursery school in which they intended to enter Stuart had refused his application for a scholarship. Instead, the school sent a bill for roughly half of the twelve-thousand-dollar tuition for the upcoming year, due immediately. They might have coped with any one of these setbacks, but the three together overwhelmed them.

"We won't send him," Anne said, her mind firmly fixed on the least of the three misfortunes. "I'll find a play group I can send him to for two or three mornings a week. I thought five half-days was too much anyway."

"Anne, we are beyond that. Of course we won't send him. We won't send the girls to their school, either."

"Public school?" Anne asked fearfully. "It's August. What good school could we get them into at this point?"

"Moving out of the city seems more sensible to me."

"Do you mean Cleveland?"

"If only we still had the option, but we don't."

The revelation that this time Charles did not intend to put on a show of considering Cleveland placed Anne on notice that he was serious. A move to the nearest affordable suburb, he said, some place with good public schools, was the only possible option.

"But our lives are here. All our relatives and friends are here, our work. We grew up here. And what becomes of the children's music school if we live in Westchester?"

"It won't be the same, but I'm not sure I mind terribly. Most children grow up to be happy without the world's fanciest musical education. And our family and friends can easily come to visit, and we'll visit them."

"But, Charles, you'd be coming home late on the train all the time. We're pretty old to be learning to drive, you know, and we don't want to; we like walking. In the suburbs you can't walk to the greengrocer or the newsstand or the shoe repair shop or the hardware store. We don't know about lawns and storm windows and roofs. We've lived in this apartment since we were married, and it suits us. The children don't know any other home. They'll be so unhappy."

"So now we'll all become normal Americans. We'll pull up our roots and put them down again, and make new friends and habits and be fine, just like the rest of the world. And if it doesn't work out the first time, we'll do it again. Anne, this time there is no choice. We'll be bankrupt if we don't move."

Charles was all the more irritable with Anne because he felt the losses they would experience as keenly as she. He abominated cars and grassy yards, could not comprehend why anyone would want a country home when the world provided perfectly good hotels. Buses and subways were how civilized people went about their business, and trains and planes were always preferable to cars. But most of all, what template of life would be visible to his children in some leafy town on the Hudson Line? Beneficent institutions and the kind of human beings who peopled them would be odd, absent ideals, not powerful living realities as they were here in Morningside Heights. What would life feel like in a world that did not set the pursuit of music or art or science or knowledge or justice and goodness at its core? What would the children become in a world in which their parents were eccentrics, startling individuals, rather than members of a modestly coherent society in which their tastes and temperaments were readable to others, even if uncongenial?

Although both Charles and Anne thought such things, Charles, unlike

Anne, allowed some mental room for the reflection that these attitudes were parochial and self-indulgent, and tried to steel himself to accept what must be accepted. They were mourning as a dread fate the kind of possibilities most people would dream of as the good life. A nice house, maybe in a historic old town, near the city . . . they had to be reasonable, not greedy and spoiled. But Anne angrily protested this line of thinking. "Parochial and greedy and spoiled? You think we're moving from materialism to asceticism? It's the opposite. Here we can live without clothes and cars and the rest. Not there. You watch, Charles." And she cried. But Charles was not yet ready to stop blaming Anne, and Anne still believed that she was entitled to a life in Morningside Heights.

"Cleveland has a symphony and a great conservatory and a university and . . . and . . ." said Charles to Anne bitterly.

"I know," she replied, by way of admitting that this would, truly, have been preferable to Yonkers or Katonah or any of those towns lining the train routes. "What if we can get the girls scholarships? Or what if we can get them into Hunter? Or one of the magnet schools?"

"We're beyond that. It's not enough. We'll never be able to pay that assessment or the credit cards, and now we're not going to be able to pay the maintenance and the mortgage, either. We've got to sell, or we could lose this place. And," he continued, anticipating her next suggestion, "your mother will never be able to come through with enough this time. It wouldn't be right, even if she wanted to."

Anne persisted in arguing for a delay in any drastic action. She would go to the schools. She would look for temporary work to pay the assessment. Perhaps another set of high-paying engagements for Charles could be found. He should at least call the agent immediately. Of course he had already had the talk with the agent, who was scrambling to recoup but not optimistic. The canceled series was to have begun in October.

"Anne, these are all stopgaps. The fact is, we can't live here the way we have until now. It doesn't work anymore. Even if it did, our children wouldn't be able to. It's probably better for them if we set up elsewhere now."

Anne prevailed to the extent of persuading Charles to give matters three or four days to settle before taking any steps. Charles, however, resolved privately to begin calling brokers, and Anne decided to visit the schools just to see what might be done.

Merrit came by that afternoon. Hearing from Anne just how badly things stood, she offered a loan. Anne was touched, but declined on the grounds that she would never be able to pay it back; an outright gift of a smaller sum she also declined, saying that it left the real problems untouched and would only put off the inevitable. Sitting on Anne's threadbare and child-scarred sofa, they had their first tête-à-tête since the unpleasant one when Merrit had first returned to New York, and, as always happens when an angry encounter is left unresolved, were plunged back into the same murky sea of pique. The timing was bad. Anne was already full of anxiety, and Merrit didn't seem herself. Something was on her mind, and she was uncharacteristically somber, even slightly unfriendly.

"What if you got a job?" Merrit demanded. Her face showed the kind of expressionlessness that conveys polite suppression of a deeply critical attitude: a passive-aggressive maneuver borrowed from teenagers, Anne thought, for she had recently been looked at in the same way by Jane.

"I could hold down a job for at most a few months, and then the baby is due. I can't work with Stuart and a new baby."

"The whole world thinks you can."

"The whole world thinks lots of stupid things."

"Good heavens, Anne. And you used to be such a good socialist!"

"Who's not a good socialist! Name me one issue I am not a good socialist about: medicine, abortion, labor unions, civil rights, environment, Bosnia, the Tutsi, free speech—unlike you, I'm even for free speech for pornographers. What is so socialist about separating mothers from their tiny babies so they can be exploited on a job?"

"That doesn't deserve an answer. You want to know your problem, Anne?"

"No," Anne said, but Merrit continued.

"You felt too guilty about competing with Charles and possibly outshining him, and later on about letting anything matter to you except the babies, so you stopped practicing and got your ambition frustrated. Then you turned your frustrated ambition into fanatic pro-child garbage. You stay home hovering uselessly over these kids, for no real reason, and spout anti–day care nonsense. This justifies your masochistic sacrifices, gives your resentment an outlet, and keeps you in line all at the same time."

"That's psychological bunk. How it really happened is that my fanatic practicing was actually frustrated sexual and maternal longings. I hate to tell you, but when I met Charles and then when I held a real baby in my arms, I simply didn't care enough about practicing anymore. I was ecsta-

tic. My mother told me she was the same, and she played better than I did.
I love teaching children about playing more than I ever loved playing. My
kids need me here, and there are no frustrated ambitions poisoning my
soul and making a lie of my life. Come on, Merrit, show me the telltale
signs of this inner corruption you see—the tension, the suppressed depression, the compulsions, the irritability."

"I confess I don't see signs like that. But all that garbage about frustrated
sexual and maternal longings—your description of women's mental life is
hideous and depressing."

"But I wasn't describing women's mental life, just mine."

"Oh come on. You took that stuff right out of Freud, collected works,
volume and page whatever."

"Well, he could be pretty perceptive."

"If you were right about things, there'd be no hope for any of us."

"What are you talking about? I'm describing my life, not offering a
theory about women. Who's more hopeful than I am?"

"Anne, you and Charles sit here on the brink of ruin, largely as a result
of all these hopeful and happy ideas of yours."

"That's begging the question—it's begging a lot of questions."

"Is not."

"Is so."

Here Stuart entered, delighted with a debate whose terms were so congenial, and joined enthusiastically in many more hilarious rounds of "is
so" and "is not" before he could be persuaded to turn his interest to Rivers,
Roads, and Rails. This calmed the atmosphere appreciably, and Anne, determined not to let a rift develop, insisted that Merrit stay for dinner, despite her lingering sense of annoyance. Merrit hemmed and hawed, saying
she *had* to go home to work, but in the end stayed. She and Anne both
liked cooking, and by the time they finished making a meal, they felt more
easy with each other. This, however, did not lessen Merrit's moodiness,
Anne noticed, or her own irritation with Merrit, which was threatening to
become permanent.

They were already setting steaming platters on the table when the doorman rang to say that Father Merriweather was coming up. No sooner had
he appeared at the door, looking full of something, and, to his surprise,
been ushered to a chair and plate, than Morris rang the bell and asked to
borrow a broom. He was working on his apartment but could not be permitted to leave without having a few bites, even though it was so early and

he was wearing a paint-stained shirt. Charles followed up the invitation with a stern warning, delivered in the foyer, to behave himself with Merrit. Morris was annoyed by this gratuitous protectiveness toward Merrit but nonetheless glad to walk in. "Don't be absurd," he said to Charles. With his tropism toward conflict, his wish to stay was, if anything, increased by her presence, while she could now find no way to back out without her motive being obvious—and in this way was forced into spending another evening with Morris. He deduced all this readily enough, observing how she concealed her irritation when she saw him and behaved with cool civility; he even enjoyed the irony of her getting trapped by the concern with appearances which he so disliked in her.

Their guests and children ranged around their table, enjoying the sight and aroma of the plentiful meal, Charles and Anne began to forget the doom hanging over them. What could be so terribly wrong when there was a dinner like this on the table and your friends and your children were all here?

"I have some news for you," said Father Merriweather as Charles and Anne filled plates and shouted directions at children. They were too distracted to listen. "I was on my way to a meeting at the Cathedral," he continued, addressing Merrit, as no one else seemed to be paying any attention, "so I thought I'd drop by instead of calling, because I have some news, some really . . ."

"Good. It's time they were converted," said Charles, looking around to be sure all were served.

"To Christianity you mean? The Cathedral?" Merriweather asked, amused. "How did you know about the problems over there?"

"We took Stuart and the cat over to be blessed on St. Francis's day and they invoked the earth goddess Maia and a lot of spirits. I mean, it wasn't even monotheism. I wanted to expose Stuey to the influence of the God of the Scriptures, not some cheesy primitive deities. What goes on over there?"

"They lost the faith."

"They lost the faith and acquired the Cathedral?" Merrit asked.

"It's changing for the better now," Father Merriweather said, smiling at Merrit, whom he thought spectacularly pretty. "Interesting that you object, Charles, since you say you're an atheist. I would have thought you'd prefer religion to be multicultural and primitive."

"Of course not. We want to reject the God of our own fathers," Charles said, "not someone else's. We don't like that tolerant, P.C. type of atheism that likes to play-act religious ceremonies. Why don't they dig up a mono-theist to install over there?"

"I think they might. We're monotheists at St. Ursula's, by the way, next time you want to expose Stuart to Christian monotheism."

"Oh, we plan to stick to storybook religion from now on. By the way, Father—do your friends call you Greg?—Morris here is going to move into Elizabeth Miller's apartment."

"Greg, yes." And he smiled again, shyly. "In fact, that's why I came by . . ."

"What's atheist?" Stuart inquired.

"Someone who does not believe in God," Charles replied.

"*I* believe in God," said Stuart. "He made the world in three days."

"Six days, Stuart, and rested on the seventh. Anne read Genesis to him," Charles explained. "It's perfect for his age."

"It's perfect for my age too," Merriweather told Stuart.

"I had been hoping you were here to convert us," Morris said, and his disappointment was only half feigned. He liked to argue, and especially liked to argue about religion with a true believer. He was always happy to see the Jehovah's Witnesses when they came to call. When they offered their evangelical pamphlets, he would insist on giving them a copy of Bertrand Russell's "Why I Am Not a Christian" in return. Then he would debate them until finally they left, disgruntled and defeated.

"No. Actually, I came to let Charles and Anne know, well, something I've learned about Elizabeth Miller. But it can wait until you're not enjoy-ing company," said Father Merriweather, thinking that Charles and Anne might regard the news as private. "I hate to bore the others. . . ." His voice, as he half addressed Merrit, drifted off apologetically.

"Not at all!" Merrit said, too sweetly and politely, feeling compulsively polite, psychologically incapable of any shred of irony, negativity, or ag-gression. My God, she thought, startled by her own paralysis; it was dis-turbing to realize how profoundly Morris could jinx her. He, meanwhile, stared at her mutely, feeling that verbal restraint fulfilled his promise to Charles. But hints of unspoken sarcasm and derision deranged his face muscles to a minute degree that only she, inexplicably tuned in to this near-invisible evidence of his disapproval, could perceive. And it was not only Morris who stared at her. That priest was also staring, though not with any hostility, so far as she could tell. On the contrary, he seemed to per-ceive her awkwardness and to feel sorry for her. At least, he kept offering her dishes and wine, and making meaningless comforting noises. Sweet, but a bit of a nerd, Merrit thought, observing that Father Merriweather had been over-encouraged by her clumsy, saccharine words.

"They're not bored," Anne assured Merriweather.

"Well, I'm afraid it's a long story. And some of it actually involves you, so . . ."

"We're dying of curiosity. Let's hear it," Charles insisted.

"But . . ."

"They don't mind," Morris said.

"Well then," Father Merriweather said. "I'll start at the beginning. I found three elderly members of the congregation at St. Ursula's who knew Miss Miller fairly well twenty years ago, when she attended regularly, and they told me the common knowledge about her back then, just before St. Ursula's more or less fell apart."

Elizabeth Miller had been a pillar of the church. She was the only daughter of parents who were, although well-to-do, the least-moneyed members of a wealthy family. She had tried to become an actress against her parents' wishes, had been in a few respectable productions—the last sometime during the Depression—including *Private Lives* and *Blithe Spirit*. Her life after that had been lonely. Her family wanted little to do with her, and she had ended up the cast-off lover of a no-good man, a misfortune from which she had never fully recovered. Her parents had also been members of the parish. When her father died in the forties and her mother in the fifties, they left her with the lease on their apartment and enough money to keep her comfortably for the rest of her life; and later she grew still richer when she inherited everything left by her mother's two sisters, who both died childless. A house they owned in the country, however, had been left by Lizzie's parents to the church, which had used it as a retreat for a while but was forced to sell it in the late seventies.

Years after her unhappy love affair, when Lizzie was growing old, she had befriended a younger member of the congregation, a Mrs. Edna Becker. Mrs. Becker's husband was a roué who had had affairs with both the dean's and choir director's wives during the peccant nineteen-sixties and -seventies. Edna had retaliated in kind and ended up a bitter, impoverished divorcée in middle age with a son rumored to be of doubtful paternity, although he was named Eugene Becker and Edna was known to have sworn to intimates that her husband, not her lover, was the father. In her misery, Edna had sought the friendship of the kindly older woman, who felt sympathy and kinship with the social ostracism Edna experienced when so many members of the congregation had begun avoiding her and her husband. Miss Miller had probably helped Edna and the boy with money, had perhaps even paid his tuition at Harvard, where the not very promising young man was admitted, no doubt only because a number of respectable Becker ancestors had been alumni. As Miss Miller got older and more frail, Edna took her affairs in hand. When Edna herself unexpectedly fell ill, her son stepped in and helped manage affairs for both of them. Edna died of her illness after some years, and from then on Becker—resentfully, Merriweather guessed, based on what he'd been told, but apparently competently—continued to manage everything Elizabeth Miller owned, except possibly a bank account of whose existence Father Merriweather had learned from Claire. This account, of which Becker might still be unaware, was the one from which Miss Miller wrote her annual check to the church and made Christmas presents to her caretakers and employees in the building. Some of those whom Merriweather spoke to thought that Becker might have felt obliged to contribute to Miss Miller's support at the end, in recognition of what she had done for him and his mother earlier on. In none of the stories Merriweather had collected was there any evidence that she had ever known satisfaction or happiness. Yet she never complained and always smiled. It was a touching story.

"So here he is, paying to keep this never-dying old woman and getting nothing but suspicion and dislike in return," said Morris.

"No wonder he wanted to charge extra rent," Charles added. "It's a case where you should look the other way."

"Maybe so," said Father Merriweather, "but this isn't all."

He had called Claire, he continued, who told him much more. She despised Becker. He had nickel-and-dimed Miss Miller more every year, until he no longer sent household money sufficient to pay for the little treats she liked, chocolates, or even for new shoes. She had so few pleasures, Claire maintained, that this was a crime. Her old coat was a disgrace. Worst of all, he had made her leave her trusted, familiar doctors for some cheaper arrangement he had made. Miss Miller didn't argue when he said the money was shrinking every year, but Claire did not believe him. All the caretakers were convinced Becker was spending Lizzie's money on himself.

"I asked her who she thought Miss Miller's heirs were," said Father Merriweather, "and she looked worried and said, 'Miss Miller's will is in a bank box, but she didn't show it to me.' A few years ago, it seems, she got Claire to wheel her to some lawyer's office on Amsterdam Avenue, where she made out a will. Then she left with it and went to her bank. She had Claire co-sign for access to her account and safety deposit box, and she put the will in the box. From then on, according to Claire, Miss Miller would occasionally send her for cash, usually for tips at Christmas or presents for employees, including Claire. But she wouldn't spend on herself—even though Claire could see on the ATM that there was a lot of money in the account. And she made Claire promise not to tell Becker anything about the cash—which was the source of some of Claire's suspicions of him. Claire has convinced herself that Becker, being a lawyer, naturally found out about the will and bank account after Miss Miller died. But I think he probably doesn't know anything about what she had in that bank. So I convinced Claire that we had to look into it, and this morning she and I went to the bank and got a copy of the will, which is why I'm here. Anne, it looks like you're one of the heiresses-in-chief."

Merrit laughed and clapped her hands, and Morris shook his head, incredulous. Merriweather handed a paper to Anne and Charles, who read it and frowned.

" 'Revoking all other wills.' I wonder if Becker doesn't have an earlier will. He wouldn't have any way to know it's been revoked. Wonder if he's probated it," Charles said.

Anne sat meditating. "It was awfully sweet of her to want us to have something. I just wish she had had someone closer to be good to. This is sad."

"Yes, it is. It was very good of her, but I don't expect we should rush off on any spending sprees," said Charles.

"Well, of course, there was probably very little left by the end, and whatever there was, we'd have to give some out to Willie and Roberto and the others, maybe to the other caretakers—Josefa and what was her name? I would guess that's what she meant, or that we could keep it if we're desperate. When she wrote the will, I guess, she was thinking she couldn't predict where things would stand or who'd be working for her when she died. I wonder if there's anyone else. Claire was her favorite."

"Anne, for heaven's sake. We can get to all that down the road—if we ever get any money, which I doubt. This is all too strange."

"I'm starting to feel bad," Anne said. "You know, I didn't really feel close to Lizzie. I wished her well, but I didn't think much about her. I barely gave her the time of day, just ordinary neighborliness. Now this will makes me feel that I should have cared more about her, and maybe she wanted me to. But even now I can't. Charles, why do you suppose she did it?"

"I suppose," he replied, "because she had no one else. Her emotional life was probably being lived out in encounters at the elevator. She liked you, or maybe she wished she'd had a life more like yours, and this was as close as she could come to living it. Whatever the reason was, I'm sure she knew she wasn't important to you, but you were the closest thing to a human connection she had left. So she left you whatever she had, and the only cost to you is a day or two of demoralizing guilt. It's a bargain."

"Well," Merriweather sighed. "I imagine you should plan on calling or visiting Becker as soon as possible. He may have property that belongs to you. I wonder what's happened to her household belongings, in fact. They should have gone to you."

Morris slapped his forehead. "My God. I think a bank statement came for her in the mail last week. I'm sure it was a bank statement. I returned that and some other stuff and had her mail stopped."

"That suggests Becker doesn't know about it, or he would have had the account address changed. Lizzie kept it secret from him, although it's hard to imagine how or why."

"It may not even have been intentional," Merrit said. "By this time, she was undoubtedly having memory lapses and other mental problems. No one gets to one hundred and three with everything intact upstairs."

"That's not true at all," Anne objected. "Talking with her was like talking with you, Merrit. She was sharp and clear. The only thing I could see wrong with her, other than general frailness, was that some days she was just too exhausted to move or talk and sometimes she just couldn't breathe and had to use an oxygen tank. I think she probably hung on to some cash as a cushion. She didn't tell Becker, because she wanted control over it. It all certainly looks as if she didn't trust him, doesn't it?"

"She could have fired Becker if she didn't trust him," said Merriweather. "But of course that might have been hard, maybe beyond her strength and resources. Much harder than getting a will drawn up. Maybe he just overwhelmed a helpless old invalid."

This reflection subdued them all. Suppose the quiet, gasping creature had been afraid for the roof over her head and could find no one to turn to, while the world persisted in regarding her as well cared and provided for. Charles and Anne, particularly, who had known her and had always thought of her as placid and unaware, found it painful to imagine her inner life as full of plots and fears and disappointments. Connivance and conflict should have been banished from a life that had moved into extra innings. Yet although it was more comfortable to think of her as unknowing and trusting in a childlike way, of course it couldn't have been so. At 103, she was still a mistreated daughter, a failed actress, a cast-off lover, and all the rest.

Father Merriweather was pensive, wondering how all these godless, decent, thoughtful people understood death. He never could get over the number of people there were in the world who didn't really understand that someday they were going to die. When he met them, he always tried to keep it from them, never wanting to be the one to break the news. How very difficult it must be, he thought, looking at all their faces around the table, none of them young anymore except the children, and the children innocently relying on everybody's immortality. How angry the kids will be when they find out death isn't just a story and that everyone really dies, when they understand that someday they are going to be alone. It would be very hard. The single adults, Merrit and Morris, were only just getting there, he surmised. For the first time, he felt toward them all a little of the compassion he thought a priest should feel for people. He himself had always known he was alone.

Such sad thoughts and feelings, however, did not go deep. Good spirits returned, inspired by the camaraderie the little group experienced in being drawn together in Lizzie's cause, and equally by the good things being served at the crowded table, for now Charles was handing around little plates of tartlets and cookies. Merriweather, in particular, whose life was devoid of any physical intimacies, found it very enjoyable to be squeezed in as he was between Merrit and Ellen, close enough to smell shampoo and hear chewing. Merrit began to feel almost happy, despite Morris. And Charles began to find humor in Anne's being designated an heiress who would inherit nothing, and on the very day when they had learned that they were essentially bankrupt. Schadenfreude, thought Anne, watching Charles draw the company into lightheartedness with jokes on this new and absurd theme. *She* was ridiculously old and had died—not us. But, listening to Charles, Anne laughed even more than the rest of them.

Charles and Anne stood in the foyer to see the company out. Father Merriweather volunteered his own and the rector's company on a visit to

Becker, and Charles and Anne gladly accepted. Merrit promised to drop by later in the week with a CD she had bought in London that Charles wanted to hear—Janet Baker singing Schubert in 1972. Morris said he'd return the broom tomorrow. And when all the guests had ensured a future occasion on which they would see the Braithwaites, they departed, with cheerful good-byes. To avoid any painful interaction with Morris, however, as soon as the three of them were in the elevator, Merrit crushed the cheer by explaining to Merriweather how Charles and Anne were in serious trouble this time. Merriweather, on hearing these particulars, simultaneously worried about the Braithwaites, marveled at people's proclivity to share any misery with a priest, no matter how unrelated to them he might be, and decided that Merrit was very cute and, despite—despite what? despite something or other, likable. Morris, too, was dismayed by the bad news, and lost the look of ironic indifference he had reserved for Merrit all evening. His life's plans had more to do with the Braithwaite household than he could comfortably acknowledge. Past forty, one didn't move across a continent just so as to live near one's best friends. Friends visited but knew better than to lean on one another. The overt understanding between Morris and the Braithwaites was that his coming to Columbia, two blocks from their home, was happenstance. But the reality was that if Charles and Anne and their children weren't going to be here in their crowded apartment on West 117th Street, then Morningside Heights—all of Manhattan, for that matter—had little appeal for Morris; and he had had thoughts of settling here permanently. "Maybe they just inherited a bundle," he hoped. But Merriweather and Merrit shook their heads. From all they'd been told, that was improbable.

The three walked to Merrit's building on 116th Street, where Merriweather wanted to see Merrit to her door. She wouldn't allow this, however. The two men walked on together, leaving her grateful to have gotten home unscathed but angry with Morris for his power to suppress her personality. Her irritation was magnified by a suspicion that he had some notion of his effect on her—whatever it was—and took pleasure in it. She perceived what a true friend Morris was to Charles and Anne, which depressed her, for it made her feel excluded from a circle of amity. What a terrible talk she had had with Anne. She had said things she shouldn't have. But she had been off balance, worrying about comments her gynecologist had made when Merrit had called to report on some symptoms; she needed to set up an appointment.

Charles and Anne called Claire as soon as the guests were gone, but she would not agree to go to Becker's office with them. They called their lawyer, too, but he was out of town until after Labor Day. It didn't matter. Merriweather was a lawyer, and was on their side, and the rector's presence would dignify the occasion.

Lizzie Miller's will had temporarily overcome Charles and Anne's willingness to face the ominous implications of the morning's bad news, and they got through the evening in tentative good spirits. They washed the dishes and put away the extra chairs brought out for the guests. Then they tiptoed past Stuart sleeping on his fold-out bed in the living room and went into their own room, which was so small that it held little besides their bed. They crawled under the sheets, heaving deep, exhausted sighs, and read, as they always did, in a scattered way—Opera News, Gramophone, and The New Yorker for Charles, while Anne had a Penelope Fitzgerald novel and an essay on the psychological effects of life in a concentration camp on children of the Holocaust, which had had her weeping the night before.

"For God's sake, Anne. Don't read that stuff if it's going to upset you again. I personally would not put myself through it."

"I just have two more pages, then I'll read the Fitzgerald. But the fact is she's almost as gloomy as this is. I always wonder what her problem is, but I keep reading. Oh, Charles," she cried, reading the end of the essay. "Listen to this. They ask this woman if she was frightened when she was a child in the camp, and she says, 'I had no fear of Germans or death. Why should I be afraid? I was with my mother, and if she would die, I would die. So? This didn't frighten me. The only fear, and that never left me, was separation from my mother."

Charles looked stricken, and Anne, whose cheeks were wet with tears again, was sorry she had read it to him.

"Why does anyone need research to figure that out?" Charles said. "I could have told them."

"No one would believe you," said Anne. "Not today. Today, no one knows things like that about children anymore. They don't want to believe that children need so desperately to be with their parents. How lucky we've been to be able to bring up our children the way we have—so far, anyway."

"But things may change for them now. Still, something like this"—and Anne inferred that he had jumped to the subject of Lizzie Miller's will— "makes you think you don't need to worry. You realize all the ridiculous solutions life might offer for your problems. We're never going to have a penny from Lizzie Miller, yet we might have—and this changes everything in my mind. Somehow, I'm more optimistic we'll manage. I mean, if riches might just rain down out of nowhere, maybe the assessment will be canceled and I'll be offered an international tour. It's a revelation: problems can be solved without merit or effort or judgment."

"It convinces you that they're not punishments for crimes like eating expensive organic apples," Anne answered, "so that being virtuous isn't going to fix them."

"Maybe there is something to that, but it would be more wifely of you not to say so. Tell me what else Claire said when you called."

"Claire said Lizzie told her I was a good mother and a kind person and Stuey shouldn't wear Ellen's hand-me-downs and the girls' coats were too big," Anne said, eyes on her page.

"Even she noticed that you bought them huge so they would last long. I *told* you you were overdoing it."

"Money spent on kids' coats that fit is wasted. Just so they're warm."

"It does seem like getting money on false pretenses. She never would have left anything to you if she'd known you spent two thousand dollars on Stuart's one-sixteenth-size violin."

"Yes she would. Besides, I did tell her that."

"Why would you tell her something like that?"

"She was curious. It's not crazy to spend money on their violins, Charles. You're stubborn on this. Lizzie was more sensible than you are."

"How do you know? The woman could hardly talk."

"Stuey played for her in the lobby one day, and I was explaining to her that you have to get a nice violin for tiny kids so they can get sound out of it, or they're too frustrated to learn. She was very interested and said, 'Lucky boy.' And she said she wished she could play the violin."

"Good Lord. That's rather sad—at one hundred and three, she's still wishing she could play the violin."

"I'm sure all her yearnings and dissatisfactions were intact, and we'll soon see whether she did anything about ours."

"I'm not holding my breath."

"I certainly don't think we're rich. But I'm thinking now that if Lizzie thought she was leaving us something, and thought there was enough for us to give people presents out of, then probably there really is something. I knew her, Charles, and there was nothing wrong with her mind or her judgment. I wouldn't be at all surprised if there's at least enough to get us out of the jam we're in right now."

"We'll see," said Charles. He was irritated by Anne's reckless optimism, which had done so much to get them into this mess to begin with. But there was no point in arguing. She'd be brought back to reality soon enough when they talked to the trustee.

# 11

HEAT BLASTED THEM as they descended the subway stairs at 116th Street, and kept them silent and enervated until the air-conditioned IRT No. 1 Local arrived. They took it to Ninety-sixth Street, where they changed for the No. 2 Express, which they rode beneath Midtown skyscrapers, Wall Street, and the river. They ascended at the shabby corner of Montague and Court, adjacent to the plaza where Brooklyn's Borough Hall, with its great columns, stood brooding over Manhattan's century of ascension and its own diminished glory. From there they walked, perspiring, down Court Street for several blocks until they came to a side street lined with odd, musty shops whose windows displayed yellowed papers and advertised investigative services, process serving, bail bonds, stationery, office documents of every kind, legal forms—state, federal, and local—and accurate transcriptions overnight. They proceeded down this street until Charles, stopping at a door, announced doubtfully, "This is it." There on a panel of buzzers was the name Eugene T. Becker, Esq., Suite 3D. They rang; the door buzzed open, and they entered. It was a walk-up, three dark, shabby flights of slanting steps and the stench of disinfectants; but at least it was cooler. Father Quincy, older and plumper than the rest, was thoroughly winded at the third floor landing and had to stop to catch his breath before they knocked at 3D. The metal door, which was scuffed and dented, as though it had been kicked and banged in some attack, had a brass plaque at eye level, which announced:

EUGENE T. BECKER, ESQ.
WILLS AND ESTATE PLANNING
REAL ESTATE
CRIMINAL DEFENSE
PERSONAL INJURY

"Versatile chap," muttered Father Quincy, wiping perspiration from his forehead with a sodden linen handkerchief.

"I'm a lawyer. It might be better if I do the talking," said Father Merriweather, but Father Quincy paid no attention and knocked at the door.

Becker opened it himself. He was an unexpectedly good-looking man, with a full head of neat gray hair, and well dressed in a fashionable tie and sports coat. A young woman, in a tight miniskirted suit with a cigarette burning beside her in a metal ashtray, worked on a computer at the side of the front room, which appeared to lack a reception desk. She glanced briefly at the visitors through eyes slitted for protection from the smoke while she continued to type. "We'll shut the door to my office in case that smoke bothers anyone," Becker said, briefly permitting a slight smile to crack a face that showed habitual lines but none that signified good humor.

"Josephine, have a messenger take that," he said to the young woman.

"You want to check it first?"

"No. Just don't make any mistakes," he said to her, and to the visitors, "My intern—a law student."

With a faint smile, he gestured hospitably toward his office. It was crammed with stacked drafts of memoranda, files, transcripts, and briefs, interlittered with stray ties, jogging shoes, newspapers, and paper hot-drink cups. He extinguished the glow of the computer monitor and, as the office had only two visitors' chairs, went out and returned with a straight-backed chair under each arm.

"So you're from St. Ursula's," he said, in a voice that Charles—sensitive to voices and what they could do—marveled at. It managed to be gravelly and silky at the same time, like liquid concrete, and Charles remembered that he had noticed this even over the telephone. Although Becker's face was unsmiling, his voice carried simultaneously the lilt of a congenial smile, a contemptuous note, and a hint of threat. It was the most thoroughly ambiguous voice Charles had ever heard. "Two of us," replied Father Quincy stiffly, in an obvious way cutting off Father Merriweather, who had opened his mouth to speak. Merriweather sighed, and Becker's eyebrows lifted slightly.

"So who are *you?*" Becker said to Charles and Anne in a voice that straddled a fence between rudeness and good-humored bluntness. Charles and Anne hesitated for a moment, not knowing how to react, and Father Quincy cut in again, firmly if pointlessly: "We'll get to that." He had taken an instant dislike to Eugene T. Becker.

Becker's face reverting to its previous taut blandness, he again addressed the priests. "You wouldn't have known old Thornton, would you—before your time, eh?"

"That's right," the rector said coolly.

Becker smiled appealingly and asked, "So what can I do for you?"

Merriweather once again attempted to assume a position as spokesman. "We understand that you served as Elizabeth Miller's conservator or trustee, and we've found something that you'll want—her will."

"Her will?" Becker tried to sound skeptical and sarcastic, but Charles detected alarm.

"Yes, from 1995, four years ago. It was kept in a bank safety deposit box."

"Who kept it? What bank?" Becker asked, attempting to sound neutral but betraying his excess interest, Charles noted, with a slight accelerando.

"We'll get to that," Father Quincy snapped.

"You're going to show me this will, I suppose?" Father Merriweather handed him a photocopy of it, and Becker read it, apparently calm.

"Oh, I see why you're here. And she's Anne Braithwaite—I remember now, the neighbors, right, with the friend who's renting the place, right, right. I get it now." Becker, unexpectedly, became expansive. "Mrs. Braithwaite, I guess you knew Miss Miller pretty well. I knew her my whole life. When I was a kid, sometimes I stayed up there with her—before your time, of course. Some apartment, eh? Like a museum, wasn't it, with the old furniture and those velvet drapes? She was a good person—the best. You moved in when? 'Eighty-four, 'eighty-five? Ah, by that time she wasn't all there anymore. You didn't know her when . . . Father Quincy, the kind of lady she was—I'll bet you didn't even know—back in 'eighty, she actually paid out of her pocket for repairs to your organ that ran six figures. You didn't know that, did you? Oh, there're lots of things like that. She was really something special."

"She was, Mr. Becker," Anne said, with her best disarming smile. "And I myself wouldn't have said she wasn't all there anymore. She just had a little trouble expressing herself." Charles knew that Anne's comradeliness was a con, but no one else did. This was the manner she reserved for bureaucrats and prickly headmasters.

Becker looked at Anne appraisingly, his face slightly averted but with eyes turned toward her. Then he grinned boyishly, shyly, from that angle, and she returned an ingratiating smile that did not, however, answer the appeal in his. With traces of his grin still at the corners of his lips, Becker glanced at the others. Then he stood up and went to a file cabinet, dug for a moment, retrieved a document, and left the room, returning shortly with what was evidently a warm Xerox copy of his own document.

"I could have saved you a long subway trip," he said apologetically (but Charles thought it possible that there was the slightest undertone of sneer), and handed the copy to Father Merriweather. The document, dated March 21, 1998, identified itself as the last will and testament of Elizabeth A. Miller and revoked all other wills. The signature looked genuine, if rather more shaky than the 1995 signature. The will left her entire estate to Eugene T. Becker

The initial reactions of the visitors ranged from deflation to mute dismay. Of course, Becker had a valid will in his file. He was her trustee, and he was familiar with all her affairs and involved in their daily supervision; he wouldn't have let her die intestate, and he wouldn't have trusted in the existence of a will he'd probably never seen, tucked away in a safety deposit box somewhere. They leaned over one another to read the 1998 will. A perilous silence ended when Father Quincy took in a breath and opened his mouth as though to speak; but this time Father Merriweather spoke first. "Well, this should settle matters. Of course, this document revokes the earlier will. But ours was so recent and so carefully preserved, you can see why we assumed it was her last word."

"Of course. Anything else in that box, by the way?"

Father Merriweather was about to speak again, but Father Quincy jumped in first.

"If we come up with anything of Miss Miller's that belongs to you," he replied smoothly, "we'll be sure to send it over."

Father Merriweather was beginning to redden. He looked helplessly at Father Quincy, who managed to telegraph to him by means of narrowed eyes and compressed lips that he should be quiet about the bank account. Charles and Anne were willing to accommodate his evident intention to keep Becker in the dark—at least for now—and remained silent.

"You people want to let me have anything you find right away, wherever or whenever," Becker said, looking around at their faces, which would have betrayed the existence of a shared secret to a much less acute observer. "Of course, I accept your good faith in coming here with this—this document today, but I'd take amiss any attempt to conceal any of Miss Miller's assets from me. The fact is, Mrs. Braithwaite, even if that will was valid, no one would inherit anything—let alone fifty thousand, twenty-five thousand dollars, whatever—" Becker shook his head. "This is just pure fantasy on her part. I told her over and over, the money was gone, but she just couldn't accept it. In fact, the estate owes me. You know, at the end, I was paying her rent and grocery bills. Listen, I don't mind. She was a good friend to me and my mother, and I wanted to do it. But I'm not a rich man, and fair is fair."

Becker began leafing through papers on his desk as he ended this speech, seemingly distracted, looking up occasionally at the group with a frank, businesslike air. "You know, I'm due in court in half an hour . . ."

The visitors by this time had risen and were walking out the door. "Thanks for your time," said Father Merriweather apologetically, and they left. Out in the dim hallway, Father Quincy proposed that they stop for lunch in a diner on Court Street to talk things over, and the others, who by this time acknowledged him as their leader, agreed.

"Well, Gregory," Father Quincy began, somewhat accusatorially, as they sat in plastic chairs at flimsy tables eating tuna on toast. "I'm wondering why you seemed to want to give up Miss Miller's money to that crook."

"I just . . ." Merriweather began, blushing, but he was interrupted by Charles.

"He's a peculiar character—makes you feel you should watch your back. But it looks like he's the heir. You think that will he pulled out is genuine, don't you?" Charles asked Merriweather.

"Definitely. Forging her signature on a will would be too serious—no lawyer in his senses would take a chance like that, especially when the gains are likely to be so small. Look, he doesn't strike me as a straightforward man either, but I've known a dozen lawyers like him. They're underhanded and tricky and hyperaggressive, but they protect their standing in the bar. They don't go in for false wills. That money is his, and this is no good. He has to be told about the money."

Here Father Quincy asserted his authority. "Just a minute, Gregory. I'm not at all sure of that. We're not lawyers. We're priests. This man merits suspicion, and I'm not going to pretend otherwise. Now, Mrs. Braithwaite, I strongly recommend you pursue this. There are too many fishy things here. Why did she keep this money secret from Becker? And she either didn't tell him about the 1995 will or she didn't tell him where it was."

"It might just be because she was an old, old woman with a few screws loose," Charles said.

"It might," Father Merriweather agreed.

"She was perfectly sane. Her mind, memory, everything was perfectly good," Anne protested.

Father Quincy chided Merriweather again. "This is a complicated situation. If we just hand cash over to Becker, you'll never get it back, even if someday you can prove that 1998 will is fraudulent. He says she owed him lots of money when she died. And how do you know he doesn't have another bank account or two somewhere holding Elizabeth Miller's assets? Let 'em take some time to dig into this a little. You could hire a private detective," he said, turning to Charles and Anne and brightening.

"No way we could pay a private detective." Charles smiled, while Merriweather blushed for his rector, who, he feared, was leading these people astray. Father Quincy felt bad about never having looked up Elizabeth Miller, who had sent them money every year. And St. Ursula's, which was experiencing growing pains, needed cash right now. Merriweather suspected that it was in the back of Father Quincy's mind that some of her money might come to the church and that this distorted his judgment. Father Merriweather suggested as a compromise that they call Becker this afternoon and tell him there was money in a bank account that had been escrowed and that he could claim it when the will was probated. This would give them a little time during which Becker could not claim the money. This plan was accepted all around, but, as Merriweather pointed out, it was a poor way to start out with Becker. Now he would know they'd held out on him, and he would be suspicious and uncooperative.

Despite his earlier protestations that all this would come to nothing, Charles felt as let down as Anne did when they returned to their lobby—which reminded them of the assessment, the maintenance, the debts, and the schools demanding their tuition money. It had been impossible not to hope, just a little, that their problems were to be solved, as Charles had said, without merit or effort or judgment. But here, once again, was the unrelenting reality. The lobby scene was dismally congruent with their low mood.

The superintendent, Mr. Morales, languid in the heat, was leaning against the entranceway when the Braithwaites arrived, and greeted them in a friendly manner. In one corner of the lobby, Albert Bernstein, with a week's growth of beard, was standing, listening like a good child to Roberto scold him for not locking his door when he came downstairs. Mary O'Reilly, clutching her walker for support, was loudly berating Willie at the doorman's post. A young woman with a wailing baby in her arms was anxious to say something to Willie but too shy to interrupt Mary. The handyman and the porter were eating lunch at the far side of the lobby, sitting in the visitors' chairs most improperly. Charles groaned, then approached Mary. "Stop browbeating Willie and talk to me, Mary," he commanded.

"What do *you* want?" she snarled, turning on him.

"I want to know how well you knew Lizzie Miller."

"Don't talk to me about Lizzie Miller. What do you care about that poor old woman? You never knew she was alive."

"We knew her. We lived across the hall for fifteen years. Anne wanted to go to her funeral, but we never found out where it was. Did you go to her funeral?"

"What funeral?"

"Wasn't there one?"

"I never heard of one."

"We thought maybe we just missed the notice."

"Never heard of anything for that poor woman."

"Do you think anyone around here would know?"

"No. What do you care?"

"It wouldn't hurt you to keep a civil tongue in your head, Mary."

"I don't want to be civil. I'm too mad about everything. I'm just too mad."

"What's the problem?" Anne said, roused from a kind of torpor.

"The light in my hall, by my door, is out, and they won't fix it. I've been down here three times, and they still haven't fixed it. It went out on Friday. It's scary without that light. I need that light fixed."

As Mary shuffled out to the street, Charles went to Mr. Morales and spoke quietly. "What's this about her light?"

"Of course we'll fix the light. The porter was away, and then he got behind in everything. Soon, he'll fix it."

"Right now. It has to be now, before she comes back. The old lady has waited three days. She shouldn't have waited three hours. Right now, so she's not upset. What if it were *your* mother?"

"Please, Mr. Braithwaite, this has already been ordered. José! Why wasn't this light fixed?"

"No ladder. They took both ladders for the work up on twelve."

"Just take a ladder from twelve and then take it right back. Tell them I said. Now, Mr. Braithwaite, you see you don't need to worry about old ladies in this building. We treat them well. And let me tell you—see the old man, Mr. Bernstein, has lots of help. She makes her own problems with her bad temper. The men don't like to go near her."

"I know it," Charles said conciliatorily. "I know it."

José marched off grumbling. Charles took bills out of his wallet and, making sure that Mr. Morales saw what he was doing, went after José.

"Try to make sure the old lady doesn't get upset about things," he told José in a low voice, putting the money into his hand, "and I'll remember you."

The Braithwaites' apartment was insufferably warm when they entered, and they quickly switched on air-conditioning. They felt disoriented and exhausted, but Charles had to practice, Anne had to give a lesson in an hour, and her mother would soon arrive with the children, whom Anne was beginning to feel hungry to see. She always began to long for them after these separations of a few hours.

"I don't think Becker had a funeral or memorial service for Lizzie, do you?" Charles said. He had intended to hole up in his studio immediately but instead sat down by Anne on the sofa, and neither could find energy to rise again. "He'll have had her cremated. Wonder what he did with the ashes. Or maybe there's a family plot or something."

"Charles," Anne began after a pause, when they had run out of talk about Becker and Lizzie. "If they give Ellen the scholarship—and I'm betting they will—and we find a little neighborhood play group for Stuart, I think we might consider taking Janie out of school altogether."

"Are you out of your mind?"

"She could get home tutoring. Her concerto competition is only four months off, in December. I know how you dislike these competitions, and I do too, but she's a child and she desperately wants to win it and I think she probably will. I did, and she's much, much better than I was. But she should be practicing more than she is. She doesn't need to be in school. Dr. Suarez promised me that she could stay involved in some things—dances and the school orchestra—so she won't be lonely. And the decision could be presented to her classmates as a professional one."

"I don't like it at all. I'd a thousand times rather have her at public school in . . . in wherever, and let her still be a child. Anne, how could you think of doing this? You've talked to her about this, haven't you? You shouldn't have done that behind my back."

"It was her idea. She brought it up, and I discussed a few ideas hypothetically with Dr. Suarez when I went in to beg for a scholarship for Ellen."

"And suppose we manage to sit this out for one more year. Then we'll still have to move next year, and we'd have a girl thoroughly off track, confused about her life and where she belongs and . . . She might skip college, and study independently. We might see her through that. But none of this is right."

"Charles, either she decides now or it is ruled out. We were reaching this point quite apart from the money question. After all, what is so wonderful about that treadmill of a school she goes to, with its three hours of pointless homework every night, where she performs miserably and puts up with nasty rich girls? There was no way we could help her avoid this dilemma. That's what the world is like now. When we were kids, you could win the competition and get straight A's in a top-notch public school. No child can do anything like that anymore. The schools are more pressured. So is the music world. This was coming, money or no. If we did anything wrong, it was long ago, in encouraging her with the piano the way we did, right from the beginning."

Anne stopped, horrified, because tears had appeared on Charles's cheeks. He wiped them off, but they kept coming. "Not I. That was you. I don't like this. I don't. I won't permit it. Anne, this time you're wrong."

Anne would not oppose him further, and the strength of his feelings made her doubt herself. "All right," she said in a yielding voice, and put her hand on his arm. Perhaps she had allowed Jane's pleading, combined with her hope of retaining their home, to overcome her own better judgment against permitting a child to choose such a radical path in life. She was willing to let Charles bring her around to this view again, even though she dreaded telling Jane that they not only insisted she stay in school but intended to move her to the suburbs.

Anne found it easier to go along with Charles, however, than to convince herself entirely that he was right. If Jane was to have the chance to become the kind of musician who had recitals in Avery Fisher Hall, she could not have a normal middle-class childhood, like hers and Charles's. No longer could anyone carve out a career like Charles's, with its leisure, moderation, and intellectual depth. And what was so wonderful about the middle-class life, which he so strongly insisted on for his daughter? You could train in medicine or law or some other profession that had long ago gone commercial and forsaken the ideals that had once guaranteed respect and security for its members—or take some well-paying, soul-squelching job. Janie had a chance to avoid that, and, unlike her more versatile sister, had perhaps only this one chance. Charles, of course, thought that Jane might grow up and live as Anne had, unreasonably assuming that she would want to. But the one thing Anne was sure of was that Jane was not like her.

# PART

## II

# 12

THE BOARD OF DIRECTORS of 635 West 117th met one August evening
in the living room of the board's president, a Wall Street broker named
Arnold Metzger. He had bought two apartments two years ago, knocked
out the wall between them, and entirely redesigned the space. Much of his
apartment was now one great flowing room, with a vast open kitchen
gleaming with enormous appliances at the southern end, a long modern
table with eight cleverly unmatched chairs in an adjacent dining area,
and, in the northern end, a separate area where six board members were
sitting on sofa segments arranged in conversational squares. A maid had set
out waters, soft drinks, and snacks, and while they were waiting for a seventh member to arrive, they admired the huge, chaotic paintings on the
walls and writhing ebony sculptures spotlighted on stands—and listened
to Metzger's wife, also a broker, fume about the building staff.

The board members all agreed that something must be done. Morales,
who was incompetent and lazy, should be fired, but they could not take
that step until they had replaced as many of the other employees as possible or the staff might all walk off when Morales did, as they were all either
related to him or indebted to him. The replacement had to be a gradual,
cautious process. The first thing would be to make them all wear their
complete uniforms. That would create a more disciplined atmosphere.
One board member, Georgia Lyons, said she thought they should wear
gloves as well, but the others thought this a little over the top. This was,
after all, the West Side, and they lived on the West Side for a reason. But
they were united in the belief that a little more respect, a little more

businesslike behavior, was in order. They would write something up, call Morales in, and explain the new, tighter dress code and the rest. This sort of thing was necessary if they were going to keep the property values up — if they were going to be able to sell to the right people. One member was assigned the task of writing up instructions on how often floors were to be swabbed, garbage removed, and the like.

"I hate to say this," said another member, "but the real problem in this building is the tenants, not the employees."

The others laughed.

"The O'Reilly woman has got to go," said Lyons. "She's insane. Just the sight of her standing in the lobby would lower selling prices a hundred thousand or two." Metzger shook his head. He didn't think much could be done about the old tenants like Mary O'Reilly, who had refused to buy when the building went co-op and lived here cheaply under old leases protected by municipal rent laws. They'd have better luck getting some of those who owned their apartments to leave. The board had to face it. There were people who were having trouble paying the last increase in maintenance, which had gone into effect a year and a half ago. Now they were going to have to pay another, larger, maintenance increase, along with assessments for the repairs, the pointing, the new boiler, the renovations in the halls and lobby, the new furniture and chandelier. A little blood was going to be spilled, which he didn't like but couldn't help. The people who couldn't swing it would just have to sell out. On the up side, they could sell high and move on north. This was New York City. The board members didn't need to be told how serious this business was, and agreed that it was unavoidable.

"Speaking of selling," said Metzger. "We've got an annoying situation in 9D, where that hundred-year-old woman died. I heard from her trustee that the place was going to be sold months ago, then I found out he rented it to some visiting professor, without getting approval. I called him up to complain and he says he needs the money to pay the maintenance and the assessment, because it turns out he can't sell until her estate is settled." Metzger thought they should ratify the rental after the fact, because otherwise there might be a foreclosure, which would tie things up forever. The tenant was unobjectionable, as far as he could tell. The trustee was not being unreasonable, but he should have come to them first. They discussed the sum such a huge apartment was likely to bring when it could be put up for sale. They all thought seven figures was likely, even without a river view. And if the building renovations were completed before it went on the market, it would bring a fortune. A nice-looking lobby, uniforms, made a big impression on buyers.

The meeting continued for at least another hour, and all left thinking that it was an agreeable, efficient group, a good board.

# 13

BY LATE AUGUST the city had suffered a record-breaking spell of tropical weather. The air on Broadway was fetid and steamy. In Morningside Heights, people who lived in the un-air-conditioned tenements east of the university went down to Riverside Park after work. Clusters of men played chess and dominoes at the stone tables at 108th Street. The benches along the promenade were filled until late at night, when the air had finally cooled the sweltering apartments.

All those tens of thousands who could do so had long since fled to Long Island, upstate, the Berkshires, the Cape, the coast of Maine, and rented farmhouses in Europe. Morningside Heights always felt deserted until the last week or two in August, when students began to return, with their computers, clothes, lamps, and books stuffed into station wagons or minivans driven by harried middle-aged parents. This year, as in all years past, Charles and Anne watched a new crop of parents and students unpack all those trunks, boxes, and bags. How meek and humble, how self-effacing, the mothers and fathers looked as they arranged to give their hopeful offspring a chance for the success that they themselves, apparently, thought they had muffed. For every parent appeared to feel insignificant at this juncture, while every new student seemed to feel the rush of satisfied ambition. Yet, Anne and Charles had often remarked, this was reversed at graduation, which had become one of life's sad endings instead of a glad beginning. Now graduation meant free fall into lowly adult status, in which love, respect, and gratification—granted so liberally to all middle-class children—were rare privileges, reserved for the lucky few.

Morris and the Braithwaites were among the unfortunates still in the city. Merritt was at her mother's house in the country. She had invited all the Braithwaites to come for a weekend, but they hesitated to expose the nervous old woman to the commotion, mess, and noise of a family with three young children. Morris had been working on his lab and his apartment. When these were in order, around the end of the week, he would visit Lily Freund in Maine and had called to tell her so. The Braithwaites, who could not afford a vacation of any sort, had put their apartment on the market and made an appointment with an agent to take them to see suburban houses. In the meantime, they planned to take the children to cool off in museums and in the sprinklers at the playground and to rent movies to watch in the air-conditioned comfort of home.

Then came a stroke of luck. A friend, a singer, had been forced at the last minute to cancel an engagement to perform at a resort hotel in the Catskills—an old place that sat beside a grand, icy lake at the top of a comfortably rounded mountain. He called just before dinner one evening, after an especially hot and oppressive day, to suggest that Charles take his place. He had already recommended Charles to the entertainment director, and, desperate for a replacement, she had listened to a CD, looked at some publicity photos, and approved. It was a matter of five or six evenings, over a period of two weeks, singing old chestnuts, solo and ensemble. Anne could accompany, and Charles could work into the program anything he thought would please a mostly unsophisticated audience. It wouldn't be an artistic challenge, but it would be fun. Best of all, the whole family could stay free for the full two weeks.

Charles relished sitting down to dinner with this bit of news, and described the place in terms that made Ellen and Jane clap their hands. Anne was almost as happy as her daughters, but Stuart thought it a bad idea to go sleeping in hotels, where there were unfamiliar beds. His sisters' attempts to change his mind by excitedly listing the hotel's allurements only reduced him to tears.

"Let him be," said Anne. "He doesn't like new ideas. Just let it sit."

"I like old ideas," Stuart wept piteously, and Ellen buried her face in her hands so as not to laugh, having been warned to respect his feelings.

"We haven't got much time to get ready, Anne," said Charles, still radiating contentment. "They want us Friday night. We'll need dinner clothes for all of us . . . will I need a tux? Surely not. Well, I'll bring it. What can you wear with that belly? And bring a pile of books. You and I should plan a few programs tomorrow morning—or maybe tonight, if you have the energy. We might have to make a run to buy music. If not, we can always send for things. Do you think we can manage?"

"Of course we can. I'll just need to get all of them a pair of shorts, and Ellen needs a bathing suit. And I still have that black silk shift I wore when I was pregnant with Ellen. That would be fine—unless it's spotted. I'll check right after dinner. Do we go on the train?"

"They'll send a van to drive us up." And here, once again, he enjoyed hearing the children squeal in their excitement. Even Stuart was reconciled by the prospect of a chauffeured ride in their own minivan, and, demanding a suitcase, he went off to begin packing immediately.

Anne called Merrit that evening to explain why she would have to decline her invitation. "How lovely! How really lovely!" Merrit cried. "It sounds so wonderful I'm tempted to come myself."

"Oh yes, think about it!" Anne exclaimed. "I'll call and give you a report over the weekend."

Anne and Charles sat up outlining concert programs and making sure they had scores for all possibilities. The next morning, packing and organizing proceeded at a frantic pace. There were last-minute telephone calls to relatives and friends, a flurry of trips to shops, the chores of closing and securing the apartment, and the rest of the vacation departure ritual—all just as it had been years ago, when they had only one or two small children, before they were buried in debt. The children were at first angelic in their excited good cheer, then, predictably, turned irritable and started squabbling. Ellen pulled Jane's hair. Stuart tore Ellen's drawing. Jane screamed at them both for making noise in the living room while she was practicing. Anne finally settled the little ones to watch *Peter Pan* while she packed.

The following morning found them ready for the van. Stuart crowed and hopped when he saw it. It was blue—his favorite color. He warmed to the driver, delighted in the softness of the seats, and his beaming parents found his joy altogether charming. The poor little fellow, Anne thought, had hardly ever been in a real car other than wretched New York yellow cabs. The girls, for once, were contented good friends, and not even above singing in harmony, with their clear, young voices, and passing the time by playing at counting cows and "I Spy" with Stuart. Jane especially, who had pleasant memories of other times like this, before the money trouble, seemed particularly full of goodwill. The sense of escape from the terrible heat and the dark threat of loss and change that had been hanging over them amplified ordinary pleasures. Everything was exquisite.

That evening, after they were comfortably settled in two cheerful rooms, Charles sang to a small, packed hall, splendidly accompanied by Anne—her first public playing in years. The audience received the performance enthusiastically, and, despite the unimportance of the occasion, Charles and Anne were glowing. "The trick, sweetest," Charles told Jane, "is always to make sure your audience knows you understand that you feel honored that they came and listened. You can't think you're above your music or them. I don't mean to fake feeling this way, the way some people do. I mean you really should feel this way." Jane took this seriously, as real-life professional advice. Anne watched the interchange worriedly, wondering if Charles realized that Jane interpreted his words as encouragement of her own hopes of becoming a public performer. The family spent the next day hiking, reading, and swimming, and that evening Charles had the people in the hall begging for encores. To crown the day, the program director of the hotel told Charles that she hoped he would agree to come back next year. "You're perfect for our crowd," she bubbled, and Charles graciously thanked her, his own words to Jane echoing in his head. In any event, he thought, enduring such compliments was a small price to pay for the chance to give his family a real vacation.

Anne grew buoyant with this news, the exhilaration of public playing, and the pleasures of the old hotel. In three days, she had already lost her careworn look and seemed to have put on weight. Suddenly she was big enough to have everyone opening doors and offering seats but not so big as to be tired. She called Merrit the next morning and begged her to visit, describing the fresh chill nights, the scenery, the quiet, and the concerts. Merrit promised to come if she could talk her mother into coming with her, but that evening she called back, obviously disappointed, to say that Mrs. Roth wasn't up to it.

Charles was glad to see Anne get a chance to exhibit her talents and also to rest, read, and walk to her heart's content, while the children, even Stuart, were occupied with picnics, hikes, swims, and boating expeditions. Now and then, however, he could not avoid thinking about the sums of cash he had to come up with in a few weeks, even if Ellen got a scholarship and they kept Stuart at home, and he could find no solution. He knew of nothing to do but sell the apartment and move to some place less expensive—and even that would not resolve the issue of Jane's musical future.

For some weeks now, when such thoughts bedeviled him, Charles had found himself growing cold toward Anne. In theory, these questions had been settled. No one was to be blamed and they were to move as soon as possible. But Charles could not stop himself from blaming her. On their income, they should have been able to make a go of it. He turned away from her in bed for the first time. They had so many years of goodwill behind them that goodwill had become a habit, hard to overcome, and Charles's alienation could scarcely be detected by an observer. But Anne worried and suffered from it. She did not blame him for anything. They understood each other, in these respects, perfectly. This vacation, he hoped, would be good for them. He'd forgotten how much fun it was to perform with Anne, who was still his favorite accompanist. Up here, he'd managed for long stretches not to lapse into sullenness. But she caught enough of the undertones of his mood to experience, at times, a wary tension that was new to the marriage.

The children, too, picked up something on the sensitive radar with which children monitor their parents' secrets. Only Jane, however, showed distressing symptoms, and Charles was not sure what they were symptoms of. With Jane there were now so many issues. Despite the strength of his feelings, Charles doubted his decision to insist she stay in school. He had trouble letting her reach for anything if he could not guarantee her success. He had trouble imagining her living in any pattern other than the one he and Anne had established for themselves, which was not much different from the one their parents had followed. Anne's mother, Helen, said that it didn't matter; the capitalists were not going to let anyone live that way anymore. The oligarchs wanted to keep all the bourgeois pleasures for themselves, along with the money, while proletarianizing everyone else, squeezing people with overwork and low pay, corrupting the liberal political forms so that they answered only to cash. They were not smart enough, she said, to realize that it couldn't work that way. You couldn't undercut the institutional and characterological supports of bourgeois life, things like public schools, arts, politics, religion and morals, and still preserve its goods and pleasures.

"What crap," Morris had said, a few weeks ago, on hearing an account of this. "How can you buy that stuff?" Morris had a placid confidence in human freedom; he feared no determinisms—social, biological, economic, political, or psychological. He was calmly optimistic. Reason would triumph, although not without horrifying backslidings. All those political people, armchair socialists like Helen especially, made up nightmare stories, and no one should pay attention. Charles wasn't sure, however, that Helen wasn't putting her finger on one hell of an ominous backsliding.

In Maine, at this very moment, Morris was having another version of that same discussion. Lily and her friends were telling Morris that psychoanalysis was dying, even though, they contended, for all its evident flaws, past and present, it was a storehouse of humane knowledge and insight. Lily argued that it was dying because its ideals were inconsistent with the way people had to think and work and behave to get along in the brave new world. Instead, they turned to the moral equivalent of psychological snake oil—drugs and fad diagnoses. Morris, however, thought that psychoanalysis wasn't doomed. This was just as silly as Helen's death-of-freedom-and-meaning scenario. All good ideas always survived—in the long run.

Morris, however, was not very interested in psychoanalysis. It was like proctology. People needed it, but who would want to be a proctologist? So how could he be seriously interested in a woman so seriously dedicated to psychoanalysis, he wondered, and her profession began to appear as a barrier to getting something going with Lily. Surely it was not possible to be intimate with someone when you weren't even interested in the thing that mattered most to her. Lily asked herself the same question. Why had they been so interested in each other, she wondered, back in Morningside Heights? Or was this present failure to connect itself an illusion? She decided to watch and wait. But their conversation flagged after this discussion, and a bored silence was prevented only by the chatter of the three friends with whom Lily shared the big frame farmhouse.

The next morning, Lily and Morris went for a walk in nearby woods that offered privacy and natural beauties that a pair of lovers should have found inspiring. But they still could not re-create the excitement they had seemed to share over that lunch such a short time ago. Lily's skin was still creamy, her eyes dark and sparkling, and her smile charming, but Morris felt nothing but ordinary friendliness toward her. This frustrated him, as he had hoped to put his life on a new footing, and had spent hours in the past couple of weeks fantasizing a future in which Lily played the female lead. Yet here in the flesh, they could find nothing and no one to talk about, once they had canvassed the death of psychoanalysis and a visit from Jonathan, who, she told him, had just left after spending a week with Lily and her friends. It took a day for Morris to conclude that the problem was that although Lily was polite and cheerful, she was emotionally flat. When Morris made jokes, she smiled dutifully, but he couldn't pull a real laugh out of her. When he tried to talk seriously, she listened with the same air of dutifulness. This was not encouraging.

They had emerged from the woods and turned down the shady path that led back to the house. The scents of earth and pine and the dappled light coming through the trees had aroused painful loneliness in Morris, and he was doubly mystified by the distance between him and Lily.

"Have you always been so close to Jonathan?" he asked her.

"We have been for years now, ever since my mother died. I don't know what I would have done without him."

"You were seventeen and he was . . ."

"A little over thirty."

"You were lucky he was around."

"More than lucky. I would have gone around the edge without him. He's the best man I know," she said earnestly.

"He's a good guy. He manages to be principled without beating people up about it." Around the bend, over the edge, he thought. But today her conflation of synonymous expressions seemed strange, not appealingly funny, and he said nothing.

"You get his number," said Lily. She respected Morris for what he valued in Jonathan. Certainly, Morris had some appealing qualities. Lily remembered what she had found attractive in Morris, but was unable to revive the attraction itself. She racked her brain, trying to understand the cause of the cool-down. Perhaps it was because he was not attracted to her? Was it her hair? Her clothes? Of course not. Silly even to think that. But still she could not put her finger on whatever it was. She saw his good points but couldn't get interested in them.

Morris, although no more successful at diagnosis than she was, as a man of experience knew how to deal with the situation. You don't push things, he knew. "Let's go swimming," he said. They swam, walked, played badminton, and talked for two more days, at the end of which they had once more achieved ease with one another and a confirmed liking.

On his last evening there, Morris, swinging on the porch swing, read a novel he had found in his bedroom, while Lily sat opposite, rocking in a wicker rocking chair and reading an article in a psychoanalytic journal. Each knew that a painfully awkward windup conversation was imminent, and hoped to be able to have it in the dark so that they could avoid looking each other in the eye. When the light was almost too dim for reading, Morris was called to the telephone. "It must be Charles Braithwaite," he said. "No one else knows how to reach me." Charles was calling to urge him to join them in the mountains, and in Morris's disgruntled state of mind, it sounded like a good way to counter his mood and stay out of the heat. Pleased at the invitation, he said he'd spend a day or two in New York and then drive out. Lily saw Morris's discomfort when he returned, and felt sorry for him. She admitted to herself candidly that she felt no disappointment that nothing had developed between them, except that she minded for Morris's sake.

"What was this woman like, the one in your department you just broke up with?" she asked.

"Not a very nice person."

"What was the attraction?"

"Truth be told, I didn't realize just how bad she could be when she was mad. I didn't mind getting mixed up with her, because I knew I'd never be tempted to marry her. She understood that, but after a couple of years she decided she wanted to marry me anyway. I just wanted someone to hang out with—she was also really . . . attractive—and amusing. I was lonely, but I wasn't ready to get married. I had things to do first. I had no money. I had to get over some hurdles in my work."

"How Victorian—to feel you had to make your way in the world first and then get married. That's not how people do things now."

"I didn't want to have a family I neglected. I told her up front I wouldn't marry her and I didn't have time for her, and she said fine. She said she felt the same way. For a long while, I think she really meant it, too."

"Do you think you'll ever get married?"

"I'm beginning to wonder."

"Was there ever anyone you wanted to marry?"

"Years ago. But she wasn't interested."

"Aha! You weren't a Victorian then."

"I never actually proposed to her."

"Who was she?"

"All right, nosy, it's your turn. I want to know your whole love history."

Lily blushed, but he couldn't see this in the dim light.

"Well, it's a very short history. I had a crush on someone in high school, but my mother died and nothing came of it. I had another crush on my analyst. And that's the whole story."

Morris thought this over carefully. "Are you saying . . . ?"

"That's right."

"You never . . . ?"

"Never."

"You got all messed up there at the beginning."

"At the very beginning, and things took a turn downhill when I lost my mother."

"And when did your father die?"

"Two years before that."

"Rough things," Morris commiserated, and Lily thought his tone of voice just right.

"I'm telling you the truth about my non–love life so that you won't go away and decide you hate me, because I like you a lot, Morris. These are my secrets."

"I'm a man of honor."

"I know. In fact, I thought maybe . . . but you showed up, and you weren't interested."

"*I* wasn't interested!"

"You know you weren't."

"You weren't exactly sending out invitations. Remember, sweetheart: the woman picks. The woman always picks—no matter how much it looks like it's the other way around. Listen to this. This gets it exactly right." Leaning toward the window for light, Morris read from his novel, " 'Any woman unless positively deformed may marry *whom she likes.*' That's Thackeray, and he was a good observer. Anyhow, you're too young for me."

"How old should your chosen one be?" Lily asked, distracted from the interesting proposition, that women initially choose men and not vice versa, by this still more interesting one about the proper age for Morris's spouse. But her tone was false, like a poor imitation of Katharine Hepburn playing a spoiled, witty young debutante of 1938.

"She should be thirty-three and a half, but anyone from thirty-three to thirty-four would do." Morris let Lily's inauthentic archness pass. He, too, could be kind.

"That's liberal enough. Shouldn't be so hard to find."

"I'm going to bed. I'm old, and I have a long drive tomorrow. Anyway, you're a nice, sweet person, Lily, although completely abnormal. I realize, one of the things I like about you is that you know you're really abnormal and you don't really mind, do you?"

"Nope. I don't mind if other people are, either."

"Is that meant for me? Doesn't matter. You're a good egg."

Morris went upstairs to his room, feeling that his unprecedented foray into the marriage market was over. He read a few pages, then, for the first time since arriving, fell asleep readily and slept deeply. In his mind the affair had just ended, even before it had begun. Lily, however, for the first time since Morris had arrived, stayed awake, restless and uncertain. She found it hard to let him go. He was admirable, smart. She also felt sorry for him, because of his loneliness and difficult circumstances, and because, she believed, he was handling things badly, messing up. It wouldn't be hard to be devoted to a man like Morris, and she might be able to help him.

In the morning, Lily stood at the door of his rental car with her hands on the open window, strangely intense. "Will you call me when I get back to the city?" she begged.

"Why wouldn't I?" he said. "We're friends. Or you could call me."

"Good. Yes. It's just that I think you shouldn't write me off." Lily blushed, as this felt brazen.

"So call." As he drove off, Morris did not know what to make of this. It seemed mechanical. He didn't really believe she was interested in him. It seemed more as though she thought she should be. This was not surprising, given that she was twenty-seven and had never yet succeeded in being interested in anyone. Whatever—he was certainly not going to take it personally and, in any event, he was not the sort to worry over things like this. If she wanted to pursue it, he wouldn't fight. She was appealing and substantial but a real sobersides.

# 14

LIFE AT THE hotel quickly took on a vacation rhythm of hikes, swims, meals, reading, and Scrabble or chess when it rained. The air smelled sweet and fresh; the days were slow and calm. Jane practiced, having been set up by the program director in an airless room on the fifth floor with an old upright. But even Jane was reduced to putting in a mere hour's playing each morning, after which she succumbed to the persuasions of other girls, who would come to find her, listen respectfully for five minutes, then beg her to come ride or hike or swim.

Three days before their stay was to end, Charles reminded Anne that Morris was due that afternoon, so they should make dinner reservations for an extra person. When they returned from a morning hike, Morris had already arrived and, with an ironic expression, was surveying the architecture, the people, and their L. L. Bean and Laura Ashley fashions. Vacationland for the repressed, he laughed, causing Anne to recall that he had been visiting with shrinks, and with one special good-looking young shrink. But he didn't have the air of a man in love. At lunch, Charles and Anne were curious to know what sort of visit he had had with Lily Freund, but nothing could be said in front of the children. Stuart, who had been standoffish when Morris first arrived, stared at him throughout the meal and at the end went and leaned confidentially against him. Morris put his arm around the boy, and his heart warmed but cooled again when he heard Stuart mutter under his breath, "Merrit."

"Hm?" Morris asked, startled.

"Merrit over there."

Morris looked, and saw Merrit standing in the doorway of the dining hall. She was scanning the room, not seeing them. Morris thought to himself that, even sweating and wearing wilted khaki shorts, she was probably prettier and better dressed than anyone within a radius of a hundred miles. All the women around here seemed to be mothers of three, or grandmothers of seven, who looked fuddy-duddy and were somewhere between slightly and seriously overweight. But there was something off-putting about Merrit's attractiveness, he thought, because you knew that no one drew so much attention to her looks who wasn't way too interested in doing so. He contrasted the slim perfection of Merrit's figure with Lily's artlessly sensual curves, intending to conclude his private debate with an unambiguous victory for the latter, but Merrit's physical presence was surprisingly argumentative.

"Run get her, Stuey," he said, sighing. He turned to ask Charles, "What is this?"

"What is what?"

"Inviting Merrit up here now?"

"Merrit's not here. What are you talking about? By God, it *is* Merrit! Why didn't you tell us you were coming?"

"I called. Didn't you get my voice mail? My mother got fed up with the heat on the farm and went back to her air-conditioning in the city. So I decided to come after all. How are you, Morris? I didn't know you were here," she said neutrally.

"We didn't get any message, but it doesn't matter. How glad I am to see you!" Anne said, to make up for the initial awkwardness. She embraced Merrit, then pulled back to look at her with motherly approval. No one did more for a pair of shorts than Merrit.

"Oh my God, how strange it is here! Kids and parents and grandparents. All families, no single people—except widows, and they're all here with their twenty grandchildren. Just look at all the families! I was here when I was eight," Merrit said. "It's unchanged. I thought it had probably gone the way of all the other resorts."

"Yes, it's a family place, a real dinosaur, isn't it? We feel normal here. At home, we always feel like a herd."

The two women went off together after lunch to see Merrit's room. As she unpacked, Merrit complained gently about Morris's presence. "He's a little better when you and Charles are around, I'll admit, but still, he's so unpleasant, Anne. Why didn't you tell me he was up here with you?"

Anne detected that something more than Morris was affecting Merrit, but chose to ignore it. "I simply didn't know you were coming," she said, "and so Charles saw no reason not to call Morris. It's just a slip-up. Oh, it's a big place, Merrit. You won't need to deal with him. Except at dinner. You've got to have dinner with us."

"I suppose. I'm sorry to be such a sourpuss, but he makes me uncomfortable."

"Well, let's just go have a swim and forget about it. He's in a bit of a strange mood, and I think his attack mode is switched off. Anyhow, Charles knows how to deal with him. You don't need to worry."

In fact, for the entire day, Morris said hardly a word to Merrit, but still managed to project a kind of disdain for her that made all of them uncomfortable and, after a while, irritated. He was quiet and sober, and Jane again took to calling him Morose. No one could shake him out of his mood; and Charles began to regret inviting him. Disapproving of Morris, however, he became conscious of his own testiness and was inspired to mend things with Anne.

"You're looking like a new woman, sweetie," he said to her. But, as he never called her sweetie, reserving that term for his children, the remark sounded false to both of them. Even Merrit and Morris noticed, and wondered what it meant.

Charles gave up, and sat silent. Anne understood it all and even credited his good intentions, and he knew she did. The thing about being angry with one's spouse, he thought, was that you instinctively turned to that same spouse for solace. Because he was angry with Anne, he wanted comfort—from Anne. Most amazing of all, she managed to sympathize with him in his anger toward her. She really felt bad for him. No wonder people didn't want to get married anymore. It made your head buzz. Morris and Merrit were lonely and afraid of something, dying probably, but Charles remembered loneliness; it wasn't as difficult as marriage. And added to the difficulties of marriage were those of raising children, the terror that Charles might let one of them fall in life, the sense that there were an infinite number of ways things could go wrong for them that he would be unable to fix. Nothing but Anne's sweet, unshakable, and unfounded confidence that things wouldn't go wrong preserved Charles from outright panic.

Merrit was chipper in an irritating, forced way, brittlely playful with the kids, and full of plans for fun, all of which Morris declined, in favor of reading or solitary walking. His only real enjoyment appeared to be in Charles's evening concert with Anne, throughout which he smiled, but afterward he seemed more glum than ever.

"Why didn't you become a musician, Morris?" Jane asked him the following afternoon as he sat on the shady veranda, reading the copy of *Vanity Fair*, its pages spotted with mold, that he had taken from Lily's house in Maine and looking up occasionally at the swimmers on the lake-shore in the distance. "Daddy says you were a good composer and pianist and could pick up practically any instrument and get music out of it. Didn't you like Juilliard?"

"I didn't like all the hogwash involved, and I didn't like giving up the rest of the world. It felt like joining a monastery."

"Daddy's not like that."

"Your daddy also has not gotten all that he's entitled to. If he weren't something absolutely extraordinary, he wouldn't have been able to hold to-gether what is in many respects a career less than what he merits." And holding it together is a balancing act, Morris thought, that is always threat-ening them with a bad tumble. He himself did not approve of trying to combine a career like Charles's with raising a big family.

"If Mommy were rich, it would have worked."

"I can't believe you said that! Anyhow, it isn't true. It couldn't have worked under any circumstances, because he refused the Faustian bar-gain. You only get invited to the top rung of the ladder if they own you—all of you. Faust, you see, made a bargain with . . ."

"I *know* what a Faustian bargain is."

Morris looked at Jane and wished she would go away. She was sitting on a banister in front of him. Her features were still childishly characterless, merely small and regular without beauties or strengths yet—unless an ex-ceptionally bratty expression counted as one. The older she gets, the less there is to like about this kid, Morris thought, and pondered the mystery of Charles and Anne's adoration of her—the way they hung over her, spoiled her, and rarely noticed what a little stinker she was, how mean, how con-vinced she was of being the center of the universe. He wondered whether getting so much unconditional parental love always turned a kid into someone the rest of the world could do without. But Morris disliked feel-ing so critical of a child, especially Charles and Anne's child.

"That's what a fancy school does for you," he said at length, stifling his aggravation. "Imagine a twelve-year-old knowing stuff like that."

"Almost thirteen. But I'm going to quit school. They're going to let me."

Morris sat up and scowled. "Who?"

"Mommy and Daddy. They're going to let me quit school and do eighth grade with home tutoring so I can practice three or four hours a day and concentrate on my career."

"No they're not."

"Well, they didn't say for sure yet, but they will. I can tell. Anyway, they don't have money for my tuition, so I'm not going back to that fancy school no matter what happens. And that way, we don't have to move."

"Listen, sis. I think you're mistaken about this. I'll believe it when I see it. Your daddy would never . . . anyhow, you better talk to your parents again before you go counting on doing anything like that." Morris stopped because he saw Merrit approaching from the other end of the veranda, frowning as she saw the serious and almost angry look on Morris's face. She took him to be scolding the child, and she had heard that he had been rough with Janie once before. Janie had an impenetrable expression on her face as she leaped from the banister and ran off, waving at Merrit, who for once turned aggressively on Morris:

"What was that all about?"

"It's none of your business."

"Don't browbeat little girls, Morris. Aren't you ashamed?"

"Merrit, we have to put up with each other for a couple of days, so I'm going to straighten you out on this one. But after that, if you have an attack of self-righteous fervor, you should just go rest quietly in your room until it passes, and also you should never use that tone of voice to me again. Jane just told me that Charles and Anne were going to permit her to drop out of school so she can practice more and prepare for a musical career, and I told her that I didn't believe it and I told her that she should discuss this with her parents again. And there is the horrible crime I committed."

Merrit was abashed at having been so aggressively suspicious. She apologized clumsily and got ignored for her efforts. Reflecting on the surprising news he told, she found that she did not regard such a plan as self-evidently wrong. There was a lot of good sense in it. "But are you so sure they wouldn't permit it? Of course, it's not for every child—certainly not the right thing for Ellen. But Jane is different. She could really make it; she could really be something."

"Merrit, this is a subject you and I would do best to avoid." Morris took up his book here, and Merrit walked away at a quick pace, feeling both hurt and hurtful, and headed past the lake toward the trail that led to the top of the mountain, despite darkening skies and gusty winds. Morris thought about calling out to her that a storm was whipping up, but felt too annoyed with her to do anything that could be interpreted as friendly. He sat and read for a while, then grew uneasy, noticing that the boathouse was closing and the horses were being led back to the stables. "Storm going to last long?" he asked a young man in a hotel uniform. "Until tomorrow at least," was the reply, "but don't worry. We'll do things indoors, dancing and all."

Morris watched the clouds thicken for some minutes more and waited to see if Merrit would reappear, then decided to find Anne. He walked toward the beach, but it had also been closed off. He went back to the hotel and called up to the Braithwaites' rooms, without luck. Then he went to the lounge and found Anne with all the children, playing Monopoly, just as drops began to pelt the windows. A chilly breeze quickly filled the room, carrying the scent of summer rain. There were flashes of lightning in the distance, followed by long, muffled rolls of faraway thunder, as the body of the storm moved toward them.

"Charles isn't out in this, is he?" he asked her.

"No, he's rehearsing somewhere, in some room they found for him."

"I'm afraid Merrit's out there," he said, after hesitating. "I saw her go off walking."

"Oh dear."

"Call her room, Anne. Maybe she came back on the other side while I was walking down here."

But she was not in her room, or in the shops, or on the veranda.

"She's out in this. Goddamn. I should've said something."

"She wouldn't have listened, Morris. You know, she'll be fine. She's a strong hiker, and she's not afraid of the weather."

"She should be. She should have her head examined."

"Just don't worry about her. She's a big girl."

"That's what you think. I'm going to go ask at the desk."

The captain was unperturbed by the news that Merrit was out walking in the storm. "We posted the storm warning this morning and told people not to walk out far. But we always get a half-dozen people who ignore us and come back soaked. No one ever gets hurt, so try not to worry about her, Mr. Malcolm."

"I'm not worried. I just thought you'd want to know."

Near dinnertime, no one had yet heard anything of Merrit. By this time, all the other stragglers had run back shrieking and laughing while sheets of rain sluiced over them. Charles, Anne, and Morris stood at an upstairs porch and stared into the dimness, listening for voices over the noise of the rain and thunder. Now they all were worried. "Someone's got to go look for her," Charles finally said. "I wish I had brought boots. I'll go."

Morris objected. "How can you go? You have to sing in two hours. I'll go." And it was agreed that Morris should don Charles's flannel-lined slicker and his own boots and set out with a big flashlight, a whistle, and an umbrella borrowed from the desk, a cell phone, and a warm sweater of Charles's for Merrit. When Morris had not returned in more than an hour, the hotel staff also began to feel concern, for by now it was night and the storm had not abated. Three pairs of searchers were sent out, all communicating by walkie-talkies. "He said she went up the mountaintop trail," Anne and Charles told them, "but that means nothing at this point. This was hours ago. Is there anything dangerous that way?" None of the paths was dangerous, they said, unless you got off them or climbed over fences and railings, and then there were cliffs to fall off all over the place. But they had never known anyone to be lost for longer than a few hours, and had never seen any injury worse than a cut or a sprain.

Morris, in the meantime, found the trail rough going. In a few minutes after he strode off, the lights of the hotel had receded, hidden behind foliage, and the noise of the wind and heavy rain on the leaves of the trees muffled his shouts. His voice tiring after a mile or so, he began blowing the whistle, shining the light about him in all directions. He went on for another mile and a half before he heard a voice faintly returning his call. Even then, however, Merrit was not easy to find. It took a series of answering calls before he tried shining the light down a hillside, where he glimpsed her in the shelter of a rock formation. She was wet and shivering, and very glad to see him. Morris, even under the circumstances, was struck by the oddity of Merrit's being glad to see him. She had injured her ankle, couldn't put any weight on it, and had a bruise on her forehead.

Merrit had begun to run back to the hotel when the downpour started, she told him, but had been blinded by the driving rain and had tripped over a root, fallen, and twisted her ankle. For a while she had sat on the trail in too much pain to move, drenched, but eventually she had limped to this mossy recess sheltered by rocks, fifty feet from the path.

"Now it only hurts when I try to walk on it," Merrit said. After being so frankly glad to see him, she turned awkward and was glad that she didn't have to look him in the eye. They both examined the ankle by flashlight. It was swollen, and tender when touched. "Mainly, I was beginning to be terrified that no one would find me until morning. I'm freezing, absolutely freezing."

Despite what she said, Morris saw that actually she was not all that frightened. He was surprised that Merrit didn't scare.

"I've got a cell phone," he said, unpacking the bag that held the dry pullover. He was completely at ease now that he knew she was all right. "I'll call and have them send one of those little trail carts for you. Tower of strength though I am, I don't think I could carry you two miles in this storm."

Released from the prospect of spending more hours alone and hurt, wet, and cold, Merrit found herself becoming wildly joyful and giddy with the relief.

"I do so hate pain and suffering," she said, and they both found this re-mark rather funny.

It took fully an hour after his call before the cart arrived, so Merrit was grateful for Charles's warm sweater, and they spread his slicker over the two of them like a blanket. Oddly, the original search party of six never found them, although they had all been shouting loudly and two of the pairs reported that they had passed the very spot where Morris and Merrit said they had been sitting.

Merrit's awkwardness with Morris had returned the next day, when he came to her room to see how she was. Anne was there looking after her and trying to keep Stuart from jumping on her bed. The bruise on her fore-head, having been swabbed with a reddish-brown antiseptic, looked shock-ing, and her swollen ankle was tightly wrapped. She was subdued, almost sad, even though she was quite all right. X rays taken at the clinic in town had found nothing broken, and the doctor said there had been no serious danger except the possibility of hypothermia if she had actually been forced to stay out overnight. It got chilly up in those mountains, and she was wet. Merrit thanked Morris in a low, formal voice. "You were very kind," she said. Morris's eyebrows rose, but he replied only that he felt sort of responsible because he hadn't warned her as she set off.

"I'd read the weather posting," she said. "Next time I'll heed the writing on the wall."

"No more throwing caution to the winds, eh?" But his voice, Anne noticed gratefully, was not so sarcastic as usual. He actually sounded almost kindly.

"No more," said Merrit, with a pro forma twitch of a smile.

"Well," he returned, more cool but polite, "the rain has let up. So I think I'm going to go out for a bit of a walk myself."

"There you are," said Anne after he had gone. "You should have let him do you a favor long ago. He doesn't dislike you so much now that he's done you this good turn. It's a psychological law: people like those to whom they've been kind."

"Great. Only you don't know just how kind he's been."

"What do you mean?"

Merrit would not look at Anne, or say anything more. Anne's lively imagination supplied a few answers but none she could really credit.

Merrit's mood did not improve for the rest of her stay. Her friends chalked this up to trauma. "A thing like that is a blow to your narcissism," Anne said, keeping private a few doubts about whether this was the real explanation for Merrit's funk. "Makes you realize you're mortal and that the world doesn't revolve around you, and it takes a while to get over that. I feel a tiny little bit that way if I just trip or bang my shin." Dinner on the last evening was quiet. Charles and Morris discussed his lab, the election primaries, and what Father Merriweather might be up to. Charles and Anne girded themselves for making the hard changes that lay before them. Ellen and Stuart, who were falling apart after two weeks away from home, bickered constantly while Jane sat and thought, apparently oblivious to everything.

The next morning, they all promised to see each other soon and drove off, Morris in his rented car, Merrit in her own car with a hired chauffeur because her bad ankle kept her from driving, and the Braithwaites in the same blue van that had brought them two weeks ago. The drive home from a vacation is always dreary, Anne thought. It reminds you of the trip out, when you were full of anticipation, and this doubles your disappointment that it's over, especially when there are so many problems at home. And comparing her own life's difficulties with those of their two friends, she wondered whose were really worse.

# 15

FATHER MERRIWEATHER HAD heavier duties in the second half of August, when the rector, along with much of the congregation, was vacationing. Sermons had to be written no matter how few congregants showed up to hear them. He tried to write sermons that were both theologically coherent and consistent with scientific truth and naturalistic explanations. One Sunday, preaching on the miracle of the loaves and fishes, he attempted to persuade the congregation that the story was an allegory, that faith couldn't be based on belief in Jesus' magical powers. He preached to a house that was less than half full, and he knew that most of his listeners thought the important thing about the story of the loaves and the fishes was that it demonstrated Jesus' power to defy the laws of nature. Through the miracle of faith, thousands of fishes and loaves could literally be created out of a basketful, the faithful believed, even though they understood the implicit analogy with the power of love, when freely given, to multiply itself.

Father Merriweather was drenched with sweat when he left the pulpit; and not just from the white polyester-satin robes he wore over street clothes in the stifling August heat, but also from the moral strain of fearing both that he might and that he might not be undermining the faith of the congregation. Perhaps the Quakers had the best policy, in insisting that the Scriptures speak to each member individually and letting each individual address the congregation as his or her conscience directed. Merriweather could no longer conceal from himself how much he disliked giving sermons, announcing the meaning of the Bible from on high—both literally and figuratively speaking.

At the same time, he had lately been noticing a discouraging likeness between his new distaste for his ecclesiastical duties and his old distaste for his lawyerly duties. He was distressed to think that perhaps he was destined twice—or maybe always—to find his mind revolting before work that other decent folk seemed to find unobjectionable. Once more, his over-wrought conscience, as it seemed to him, ruined his peace and prevented him from accommodating a perfectly acceptable world. Even worse, he experienced his own beliefs as an implicit condemnation of people who did not share them.

From a social point of view, moreover, the priest's collar seemed to rule out every woman he might be interested in. Churches, priests, and God were a big joke to most sophisticated people of his generation. Add to that his poverty and unimportance—he couldn't even imagine any pretty, smart woman, like Merrit Roth, for example, being religious or even sufficiently tolerant of religion to get mixed up with someone like him. He ran down the list (and it was a long list) of single women at St. Ursula's—not that he'd actually ask out a member of the parish, of course, but just hypothetically—and there wasn't one who glowed in his memory the way Merrit did. But she was heartbroken, or at least sad about something. Perhaps he'd ask Anne Braithwaite about her.

Father Merriweather had no distaste for his work in the soup kitchen— for keeping the books, lining up the volunteers, washing dishes, filling plates, or counseling the hungry visitors. He worried only whether it was the best way to serve the poor. Those who came for a meal were almost without exception impoverished elderly people or people who were in-sane, retarded to one degree or another, or incapacitated by addiction. Or they were people with a criminal past and had spent so much time impris-oned that they lacked even the most basic social skills and connections. All of them had long histories of convoluted relations with the welfare system, and were always trying to cadge Metrocards so as to be able to crisscross the city to deal with its different agencies. Over and over, they were caught between two or more different sets of officials, each insisting on the other's action as a condition of their own. Many of them lacked the mental power necessary to negotiate the maze of rules and offices; many lacked the physical stamina. Father Merriweather was always begged to call the dif-ferent bureaus and straighten it out or to find them a way to get somewhere or to go there himself. He listened to the stories and offered advice, wrote down the phone numbers of agencies and the addresses of charities with goods to give. He handed out the Metrocards donated every Sunday by the congregation. This was never enough, however, to help people with the dire and complicated problems of the soup-kitchen clients, and when these efforts failed to bring comfort, Father Merriweather had to tell the people, "I can only give you food. It's all I have to give you."

Merriweather, who spent most of his days puzzling over such religious, social, and moral dilemmas as these, discovered that he found it soothing to spend a little time pursuing facts that could shed light on Elizabeth Miller's will and her relation to Becker. For here at least duty was clear. The suspicions voiced by Father Quincy had been ratified by the small private investigation Merriweather had undertaken. He had quickly discovered that on three occasions Becker had been subject to disciplinary proceedings by the Bar Association Ethics Committee. He escaped without reprimand twice; and once he had actually been suspended from practice but subsequently reinstated. Becker's suspension was the result of his dealings with the estate of an elderly woman for whom he had been appointed guardian after she had been declared incompetent. Moral, as opposed to legal, wrongdoing was not so clear in this case, so far as Merriweather could determine; Becker had certainly defied the letter of the law, but it seemed he had done so at the behest of the woman's daughter under ambiguous, partially exculpatory circumstances. The two other cases involved questionable fee arrangements. But Becker had apparently convinced the committee that he'd done nothing unethical. Merriweather could find out little about these cases. In the suspension case, there was, perhaps, a violation of the professional code of ethics but not, in Merriweather's opinion, a crystal-clear one. He was surprised that the penalty was suspension rather than reprimand, but maybe that reflected the committee's impatience with a man who habitually operated too close to the borders of the permissible. In the wake of these difficulties, Becker had been thrown out of the small firm in Manhattan where he had practiced, and had then opened his own office in Brooklyn.

Although they had been regularly reported in the Law Journal, Becker's legal travails were not well known at St. Ursula's, even among the members of the congregation who remembered his mother. Only one elderly woman, who was married to a lawyer, had heard her husband talk about the trouble that Eugene Becker was in. That hadn't surprised them, she said, because he had always been in trouble as a boy. You couldn't have expected anything else, considering the way his parents had carried on and neglected him. The family had once been very proper, too, but they seemed to go all to pieces. "The father left her and disowned the child," she told Merriweather, "and she fell apart and paid no attention to the boy until it was too late, and then, when she was getting on and not so well, he got the upper hand of her. I'll bet you it wasn't any picnic for her those last years, having to lean on him. She hadn't ever really cared for the boy, and that's why she let him run all over her—because she felt so bad about how she'd behaved." Becker's professional difficulties, however, Merriweather guessed, were never known to Elizabeth Miller, who was not a reader of the *Law Journal* and had lost touch with everyone at St. Ursula's.

If there had been misdeeds in Lizzie's case, Merriweather had decided, they would have followed the pattern of the earlier ones. In the past, Becker's conduct was at least arguably legal, or could and would have been legal under slightly different circumstances. He had told lies, but these, in the same way, were just stretches, embroidery, never so elaborate as wholly to alter the underlying fabric of facts. Was this, Merriweather wondered, evidence of a conscience at work, restraining angry greed? Or was it simply evidence of a well-functioning sense of self-interest seeking to avoid detection? In either event, did this imply that Becker would or would not actually write a fraudulent will and forge a signature? Perhaps Becker reasoned that Miss Miller owed him for all he had done. Of course, Claire, Monique, and Anne Braithwaite could formally challenge the will and try to find the witnesses who had signed it, but Merriweather felt sure that the latter would either be unavailable or would swear that they signed it in the presence of the testatrix whether or not they did. Becker could be relied on to see to these details.

Merriweather also puzzled over why, if in fact the will was fraudulent, Becker had waited until 1998 to write it. In 1998, Elizabeth Miller had been 102 years old. Had Becker learned in 1998 that she had made the 1995 will that left him nothing? Or had he then learned that she had a little money in the bank that he might not be able to get his hands on unless he was her heir?

Father Merriweather had described Becker's disciplinary history to Father Quincy two or three days after their meeting with him. The rector had felt smug upon hearing that his intuitive assessment of Becker's character was backed up by objective evidence, and once more insisted that the heirs would have been foolish to give up the money in the bank to Becker—who had been furious when he learned that they had escrowed it. Merriweather, however, knew that he had to have much more than this to convince Anne Braithwaite and the others that they should contest the 1998 will. He and the rector planned to bring the matter up at a meeting with the bishop that was scheduled for just after Labor Day. In the meantime, the Braithwaites had put off taking any action until their return from vacation, and Claire and Monique insisted on leaving things in Anne and Merriweather's hands. They were afraid of Becker.

Merriweather took advantage of this delay to launch an investigation of Becker's financial situation. He was fortunate in that the court records of the disciplinary proceedings against Becker contained a good deal of information about his circumstances up to the time when he was suspended from the practice of law for a year. Father Merriweather was pointed in the right direction by the clerk of the court, who was a churchgoing man. The clerk was in late middle age, a lean, knife-sharp man with sallow-tinged, bloodless, leathery skin and Abe Lincoln features. He respected the law, judges, teachers, mothers, and clergy of any denomination. But he had the melancholy cynicism of the good man who has had to observe too many people's sins and crimes and who has personally been the object of a thousand ruses, lies, and scams. He took the nervous clergyman under his wing, getting him copies of documents and helping him interpret them, leaning over the old oak counter to point out important parts. "I'd love to know why you're so interested in this guy," he said.

"I don't really think I should say anything, Mr. Mahoney," said Merriweather, "except that I'm trying to figure out whether I should be suspicious of his conduct in another matter."

"It's hard for me to imagine circumstances in which I *wouldn't* be suspicious of him, but then it's your job to think the best of people, isn't it. Look at this. It's pretty clear that basically he sent this old lady with Alzheimer's into the poorhouse and pulled the wool over the daughter's eyes somehow."

"I thought the opposite. It looks to me as though his violations were just technical, and he meant to do right by them."

"Are you kidding me?"

"I don't see any proof he spent a penny of the money personally."

"No? You're a hard man to convince, then. All you gotta do is look at this record of withdrawals." The clerk pointed at a list of figures that had been submitted at the disciplinary hearing that resulted in Becker's suspension. "These sums don't make any sense if they were for taking care of

an old lady. The timing, the amounts—and see here how the dates corre-
late with his own expenditures, see here these investments, a new car . . ."

"Oh, I see. Yes."

"I should think so. You say you're a lawyer, but you never actually practiced law, didja, Father?"

"Well, in fact, I did for a few years."

"I can understand why you decided to go into another line. Now look
here, here's his financials from that year. Look at this. Lists a dozen different chicken coops this fox was in charge of. And the guy is legally back in
business."

Merriweather looked at the lists of figures and was surprised to see the
sum of $10,700 payable to Becker as guardian for Elizabeth Miller.

"Well, that seems like a large sum, Mr. Mahoney . . . especially since . . .
What do you think would have happened to this guardianship while he
was suspended?"

"Hmm. Well, as the guardian of an incapacitated person, under the
statute, maybe nothing. He didn't hold that position as an attorney. Anyone can be the guardian of an incapacitated person."

"How did he get to be her guardian?"

"Someone files a petition, and then there's a hearing."

"Is it possible for a third party to find out what property the guardian
manages?"

"The guardian is supposed to file a report with the court."

"And that information would be stated in the report?"

"Sure. Let's have a look."

The clerk left and was gone so long that Father Merriweather began
to ask himself how long he should continue to wait before asking the
drab woman working at a desk behind the counter to make inquiries. But
Mahoney finally reappeared, still poker-faced, bearing another thick file.
"Well, he's made some attempt to follow the letter of the law—except for
one thing. He's not the guardian."

Father Merriweather was stymied by this announcement, and stood
considering it for moment, wondering how to correct the clerk without appearing disrespectful. "Well, actually, Mr. Mahoney, I don't think there's
any doubt as to whether he's the guardian. My concern is only about his
reliability in . . ."

The clerk cut him off but spoke patiently. "Someone named Edna
Becker is the guardian. Eugene Becker shouldn't have any income as

guardian at all. I don't get this." He had opened a folder and was tapping his finger on it, showing Father Merriweather where the ". . . Court hereby appoints Edna Becker . . ."

"I've gone through the whole file," said Mr. Mahoney. "Edna is appointed in 1984. Eugene has no appointment."

"Edna was his mother. She's dead."

"You sure about that?"

"Positive. I didn't know her, but she was a member of our parish. She died eight or nine years back."

"Aha. He slipped one over on us, making sure we didn't revoke the guardian's appointment." The clerk flipped pages and read off signatures. "Edna Becker, Edna Becker, E. Becker, illegible Becker, Eugene Becker, and no one ever noticed. They're not really focused on the signatures when they review these things."

"He kind of slipped in there, eh? He probably still signs his mother's name. Or maybe he uses a power of attorney. I'll bet he was doing everything when his mother was still alive."

"Mm-hm. Something like that. Well, I can't let this drop now, Father, now that I know this. I'm sorry I have to blow your cover here." The clerk was dexterously stacking and closing the Becker files.

"No, it's all right. It had to come out."

"You wanna tell me what this is all about?"

"Let me go back and talk to my rector, and I'll be back in a day or two. You'll do what you have to, of course. But in the meantime—can you tell me what he was managing for Miss Miller?"

The clerk reopened one of the files, leafed expertly through its contents, and read, frowning. "Well, she's got some stocks and bonds, an annuity, this and that—or at least he claims she does," he said blandly. "Is she in a nursing home or something? She must be a hundred."

"She's dead. Died this spring at one hundred and three."

"Well, well. You don't say. The judge is going to want to talk to you, Father Merriweather."

"Of course. My card."

Father Merriweather left the courthouse and rode the subway uptown. From St. Ursula's, he called Father Quincy, who was vacationing in the mountains. Father Quincy, in turn, straightway called the bishop at the shore. The bishop, like Father Quincy, suspected that the 1998 will was forged and thought the parish should do whatever was possible to protect

Miss Miller's intentions as expressed in her 1995 will, sort of act *in loco familiae*. An elderly man himself, the bishop remembered quite well the country house Mrs. Miller had left to the parish so many years back. He'd actually attended a couple of retreats there, thought he could even remember meeting Miss Miller on this or that formal occasion, just to shake hands with, but of course he couldn't be sure. It was all so long ago now.

The bishop himself telephoned Merriweather and they spoke at length, finally agreeing that Merriweather would continue to assist the heirs under the 1995 will, if they wanted him to, and would in any case go immediately back to the court and tell all that he had learned, without waiting to be called in. The church might eventually get its lawyers involved, but for the time being there was no reason why Merriweather shouldn't pursue this, if he'd like to, to the extent he had time after his clerical duties. Merriweather was glad to be able to, but couldn't help wondering whether the rector and the bishop didn't encourage him, at least in part, in hopes of a tangible reward. Didn't they suspect that Lizzie's estate consisted of more than some forks and spoons? Perhaps. But, Merriweather reasoned, that didn't make it any the less the right thing to do. Nor was there anything wrong with hoping for money for a struggling church. It wasn't as though it was going to line anyone's personal pockets. No, they were doing just what they ought to do, yet Merriweather couldn't help feeling rather shamefaced about the church's motivations.

# 16

MORRIS WAS LOW when he returned to the city—not so low as he had
been last year when the troubles with Joey Delano had erupted, but low
enough that he wondered whether he had made a serious mistake in coming to New York. It was not just the lonely prospect of working through the
Labor Day weekend to get ready to launch his new series of experiments
as soon as the students returned. Living next door to the Braithwaites had
him constantly either worrying about them or envying their domesticity
and feeling like a third wheel. It seemed he would be running into Merrit
Roth around every other corner for the next two years, continually having
encounters that would leave him upside down. Morris wished he'd let
someone else go find her up on that mountain and that it all hadn't happened. He understood that she was ashamed of herself, humiliated, partly
just because she had lost control and let herself go and partly because she
had done so with Morris. Morris's intimacy with Charles and Anne made
the memory feel claustrophobic, almost incestuous; and, although Morris
was all but immune to embarrassment, he found the whole thing embarrassing. Everyone knew he didn't like Merrit, and that she neither liked
nor respected him. Merrit thought him a social incompetent and an academic failure, someone whose flaws of character prevented him from succeeding in science and society. He knew that Merrit felt superior to him,
and to most men. Her romantic life had been a series of affairs with men
whose high status allayed any danger that she would feel above them. This
was not very original, since, as everyone knew, 99 percent of all ambitious
women did the same. But Merrit was more aggravating than most of them,

Morris thought, because she actually believed that successful men were smarter, handsomer, and better—which is how she could end up totally blindsided by an idiot like Brendan McGarry.

In fact, when it came to men, Merrit was a fool, and he could have enjoyed explaining to her, at length, just how and why, if she would have given him a chance, which she wouldn't. He suspected, too, that she blamed him for the incident on the mountain, and that ticked him off. Why did she have to be so determined to disavow and condemn? If she'd loosened up, they could have laughed about it. Maybe they could even have revisited the scene, and Morris did revisit it in memory just then, with covert pleasure. But with an effort of will, for the twentieth time, he deflected these thoughts. The upshot was that he didn't think he could get angry with Merrit anymore, despite her flaws. Now he saw things more as Anne and Charles did. She was in for some misery, and more and more as time went on. But, with the loss of his anger, Morris stopped finding satisfaction in this insight. It began to sadden him, and he began to wonder if his own future would be much different from Merrit's.

Morris began thinking about Lily, but this was almost as melancholy as thinking about Merrit. When he remembered that last morning in Maine, it made him feel as if he were wading in molasses. He liked her. She had a lot to her. But somewhere in the back of his brain, he detected a tongue-tied anger that had something to do with Lily. Maybe what it is, Morris thought, is that I just hate women. I hate them. Merrit, Lily, Sam— they're all impossible. He considered asking one of his sisters to fix him up with someone who wouldn't be impossible, then remembered how impossible his sisters were. But he loved his sisters, so perhaps he could love a wife. This thought was cheering but, paradoxically, increased his loneliness. Morris longed for the comfort of another soul nearby, someone who knew all about him, someone he knew all about; and for the dozenth time since he had moved into 9D, he had an odd sensory episode, experiencing the dead silence in his rooms not as the absence of sound but as his own deafness. He dropped a book for the reassurance of hearing it strike the table.

He switched on his computer, was comforted by its familiar faint whirs and beeps, and checked his e-mail. Among the twenty or so waiting messages were, he saw with dismay, two from Joey Delano, one with an attachment. The first note said, "Urgent! This is a paper the gang at Duckworth's lab is coming out with in the next issue of *Biologica*. I got hold of this

copy and thought you should see it. I wanted you to know I'm not all bad."
The paper was, of course, virus-infected and had to be cleansed; Morris
wouldn't put it past Joey to have done this on purpose. Morris began reading it anxiously and was appalled to find in it a direct attack on Morris's
new thesis on genetic imprinting, which Duckworth, for some reason, presented as a hypothesis he had thought up himself and then rejected. He
presented it speculatively and demolished it speculatively. He even discussed hypothetical experiments, similar to those Morris had actually
completed, and, if Morris wasn't mistaken, alluded hypothetically to results of Morris's experiments that had never appeared in print or been publicly discussed by Morris—although his close associates, including Sam
and Joey, knew about them and knew where he was going with them.
Those slimy bastards weren't satisfied just to squeeze him out. They
wanted to make sure his adversaries had all the ammunition against him
that was possible. He had never heard of anything like this. Morris struggled to contain tears of rage and frustration.

When he had recovered enough to read further, he looked at the second
e-mail from Joey. "Watch out! That attachment I sent you has a virus. I
wouldn't put it past the bastards to have done that on purpose. I want to
tell you a few things about this. Please call me. I owe you something after
last year. (415) 555-2137."

It was almost three in the morning, late even on the West Coast, but
Morris called Joey anyway.

"Professor Malcolm," answered a groggy voice. "Oh, I'm glad you
called." And then Morris heard faintly, "It's okay, Mom. It's for me. First, I
want to say I'm sorry for everything that happened. I want to explain . . ."

"Forget explaining. Tell me who the hell gave Duckworth my data and
why."

"It was Schmidt. Sam put him up to it."

"Just plain malice? Why would Schmidt go along with it?"

"They got it on this summer."

"Sam and Schmidt? You can't be serious. He's sixty—he's married. His
kids are her age."

"Seems likely, though."

"He's ugly. He smells."

"She has to have someone, and he's top dog."

"Oh man, oh man."

"He left his family up at the lake, and spent the summer in town, which he never does. She never left. They're always at lunch together. They're always in the lab together at midnight. They're . . ."

"All right, all right. So what was the point of handing my stuff over to Duckworth? What do you know about that?"

"Do you have a cold?"

"Allergies," Morris said, swallowing tears.

"Well—you know this already—Sam hates you now, really hates you. And Schmidt, being new, didn't know much about you or your work, but—this part is guessing, of course—he probably felt a little jealous, because he has a big thing for Sam. And I think she showed him some data she had copies of."

"But where would she even get that stuff?" Morris exploded.

Joey, however, was unrattled by Morris's temper. He continued his recital in a manner at once sincere and earnest but somehow double, disingenuous. What Morris had eventually learned about Joey, during the Stanford fiasco, was that his craziness consisted, in part, of having no identity whatever, so that he was not capable of fully meaning anything he said. Joey would make Fagin look straightforward. And he had uncanny skill at figuring out what other people were up to.

"From me," Joey said. "Sorry. I had no idea at the time what she was up to. And she knew Schmidt was going to be seeing Duckworth at that Norwegian conference. So she seems to have convinced Schmidt that he should talk about all this with Duckworth—you know, describe the data and where you're going with it so that he can respond in this big paper he's coming out with, the one I sent you. So maybe Duckworth never actually saw the data, but Schmidt probably told him everything. Now there's a fuss about this around here. The paper is circulating. People are wondering what's going on. It seems Schmidt is going around saying you didn't think up this hypothesis and that you actually got it from Duckworth. You just borrowed it and tried to prove it, with a lot of worthless science. He claims he and Duckworth had an interesting and fruitful professional discussion and he did share with him his understanding of your research. You know, he's big on that—'science is dead if there's no open discussion and free sharing of information'—that kind of thing."

Now Morris got the whole picture. He knew these people, especially Sam, and thought Joey's analysis was probably accurate. "So they made sure Duckworth would get credit for ten years of my work," said Morris. "If in the end I prove I'm right, they'll say I got the idea from him. And if I'm wrong, I don't even get credit for finding that out, because he says it first, in print, actually using my stuff to do it. Oh my God. How do you know all this?"

"The secretary, Barbara, told me some of it, and I got the rest out of Sam."

"But there are people there who know this is all lies. Isn't anyone speaking up?"

"There's a bit of heat. Barbara, for one, is on your side, and me. But we're not flying our colors, so we can get info for you."

"Christ."

"Also Tina Spinelli and Pasternak. The trouble is, you know what a wimp she is, and Pasternak's so incoherent. Even so, Schmidt is a little worried. But I guess he thinks it's just your word against his—and Sam's and Duckworth's."

"Joey, why are you getting involved in this? And what are you doing back in the lab anyway?"

"See, that's what I want to tell you about. Last year I had a manic response to this antidepressant I was taking. You remember when I got the tattoos? And those Russian wolfhounds?" Here Morris detected the ghost of a snicker behind Joey's voice. "Until I figured out what was happening, I did a lot of damage. I'm sorry. I'll always be sorry. It all stopped when I stopped the medication." Morris knew that as far as Joey could mean anything, he meant this. He was making a great effort, aided in doing so by his love of mischief, which made him delight in the possibility of exposing Schmidt and Sam.

"That's some story," Morris said.

"Do you believe me?"

"It's not hard to believe."

"I got so much medical testimony that they took me back. Also, I think the people who are mad at you don't really mind what I did all that much. I'm applying for post-docs, and they're writing letters for me saying I'll be all right. But I don't want you to think I think I'm really sane now. I'm just back to my used-to-be. I've always been crazy. They tell me my psychiatrist should have known this was the wrong drug for me."

"How a biologist can take drugs like that is beyond me. You know there's no science behind them. It's just voodoo." Morris wanted to make some forgiving gesture toward Joey, but this was all he could manage—so far, anyway.

Morris went to bed, but lay awake trying to find a way to undo the catastrophe and inventing florid schemes of vengeance. Perhaps he should call the editors at *Biologica* and explain the situation. If anyone at the Leland Center would back him up, that would help enormously, and there were many people at other institutions who knew the truth and would support him. He despaired at how much time was going to be wasted in rages, explanations, and soul-wrenching political machinations, time that he wanted to spend in the lab, bringing this work to its conclusion. He had had such a good chance of being right, and of being first—except that Sam didn't want it to happen. By spreading rumors about him, she had almost prevented his being funded, and when that didn't work, she had tried to undercut the work itself. The only thing she hadn't been able to accomplish was to ensure that someone else actually did the same work and got there before he did.

He had been asking for it, getting mixed up with her, knowing—as he had known—that she was not the decent solid-citizen type. He had also known that sooner or later he would hurt her and arouse her rage. From his present vantage point, it looked to Morris as though he had done everything but sit down at a drawing board and design his current dilemma. Worse, the idea that he had intentionally involved himself with someone because he knew he couldn't like or respect her well enough to marry her began to seem revolting to him, and his troubles to seem like punishments for miscreancy. He had behaved unkindly, cynically, imprudently; he had known that, morally speaking, she was a weak reed. And look at the cascading series of injuries he had set in motion—all the way to Schmidt's wife and kids, even a blow at whatever was left of the spirit of science. This had all been done, moreover, in the name of decency. Morris had told himself he wasn't going to mistreat a wife and family; this, he had concluded, privileged him to have mutually exploitative relations with another human being. Full disclosure made everything all right, even when he knew that someone was actually banking on his behaving humanly, despite his announced intentions not to. Why, then, did he feel so superior to the Brendan McGarrys of the world? Or the Merrit Roths for that matter? Once more, his encounter with Merrit on the mountain passed through his mind, this time causing him not just embarrassment but excruciating guilt. How could he have taken advantage of her the way he did! He ruminated obsessively, for hours, on a novel he had once read called *Harry, the Rat with Women* but couldn't remember who wrote it.

At sunrise, Morris was still awake and had found no peace of mind. He watched the light grow full, then showered and headed for the lab. He intended to call Schmidt, and if Schmidt would not promise to call Duckworth and *Biologica* to do so himself. Before this, however, he would line up his backers. And before he did anything at all, he thought, he had to call Sam.

# 17

MORRIS WAITED SIX hours, until it was ten A.M. on the West Coast; then he dialed Samantha's lab.

"Morris!" she said, recognizing his voice immediately. Morris heard the tension in hers. "Morris, you heard about this."

"Let's get to that in a minute."

"It doesn't really mean much, you know. You have no reason to get in a snit about this."

"Sam, I want to talk about something else first." But Morris felt his carefully rehearsed expressions of remorse begin to seem unutterable.

"I don't."

"I have something to say to you," Morris said. "I'll bet you'd rather not make me fly all the way out there to say it." He instantly regretted the suggestion of threat in these words. He'd meant to be nothing more than sarcastic.

"So," Sam replied, sounding more relaxed, "what is this important subject you want to talk about?"

"I want to tell you—all this happened because you and I never should have gotten together, and it's all my fault. I shouldn't have gotten involved with you, given the way I felt. I told you honestly what my feelings were, but I knew you'd eventually get burned anyway, and you didn't know it. My attitude was that this was your lookout, not my responsibility, but that was wrong and I'm sorry."

"Give me a break, Morris. You're about as capable of remorse as my cat. What are you up to? You think maybe I'll do something for you if you hand me garbage like that?"

"No, I'm trying to be serious, and you're making it hard. Let's try to look at this for a minute."

"No, I don't want to look at it. I really don't. I've got someone new in my life. I just want you to get lost."

"Let me say this another way . . ."

"Don't bother. All your fault! Even your apologies are nothing but colossal egoism, disguised attacks. I don't want to hear it." Morris had heard her say that, in that tone of voice, before, and on those occasions she had always walked away and slammed a door. For a moment he feared she would hang up, but then he heard the soft clack of her computer keyboard. Was she actually answering e-mail while he was trying to have this serious talk with her? Of course she was doing it on purpose, to show her indifference and annoy him. She knew how he hated her habit of typing when talking to him on the phone. But Morris refused to take the bait.

"The fact is," he said, "I knew it, I mean, what the big picture was, from the beginning, and you didn't. So it's my fault—I took advantage. That's all I mean. But you don't want to understand, so forget it. But no matter what I did, Sam, you shouldn't have put Schmidt up to this. You shouldn't let these personal things corrupt what we're all supposed to be doing. I'm ready to agree the real bad guy here is Duckworth. But he had a lot of help and encouragement from people who were crossing lines they shouldn't have. I imagine you took little shots in the dark and got a bigger hit than you expected, that's all."

"The teachings of Saint Morris."

"Stop it. You sound like a ten-year-old. Look, I know I'm responsible for a lot of this mess, but that doesn't mean I won't try to stop that article from coming out if I can. And here's the main thing I have to tell you: if it comes out that you did this—and it might, I'm not going to protect you—no one will be on your side. And your career, not mine, will go down the tubes. So you want to be careful. You've got a chance to stop it all now, before you get in too deep. In your own interests, you should go to Schmidt, or Duckworth, or whoever, and try to head this thing off."

"Oh please. I *thought* it would come down to this."

"It's the best I can do."

"Which is probably the pitiful truth. When could you ever do anything right? You're a small man with big pretensions, Morris. You're a second-rate scientist. You've never had an original thought in your life. You've never done anything that mattered, and you never will."

Morris, so furious that he was shaking, hung up on her. But it was done, and it reduced his choking sense of remorse to the point that he was able to eat the sandwich he had brought for his lunch. She felt better the minute I got mad at her, he reflected gloomily as he chewed. By that evening, his anger was all but burned out, and he gave a calm report of the story to Charles and Anne, who were irate in proportion to his failure to be irate. It was unnerving to see Morris laid so low, practicing a feeble stoicism, and so terribly lonely.

"What *will* it do to you if the article actually comes out?" Anne asked him.

"It would make it difficult for me to prove I was the one who actually dreamed up this whole theory and hard to get funding to pursue it further. Even if the work turns out favorably, I'm going to have a hard time convincing people I'm right, because Duckworth's account is sleazy in ways you can't easily tell when you read it. First impressions are powerful, and I'm already up against ideas that are entrenched. None of these things are necessarily fatal—in the long run I should be able to make a pretty good argument against Duckworth—but they make everything hard and unpredictable. I just don't know what's going to happen."

Despondency and lack of sleep had aged him ten years, Anne thought. She felt a hollow ache inside just looking at him. Anne guessed that what had really sunk him was not the damage to his work and his professional plans so much as the knowledge that he had inspired such active, murderous hatred, and as a result of permitting himself a corrupt intimacy. Oh, this was a man strangling in guilt, mercilessly punishing himself. But those were things she could not say. Instead, she laid her hand on his arm and said, "I think it's going to come out all right, Morris."

He gave a weak snort of disagreement, but Anne persisted. "It has to straighten out, because too many people know the real facts. Her character is going to emerge; the anomalies are going to accumulate."

Charles agreed with this analysis. "The real problem is that it will take time."

Morris, however, was far from sure that he would eventually be vindicated. He was only an optimist about larger forces and trends. When it came to individuals' fates, it seemed, he was stubbornly fatalistic. "It's because he feels too guilty," Anne told Charles when he had gone. "He can't yet permit himself to think he'll ever be off the hook. But notice he has no plans to give up, stop working. He's still in there fighting."

Morris, pleading exhaustion, did not stay for dinner when pressed, and

crossed the hallway. He found a message from Lily on his answering machine, returned her call, and spent an hour on the telephone with her. Her
comprehension of the scientific and psychological issues and her calm
common sense were reassuring and soothing. He felt much better after
talking to her, and they arranged to meet for dinner the next day. He also
found another e-mail from Joey:

"Barbara said you called Sam at the lab, and I feel pretty sure she listened in on the conversation since she suddenly thinks you're a prince
among men. She says your call to Schmidt scared him, but it's not going
to work. He's just digging himself in deeper, going around saying that
you're deluding yourself and you don't have the mind or character of a true
scientist."

Three days later, the whole story went the rounds at Columbia, after
Joey called a post-doc there who had done graduate work at Stanford. But
Morris had wisely told all, before this, to the head of the department, Barry
Horowitz. Horowitz had worried that Morris was the sort of man who
made trouble around him. But he worried less when Morris assured him
that there would be no fireworks. He intended to press everyone involved
to do what they could to get the article withdrawn or revised, but if that
failed, Morris would simply repair the damage as well as he could, he said,
when he brought out the complete research. The data Duckworth was
discussing—and this was what grated most—was not only preliminary; it
was misleadingly partial. "He's the one who's hard to figure," Horowitz
said, puzzled. "I know him. Why don't I give him a call?"

This, too, was done, with the result that Duckworth refused to consider
withdrawing or revising the article. He insisted that nothing in it had
drawn on Morris's work, and strongly implied that he had actually suggested the whole business to Morris when Morris was his post-doc years
ago. And, after all, he said, these were in the end communal endeavors. All
these proprietary attitudes about ideas! What sense did it make for Morris
to claim originality when he'd learned his entire framework of thought
from Duckworth and others? Duckworth had already discussed all this
with the editors at *Biologica*, and the majority opinion, after reading the
piece, was strongly in accord with Duckworth. Horowitz thought he got a
hit when he suggested that Morris could document his own origination of
the idea. Duckworth hesitated at that point, but in the end he was not to
be swayed. Horowitz then went so far as to call *Biologica* himself, but the
editors were intransigent. They were beginning to be too scared to think

straight. Horowitz conveyed all this to Morris, who realized that Horowitz believed him, Morris, over Duckworth, simply because he trusted him. For this Morris was grateful, but he doubted that the rest of the world would be so kind.

Horowitz was one of a handful of people who really understood where Morris was going with his new work and the ingenious route he hoped to take. Fascination with Morris's hypothesis was what had originally led Horowitz to do everything he could to get Morris to Columbia despite the unpleasant reputation he had acquired at Stanford's Leland Center. Part of his faith in Morris's story derived from reading Duckworth's new article, along with many of his older ones. In the arguments against Morris's thesis he detected dishonesty and weakness—there was some kind of twisting in it. The mind that could produce the *Biologica* essay could never have invented Morris's theory. Besides, what Morris had said in *Scientific American* about Duckworth's latest ideas—that they shifted into nonscience—was obviously true. Duckworth was mixed up about what he could prove and what he couldn't, what he knew and what he didn't. A man who wanted to impress people so much that he confused facts with fancy fictions was far more likely to be a cheat than was a hard-nosed, straight-thinking man like Morris.

Horowitz walked out of the interview convinced that Morris was telling the truth, and he considered himself a judge of character. Yet he still debated whether this latest incident showed that Morris was a lightning rod for trouble or confirmed his impression that the Leland Center was a troubled place which Morris was well quit of. He was impressed with Morris's restrained response to what any fool could see was an outrage.

# 18

ON A PLEASANT September day, Merrit boarded the M4 at 116th Street clutching a copy of *The New Yorker*, which she had just bought at the newsstand. She riffled the pages until she found three columns describing a conversation with Brendan McGarry over lunch at Babbo. The article gave as much detail about the post-Italian food as it gave about Brendan's discourses on the post-Internet world. That was Brendan for you: so anxious to be first among trend-spotters that he killed off trends when they had barely gotten started. This explained why he had canceled lunch with her, she realized as she read. He had said he couldn't make it because he had to meet someone at Babbo. The bus waddled up Broadway, careened onto 110th Street, and then wheezed and snorted its way down Fifth Avenue to Eighty-second Street. Dr. Freilich had been away for only a month, but in that short time Merrit had collected at least a year's worth of miseries, one after another—major life crises, tawdry love-life incidents, minor atrocities, ending with this one. She catalogued them in her mind. There was so much to tell that she'd have to leave some out.

Dr. Freilich was there, fresh, crisp, unruffled, noncommittal, and there was the faint, comforting odor of cigarettes and cigars smoked long ago — evidence of decades of bad nerves in scores of analysands—and now exuding permanently from the floors and walls and aged furniture in the waiting room and the office. Merrit couldn't yet bring herself to talk about her biggest issue. She began, instead, by describing her realization on reading *The New Yorker*, and soon, hearing pages turning behind her, realized that Dr. Freilich was searching through his own copy of *The New*

*Yorker*, which made her feel petulant. Where was this neutral, evenly hovering attention he was supposed to be paying to her free associations? Merrit shut up, and inferred from the noises behind her that Dr. Freilich was reading. "What is this," he finally asked innocently, "about his having written himself out of London?"

"He's alienated a lot of people there. But also he means he's pretty much done things there and wants new horizons, so he's coming to New York."

"Has this anything to do with you?"

"Not really. He's moving here with his new girlfriend, who I've heard is pregnant. They say he's going to marry her. He does seem to want to keep me on a string, but not too tightly."

"You've seen him?"

"I hate it when you ask all these questions. No, but we've been e-mailing. He says he can't give up Sybilla—his fiancée—or me. But I'm finding I can give him up."

Silence.

"It's depressing to think I ever took him seriously. I must have been crazy. I mean, this man is a moral midget—a phony. Why can't I find words to describe it?"

" 'You were crazy so you fell for a moral midget' seems to say it."

"It's not just talk. There's something really wrong with me. I mean, I have a screw loose. Only a woman with a screw loose could look Brendan in the face without laughing. It's almost frightening."

"Almost?"

"But you're being sarcastic. I mean it."

Silence.

"If we can agree I'm really nuts, that's progress. Because when I met Brendan, I went off the deep end. I was convinced he was godlike, perfect. There were holes in my brain. I was delusional."

Silence.

"He said I made him feel alive, and I thought I had brought a corpse to life. I mean *really*. Whenever I came across any signs that he hadn't actually been quasi-dead before I came along, I would have a feeling that this was a little odd. I couldn't exercise any critical judgment at all about the way he acted or what he said. If he said he had to break a date to see his masseuse, I never argued. He told me he would not have children because the world was too dangerous and evil, and I felt guilty for wanting to bring children into this dangerous, evil world. It goes on and on."

Merrit dredged up the unsavory particulars of her relation with Brendan for nearly thirty minutes. She wept. Dr. Freilich, finally, ventured to say that her irrational idealization of this flawed man, and the fantasy of restoring him to life, had something to do with her father's death and her age when he died.

After some back-and-forth that gave flesh to what he had said, Merrit said, suspiciously, "But how obvious that is. You're saying I reacted to Brendan as though I were five years old and in the throes of an idealizing love for my father when he died. Actually, you said that before, but I didn't get it. Well, I understood it, but I didn't necessarily believe it. I wonder why."

She pondered for a while. "So I guess we're done."

"What do you mean? The hour isn't over."

"I mean we got it. That's it. You said we could figure it out fast. I admit, I'm amazed." Merrit heard Dr. Freilich exhale.

"But it's not that simple. There'll be things to work through, and there may be other issues."

"Oh sure. But really, I think this is the big one."

"It seems to be a big one—and we know very little about it. You've never talked about your father's death in here."

"That's true, isn't it? Dr. Freilich, there are only five minutes left and I haven't told you some things. Big things."

"This isn't a confessional, you know."

"No, I don't mean misdeeds. Well, actually, maybe one thing is that. But what's most on my mind is a gynecological exam I had in August, while you were gone. It looks as though I'm going into early menopause. Dr. Crowley says it's doubtful I would be able to get pregnant anymore. I'm almost thirty-nine, but my mother didn't have this until she was fifty-three. I thought I still had a little time left."

Dr. Freilich, for once, she detected, was disturbed by her news, and Merrit found his reaction both gratifying and unnerving. She left his office with a shaky feeling. Her gynecologist's negative report had left her shattered, although she had been deprived of the hope of children even before this, by her pessimism about ever finding someone to settle with. She was shocked to learn how deeply her ideas about love were entwined with those about bearing a child—so much so that now she could hardly imagine wanting a man without wanting his child. She wished she had talked about her bizarre encounter with Morris, memories of which continued to torment her now, weeks after the fact. On second thought, however, she realized that the entire incident with Morris could be chalked up to August madness—when the shrink is away, the analysands act out. At this point it was water under the bridge, she decided, with some relief. Her embarrassment was not really something she needed Freilich's help to deal with.

She boarded the M4 on Madison, and, as the bus groaned its way uptown, her mood altered yet again. She became aware of an inner pressure, some wordless feeling that had been with her, unnoticed, since childhood; and no sooner had she noticed it than it vanished and she felt, instead, eerily alone, released, with no particular reason to go anywhere or do anything. She disembarked at 116th Street and went straight home, because she could think of nothing else to do. She looked at the notes on her desk, the file list on the computer monitor, the books she had been absorbed in. It all seemed to belong to someone else. For months, she had been tortured by her inability to make real progress with the new book, and now the sense of compelling reasons to proceed with it had dissipated completely. She did not care at all.

The following morning, she visited Anne. "I don't want to burden you," Merrit said tearily, "but I'm having a kind of taking-stock. I feel so lost. I look back at the past twenty years, all the years since I left home, and there's nothing but love affairs that started out zingy and turned bad, and trying to get noticed and read. I still don't feel I know what I should be writing about, even though I've published so much. But you look back, and there was the music and Charles and all the children, and it all builds and links up. It's all part of you. I don't have anything like that. The things that happened to me aren't part of me, never have been. And the worst is, it will just go on like this forever. I'm going through life behind a glass. And nothing can reach me, nothing can touch me."

Anne made concerned noises. "Why not see a fertility specialist?"

"Anne! It's not just that. And what would be the point? I'm single. Who would be the father?"

"You've been to see Dr. Freilich today?" Anne asked.

"I'm going this afternoon."

"Good. You'll talk about all this again."

"But what's going to happen to me, Anne? It's not just no babies. Everything is wrong. Everything."

"Merrit, I think it'll probably be all right," Anne said, feeling foolish but incapable of believing the worst or withholding comfort. Let Merrit's shrink get to the meaning of things.

When Dr. Freilich opened his door to her later that day, Merrit saw his brows lower a fraction of a degree as he observed her. What did he see? That she looked terrible, with hair pulled back into a stubby brush, and ill-sorted jeans and top? Merrit didn't really care. She said no word of greeting, but when she settled on the couch, she was talkative.

"I keep getting older outside, but inside nothing changes. I'm still twenty." She described the eerie time in her childhood just after her father had died, and what her mother was like, then and now.

"Did I tell you: my mother *adored* Brendan. What kind of mother adores Brendan? She never really cared whether I got married or not. She's not at all the kind of mother who asks you when you're going to give her grandchildren. I was always glad about that. I thought I was lucky to have a mother who let me live my own life, and I thought we were really close. I call her twice a day and spend every vacation with her and I have dinner with her three or four times a week. Some of my friends think I don't have my own life, and maybe it's true. If I'm not in love, I'm with her. I thought she never asked me about getting married and kids because she didn't want to pressure me. Now I'm not sure she ever cared. When I was a child, I always assumed she loved me but, objectively, she acted as though she didn't even like me very much. She still doesn't like me very much. I used to compare her to Anne's mother, and I thought that mine was just, somehow, maternally inept. But in retrospect . . . she had no hopes for me, she didn't take pleasure in me—the way Anne does with her children. You know, Dr. Freilich, all these are psychoanalytical chestnuts. Here I am going on thirty-nine when I finally realize that my mother didn't love me. I never knew that before. Why? I've got lots of friends who come from wacko families, but they all know it, and I was oblivious. I had on blinders, earplugs. I never had a clue. Why was that?"

"I would guess that it was defensive ignorance. A child who had already lost her father would be doubly terrified if forced to question her mother's affection or strength and judgment. Time is up."

Merrit expressed her irritation at this abrupt termination in body language, but she said good-bye. She didn't quite know what to do with herself when she left.

# 19

THE BROKER DELIVERED potential buyers to view the Braithwaites' apartment several mornings each week. Charles and Anne dreaded the viewings but hoped to sell soon, because Anne's mother was now paying their deficits and they planned to repay her from the proceeds. On weekends they toured houses for sale in leafy towns in Westchester, New Jersey, and Connecticut, driven around by local brokers, who picked them up at the train station. Viewing houses was as upsetting as having their own apartment looked at. Each visit to another suburban house plunged them into dark imaginings of a strange, weightless life, without the people and places and habits that moored them in the city. They would tell each other that they would put down new roots, but they didn't fully believe this, having never yet succeeded even in imagining what it might be like. The result was that it was difficult to find a place that attracted them; and it was equally difficult to find one they could afford. In any event, they could not buy before they sold, so these trips to the suburbs were undertaken by way of education, as the brokers put it, to learn what they liked and get a feel for prices. September went by, however, and no buyer had yet made a satisfactory offer.

When school opened, Ellen went back on a full scholarship. Stuart laid his head on Anne's lap and sobbed quietly when he was told he was not going to the nursery school he had been looking forward to for more than a year, his anticipation primed by teachers' visits to him at home and his own visits with Anne to the school. Charles and Anne found his grief unendurable. The next day Anne went to the director and begged to let Stuart come with tuition unpaid for the time being; they could pay when they sold. This proposition was put so persuasively, and Stuart's distress conveyed so movingly, that the director agreed. Stuart was restored to smiles even though Anne told him that it would not be forever, that they were going to have a new home too far from this school.

Anne had tried to find a place for Jane in a good public school, but two days before classes began, in mid-September, Dr. Suarez, the head of the school both girls had been attending, called and insisted that Jane return. Anne was touched by Dr. Suarez's determination to protect Jane, who was, after all, an indifferent and often troublesome student. Dr. Suarez, too, agreed to permit them to delay payment until they sold their apartment. When Jane, however, learned that her plans for staying home were to be overturned, she stormed, ranted, and was twice sent to her room to cool down. After two weeks, during which Jane's behavior at school and home was abominable, Charles and Anne called in Anne's mother, who hardly bothered to disguise her preference for Jane among her grandchildren. Helen forcefully argued Jane down, pointing out that her mother, Anne, had won the concerto competition not only while attending school full-time but even while making an outstanding academic record. To give the family some relief from the tension of Jane's rebellious unhappiness, Helen took Jane home with her for a couple of days, during which time she indulged her unceasingly and insisted on the wisdom of her parents' decision and the importance of her education. She even got Jane to agree to try to learn a little this coming year. Jane returned with boxes of new clothes and a tantalizing assortment of diaries, pens, pencils, and notebooks, reconciled to being a schoolgirl.

This resolution, however, created a new predicament. When Ellen saw that Jane had been rewarded for what she regarded as willfulness and foolishness, she broke down and cried into her pillow. "I never get anything, not even if I'm good," she told Anne in a broken voice, "and Janie gets everything just for being bad." Anne, who had been dismayed to learn of Jane's shopping trips, told Ellen that she should not cry yet, because she thought someone had plans to buy her some presents too. "Really?" Ellen said hopefully, through sobs. Anne then left Ellen's room to discuss with Charles just how this could be brought about.

Charles, gloomily, pointed out that the proceeds of the sale were going to go to pay so many debts that they would be forced to assume a sizable mortgage on the house they would buy. But when it came down to it, he could not endure that the children should have to change schools twice in a matter of months. He did not see what else could be done. And yes, god-dammit, Ellen would have to have presents. What was Helen thinking of? But you couldn't blame her. She was just trying to make the pill go down easier. And, really, where would they be without Helen? She was always handing them money—and she was not a rich woman—never complained about it, never saw anything wrong with the way they lived, never came be-tween them. Still, the sense that their indebtedness was growing rapidly made Charles anxious to make the move they all dreaded.

"There's something else, Charles," Anne said. "I went to get Stuart a bigger violin. I gave fifteen hundred plus the trade-in for it. You know, it's just like money in the bank. It appreciates. It'll mean we pay less when we finally get into full-size . . ."

But Charles had walked out of the room.

It was a week or so later, while Charles and Anne were in a state of great suspense, expecting a call from the broker about a bid, that Father Merri-weather phoned to report what he had learned in his investigations. Charles picked up first, in his studio, and Anne ran in to listen, thinking it was the broker. Merriweather's information was annoyingly ambiguous. Becker hadn't legally been Lizzie's guardian, which meant that all his dealings with her property were illegal in a formal, technical sense, but didn't prove he had really robbed her. It was possible but not certain that Becker had lied when he said Lizzie had nothing to leave anyone. He had once been suspended from practice for dishonesty in dealings with the property of another elderly client, but Merriweather was not sure how cul-pable he was in that instance. Nonetheless, the 1998 will in his possession was probably valid. Under the law, doubts like these about his character or his honesty in dealing with Miss Miller's property would not be sufficient to overcome the presumption in favor of the will's validity.

Now Charles and Anne reversed their positions. "Of course the 1998 will is the valid one," Anne said. "Nothing else makes sense."

"But then why didn't she make the 1995 will in favor of Becker? Why did she have to arrive at the age of one hundred and two before she finally realized she wanted to be nice to him?"

"Maybe the 1995 will was a whim and she thought better of it. Maybe there was a quarrel and she relented."

"Then she would have torn up the 1995 will when she made the new will," said Charles.

"She was old, and legally there was no need to tear it up."

"At any time, she could have had Claire run over and retrieve it for her and then she could have torn it up. That would have been sensible, and you're always saying she was so sensible."

"I don't know, Charles. It's all a mess. I don't want to be chasing will-o'-the-wisps anymore. It upsets me." Anne sat down at the piano bench and played a few lines of the Mozart piano concerto that Jane would perform in the competition.

"That's lovely, Anne. It makes me realize that Janie doesn't really get it yet, does she?" Charles had come to stand by Anne and listen; but Anne wanted no praise that diminished Jane's efforts, and she stopped.

"Not yet, but there's plenty of time. She'll get it by December."

Charles was not sure he agreed; he thought that the temper of those Mozart piano concertos was always difficult for children to grasp, and particularly hard for a child with Jane's stormy nature. But this was the sort of thing you couldn't argue about with Anne. She had been pleased with this choice, perhaps, in part, because she herself had played Mozart in the competition. Charles reverted to the subject of Lizzie's will. "It upsets me, too. But now I'm beginning to feel convinced that the cash, legally, probably belongs to Claire and Monique, although I doubt there'll be much of anything else left after they get it. Lizzie didn't like Becker. She wouldn't have left him everything she had. She wouldn't have kept a bank account and a will secret from him if she intended to make him her heir, either. Anyway, we get a free ride. Merriweather's pushing things along. We don't really need to do anything. If it should turn out that there's any money there, you'll agree to give the church something out of the inheritance. That's what Lizzie would have wanted you to do anyway."

"I still say that if that will were valid, she would have left me a letter or instructions about whom I should make gifts to. She would have assumed I knew nothing about the church."

The telephone in the studio rang again, and Charles picked it up and listened to the broker's description of the outcome of the latest showing. "She says that last couple bid," he told Anne, "but way under our asking price, and they say they need to know right away. I think we should take the offer and cut our losses."

"Absurd! She must have told them we're desperate. They need to know right away! I think we should try another broker."

"Anne, we can't hold out much longer. We're getting in over our heads more every day. And I'll tell you something else. I can't spend all day on the telephone and . . ."

"Don't say it! I can't stand it. I had to get the kids settled, but now I'll take over. You'll be ready for rehearsals. You know, sweetheart, whatever else, you've never sounded better. How was your driving lesson this morning?"

"Don't change the subject. I hope you mean what you just said, because it's obvious that you've been stalling—"

"I haven't!"

"—over this. And what's going to happen is, you're going to run us into so much debt that moving won't clear us. We're going to be just as badly off after we move as now."

"Don't talk to me that way, Charles. You sound like you hate me."

"Don't be silly. I'm angry and worried."

"You've been angry for weeks. When will you stop?"

Charles did not answer or look at her, and began instead to search for his place in the pages of a book of music on the stand.

That night, while Charles slept beside her, Anne lay awake contemplating the reasons for his persistent anger. She suspected that no matter what he said, it wasn't about her extravagance. She really had spent too much, of course, but all her excess spending didn't account for more than a fraction of their shortfall, which Charles, who was clever about money, knew perfectly well. Charles himself insisted on most of the discretionary spending, on the schools and the lessons, for example, and the assessments and maintenance increases were not her fault. Really, Charles was angry because he thought she had reneged on some basic promise, a cornerstone of their marriage—that milk and honey would flow. Yes, that's what it was. In Charles's mind, Anne had promised that prosperity, plenty, and enjoyment were permissible. And now, when they had to give things up, he reacted as though she had broken her word—as though he was losing not just an apartment but all the satisfactions that Anne had insisted he should expect and enjoy. He'd never forgive her if they had to move, and he'd never forgive her if they didn't move. Anne couldn't quite see a way out of this, other than to convince Charles that this was what was going on, but Charles was not usually amenable to such explanations.

By the middle of October, the apartment remained unsold, Charles was still antagonistic, and he still could not drive well enough to pass the Department of Motor Vehicles test. Two mornings each week, he trudged stoically down to 106th Street for another driving lesson with a man from Costa Rica who was beginning to regard Charles as a freak of nature in his baffling incapacity to master simple mechanical skills. If they really intended to move in a couple of months, he simply had to learn to drive, Anne thought, watching him leave for his lesson one morning wearing an expression of combined anxiety and determination that brought to mind movies of soldiers preparing to land at Normandy on D-day. Perhaps she should have taken lessons too, but they had decided she should wait until after the baby came.

Anne had an appointment with the obstetrician that morning, and she rode the bus there, feeling the baby kick vigorously and trying to imagine its future in Larchmont or Englewood. She was not sure she knew how to raise a child in places like that. How far her mother and brother and Merrit and all her friends would be from there . . . or wherever they ended up. How odd not to walk the city with the baby in a stroller, not to join the group of mothers, nannies, and babies at the playground at 112th Street and at the bagel shop, or on walks down the Riverside promenade, or at the sprinklers. And the museum and all the concerts—these would be rare treats instead of daily, weekly life.

When she returned to Morningside Heights, Anne got off the bus at 112th Street, walked to the post office, where she bought stamps, then continued north on Broadway. At 113th Street she saw the soup line extending from far down the block to the door of St. Ursula's. A young woman with a sobbing two-year-old boy came out of the church and, pulling the child into a stumbling run, walked quickly to the curb and waited impatiently for the light to change. How horrible, thought Anne, watching the two of them at the corner, to have to come here to feed your child. She probably had to drag him, both of them irritable and hungry, all the way from God knows where to get him a little lunch. The woman was disheveled, and the child's dirty face was streaked with tears. Just as Anne was walking past, the woman struck the boy hard across the back and face. Anne stopped, appalled, sickened by the sound of the blows. The young woman scolded in a low, deadly voice, "Stop that noise!" But the child wailed even more loudly in pain and terror; his screams became strange, like nothing Anne had ever heard in a child's cry. Anne stood helplessly, her eyes filling with tears. The woman seemed to go into a frenzy at the boy's eerie cries, and began striking and shaking him even more brutally, until an old, drunken-looking man in the soup line staggered toward them and rebuked her in a slurred, high-pitched nasal voice. "No, don't hit the baby. Oh no! Oh, don't hit the baby." To Anne's astonishment, the woman stopped, grabbed the child's arm again, pulled him across the street, and disappeared in the crowd. Anne stared at the old man, who did not seem to notice her, and saw that he was emaciated, that his eyes were yellowed and red-rimmed, his gums mostly toothless. Then Greg Merriweather was at her side.

"What happened, Harry?" he asked the old man. But the old man was taking a while to organize his thoughts, and Anne answered first, describing how the woman had beaten the child. "This man told her to stop, and she did, and then she ran off. I just stood there. I suppose . . . I should have done something." Anne felt her legs trembling.

"I lost my place in line," worried the old man, in his peculiar treble voice.

"No, no. I'll tell them. You go right back up where you were," Greg said. "I've got to run back in, Anne. I'll call."

Anne continued up Broadway until she came to 116th Street, where, still shaken, she was inspired to stop at Merrit's building and ring her buzzer.

"Come up, Anne," said Merrit over the intercom. Surprised welcome was perceptible in her voice even through the static.

"No, you come down. Come walk with me."

"Five minutes" was the pleased reply.

They went to Riverside Drive and strode briskly down the promenade. Cool, fragrant air blew in across the river, and swatches of bright-colored leaves, the first of the season, had appeared here and there overnight. Anne was disturbed by the juxtaposition of such prettiness with the misery she had just witnessed. She told Merrit what had happened in front of the church.

"I'm ashamed. I just stood there," she said.

Merrit, however, thought Anne's reaction was understandable. You never know what to do when you see something like that. You might make things worse if you interfere. But Anne still thought that she'd behaved badly. She wasn't sure why, but she had been tongue-tied.

"When I really felt bad is when Greg Merriweather rushed up out of nowhere. That's his church, and there he is, taking care of Harry and all those other hungry people. *They* all know you don't stand by and do nothing while someone beats up a child. I'm useless as a citizen. I get everything wrong lately. Maybe I always did, only now, for some reason, I mind more."

"You're older. You have all these kids depending on you. You're becoming more cautious, as you should—especially when you're pregnant."

"That had nothing to do with it, unfortunately. Anyway, I'm equally useless as a wife and mother. At least one of my kids has some desperate problem all the time. Now it's Ellen."

Anne told Merrit the story of Ellen and her tearful envy. "So I'm off shopping this afternoon, if I can get someone to watch Stuart after lunch."

"It shouldn't be you, Anne. She should feel that someone outside the family gives the presents. I'll do it."

"No, no. I couldn't allow you to do that. Absolutely not!"

"But I really want to. I'd love to take Ellen. I love little-girl clothes and all their school things. Oh let me, Anne. She'd love it too."

"She would, and I'm tempted, but I can't let you go to this expense. Charles would never agree."

"You give me the money, then, and I'll take her. I won't tell her you gave me the money."

"No, we can't trick her. She'd smell it."

"So you do have to let me buy the presents. Look, you can take me shopping later, Anne. You can buy me things. Or if not that, something else. It'll balance out somehow."

On impulse, despite a feeling of shame, Anne agreed, not because she was so impoverished, but because she could not resist these delicious pleasures for Ellen. Charles's and her own pride could suffer a little in this cause. They agreed that Merrit would take Ellen on Friday or Saturday, or perhaps both days.

"Do you think she'd like to stay over at my place on Friday night?"

"It's possible. Are you sure you want the trouble?"

"This kind of trouble, yes. You tell her she's invited to sleep over as well, so she'll feel more free to say no if she's too shy."

When Ellen heard that Merrit, whom she greatly admired, would like to take her shopping, she twirled and skipped. Of course she wanted to sleep over at Merrit's. She was all delight at knowing that she, for once, was the chosen one.

Anne told Charles about these arrangements at the first opportunity, which, however, did not occur until the next morning, when the children were at school and she and Charles were walking to her brother's apartment on Morningside Drive. Paul and Greta had been begging them for days to come and try their new piano, which they had described rhapsodically — a 1919 Steinway, A-model, splendidly rebuilt, with a delicious, mellow tone. Anne's piano, too, was a restored A-model from 1926, and Paul had always envied Anne hers, a gift from their parents on her graduation from Juilliard. He played well, but had never been as serious about it as Anne. "All right," Charles had said when Anne got back from dropping off Ellen. "Let's waste an hour or two this morning and go see the piano."

Anne was delighted to go. It was rare that the two of them got out of doors together in daylight hours without any children. It made her feel free and light; she held Charles's hand, and chattered happily about Merrit's plan for Ellen. "She's not gotten all complicated yet, has she, Charles?" Anne said. "She's still young enough that you can fix it for her; you can make it absolutely, completely right."

"I wish you hadn't agreed to this, Anne. It makes me uncomfortable. But it's nice of Merrit. What's new with her lately?" Charles had been troubled on learning from Anne of Merrit's infertility. His first thought, like Anne's, had been that she should begin scrambling for a medical solution. Merrit, however, refused this option, insisting it made no sense for a single woman entering middle age. She hadn't talked about it the last few times Anne had seen her, but she lacked energy, and her looks had begun to go off. Her hair didn't hang right. She had put on a few pounds. She didn't seem to be writing much lately, or seeing anyone new. If she talked at all, she talked almost entirely about her analysis. Charles worried, but Anne was hopeful. "Just watch," she said. "Give it time."

When Anne told Charles about the child being beaten near St. Ursula's, and about Merriweather and the old man, Charles was riled.

"What do you mean you just stood there?"

"I mean," Anne replied, "that for some reason I didn't say anything."

"How can that be? You just didn't think you should be interfering?"

"Charles, I feel bad enough as it is. I can't justify it. I don't understand why, but I just couldn't think of what to do."

They walked the rest of the way in silence — across the Columbia campus, down Amsterdam Avenue, along 115th Street to Morningside Drive, past the rocky cliffs of Morningside Park. This was a favorite walk for both, and Anne had a particular taste for fall foliage on an overcast, cold day, as this one was; but the feelings aroused by their earlier conversation checked such pleasures. Anne wished she hadn't told Charles about the incident. She knew he had an inner account book, where he kept a record of her moral flaws. This would be a huge new red-ink entry in the columns for egoism, excessive regard for self, indifference to the sufferings of others. Was it, as Charles thought, that she simply thought she had no right or duty to intervene? No trouble or shame is too great when it's her own child's feelings to be protected, but she doesn't think it's her place to save someone else's child from a serious beating? Charles, in his new unfriendliness, would see it that way.

Yet she had not been indifferent, or fearful for her own safety. Perhaps she had been paralyzed by horror. She had seen many sad things on city streets, and read about other things, but never anything like this. It had happened so fast—she had been unable to take it in. When the old man came up, she was only beginning to register the scene as real. This was culpable, but not in the way Charles thought. Her horror, her ignorance of the feelings and sufferings that had so shocked her, her protected life, with its privileges of inexperience and innocence—all this produced an inability to comprehend and react to what was before her. She resolved to try to explain to Charles the nature of this weakness and cowardice, without excusing it. If he was going to convict her of crimes, the charges should at least be accurate.

When Anne was growing up here, the neighborhood had been full of poor people, but poverty then wasn't as hard or mean as now, it seemed to her, even though things had gotten so plush. In the sixties and seventies, lots of apartment houses in the neighborhood were still SROs, full of welfare people, addicts and drunks, and the kind of indigents who were poor only because they grew old. Those places had been rough. When Anne was a child, she hadn't been allowed to walk down the SRO blocks, where you saw quarrels and drinking on the stoop and you could get mugged.

Most of the SROs were gone now, pushed out by Columbia and other powerful neighborhood institutions. So poor people landed on the streets when they couldn't manage the rent anymore; they slept on church steps or in subway stations. Anne had seen old people who lived in her own building stealthily pick the trash in the basement and then get on the elevator with a laundry hamper or bookshelf or chair that someone richer was discarding—praying, no doubt, to get safely home without the humiliation of being seen by the former owners. The trash room was filled with valuable things that people threw out just because they had bought something new. Anne's eyes filled as she thought about all this. Lately, she was always weepy.

That woman beating her child—she was only a girl, really, maybe only seventeen or eighteen. From the way she hit the child, and the way he cried, you knew it had not been the first time. There was no way to save the child from such beatings, short of massive interventions by wise, kind people with the resources to devote days and years to that poor girl and her baby. Sometimes you could prevent her from beating her baby on the street, which is what happened yesterday, but she might beat him all the more at home, having been humiliated in public. You didn't know. The old man had acted on impulse when he begged the mother to stop. Charles thought Anne should have done the same: she should have stood up for benignant principles. This would not really solve anything, but to stand by and say nothing, to fail to prevent a moment of pain only because you knew that it was part of a lifetime of pain, was barbaric. Maybe what I'm really guilty of was failing to take a largely symbolic act, Anne reasoned, walking with Charles up to the entrance of Paul and Greta's building. She wiped the tears from her eyes with the back of her hand as Charles rang the buzzer.

She explained this reasoning to Charles as they walked home, after having played the piano and praised not only the instrument but also their infant niece and two-year-old nephew, and the carrot-zucchini muffins with coffee. But Charles did not think this was adequate ground for absolving Anne until he discussed the incident with Greg Merriweather, who mentioned it when he called that evening. Charles, describing Anne's guilt over it, played advocate for her—to her surprise. "It was a symbolic act she failed to take," Charles said, while Anne listened with interest. How very accurately he made her argument. She hadn't been sure he was really listening.

Merriweather, however, laughed at this, Charles told her afterward, and said, "I don't disagree with the analysis, but the fact is that she really did take a symbolic action. She was standing there with tears on her face, holding out her hand toward that woman—I saw when I was running up to them. I didn't see the hitting, and Anne says she stopped because Harry told her to stop. That could be, but she looked at Anne, too. I saw that part. Whatever. Nothing could have been more eloquent than Anne standing there with her hand out. I've had that picture in my brain all day. Talk about a symbolic appeal."

Charles was taken aback by this account. He should have known it had been like that. What a different picture of Anne from the one he and she had agreed on!

"Why didn't you describe it the way it really happened?" he asked her resentfully. "You've been unfair to both of us."

"I don't remember reaching my hand out or anything like that. I only remember that I didn't rescue the baby." Anne couldn't help feeling a little better after hearing what Greg had said, but she did not acquit herself. What Greg saw was something he projected onto the scene. Charles, moreover, now had a new reason to be cool toward her, and he spent most of the evening in his studio with the door closed.

# 20

ONE BLUSTERY AFTERNOON in late October, Merrit wandered down Broadway and turned onto 112th Street, where she stopped into Labyrinth Books to see what the latest crop of dark and obscure postmodern theoretical books was about. Nothing looked particularly interesting, not even her own book, *Medieval Child-Rearing Practices*, which she saw propped upright on the Women's Issues shelf. Back on Broadway, she went to Papyrus and bought a paperback of *Middlemarch*, and then to Global Ink for *The Independent*, which she had gotten into the habit of reading in London. With her stack of printed matter she made her way to the Hungarian Pastry Shop on Amsterdam Avenue, where she curled up in a corner, sipped coffee, and read herself into oblivion. They never cared here how long you stayed. Merrit had done this so many times in the past few weeks that the notes and books lying on her desk at home had grown dusty, and she no longer responded to telephone messages from her editor.

She stayed long enough at the Hungarian Pastry Shop to get deep into *Middlemarch*, a book that had haunted her late twenties and early thirties, when she read it anew every summer. This time was different. Sometime in the past five years, Merrit had outgrown *Middlemarch*. She detested Dorothea, had no sympathy for her willingness to marry Casaubon, and thought Will Ladislaw a juvenile fantasy. She reproached the author for her stick-figure characters, false psychology, and punitive moralism. Merrit frowned deeply. "Oh, *Middlemarch*! She's frowning at Casaubon," said voices, and she was momentarily annoyed at this misdescription of her feelings, before becoming aware of long, thin bodies bending over her. It was the Smith-Smythes, appearing taller than ever from Merrit's vantage point at the low table. She stood up, smiled, and shook their hands, and they exchanged formulaic words of greeting: comparisons with Starbucks, the lateness of autumn, global warming . . .

"Actually, Merrit, it's a wonderful coincidence seeing you here, because we intended to call you when we got home."

They wanted her to sign a letter of public protest, which they waved before her, hot from the printer. This was somewhat disappointing for Merrit, who had briefly hoped that the call would have been more along the lines of an invitation to a party. Instead, she forced herself to look serious and interested as she scanned the letter, which had something to do with nuclear weapons in Eastern countries. The occasion for writing the letter, however, and its intended audience, remained obscure to her. She twice attempted to get them to tell her, without appearing stupid, but with bland stubbornness the Smith-Smythes refused to name the provocative event and insisted on assuming that she knew all about it. "Where will you publish it?" she asked. "There are a couple of possibilities," they said.

"Well," Merrit began, "may I take this copy home and read it when I'm a little more wide awake? I'd like to understand the gist of it better. I'll call you . . ."

"Sooo sorry," they said, "but it has to go on the fax this afternoon." They plucked the letter from her hands, said a rather cool good-bye, and left. Merrit recalled Morris's distaste for this pair, and had to admit that he was often quick to spot phonies. She would have been more willing to admire his discernment had it not told against Merrit so often. But here they came back. "Forgot!" they said. "We're having a party in a few weeks. Saturday, the sixth, eight-thirty. Could you come? Oh, lovely! We'll send you an invitation." Actually, they weren't so awful. You could put up with them well enough to go to their party. Really, it was more manner than anything else. You couldn't object to their political positions, as far as she knew anyway. Besides, at a party, you didn't really have to be friends the way you did at a dinner party, like the one at Jonathan Riesbeck's. What a likable person his cousin Lily was. Merrit had seen her several times in the neighborhood since that evening. They had briefly chatted, exchanged telephone numbers, and talked about getting together.

I'll ask her to go to the movies, Merrit thought as she walked home.

Lily was pleased to hear from Merrit and glad to accompany her to the movies. Happily, the Thalia was showing *Sense and Sensibility*, which both of them had missed when it first came out. "Wonderful!" they said afterward, but then fell quiet. The tale of courtship and marriage left Merrit aching with loneliness and in the grip of a now nearly constant fear that her life had assumed a permanent hollow shape. Was she going to become one of the Morningside Heights spinsters she had been observing her whole life? Learned and accomplished, sharp, smiling but aggressive, attractively middle-aged, childless, and single. There would be the tasteful little apartment—Merrit had that already—occasional affairs, growing more and more rare until they tapered off, at around age fifty. At the menopause? Oh God! She had never thought of that before. So it was all about fertility! The whole world knew it, and she had never caught on. And, taken unawares, here she was, weeping with longing at the sight of babies, borrowing children from her friends, and disqualified from the game.

Fearing that the meaning of her own silence was all too obvious, Merrit could not read Lily's. The crisp fall evening was lovely, and they decided to walk home from Ninety-fifth Street, taking West End Avenue, where it would be quiet and uncrowded, as far as 106th Street.

"The age of courtship has advanced, hasn't it?" said Merrit finally, after they had walked a block without speaking.

"I'm not sure," answered Lily thoughtfully. "At least the age of marrying has."

"Well, according to Margaret Mead," said Merrit, "the marrying age determines the age of romantic feeling. She once wrote about an aboriginal people whose girls are married at about age five and then reared by their husbands' families. The marriages aren't consummated until the girls are sexually mature, but the men's hearts start racing for five-year-olds, not grown women."

"I don't believe it," Lily said stoutly, which surprised Merrit, who had thought the story had the ring of truth.

"Well, you may be right," said Merrit. "You psychoanalysts still hold to psychological universals, I suppose?"

"Modified by cultural and familial milieu, of course. It's never shut-and-dried."

Merrit sensed something vaguely wrong with this speech but was too polite to mention it. "But what do you think?" she said. "If people can put off marrying until after thirty, can they put off falling in love as well?"

"I've been wondering about this lately. I think that the older we get, the less likely we are to fall in love. Not only are we less naïve, less likely to idealize someone when we're older, but there are constitutional and biological factors involved that make it harder for older people to fall in love. I don't mean impossible—I've seen it happen—just less likely. The sap is high in an eighteen-year-old, and the drive for independence from parents—and therefore the need to link up with someone new—is very strong. All this creates feelings ready to be transferred and powerful motives to transfer them. The forty-year-old, on the other hand, has long since negotiated independence, has found security and narcissistic satisfactions in a variety of other ways, has lower drives and less energy, has lots of sublimated satisfactions drawing off some of the heat, and is more aware of consequences."

Merrit scarcely reacted to the rather pedantic tone of this speech, so intent was she on Lily's thesis. "Go on," she said, sinking, but intrigued by this lengthy list of inherent detriments to middle-aged romance. Why, Merrit wondered, hadn't she ever heard anyone say any of this aloud before? "So you think the *mariage de convenance* is the only form middle-aged marriage takes?"

"Not the only form," said Lily, "but the usual one. Don't you agree? Both parties have their own money, maybe older children. Companionship is what they want most. They find an attractive person they admire and respect. Of course there are limits on the strength of the connection in that kind of marriage. Sex is comfortable, but the passion is limited. They part too readily over differences that people in love would struggle to contain."

"Good heavens, how depressing!" Merrit sighed. She was simultaneously grateful and resentful that Lily, lost in a kind of professional abstractedness, seemed oblivious of Merrit's age and the import of her views for Merrit's chances in life. When Lily started expounding on themes connected with psychoanalysis, it seemed, her sensibilities got blunted.

"But," Lily continued, "these are averages. There are people who first fall in love in middle age, and they really fall, dramatically. I've seen this happen with both men and women who go through psychoanalysis. I think the energy that is sometimes released when neurotic conflicts are worked through is truly enormous. You see these people, and they're like kids—head over heels, overwhelmed with sexual passion. They tend to be people who had led constricted adult lives."

"You're overlooking the problem with women's biological clocks."

"Fertility is just a mechanical problem. I'm more interested in the psychology of late love, and the obstacles to it."

"It's a very serious mechanical problem." Merrit was not entirely able to prevent a note of bitterness from entering her voice, but once more Lily showed herself surprisingly tone-deaf.

"Oh yeah. Like death and disease. But going back to the falling-in-love question," and Lily hesitated for half a second, "consider someone like Morris Malcolm."

Merrit tensed; she was ill at ease discussing Morris after what had happened but anxious to hear him talked of. Yet it was odd that Lily would have any opinion of him; she hardly knew him. Still, unable to resist the rare opportunity to hear him spoken of by someone less prejudiced in his favor than the Braithwaites, she said, "By all means, let's take Morris Malcolm."

"Actually, I have something to tell you that might surprise you—or perhaps you know already. Morris and I have been seeing each other for a couple of months now. Yes," said Lily, acknowledging with some embarrassment the pained expression Merrit was too surprised to suppress. West End Avenue had been dark, but they had reached the corner at 106th Street and were waiting to cross to Broadway, standing beneath a streetlight, which suddenly illuminated their faces. "I know we haven't been terribly public about it. I thought maybe Jonathan had told you. In any event, it was another reason I was glad you called. Of course I had hoped to get to know you, but I know hardly anyone, except Jonathan, who knows Morris. I wondered how you would react."

Merrit, however, had not seen Jonathan since the night of his dinner party, months ago. They had spoken by phone a few times, but there had been no reason to mention Lily or Morris. Merrit was more than disconcerted by this disclosure. Had Morris already been seeing Lily in August, at the time of that wretched incident on the mountain? She wouldn't put it past him. She felt some indeterminate undertow of anguish, the sources of which she could not identify.

"Do Anne and Charles know?" Merrit inquired.

Lily wasn't sure, but she wouldn't be surprised if they didn't. It would be like Morris to keep them in the dark under the circumstances. Lily had never met them, although she would like to. She knew that Charles Braithwaite was Morris's best friend, but Morris had avoided getting the four of them together. The reason, Lily said, was that both Lily and Morris were unsure of where they were going together—at least until very recently.

Merrit waited expectantly, passing on the opportunity Lily had clearly offered to ask questions.

"He asked me to marry him. Just two days ago, actually."

Now Merrit was more than shocked; she felt wounded. Morris, a man older than herself, had asked a twenty-something to marry him? It was the first time that she had known a man of her own generation to do something like that. Somehow she had believed that the days when middle-aged professional men married women fifteen years younger had passed, that intelligent men her own age would never act that way. Brendan, yes, but then he was of the older generation. Of course, Merrit had long known that Morris was a social Neanderthal—everyone knew it—but nonetheless, this news made her feel hopeless, even betrayed. How could the world be so unfair as to reward Morris—forty-plus, bad-tempered, unreasonable, dense, not even good-looking—with this beautiful and brilliant gem of a young woman while slamming all the doors in Merrit's face? Here was someone her own age behaving like an archetypal midlife man: preying on the children, rejecting his own generation. Yet Merrit knew he would be nothing but admired. She saw it all. Charles and Anne, worshiping Morris, would accept anyone he chose to marry. They'd all be friends and have a dozen children among them and start to find it uncomfortable to have Merrit around. Yes, Morris would be rewarded for imposing this unworthy marriage on Lily, and Merrit would lose her best friends. These thoughts passed through Merrit's mind quickly, but even so she realized she had been silent too long.

"Well, I'm waiting with bated breath," she forced herself to say, turning as she walked to smile at Lily. "Did you accept?"

Lily, evidently relieved, scanned Merrit's face intently and then replied, "Yes. I did. But I'm having serious second thoughts."

"Because?"

"I'm not sure he's in love with me. I wonder if he's not one of those middle-aged men who'll never fall in love."

"I wonder if he's ever been in love," said Merrit.

"I think at least once. Now, there's another thing most people underestimate—not Jane Austen, though. The power of falling in love! It's very hard to get out of love once you're in—I confess this is an issue in my own analysis. Still, I tend to think psychotherapists too readily assume that being unable to fall out of love is always maladaptive, conflictual, and all that. Of course, when serial monogamy is the social rule, not the exception, you have a reality situation that's often hard on people who fall hopelessly into love with one person for the rest of their lives. But it's not that simple." Lily spoke with an earnest gaiety that, to Merrit's ear, sounded slightly forced, but once more Merrit was too distracted by Lily's theories to pay as much attention as she otherwise might have paid to Lily herself. Merrit was distressed by the idea that the opportunities for romantic love were limited by its very nature. For surely that was what Lily meant—as though things weren't bad enough under Merrit's own unexamined views, in which the big difficulty was to find the Right Person.

"I can't believe that you, a psychoanalyst, believe in hopeless lifelong romantic love," Merrit said.

"Oh no—we all believe it happens sometimes, but most analysts—so it seems, anyway—think it's bad, unhealthy. I think I'm unusual only in questioning whether it always is. And when a beloved object is not dead but unavailable and might continue to be the recipient of your affection, anger, whatever—the whole moral and psychological picture is different in ways that psychoanalysis should pay more attention to."

"You mean psychoanalysts don't pay attention to the difference between unrequited love and love for someone who's been sent to Siberia for thirty years? Now it's my turn to say I don't believe it. Anyway, assuming you're right about psychoanalysts, Jane Austen agrees with your colleagues, not you. Look at Marianne, happily marrying Brandon after being so in love with Willoughby." Lily was being so evasive about something that Merrit was not quite sure what she was talking about. Merrit furtively searched for clues in Lily's face. The thought crossed her mind that Lily knew something about what had happened between Merrit and Morris. This idea induced mental flinching, but it couldn't be true. Morris was the close-mouthed sort. On the other hand, maybe when it came to his fiancée . . . Again dismissing this possibility, Merrit felt guilty about concealing from Lily what might be evidence of poor character in her intended. However, if Lily was going to hide behind high-flown generalities, surely this negated any obligation on Merrit's part to be frank. In fact, perhaps Merrit had no right to tell anything. And perhaps Lily and Morris had not yet been involved when the encounter on the mountain had happened. In that case, as angry as Merrit felt about Morris's folly in pursuing this much-too-young woman, she still recognized that he had a right to expect her to maintain their secret, and she was not deficient in her sense of honor. And even if Morris and Lily had already been involved, it was Morris's place, not Merrit's, to tell Lily.

"No, I disagree," Lily was objecting, with some heat, while Merrit weighed these pros and cons of the morality of disclosure. "In the novel,

Marianne only liked and respected Brandon; she makes a good marriage with him even though she *isn't* in love."

"Not initially, but she could never do anything by halves and ended by loving him fully. And do you remember that character in *Persuasion* who is so unhappy and thinks he's going to mourn his deceased sweetheart for the rest of his life but falls in love with someone else before the year is out? Jane Austen doesn't buy into this romantic lifelong love stuff."

"But she surely does. She just doesn't believe that it's the only basis for a good marriage. Don't forget Anne Elliot and Captain Wentworth. They're still in love even after not seeing each other for eight years. Jane Austen thinks falling in love is often, or even usually, permanent, and she would be astonished at the idea that you'd expect it to happen over and over again, especially later in life." Lily argued with great energy and seriousness now, holding up a pedagogical finger as they strolled past the drab shops on Broadway north of 110th.

"I'm astonished that anyone could ever believe that falling in love might be permanent and irrevocable. What a terrifying world it would be if that were true! But speaking of Morris," Merrit responded nervously, determined not to lose this opportunity to analyze him, "I've never heard about him being in love with anyone. The stories are always about Morris getting mixed up with some woman he doesn't love. Who was this love of his?"

"I'm not sure which one it was. I'm just guessing—I just have a feeling about it. When I asked him, he got grumpy and said he doubts there is such a thing as falling in love. People often say that when it's never happened to them, but Morris acts more like a disappointed lover than someone who's never loved anyone. Yet I don't understand why he wouldn't just say so if that's the case. It's not to save my feelings. But maybe I'm wrong, or maybe he's just . . . just too middle-aged. Or maybe . . ."

Merrit did not ask Lily what other hypothesis she might have. Was Lily implying that Morris was not sexually interested? Merrit knew that sometimes, at least, he was very interested. Or maybe he was only sexually interested when he was not in love; according to Anne, that was how it had been with that woman Sam. But it was crazy to think he'd have that type of relationship with someone like Lily. Besides, he'd asked Lily to marry him. Or maybe Lily was right. He was just crazy enough to nurse a crush for years and years and let it get in the way of making a better marriage than he could ever possibly deserve. The long and short of it was that none of it made sense.

"I don't know if his love is eternal, but I think his grudges are," said Merrit. "You're confusing me, Lily. If you doubt Morris, why did you say you'd marry him so quickly? Why not discuss your doubts with him? You must be very much in love if you can't take a couple of weeks, or even a couple of months, to think this through. You're young. You only met this man a few months ago. What's the rush?"

"Well," Lily replied, "my only real doubts are whether I could offer Morris a happy marriage, kids, and all that. I'm sure I want to marry him. I'm not sure I should, actually, for his sake."

"Did you really just tell me that you'd marry him, even if he didn't love you, so long as you were sure that wouldn't make *him* unhappy? Lily, be sensible. Frankly, I think Morris is a complicated, difficult man, and with you he might have a chance for a reasonable marriage. It would have to be someone like you. The average woman would find him too daunting. But you could do it. I just can't help wondering why you'd want to."

"You and he don't get along, I saw for myself," said Lily, her voice diplomatically gentle.

"Many people—women—do not get along with Morris," Merrit declared, then wished she hadn't.

"He gets along with me. I see the irritability, but I think he's unusually empathic with women."

Merrit wondered how a psychoanalyst could be so blind to the character of her own fiancé, but said nothing. Morris empathic—why didn't Lily have enough sense to avoid psychoanalytic jargon?—with women! She must really love him, even though half the time she sounded as though she were defending marriage without romantic love. No doubt it was all for the best that Lily think well of Morris if she was going to marry him, but Merrit still could not comprehend why she would want to.

"Merrit, would you mind my asking you not to mention our engagement to the Braithwaites just yet—since Morris probably hasn't told them?"

"Of course not. He should tell them first."

"Here's my street," Lily said, gesturing down 114th Street. "Good night, Merrit. Let's do it again soon."

"Let's. Good night, Lily." But as soon as Merrit was alone, she became aware that sometime in the course of the evening she had developed a tinge of bitterness in her feelings toward Lily. What a strange conversation, with Lily alternately assuming the role of the psychoanalytic authority and then looking to Merrit, the older, experienced woman, for reassurance about her love life.

Lily, too, felt unsettled and drained by their talk, and, when she got home, was glad to find a message from Morris on her answering machine. Something had gone wrong, he said. Lily was flattered that such a man had chosen her for a confidante, proud that she was such a good one, knowing how to listen and when not to talk, knowing not to offer false comfort.

When Morris had hung up the phone after leaving his message for Lily, however, he had been thinking that he rather liked a little false comfort now and then. Neither Charles nor Anne understood anything about his work, but that didn't stop them from being certain that it was brilliant. Anne, especially, was optimistic and had an unchallengeable faith in Morris, and Morris found himself taking great comfort in her opinion. She had said to Morris, "I'm not just talking. I'm sure of this, because I know you so well. I know that you know you're on to something, and I know how the world goes too." He didn't let on, but her words actually made him feel much better.

Now, with Lily, Morris had someone—for the first time since his breakup with Sam—with whom he could go into the scientific minutiae, and that had its own comfort. Lily, who at one time had had a special interest in heritable mental illness, had a strong background in genetics. Her judgments were scientifically informed, and her response to Morris's fears and angers on this subject, while warm and understanding, were also professionally distanced. Lily was capable of intimacy and closeness, Morris saw, but she'd decided that this was the way to relate to his present dilemma, and he had to admit he always felt better after he had a talk with her—not in the same way he did with Anne. Lily helped him get clear on things, and wasn't that more important?

This day had brought Morris a fresh calamity. Sitting in the lab sometime after dark had fallen, with his post-doc and a graduate student, Morris stared gloomily at a computer monitor on which were displayed the catastrophic figures. The results of the last run of measurements had been carefully calculated and were not at all what he had predicted. His hypothesis was not confirmed. They had spent hours considering all the possibilities: machine malfunction, contamination, miscalculation. They had recalculated, reviewed their notes going all the way back to the first day, and could find no error.

Morris now repeated what he had said that morning, fifteen minutes after first reading the disastrous outcomes. They'd give it a day or two, to be sure they weren't missing something, and then they'd start over, from the beginning. However, Morris felt fairly sure of the integrity of these initial results. He was going to get the same results when he repeated the assays, and he had no idea what they meant.

Lily heard all this an hour later, at midnight, in Ollie's at 116th Street, shouted over the din of the crowd. Morris always insisted on Chinese food at Ollie's when he was in a hurry, because the service was fast and the shuttle bus back uptown to the lab was right across the street. Lily's face didn't show it, but Morris's news momentarily shook her. The thought crossed her mind that Duckworth might be right, that Morris's speculations were simply ill-founded. That might be so even if Duckworth's discussion of them in the *Biologica* article was unethical—which she did not doubt. She, personally, did not care if Morris was right or wrong or whether he was ignored or earned fame for his efforts, but she wanted to believe that he was a sensible man exploring reasonable ideas. Neither of them talked for a while, and Lily thought things over, scientifically. She had a very clear grasp of Morris's hypothesis, and she had read the Duckworth article. No, she decided finally. Whatever the ultimate results, Morris's ideas were sound and merited the kind of exploration he was giving them.

"I've thought it through, back to the beginning, and I simply can't doubt that you're on to something," she said. She gave a deft step-by-step summary of what Morris's tests were supposed to show about insulating genes from imprinting mechanisms. She understood precisely why the results were anomalous, predicted neither by the Duckworth theory nor Morris's.

Morris nodded agreement. Her train of thought tracked his own that morning. She was wonderfully clearheaded. It was a pleasure to talk to someone whose faith in him was realistic, not emotional, as Anne's was.

"Do you want to be married?" Morris asked.

"I take it you're asking abstractly," Lily replied with a small smile, "since you've already asked and I've already agreed in the particular."

"Remember when I told you that men say the words first but the woman actually picks?"

"Oh yes. The Thackeray theory of courtship," said Lily mildly. "I don't buy it. But the answer to your question is that I don't aspire to marriage as a goal the way I see some people do. It's just that I want to marry you." Her thoughts returned to her conversation with Merrit about Jane Austen and love. How odd that he should now approach the same subject so directly.

"This may sound funny, but I don't quite remember: did I really ask you or did you ask me?"

"I think you asked me. Yes, I know you did. We were in my apartment, and you said you thought we'd make a good married couple. And I said . . ."

"You said . . . ?"

"I don't exactly remember."

"Neither do I. But then we were engaged. It's a shame that all this trouble has to happen now, when we're engaged. It's not fair to you."

"Oh, Morris, I feel the exact opposite. I'm so glad you don't have to go through this alone." And Lily blushed, wishing she hadn't said this. Perhaps it sounded as though she took him to be weak, unable to handle trouble on his own. "I mean, I'm glad I have a chance to help a little. It means a lot to me. And I'm getting to know you in a different way, a real way, instead of the usual stuff—movies and dinners and stiff introductions to old friends and all that." She gave him a hopeful smile, but Morris shook his head.

"I guess I wouldn't mind a little of the usual stuff. We should act more like engaged people and make normal plans, talk about how many kids we want. How many do you want, anyway? Just stick to the single digits," Morris said in a playful tone. He wanted to try to have a few laughs. Wasn't getting married, after all, a bright spot in all this mess?

"Oh, whatever you want, I guess. One or two? How many do you want?"

"Come on. Don't you have some theory about sibs and only children that requires exactly 2.3 or 3.2 of them or some version of motherhood that requires just so many children to work out? I like big families myself, but—"

"You want a big family? I didn't know you—"

"—I don't see how we could afford more than one or two—especially if we live here in New York."

"—wanted a big family. But we both *do* want to live here, right?"

"Definitely, if we can. But if things keep going the way they have, the prospects for a job here for me are not great."

Lily was dismayed at the possibility that Morris might be forced to take a job outside New York, and she knew that he was waiting for her to say something.

"Some people commute. One goes up to Boston, to Philadelphia, even to Pittsburgh," she said.

"Can't see doing that."

Lily had to think about it for a few moments. "It would be very unpleasant. We should rule it out," she said, at last, her voice amiable and emphatic.

Morris gave her an approving smile, and called for the check. "No good?" asked the waitress, gesturing at the uneaten food. "Wrap it up?" But neither wanted it.

Lily waited with Morris for the shuttle bus to arrive. They chatted once more about lab matters, and exchanged a quick kiss and hug before he hopped on. Riding uptown, Morris reflected that, very often, people with commuting marriages didn't really want much marriage. Therefore it was a good sign, of her feelings and of common sense, that Lily agreed that it should not be an option. But, he noticed, it did strange, conflicting things to his ego to learn that Lily wanted to marry him and otherwise did not particularly want—"aspire" she had said—to be married. Theoretically, that should have made him feel good; it proved she was marrying him for himself. In practice, he felt a little queasy about it. Morris suspected that Lily, despite her sophistication, had a lot to learn about what she wanted and didn't want. She was awfully smart and good to talk to. Her combination of sensuality and sexual reserve was enticing, entrancing, especially the way the reserve was slowly diminishing as their intimacy grew. Morris could not help feeling that in deciding to marry her, he had done something good.

# 21

THE BRAITHWAITES HAD seen little of Morris for two weeks. Charles was frantic, juggling rehearsals and his and Anne's efforts to sell and buy real estate. Twice they had been on the verge of a sale that had fallen through, and their anxiety was mounting with their expenses. Morris was equally busy, as Duckworth's article had spurred him to work day and night in hopes of finishing his experiments sooner than he had planned. He set up a daybed in his office at the lab and often slept there for a few hours, rather than waste time shuttling back and forth to his apartment.

One morning, as Anne left to deliver Stuart and Ellen to school, she encountered Morris leaving his own apartment with two young women, who smiled at her in a friendly way as he locked his door. "Anne," he said, fumbling with a huge cache of keys. "Anne, my sister Melanie is visiting for a couple of weeks, with her friend. This is Melanie, and this is Cicely MacPherson. Anne Braithwaite—Melanie, this is Charles's wife." Melanie, evidently, was Morris's youngest sister; she and her friend looked about twenty-five. Melanie was tall and sandy-haired, pleasant-faced without makeup, and remarkably—almost comically—similar in looks to her brother. Cicely was roughly the same physical type, but far prettier than her friend. Anne greeted them warmly while Ellen stared wonderingly at the resemblance between Melanie and Morris. Stuart, however, noticed only that both Melanie and Cicely were sweet-faced young women. When they turned to the tiny boy and admired his backpack, he swelled with pride. "I go to school," he said, with huge passionate eyes, and they were charmed. Morris hurried them all out, because something, somewhere, was otherwise going to run too long and they had to get to the lab.

"Well, imagine," Anne said. "A female Morris clone."

"Mommy, they looked exactly alike," said Ellen.

Later that morning, Charles was pleasantly distracted from his worries by the news that Morris's sister, whom he had met long ago when she was a child, had actually appeared in New York. "Let's have them all to dinner," he suggested, and Anne, curious to have a chance to observe any relation of Morris's, phoned him at his lab. He was happy to accept, knew Melanie and Cicely would be too, and they settled on the coming Saturday night.

Anne decided to invite Father Merriweather, too. She had noticed that he was lonely and that he had hit it off with Morris. She disliked inviting Merrit when Morris would be there, but could not see how to avoid it. "Just tell her," Charles said, "that Morris and his sister are coming and that she's invited, although you'll understand if she doesn't want to come, because she never has a good time when he's there." Anne did this, and Merrit was happy to be able to say she was busy that night. Still, she resented the fact that Morris and his sister were favored guests while she was invited, evidently, only through politeness. They preferred him, she felt, only half recognizing her thought as childish and unfair.

That Saturday night at eight-thirty, Merrit walked around the block to the Smith-Smythes'. They lived in a grand apartment, with large rooms overlooking the Hudson, in a venerable building on Riverside Drive. Merrit deduced from the noise audible through the door and the overflowing coatracks in the hallway, that this was not a cozy evening with a few friends and a home-cooked meal but a typical catered dinner. When she entered, waiters were already circulating through a crowd with trays of drinks and hot hors d'oeuvres; an enticing array of cold ones was set out on serving tables. Lush bouquets of flowers bloomed all around, and everything was chic and abundant. In an hour or so, the guests would sit down, six at a table, and waiters would serve them. The ritual was reliably fixed and comforting.

More than an hour earlier, the Braithwaites' guests had assembled in their cramped living room, and their dinner began at the moment when the Smith-Smythes' first guests were just arriving. Even now, when money was so tight, Anne's table was crowded with good things—superb wines, caviar, lobster, truffles, hand-made chocolates, organic greens flown to the city that morning. Charles had exploded when he saw the preparations, but, Anne argued, when your debt amounts to six figures, what's the point in trying to save a few hundred here or there? They could still afford to eat well. The guests, at least, were happy enough with what was provided. They ate heartily and talked loudly. Stuart repeatedly left his seat to go stand at the elbow of one or the other of their tolerant female guests, whose admiration he hoped to win with fascinating disclosures about family life. Snatches of these reached Charles and Anne, who listened, heart in mouth, while trying to appear indifferent, and they were sure they heard him saying that Daddy was going to move to the country but not Mommy. They sighed in relief when it was time to send the children to watch a video in the bedroom and real adult talk could begin.

At the Smith-Smythes', the talk was intensely political and academic. Bosnia, Sierra Leone, and the proper response of the United Nations to civil war and terrorism were debated by a group that included Chalmers Smythe. Arcane points of United States and West Indian slave history were argued in a group that included Teresa Smith. A third group was devoted to gossip about academic superstars, at least three of whom were visible at the other end of the room.

Merrit yearned wistfully for a partner as she stood at one side of the room, trying to decide where to establish herself. It wasn't the sort of party where you would be introduced to anyone; you had to fend for yourself. She stood at the edge of the first group for a quarter of an hour without finding a comfortable social or conversational hook, listened briefly at the second, then went to the third and was alarmed to learn not only that the talk had turned to Brendan McGarry but that McGarry himself was expected, along with his new, pregnant wife, of whose legal existence Merrit had not been aware until that moment. Before Merrit had an opportunity to digest this news or form a plan of action, she saw Howard Kappell gliding around the room, vulturelike. It was a nightmare.

When she thought about it, Brendan's presence at this party was predictable. It was full of his sort of people. Merrit had no hard feelings against the Smith-Smythes for putting her in such a difficult situation. She assumed they knew nothing about her history with Brendan. The Smith-Smythes, however, not only knew but had discussed the possibility of forewarning Merrit or not inviting one or the other. Teresa, finally, reasoned this way: "Look, this is our only chance to get McGarry here, and I only got him to accept by hinting that Merrit was coming. It's no big deal."

Merrit realized that she had to decide, fast, whether to stay or run. If she ran, Howard would spend the rest of the evening telling anyone who'd lis-

ten that poor, pitiful Merrit had shown up and then fled rather than encounter Brendan. If she stayed, she would have to appear . . . She was not
sure how she would have to appear. The point was to avoid looking like another McGarry victim in the presence of the victorious pregnant wife. But
how?

Her eyes scanned the crowd. Within two minutes of hearing the dangerous news, she had a plan ready. She saw a man, good-looking, young but
surely near thirty, she thought, and with no wedding ring. He was standing
alone at the edge of the slave-history group, listening with a disgruntled expression, clearly too shy to interject his opinion in a debate among heavy-
weight scholars. Junior faculty at Columbia, Merrit guessed, and sidled
over. "Looking for lessons in the sociology of truth?" she said, and smiled.
The young man, surprised, responded awkwardly. "Hm? What? Oh!" And
he laughed and was silent, unable to think of anything to say. Merrit, calm
and sure of herself, understood that he was simply awkward. "Are you a his-
torian? Slave history?"

"I've been writing about the black migrations from the South to the
North in the twentieth century, and the social history of the lives of the mi-
grants in the North." His voice was deep and pleasant, and his manner,
even with its remnant embarrassment, was dignified.

"What is it they're saying you think is so wrong?"

The young man introduced himself as Jeffrey Mayhew and asked Merrit's name, then summarized for Merrit his views about the way rural black
families had functioned when transplanted to the cities and explained how
this differed from what seemed to be assumed in the discussion taking
place a few feet away. He seemed likable, appealing, well worth listening
to, and not at all full of himself. Merrit had approached him with a smile
that was over-bland because it had to conceal her predatory motives; now,
however, she was able to give him a dazzlingly authentic one.

They went at their subject with so much energy that several members of
the group turned their attention from the gray-haired debaters at its center
to the handsome younger pair at its perimeter. "Leo," one of them said to
the other. "He says I'm right and you're wrong." Jeffrey overheard this and
shook his head. "Both wrong," he told Merrit, confidingly, as Leo Mi-
lanese, the grand old patriarch of slave history, made his way toward them.
The discussion resumed with Merrit and Jeffrey Mayhew at its center, and
Merrit began to enjoy herself. She added a few sharp comments to the discussion, which followed Jeffrey's poised responses to a series of challeng-
ing questions; and despite the presence of the listening eminences, Jeffrey

continued to address his words more to Merrit than anyone else. When dinner was announced, he playfully took her arm. She glowed as they walked toward the tables, still absorbed in their conversation when, there, suddenly, was Brendan McGarry's famous ironic smirk. "Brendan! Good Lord! How've you been?" And she smiled in a friendly way, shook hands to avoid a kiss, and, after brief introductions, moved off, still arm in arm with Jeffrey Mayhew. Brendan looked slightly sour, and his wife, a very young woman—not past twenty-two, Merrit guessed—with a protruding belly, looked tense and sad behind her taut smile. Merrit felt warm and happy. The crisis was weathered, and Jeffrey Mayhew, who seemed to take her to be his own age, was good company. She was being admired and courted at a party where everyone counted, and she'd upended Brendan.

She would not face the fact, until later, when she was home alone, re-morseful and self-disapproving, that Mayhew was considerably younger than she and that the successes of the evening were less than laudable and sustaining. The thing about being single, she repined, was that it con-stantly tempted you into low-life behavior. But would it really have been better to endure Brendan's condescension and be publicly identified as an object of pity? Who was harmed by her little maneuver? In fact, she had saved face, and it was important to save face. Yet, she knew, there were those who never lost face, no matter what happened. Anne Braith-waite could vomit in the street with complete self-possession, without even glancing around to make sure that no one she knew had seen her. Merrit's discomfort kept her tossing and turning until dawn.

At the Braithwaites', Father Merriweather was enjoying himself im-mensely. After only a year in New York, he still had few friends here, and everyone at church was either a member of his congregation or too old or probably unable to tolerate what he feared was his growing ambivalence about his new vocation. But among the people at the Braithwaites', he felt accepted. Yet just as he found himself wondering, for the tenth time, why he felt most at home with this crew of atheists and why they were so god-less, he learned that not all of them were. Melanie, Morris Malcolm's younger sister, was a churchgoer. She was bright, too—studying philoso-phy in graduate school in Indiana. And her friend was another philosophy student and a Quaker, she said. Morris made jokes about his sister's reli-gion. He could not understand how she remained under the influence of their parents to such a degree that she would continue churchgoing at her age. Too bad she hadn't studied science, he said.

"That wouldn't have made any difference," she retorted.

"Philosophy," added Cicely, "has far more potential than biology to undermine religion."

The priest and the two students shared theological interests, and the discussions, lubricated by wine, became uninhibited, as Morris loved to argue with his sister and to tease Merriweather. They had a rip-roaring, sophomoric go at the problem of evil, with Merriweather defending Morris's hard-line scientific point of view but interpreting this as consistent with all his own religious tenets.

"Anyway, it's philosophers who invented the problem of evil," said Merriweather when the argument had run its course. "They're the ones who pose these silly dilemmas: how can there be evil if God exists and is both infinitely good and infinitely powerful? But in the Bible, it *says* God creates evils. It doesn't say he creates only good. He's the only God, and he's good and powerful, is all it says. Anyway, why cast the problem in terms of these incoherent medieval ideas of *perfect* goodness and *perfect* benevolence? Why try to explain the totality of human misery instead of one little piece of it? And why would there be one explanation, since there are so many different kinds of misery? The Bible always talks specifics: here is this man or this woman, with this specific suffering, which arose for these specific reasons, and it lays out just what God says or does about it. It helps you locate the problem—place the individual in the community and both of them in relation to God. The point sometimes seems to be that you should be able to get rid of the suffering, that it's caused by sinning. Other times, it's about how to transform it or understand it or endure it and what kinds of mistakes or missteps, ungodliness, put it beyond bearing or frighten us too badly. There's not just one answer. There isn't a single problem of evil. Every individual life has its own—lots of them."

"So you're going to cop out on me, and end up in pure common sense—just as I suspected," said Morris.

"Not exactly," objected Merriweather, but to convince Morris, he would have had to explain more of his religious beliefs than he wanted to in this social gathering. He was grateful that Morris at least gave him that much credit, and pointed out, agreeably, that there was no enormous gulf between them on these issues. Morris, however, refused any rapprochement. He insisted that Merriweather's religion was reasonable, but only because it was utterly useless. What did it add to common sense? Nothing.

When the guests were gone, Charles and Anne, warmed by wine and conviviality, had a friendly interlude, washing dishes with comradely affection. She saw him studying a sales slip from Dean & DeLuca for the caviar and the greens, which she had carelessly left on the countertop, but he sighed and said nothing about it.

"Nothing like having graduate students over to get a silly argument going," he said genially. "I haven't heard anything like that in years, but it was fun, wasn't it? Morris and Merriweather jumped in like kids. What a sweetheart Melanie is! I started thinking she was good-looking by the time she left." Charles and Anne had been fascinated to see Morris's demeanor soften with this youngest sister, born when he was a teenager.

"How nice he was to her!" Anne smiled. "When she said she wanted to go dancing, he said he'd take her to some clubs, although I'm sure he'd rather be boiled in oil."

"He was fatherly."

"I knew he had it in him."

"I didn't. I'm sort of dismayed," said Charles.

"For heaven's sake, why?"

"It makes me think how unhappy he must be, how lonely."

"I suppose so," said Anne, "but I think that's recent, and maybe it's for the best. Maybe he'll do something about it."

Charles dismissed this hopeful comment with a scornful wave of his dish towel. "What do you think is happening with that psychoanalyst woman?" he asked.

"He didn't say. I didn't ask. I had some thoughts about Cicely and Morris. She was smart and attractive."

"I did too. He could do worse." But Charles's voice was not as enthusiastic as his words.

"But not really his equal."

"When you're Morris, it's not easy finding an equal. But his sister, now . . ."

"Oh yes! No wonder he's so spoiled if they're all like that—his sisters, I mean," said Anne. "But Morris will get married—unless he's hit by a truck."

"Anne, your prophesies are aggravating. You have no special insight into Morris's future."

"I know I don't know, theoretically, but . . . actually, I really think I do know." Anne covered a laugh with her hand, seeing how irked Charles was by this pronouncement.

"You have this conviction, you mean, without any basis in fact."

"The basis is my knowledge of his emotional capacities, and my familiarity with what has happened to every single person I have ever known who has had them."

"Then how do you explain his arrival at middle age as a bachelor?"

"Oh, he's just a late bloomer, or maybe it's closet religion or something like that. You watch."

"How about Merrit?" Charles asked after a few minutes' reverie. "Will she also marry—inevitably?"

"Merrit is conflicted about marrying. Morris isn't. It's no accident that she never falls in love with someone who'd make a good husband and father. But you shouldn't ask if you're going to resent the answer."

"What I resent is that you allow nothing for externals or sheer luck. You think whether and whom people marry is entirely determined by psychological depths."

"Not entirely, but mostly. Yes, I feel sure that's how it works."

"But," Charles protested, "even if that were true, I think you've got the two of them reversed. It's Morris who is cagey and ambivalent in his relationships. Merrit throws herself into them wholeheartedly. It's not her fault that she hasn't managed to find someone worthwhile. I don't know anyone—not one single man—who I think would make her a good husband. Ask yourself—in your entire life, how many people have you met whom you could marry?"

Anne looked distant, then began counting on her fingers. "Well, I can only think of four offhand, but . . ."

"Nonsense! You've never wanted to be married to anyone but me."

"That's not what you asked me. Of course, after I'd met you, I didn't want anyone else. I'm guessing about what could have happened if I hadn't met you."

"Greg Merriweather seems like a marriageable sort," Charles reflected, "and he doesn't seem to have anyone, either. At his age we had been married seven years and had Jane and maybe another one on the way. He's lonely, too. You'd think he'd find someone."

"He asked me about Merrit—what was wrong, where was she? Isn't that interesting, that he noticed something was wrong? He's what you imagine a clergyman should be, isn't he? Now, he's someone who might simply have a hard time finding someone, even though, psychologically, he seems to be so marriageable. There are so few bright young women with even a tolerance for religion, and he'll always be broke. There are some real, ex-

ternal problems for you. But speaking of the psychological depths that determine who marries who, I have an idea about why you're so mad at me."

"There's no particular mystery."

"It's not really my fault that we have to move, and you know it—
although I agree I should be more careful."

"I've never blamed you."

"You know you have. The real reason you're mad at me . . ." Anne
paused, foreseeing Charles's scorn. "The real reason is, you think that I
told you that you could have everything you wanted. That's got something
big to do with why you married me. And now you think I've reneged. But
I never did. I thought that you should take things you had a right to—that's
all."

Charles's face showed his distaste, and Anne gave it up. She hadn't
found the words for it. They dropped the perilous subject. Neither had energy for a quarrel. They looked in on the children, switched off the lights,
and went to bed in silence.

# 22

THE BRAITHWAITES SLEPT late the next morning. The children finally woke their parents at nine, when Ellen and Stuart climbed into their bed, demanding breakfast, and Jane stood by, in awkward adolescent dignity. Charles felt a little the worse for the extra wine the night before, and groaned when Stuart's soprano sounded in his ear. Anne was getting to the late stage of pregnancy, with its increasingly broken sleep. She could have used another hour in bed but instead pulled herself up and out, grasping Jane's hand. Putting her arm around her, she noticed that Jane had grown slightly taller than she was. How odd that a daughter of hers was going to be tall and willowy. Stuart and Ellen were going to be short, like Anne, with her small hands. But Jane was her father's daughter in every way. How good that she had his ample hands.

That morning's breakfast was like hundreds of other Sunday breakfasts in the Braithwaite home. Charles went out, unshaven, for fresh bagels and three newspapers, some part of which everyone but Stuart soon settled down to reading. The morning was peaceful, but with a tinge of melancholy and suppressed anxiety, Charles realized. The children felt the malaise, the impending loss of such Sunday mornings in Manhattan, and they were warding it off with virtue. Anne was strained, as was he.

Sunday was the day when they had to show the apartment most often, and they dreaded the broker's arrival. Today, the broker had predicted, would be the last showing. She had buyers who were ready to swallow the price. They had to; it reflected the market. But that was a few hours off. A quiet morning could still have been enjoyed, but the telephone started ringing shortly after ten. Jane had two calls. Then Merrit called Anne to report on the Smith-Smythe party. Charles listened to Anne's side of the conversation with dismay.

"Just how young is he? . . . Well, hmm. There's no reason not to be friends, is there? . . . I can see how you'd feel a little guilty. You just have to tell him how you feel, that's all."

Charles looked at Anne sourly when she hung up. "So how young is he?"

"She thinks maybe thirty."

"Why is she giving this two seconds' thought? That isn't workable for Merrit."

"Now wait. Are we so sure of that? Hmm. Yes, we are. She won't fall in love."

"Who is he?"

"An assistant professor at Columbia, history department."

"For heaven's sake, Anne!"

"Why are you getting mad at me?"

"Because you didn't tell her to grow up!"

"Why don't you do it? Just call her back and tell her to grow up."

"It's unbearable, watching her life deteriorate like this. I wish Merrit would go back to London and . . . and seduce prime ministers, or Royal Academicians, or whatever it is that makes her happy."

"Charles!"

"I'm sorry. I feel irritable today."

"I'll tell you the rest later, then."

The telephone rang again. Could Charles stand in for Raffaelo Cordara tonight and sing Don Giovanni? Cordara and his covers had all come down with something intestinal that had felled nearly a quarter of the cast. Charles had had such calls before. He could certainly sing Don Giovanni. He'd done it for a small opera company in New Jersey just a week ago. He didn't mind the chance to sing a major role at the Met—not at all! The reviews would probably say, "Braithwaite, standing in for Cordara, turned in a workmanlike performance." Some of his friends continued to be surprised by these reviews. Charles had ceased being surprised years ago, even though occasionally they still angered him.

"Anne!" he shouted, and strode into his studio, where he began digging through precarious stacks of scores. "I'm going to sing Don Giovanni tonight. I need . . . here it is."

"Charles!" Anne smiled, but said nothing more. Charles was already moody, and he was always infuriated when he got a whiff of Anne's fantasy that he would someday be a star at the Met. It made him feel like a failure. Anne knew that Charles's career, in its present shape, was the kind of success that he had not only accepted but, to a great extent, had intentionally shaped. She felt the betrayal in her wishes for his glory. So she said nothing, but privately believed that Charles's genius could not go unrecognized. Charles, on this occasion, knew Anne's thoughts, and they upset his equilibrium. He found himself indulging in a few of the same fantasies as Anne, and he knew that he could not afford to do this.

The telephone rang again, and it was Morris, who reported that when he got home after leaving them last night, he had found a telephone message from two of the graduate students who were overseeing a repeat of the last stage in the earlier experiments that had produced anomalous results. The new results were precisely the same as the first ones. He still had no theory to account for the unpredicted outcome, and his brain felt inert. But until he could make sense of things, there was no point in beginning the next, final, set of experiments. Morris no longer had any idea what they would prove.

Anne commiserated; however, she feared that she was not sufficiently responsive to his trouble. She was feeling too buoyant about Charles's performance. Tactfully, she changed the subject and asked Morris if he wanted to come. Despite his worries and exhaustion, he rallied his energy to show enthusiasm and told Charles, who had picked up the phone in his studio, that he would be there. "Take a nap and maybe you'll see a way around this," Anne said, and hung up, intending to go to the other phone to call her mother, Merrit, and everyone else who might want to come.

"Why not begin the next set of experiments anyway? Get them going while you try to figure this out," Charles said.

"I'd be doing them blind. I wouldn't know what they meant. They'd be worthless. If I figure out what's going on, I may want to redesign the next set completely."

"So you'd do them again. What do you lose? How expensive is it?"

"It might be doable. I'm just too tired to think. I'll mull it over."

The doorbell rang just as Charles hung up. The broker had arrived, with a man and a pregnant woman, both young and smiling. The man said that he'd gone to Columbia Business School, and he'd loved it, loved the neighborhood, would love to move back. Great neighborhood. Great for kids. Great parks. Right now they lived on the East Side, but it wasn't so great.

"Good restaurants, though," said Anne helpfully, "and close to schools."

Yes, the restaurants were great, but there were some great schools on the Upper West Side too. So the Braithwaites had decided on the 'burbs, had they? The young couple really loved the city life. No suburbs for them! Really, they were very urban types, although they'd never realized it, and they thought growing up in a city could be really wonderful for kids. Anne agreed. They were wandering through the apartment now, and Anne regretted not having had more time to straighten things up. There were still coffee cups on the table, and demoralizing shards of bagels and lox. The beds weren't made, and newspapers were everywhere. From the studio came, tenderly but at ear-splitting volume,

*La ci darem la mano*
*La mi dirai di si*

and Anne rushed to close the door.

The young couple exchanged looks; they were clearly disappointed by what they saw. The broker frowned at Anne behind the young couple's backs, and Anne shrugged helplessly. "You can do wonders if you get an interior decorator," the woman said to the man. "That wall could come out." But Anne could see that there would not be an offer.

As the broker ushered them out, she snarled to Anne behind their backs, "I'll have the next ones here in half an hour. Can you do something with the place?" Anne said she would try. Charles emerged, looking hopeful. "Well?"

"It was too messy," Anne said. "She told me to do something about it before she comes back with the next ones."

"For Christ's sake!" Charles roared, slamming a book of music on a table. "Ellen, Jane, Stuart! We're going to help Mommy make the place neat."

"Charles, go back and shut the door. We'll handle this. Kids, Daddy's tense because he's just heard they need him to sing Don Giovanni at the Met tonight."

"Daddy's Don Giovanni? Can I come? Please!"

"I don't know yet, Janie, but I think so." As Anne tidied up, she began to doubt. She knocked on Charles's door.

"Are you sure he wanted you to sing the Don? Maybe he meant Masetto."

"Anne, what's wrong with you? Of course he didn't mean Masetto. I'm replacing Cordara. There is not the slightest ambiguity."

"I just can't believe it, I guess. It seems too good to be true."

The doorbell rang again, and Anne rushed to readmit the broker with a second couple, who were middle-aged and unsmiling. Anne ushered them in politely. Stuart appeared in underpants, a T-shirt, and boots, his hair plastered down with water, which he considered the essence of good grooming.

"Stuart, you good boy! You got dressed all by yourself! And you . . ." Anne here, seeing Stuart's efforts as a caricature of her own attempts to make a good impression, wanted so much to laugh that in order to stifle it, she stopped talking. But giggling continued to rise up in her with such mad energy that she had to leave the room to give way, concealing her real motive for her abrupt exit by taking Stuart off to find trousers.

"That noise is my husband," she said helpfully when she returned, as a burst of fierce vocalizing traveled down the hallway and again she dashed to close the door. "I didn't want you to think there was an opera singer living here or anything. I mean in the building. Of course my husband lives here." And, fearing a relapse into uncontrollable hilarity, she thought it best to give it up.

"Your husband is an opera singer?" the man asked.

"Yes. He's getting ready for a performance tonight. I'm sure he wouldn't mind an interruption if you'd like to see his studio. It's soundproofed, if you have any need for a room like that—maybe for kids?"

They shook their heads. They'd probably take that wall out, to enlarge the living room. Anne nodded vigorously. "Well, I'll bet that would be, um . . ."

"Much more contemporary looking."

The broker summoned them to look at the bedrooms, and Anne began to grow tense. The couple did not seem to feel any enthusiasm. After fifteen minutes spent looking at the bedrooms, closets, and bathrooms, they emerged and said they thought the place was overpriced, and it looked as though they'd have to put in at least a hundred thousand to renovate it.

"Really?" Anne asked, astonished. "I'd just paint and plaster a bit, myself. The kitchen appliances are brand-new."

"Well, Kitty is a gourmet cook, and she wants some special features.

We'll need a lot more closet space. We like modern bathrooms. Of course, we'd keep these moldings, and the parquet floors just need to be worked over. But we'd have to take out a couple of walls, gut the kitchen and the bathrooms, and build new closets everywhere. It would cost a fortune."

The broker swooped down between them and Anne. "Let's go get some coffee," she said to them. "I'll call you, dear." And out they went.

Charles reappeared. "Well?"

"Who knows? They said they'd have to do renovations that cost a hundred thousand and the place is overpriced."

"What!"

"That's what I said. Why do people like that want to live here anyway?"

"The market is forcing them into places like Morningside Heights. They're looking for space."

"They're going to love Mary O'Reilly and Mr. Morales . . . Charles, I'm taking the kids and going to Mother's. I'll come back around five. I hope you'll take a nap."

"That's my plan."

By curtain time that night, Charles was in costume backstage. Scattered among the audience, looking around at the worn and dated finery of the mid-twentieth-century opera house, were Anne, Stuart, Ellen, Jane, and Helen; Merrit and Jeffrey Mayhew; Morris, Melanie, and Cicely; and, at the back of the third balcony, Merriweather, who had borrowed money for his ticket from the rector. There were many others, too, who were delighted to have an opportunity to hear Charles in a major role. Anne intended to let the children sleep in and go to school a little late in the morning. Raffaelo's wife had sent over tickets so they had had to buy only two, although Anne would have bought as many as she had to. This was an occasion the children could not miss. If only Charles hadn't stayed up so late last night. He was tired. But he'd gotten his nap, and he had amazing stamina. Some inner reserve always got him through this kind of thing.

When the overture began, Jane gripped Anne's hand so tightly it hurt. "Mommy, I think I'm going to throw up," she whispered.

"Don't be silly," Anne said. She wondered whether Jane might feel envy, along with love and pride, about her father's success. Stuart crawled out of his seat near the end of the overture and got into what remained of Anne's lap beyond her belly and dozed until Charles appeared onstage, when he sat bolt upright, enthralled, during the sword fight, which Charles conducted with such grace and flair that Anne knew he was enjoying himself. But Stuart was asleep at the end of the trio, and Helen took him on her lap so that Anne could get comfortable. Anne had never heard the trio sung more beautifully, and thought that not only Charles but the entire cast had won over the audience completely. There were a couple of muffs, to be expected under the circumstances, but they were handled with poise. At the intermission, Anne, desperate, ran to the ladies' room, where the line was so long that she was still in the corridor when the warning bell rang. She had to plead to be allowed to cut in line, and then ran back to her seat just as the lights went down.

The performance sparkled from start to finish. Anne was relieved that Stuart slept through the finale, in which Charles got dragged into the smoking, glowing hell beneath the stage. Charles had sung and played his role so well that even his friends and longtime admirers were impressed. Morris, despite his exhausted, drawn face and puffy eyes, was beside himself with excitement and, when they were all backstage, enveloped Charles in a strangling bear hug that scarcely did justice to his feelings. Janie stood by shyly, observing other members of the cast, until Charles turned to whisper something to her, to which she replied with shining eyes; so, Anne thought, that was all right. Merrit watched from the doorway, blew Charles a kiss when she caught his eye, then left, her hand on Jeffrey Mayhew's arm. He was certainly appealing looking, Anne thought, observing the tall young man, who was shyly smiling and observing the celebratory scene with amused interest and pleasure, and occasionally bending down to say something in Merrit's ear. He looked substantial but terribly young—oh dear. Morris, too, observed this pair with curiosity, and something like a pained frown. Charles, characteristically, grew more silent in his triumph, with nothing but a slight smile at the corners of his lips to indicate the inner state of affairs, but Anne knew how rarely that particular expression appeared on his face. And then her eyes rested on Ellen, who had stayed awake throughout the entire performance. The child was very tired, and showed the only unhappy face in the room. "What's up, beloved?" she asked, bending down so that she could hear the reply. "I want to go home now," Ellen said.

"We'll go right away," Anne said. She would rather have stayed to savor this rare moment of glory, but her sense of maternal duty won out.

They all slept late, and Anne took the children to school at midmorning, while Charles looked on the Internet to see if any reviews had come out.

"I don't want to be a musician when I grow up, Mommy," Ellen said on the way to school, after they had dropped Stuart.

"You don't have to be, dearest, but I want you to continue to study music anyway. You're very good at it, and it will bring you pleasure your whole life."

"But you like Stuart and Janie better than me, because they want to be musicians." Ellen looked away from Anne, and her face was contorted from suppressing tears. Anne ached for her, and then experienced such piercing guilt that she felt weak and slumped for a moment. She feared that Ellen was right. She was wrapped up in Jane's music, and perhaps a little in Stuart's, too. Her relation with Ellen had always been different.

"Not so!" she finally replied dramatically, with conviction. "Nope. That's a mistake." This response was too long in coming, however, to be very persuasive to this, the savviest of Anne's children. Ellen sensed that her mother's hesitation was evidence of self-doubt, and this fed her fear and anger.

"It isn't. Music is all you care about."

"On the contrary. I'm not even a musician myself, really, am I? I just like teaching kids. I love music, though. Sweetheart, I couldn't say this to all my children, but I can say to you—and this conversation is between you and me, right?—that you can do just about anything you want when you grow up. You have many talents. Janie has many competences, but she excels only in music. I don't value what Janie or Stuart does more than what you do, but you're right that I'm more involved with it, whether or not I should be. Frankly, I think you're better off than either of them. And I don't love any of my children more than any of the others."

Anne wondered if she had gone too far in saying these things, but Ellen, after reflecting, was mollified, if not entirely ready to end her attack. She was intuitive, and knew without much explanation that Anne couldn't help wanting Jane to have the career that she, Anne, had forsaken, and Ellen also realized that it wasn't right for her mother to do this. Kids know these things, Anne thought, still feeling shaky around her knees.

"I want to be like Merrit when I grow up, and write books."

"How happy Daddy and I would be if you did that! We would be so proud! So keep up your good work in school, but keep up with your violin in the meantime, too, because you'll be glad when you're grown up— I promise you will. You know, sweetie, I love all my children very much, but of all my children, I've always thought that you're the one most like me."

Ellen did not conceal that this was a satisfying thought, and at length responded briskly that she thought she was too. "I look like you, and I think like you," she said.

"Yes. And it might look as though Janie gets more attention, because I have to try harder with her in so many ways. And then Stuart is younger, so he needs more time with me. But he doesn't get more than you got at his age. If anything he gets less, because there are three of you now."

Ellen, Anne saw, was reassured, after having felt excluded from something important the evening before. And, seven-year-old that she was, she abruptly dropped this shattering topic and moved blithely to the subject of the annoying girl in her class who cried if she lost a chess game.

Anne told herself that she must remember to ask Charles to show some special attention to Ellen. And what about Charles? He had at times injected some extraordinary ambiguity into his voice last night, with great effect, some remarkable blending of gravel and silk, boyish appeal, and evil. It was a new interpretation of the role, quite unlike what he had done with it a couple of years ago, the last time she had heard him in it, or, for that matter, unlike what anyone else was doing with it. It was odd that a family man, a mensch like Charles, could sing Don Giovanni so seductively. Yet he made you hate him; Charles understood why his seductiveness was despicable—and Cordara didn't, because he didn't understand what villainy was. Cordara didn't really believe in it, Anne thought, and so his Don Giovanni came across as childishly mischievous instead of evil. Why was it, then, that Cordara was the star while Charles was ignored? Was it because of Anne and all her children that he didn't walk out onstage to that applause every night? Didn't she keep him constantly strained and exhausted with her demands and babies? Remembering her hysterical laughing fit that morning, Anne feared that she had undercut the broker's efforts to sell their apartment and began to feel worried about Charles. She must help him. When she got home, she checked with Charles, then called the broker and told her they'd drop the price by fifty thousand dollars. In that case, the broker responded, they probably had an offer. She'd get back to them. But, Anne thought, hanging up, after Charles's performance maybe they wouldn't need to move.

# 23

WHEN MERRIWEATHER RETURNED to the court, Mr. Mahoney accompanied him to the chambers of Justice Ruth Jacobs, a white-haired, frail-looking woman newly appointed to review the Miller file. That afternoon Justice Jacobs sent a letter to Becker by messenger, demanding that he appear in chambers the following morning at nine. This did not worry Becker. Having several clients with matters in this court, he realized only after he arrived at the justice's chambers that the summons concerned Lizzie Miller. Justice Jacobs, attended by Mr. Mahoney and a court reporter, who recorded the entire interchange, opened the interview by demanding to know whether Becker had submitted Miller's will for probate and when it had been made. Becker's replies were calm. The will was made sometime in 1998, he couldn't recall the exact date, and he hadn't yet submitted it for probate, but as he was the sole beneficiary, no one was discommoded. Why, the justice wanted to know, had Miss Miller made a new will in 1998, when she was 102 years old?

"I can only guess," Becker said, adopting a candid tone. "In fact, I tried to convince her that she didn't need a new will, because she had a 1989 will that made me heir if my mother predeceased Miss Miller, which she had. But she insisted she wanted my name in it, so we made a new one. I thought it was no big deal."

But, Justice Jacobs asked, mightn't it have been wise, under the circumstances, to keep a copy of that 1989 will just to establish that Becker stood to inherit if his mother predeceased Miller? "I myself would have done that," Justice Jacobs said, "because otherwise it might look suspicious."

Then things got nasty. In fact, as Becker later told Josephine Slevinski, the young intern in his office, Justice Jacobs had said she had reason to believe that Becker had been less than truthful with the Court, and, given his track record, the Court would take no chances. Becker, however, omitted the remark about the track record when he told the story to Josephine, who did not know that the ethics committee had taken disciplinary action against him. Instead, he told her the upshot: that the judge wanted delivered to a court-appointed conservator every single deed, title, bank account, proof of ownership, power of attorney—every single scrap of paper in his possession related to any property of Lizzie Miller's—tomorrow morning. He was forbidden to engage in any transactions with respect to any such property. And he should not give the Court any reason to believe he was concealing or disposing of any properties, or evidence of properties, in the interim.

"The only explanation," Becker said, "is that those Braithwaite people went to the Court, or maybe that priest. Anyway, we've got to pull out a copy of our last annual report to the Court on Miller and make sure that everything we send them matches perfectly—if we can. I sold some stocks. I'll have to include records of that transaction. But you send them *nothing*—you hear me—*nothing* not listed on that report."

Justice Jacobs hadn't asked the date of Lizzie's death. Maybe she just wouldn't realize that he had filed the last guardian's report without disclosing that she had died. He hadn't wanted anyone looking over his shoulder or revoking the guardian's appointment. Could he falsify the date on her death certificate? No, those people would catch it, if they were going to contest the will—and undoubtedly they had told Jacobs that there was a 1995 will. Becker now remembered, for the first time in years, that legally he was not Lizzie Miller's guardian. He had been in charge of Lizzie's affairs for so long, he had forgotten that he had gained his authority by usurpation.

Becker had taken over acting as guardian, replacing his mother when she became ill, as a reluctant favor to her and Lizzie. He hadn't wanted to, but they had begged him, pointing out that everything they had would be his one day. He had not bothered to get himself appointed, because it would have been trouble; it was simpler just to stand in for his mother. Becker, who was in general prone to excessive optimism, for once felt tense. Still, there was a chance the Court wouldn't notice; Justice Jacobs hadn't mentioned it. Maybe they wouldn't even have all the records for earlier years after all this time; maybe they wouldn't bother to dig back. If they did notice, he would just have to say he'd always done it for his mother and . . . and that he felt obligated to continue and didn't want the trouble of filing new papers—that's all. This was what he had said to himself years ago. And what if they asked him why there was so little left in the estate compared to what there had been? He would say that he'd had to sell things off to pay her medical bills, caretakers, and all that, and that she'd given a lot to charities. And he'd say that he filed a guardian's report when she was dead because . . . he'd think of something. If worse came to worst and those people won a will contest, they'd get what was disclosed on his last report, which wasn't much. None of the reports had ever listed her apartment among her assets, and he'd stay quiet about it. Chances were they would never discover that she had owned it. If they hadn't found out after all these years, most probably they never would. Of course, they could easily learn the truth if they bothered to go look it up, but why would they? Lizzie thought she was a renter, and they had no reason to doubt that. His having cashed those annuity and Social Security checks was a different problem; but let the government come after him for a few bucks— so what? That had nothing to do with the will or the heirs.

His mother and Lizzie had roped him into all this. For years he had put up with their whining, with their incomprehension and stubbornness and ignorance, endless paperwork, quarrels and annoying telephone calls, and, finally, threats of disinheritance—after he'd spent years and years tending to their nonsense. The idea that, after all this, some stranger should step up and claim the property put him in a fury. He was pacing the room while he thought this through, and Josephine, sitting at the computer and making halfhearted efforts to resume her work, observed him, resentfully and suspiciously, out of the corner of an eye.

"This is going to take some time," she objected. "I have classes tonight."

"I don't want to hear about your damn classes. Let me tell you, whatever kind of trouble I'm in, you're in. You want to practice law someday? You'd better make sure the judge likes what we send her in the morning."

Surprised and angry, Josephine nevertheless started pulling open file drawers and slamming documents down on the desk. Becker himself went home to dig through papers, and returned to add documents to those that Josephine had gathered. It was nearly midnight when Becker tucked a foolscap accordion folder under his arm and said, "All right, let's go." Josephine begged to be allowed to accompany him to court in the morning, but he refused. This also annoyed her. He had promised to give her plenty of courtroom experience, and he had never let her go to court, not once. When she angrily pointed this out, he ignored her.

The following morning, Becker carried the fat folder to the judge's chambers alone. The clerk accepted it, and handed him a letter from the judge that relieved him of any rights he may ever have had to act as guardian for Elizabeth A. Miller, deceased; Becker saw that it was awkwardly worded, so as not to imply that he ever had been guardian at all. So that was that. They were on to him on that one. He pretended to be outraged and insulted, but the clerk continued to look at him blandly.

Now he couldn't lay his hands on anything until he probated the will. He should have moved faster, but initially he had delayed selling the apartment, betting that he could get much more out of the place after the building's repairs and renovations were complete, or at least under way. Later, he had been afraid to act because those people had showed up. In fact, probate would be easy; he wasn't worried about the outcome of a will contest. Then, in theory at least, he could reclaim everything the court had just taken from him, which, after all, was peanuts. The judge would be angry about the guardianship, but in the end that came to nothing unless they could prove he had robbed the estate while she was alive. He would say Lizzie gave him everything, little by little, so he wouldn't have to pay estate taxes on it; and they'd quickly realize that he himself had no money and they weren't going to get anything out of him. But the fact was, it wouldn't come to that. These people had no money to pay lawyers and accountants; they'd soon become convinced the estate was just peanuts and they'd back off, or he could cut some kind of cheap deal with them. The only real risk was that they'd find out about her apartment, but the place was valuable enough to make it well worth it to take this chance. He was a man with a sense of general grievance so strong that he felt entitled to restitution, and he was readily convinced that what ought to happen—where his wishes were concerned—would. They owed him that apartment, he thought, encompassing in this "they," in a vague way, all those who were responsible for his lifelong sense of deprivation and injustice. Things would be all right. The bottom line was that the old woman stayed in her place with around-the-clock attendants until the age of 103. Just what had *she* been deprived of?

# 24

AT BREAKFAST ON the Thursday following his performance, before they had wakened the children, Charles read the *Times* review to Anne:

> Charles Braithwaite, called in as a last-minute substitute, portrayed a seductive, handsome, and despicable Giovanni. Braithwaite, a man whose fame has never equalled his talents, has a uniquely appealing, complex quality of voice, in which every element was used to subtle effect. He wasted no opportunity to give melodic pleasure and rose to every vocal challenge with ease, energy, a rare depth of intelligence, and such charm as the Don himself might have envied, leaving listeners torn between enchantment and outrage at his crimes.

Unfortunately, it was written by someone they had never heard of, whose opinion would matter to no one. The reviewer who would ordinarily have written up the performance had probably gotten word that Cordara wouldn't go on and decided to stay home. So maybe *Opera News* would publish something nice in a month or two, and that would be that. Anne's fantasy of stardom for Charles, and the last-minute salvation of their home and life in New York, was extinguished as soon as she saw the flimsiness of the three sentences bobbing in the sea of print. Charles, on the other hand, was thoroughly pleased. "That's a nice little review," he said complacently. "Don't you think?"

"No, I don't think it's nice. I think it's mind-boggling that an accident like this, the fact that it's some nobody's tour of duty, determines our lives and the size of our bank account and . . ."

"What are you talking about? Anne, I know you had a wild idea that something might come of this, but that's not how the world works. And, as you know, I have just about as much career as I want. I'm sorry if this is not good enough for you, but remember—that's your problem, not mine."

Anne's discontent gave way to remorse. She knew that with this outburst she had again broken faith with Charles, breached the unspoken marriage contract, and for a moment she felt desperate. These thoughts were easily readable on her face. Charles observed her as she picked up the newspaper and read the review again. She looked haggard, with her tired face and swollen body. He had never seen her look so old. He felt sorry for her in her guilty sufferings, and then was swamped with his own guilt.

During the past few days, Anne had striven to be upbeat about the move but managed to achieve only a cloyingly counterfeit cheer, to which her family, being accustomed to the real thing, had reacted with a mood of eerie foreboding. Anne knew it. She had to reconcile herself to the changes or she would wreck them all, and to make her family unhappy was worse, even, than moving to Hoboken. A painful inner struggle brought Anne near to the point of accepting the move. She suspected that perhaps such a great struggle should not have been necessary, and felt the crack in her armor of self-approval deepen.

That evening, during the bustling period devoted to homework, practicing, and baths, Anne tried to mend things. Charles had signaled his availability by sitting on the sofa with the unread portions of the morning paper. Stuart, with wet hair and wearing pajamas, knelt on the floor near Charles, arranging plastic dinosaurs in obscure patterns and whispering to himself. Ellen leaned against Charles, frowning in concentration, as she did her half-hour's assigned reading. Jane sat at the piano, playing two bars of Bach over and again, at different tempos and in different rhythmic patterns, which her parents greatly approved without saying so; she would probably have stopped if they had said anything. Anne watched the harmonious scene of innocent activity for a moment and felt buoyed up by goodwill.

"Are you almost finished, Ellen? Your turn," she said. "Won't it be wonderful when we have two bathrooms and the kids all have their own rooms?" These were Anne's first affirmative words about the move.

"You know, maybe I'll have to have a studio in Manhattan once we move," Charles said. "I could put a daybed in it and sleep over sometimes, when I need to be in early the next day or if I finish up very late." He knew that Anne would dislike the idea of his having something like a separate residence in the city.

Anne felt quite as wounded as he had intended, and looked at him gravely. "A studio will be expensive. How are we going to afford that? You're starting not to make sense, Charles."

"I forgot," Charles said, ignoring her. "Merriweather called while you were out. He wants you to call Claire and just see if she can remember anything else that might help, and make sure she knows there's nothing to worry about. He called her, but he says it would help if you did too."

Anne called Claire, and after comparing notes on the latest developments, they revisited the question of why Lizzie got the idea to write a will in 1995. Claire thought Becker had visited Lizzie that year. She didn't know why; his visits were rare. But maybe he had gone up to tell Lizzie that the money was running out and that she'd have to go to a nursing home because the apartment with all the attendants cost too much. Lizzie was always afraid of being sent to a nursing home. Maybe she thought he was robbing her. Even before that visit, she didn't like him, Claire said.

"Do you have any idea why she would have made another new will in 1998?"

Claire had no idea. She was sure, however, that Lizzie had never said anything to her about a new will in 1998, or any other year, after the one in 1995. Anne could tell that Claire liked having priests and lawyers hanging on her words and liked talking woman to woman with Anne on these fraught subjects. She particularly enjoyed the psychological aspects of their discussions, Anne noticed. She perked right up when the subject had anything to do with underlying motives or fears, and she liked to draw Anne out on these matters.

"That old lady was not as simple as people think," Claire said confidentially. "I mean, just because she's old she's not . . . you know?"

"I do. I certainly do," said Anne. "She thought things she didn't say, and she didn't take people at face value."

"That's it," said Claire. "She was no fool. You know what she said once? She sent me down with a tip for Willie, for something he did for her, and she says, 'He respects money too much, but he knows he shouldn't, which is better than most people.'"

"Did she really?" Anne said. "I wish I'd known her better." The story did bring Lizzie back, and gave Anne a moment's bad feeling.

"Yeah," said Claire. "Me too."

"I can easily believe that Becker was robbing her," Charles said when told of Claire's speculations on what prompted Lizzie to write the 1995 will. "But he will have spent everything he stole. There'll be no way to get back a penny of it. It's guaranteed the fellow is not sitting on any big bank or brokerage accounts just waiting for a court to come along and claim it for us. But let's call Merriweather and tell him what Claire said. It makes sense to me."

The following morning, both Charles and Anne were at home when the broker called to let them know that they had two offers on the apartment. The higher one was from the young couple who had visited on Sunday. After phone calls to their lawyer, Charles and Anne accepted it.

"Charles," Anne said, when the shock of this had abated. "Let's try Washington Heights or even Riverdale. Please, just consider it. They say the subway ride to Lincoln Center is really quick from Washington Heights, and there are a couple of good public schools there. The kids would still be close to the music school, and we wouldn't need a car. We wouldn't have to have a yard."

"But we want a yard. It was your idea. We agreed on this a long time ago. If we couldn't live in Manhattan, you said you wanted to go out to the country and let the kids have that kind of independence. And you yourself said the public schools in Washington Heights weren't good enough."

"Let's just look. What do we lose?"

They began scribbling numbers on papers. They subtracted the amount of their mortgage and debts from the amount of the offer, and started scouring the Sunday *Times* real estate section to see what sort of place they could afford in other neighborhoods and boroughs. They called the broker to see what she thought. Now she was friendly and accommodating. Yes, she had always thought a place somewhere else in the city made far more sense for them. She had some *gorgeous* places to show. They *had* to see one especially—four bedrooms, three baths, fireplace, private courtyard. The kids could walk to school, terrific delis and cafés right around the corner. A real neighborhood! The place was really exciting, and lots of families with kids lived there. Charles and Anne were unable to resist. Fantasies of life in a new, affordable New York neighborhood possessed them. It sounded entrancing: all that space, the kids walking to school, and nice shops on the block. But such fantasies did not survive three exploratory trips to Washington Heights and Anne's vigorous research into schools.

"We're being pushed out of here before the place is really nicely gentrified," Charles grumbled back at home after one of these trips. "Drunks are still relieving themselves on the wall of our building, the doorman won't wear a uniform—and we can't afford to live here. Why can't we get some drugs going on this block—a drive-by shooting or something? Wouldn't take anything fatal—just a flesh wound or two. That'd squelch the assessment fast enough."

Anne's mother cried. She reminded them that they would have her apartment someday. "You should just move in with me," she wept. "I'm glad your father didn't live to see this."

"We couldn't possibly move in with you," said Anne. "You've got a life. The kids would drive you crazy if you had them around full time. We'd all drive each other crazy. Out of the question."

"My parents left Brooklyn because it got unsafe in the sixties," Charles said. "Now we leave Morningside Heights because it's too safe for the likes of us."

"What about Brooklyn?" Helen sniffed. "How about Park Slope?"

They shook their heads but offered no explanations. They were no longer willing to discuss schools and co-op prices with Helen. They would call the out-of-town broker again in the morning.

# 25

JEFFREY MAYHEW AND Merrit were sitting on the sofa in her living room, tousled and barefoot. It was early morning, they were drinking coffee, and he was trying to convince Merrit to marry him. She turned him down, but not with any enthusiasm. "So we'll have a baby right away," he said, when Merrit pointed out the consequences of their age difference. She shook her head, but didn't tell him that she probably couldn't have babies. She felt as depressed as she had ever felt in her life.

Merrit had talked the whole thing over with Teresa Smith, who had called her for lunch a couple of times. She and Teresa had developed the sort of lunching relationship in which women discuss their most intimate secrets in a quasi-impersonal way, as the common property of women. Teresa, fiercely progressive on every sex-related issue, was in favor of Merrit going forward in a relationship with Jeffrey. "Eight, nine years! What difference does that make!" she had protested against Merrit's doubts. "He's right for you in every conceivable respect. Merrit, you can't let yourself succumb to that kind of prejudice." And as for the baby problem, Teresa suggested that egg donation was the perfect solution.

Merrit herself thought that Jeffrey was the man she should have met when she was thirty: a mensch, a thinker, a good father for her children and partner for herself, someone she could be good to and good for. And as though to punish her for her wickedness, fate trotted him out now: See? Aren't you sorry for the way you've behaved? Not for you! Jeffrey had been proposing marriage for a week, and she had been refusing steadfastly. But she had not been steadfast enough to refuse to see him, and therefore he continued to hope that he would prevail, given time. Anne pointed this out to her when Merrit came by later that day. Merrit agreed. She'd have to stop seeing him.

The lamentations on Dr. Freilich's couch had continued session after session. He had said next to nothing. On this afternoon, he finally asked her, "Are you in love with him?"

Merrit thought about it. "No," she said, after a pause.

"Then what is this grief all about?"

"That it would be wrong to marry Jeffrey. That I'll never be a young woman finding a young man to fall in love with and have kids with, the way Anne did."

"Who says it would be wrong?"

"Don't you think it would be bad?"

"I'm your doctor, not your moralist. There are advantages and disadvantages for you with this man, as with any man. I myself would on the whole regard his being eight years younger as one of the disadvantages, but what is the rest of the story?"

Merrit's heart beat fast. "You mean I should seriously think about this?"

"Of course!"

"You really don't think it would be wrong?"

"Me personally? No, but I must repeat that as a moralist, I have little to offer."

"Are you serious about this? So I can get married?"

"You can get married."

"I can?"

"Get married? Of course. Why not? Everybody does." Merrit fell silent for several minutes.

"But, you know, I don't really want to marry Jeffrey."

"I suspected as much."

"He's just a kid. I'm not in love. He can't match my experience, my maturity. I keep having to stop myself from saying that I already went there, did that, used to think that way too but don't anymore."

"But you can dally with this man and torment yourself with images of forbidden fruits and impossible hopes . . . playing at being a younger woman and finding a young man to love and marry."

Merrit felt a sudden intense illumination of dark places in her mind, where twisted ideas had skulked unnoticed and unchallenged. There it was, Merrit thought, exposed to the light—the grotesque, misshapen conviction that had deformed the shape of her entire adult life. She felt transformed.

"So that's it. We're done."

"What do you mean?" asked Dr. Freilich, astonished.

"I get it. I see what my problem has been. My big hang-up was—I felt that I was forbidden to marry."

"Well . . ." he said, and Merrit heard him sigh. "You've had a couple of other insights in here, and each time, you've decided that we were done. Who knows what else will turn up?"

"Don't think I don't realize you're being sarcastic. Anyway, so what if I can get married? There's no one to marry. It's all too late."

"There you go again," Dr. Freilich continued, voluble for once. "This is a perfect example. When you're finally willing to admit that things have turned out the way they have because of your own unconsciously self-defeating thinking and behavior, you insist it's too late to fix. That's classic. It's the same neurotic conviction, with a new disguise."

"How can you try to palm off that nonsense on me? They write that kind of thing in women's magazines. It's all clichés. I can't believe you actually referred to my unconscious beliefs and called me neurotic."

"Why did you come to a psychoanalyst then? Aren't they rather famous for talking about those things?"

"Let's not have that argument right now. I'd just like you to name one, *one man* I've mentioned in all the hours I've wasted on this couch, just *one* who was a real possibility whom I ignored."

"So now you're backing off. Tell me, where do you suppose you might have gotten the idea that you weren't supposed to get married?"

"It's my self-hatred, I suppose," said Merrit. "I don't believe anyone could love me."

"But you don't hate yourself. You don't doubt your lovability. I'm surprised at you, of all people, speaking such nonsense, adopting the psychology of trash journalism. The truth is far more interesting. You don't hate yourself, but maybe you would hate yourself if you found someone to love and marry. That's the problem. You'd experience overwhelming anxiety, guilt. As it is, you're a good girl. A very, very good girl, and you rather approve of yourself."

"Oh please. That's trash psychoanalytic irony. I'm supposed to be impressed, I suppose. I don't believe it."

"Believe it."

Merrit would not respond for several moments to this offensive interpretation of her character. Merrit was *not* a "good girl." She had always been someone who broke the rules, went her own way, defied the conventions. It was as if the man didn't know her at all. She would simply stop talking about any of the important things on her mind.

"You know, speaking of clichés," said Merrit, "after Jeffrey went home, I spent two hours cleaning my kitchen cabinets. Such a girl thing to do! I don't know what came over me. I took everything out and scrubbed the shelves. I even washed the outsides of all the different bottles of oil and vinegar. And I put them back, all sparkling. I kept going back to open the cabinet doors just to see how pretty all the different shades of gold and green and burgundy looked."

"I'm sure they did look very pretty," said Dr. Freilich, encouragingly.

"Oh," said Merrit, blushing as she realized that what she had said was open to sexual interpretation.

"Time is up," said Dr. Freilich.

Riding the M4 home, Merrit regretted having entrapped Jeffrey in a hopeless, neurotic dead end; she had never had any intention of being seriously involved with him. When he came over that evening, she finally spoke honestly to him, without a double message. He was furious; she was repentant. He stormed out but, she thought, he would forgive her eventually. She picked up the telephone to call her mother, as she did almost every day, then changed her mind. She called Anne and told her the whole story. Anne showed interest despite the trying events of her own day. Merrit was changing, Anne thought, becoming unguarded and uncertain. In some ways, this made her seem more like her schoolgirl self, a persona that had disappeared when Merrit was about thirteen.

Anne always told Charles everything that Merrit told her, and Charles told Morris everything that Anne told him. So not long after these events, when Charles and Morris sat at Morris's kitchen table, Charles conveyed the gist to Morris, who was intrigued.

"That's the guy she was with at the opera?" he said. "I thought he looked like a kid. I'm surprised she didn't jump at the chance to make a big feminist point about younger men being okay."

"You really think Merrit would get involved with someone just to make a silly political point? C'mon. Anyway, women don't fall for younger men. I don't know any woman who really likes being with someone who's more than five or so years younger. Men do, not women."

"I don't know," Morris said. "It's overrated, the thing with younger women. I like women my age. But I want a few kids. It's purely practical."

"You waited too long," Charles said with a hint of severity in his voice.

"No kidding. Did you also notice that there wasn't any room for a wife and kids in the garrets I've been starving in?" Morris said. But he was not offended, and Charles felt encouraged to continue, half exhorting and half reprimanding.

"It may take years to get where you want to go, and you don't have years," Charles said. "You're at the point where even five years make a big difference. Don't wait until you're closing in on fifty to have babies. This is good advice I'm giving you, Morris. What's wrong with that psychoanalyst, Lily? Or how about Melanie's friend, Cicely?"

"Cicely—you have to be kidding. She's just a kid, and even if she wasn't, I couldn't get interested in someone like her. She's a real Indiana girl— everything I wanted to get away from. And she has no edge. I like a little bit of edge." Morris's voice sounded wistful, and Charles's heart went out to him. "But Lily is another matter."

"Or if Lily doesn't do it for you, look around. You can't just work all the time, you know," Charles said. "You've got to circulate. You want me to try to fix you up with a singer I know?"

Morris shook his head. "No thanks. Patience, Charles. I know what I'm doing, and I'm not working all the time."

"Appearances to the contrary, eh?"

"Never trust appearances."

# PART

---

# III

# 26

IN THE WEEK before Thanksgiving, there were signs of impending revolution at 635 West 117th Street. The Braithwaites, who had come as newlyweds, had been forced out—after fifteen years! The news was gossiped up and down the elevators and in and out of the lobby. They had sold to some Wall Street couple, and were going to move to the suburbs right after their baby was born. And they weren't the only ones. The couple with the baby down the hall from the Braithwaites and the family on twelve were both looking to sell. Victor Marx confessed to Charles that he and his friend, too, were getting scared and thinking about looking for a new place. The maintenance here was just too steep for them with nothing but their Social Security and some irregular income from his writing. That new assessment had pushed them right over the brink, and, the way Vic read things, it wouldn't be the last one. He suspected the new board had big plans to upgrade the building and clear out the riffraff. Who would ever have thought that buying an apartment in this building would turn out to be such a disastrous mistake?

"Maybe Queens," Vic said one day in the lobby. "I tell you, though, I don't think I've ever been to Queens. I was born on the Lower East Side, and I've been here in Morningside Heights since the forties. I know you should be flexible, but at my age I'm not interested in learning all over again where there's a dry cleaner you can trust and which grocery has ripe tomatoes. If we get sick out there, our doctors are all the way over here. My niece wants us to move to Ohio. She teaches there. But I don't know a soul in Ohio, and we're too old to learn to drive. I don't like to admit it, but a major move like that is really hard on you when you're closer to eighty than seventy. And I'm not dead yet. I mean, I still gotta work, gotta write. I need a library. I'm supposed to schlep from Queens to the library?"

"We looked at Queens last week," said Charles, suppressing the eruption of anxiety aroused by Marx's plaint. He was surprised to hear that Vic, so lean and light on his feet, was that old. "Don't rule it out. You can get some bargains there, and it's not as far from everything as you might think. But we think we're going to take the plunge. We're looking in Westchester and New Jersey." Charles forced himself to speak calmly, but he felt like laying his head on Vic's shoulder and crying.

"That's all right, Braithwaite. That's good," Vic said paternally. "You're still young enough to make a change like that. But I don't envy you. Westchester. The one I really worry about is Mary O'Reilly. She's an old bat, but she doesn't deserve what's happening to her."

"What's happening to her?"

"She's getting threatening letters from the board about what they call her indecorous conduct. You know, she rents. Never bought. The owners want her out of there so they can sell. The board wants her out of there. They want to make this into a fancier place. They can't have Mary bringing in her crazy friends or screaming at the doorman in the lobby or Al hanging around looking like an extra from *The Grapes of Wrath*. They've tried bribery. Now they'll pay a good lawyer and go to housing court, and prove she's nuts and out she'll go. And that's Mary's death sentence. Literally, you know, it'll kill her. Old folks dying, that's the trade-off if you want to keep co-op prices rising. Al, he's got a little money. They don't want him, though, because he's massively depressed and stands in the lobby all day looking for someone to talk to. They want him to sell. They told him: he should sell and move into a retirement community. He doesn't have anyone to look out for him but Willie and Roberto. Willie tells him don't sell, ignore those letters, and go to Tom's and get the turkey special for dinner. And that's just what he does. He does whatever Willie tells him."

Charles was pained by this recital, delivered in a dry, calm manner. He admired Vic's self-possessed drawl all the more because he detected the fine tremor of anxiety in it, and replied in the same style. "You think Willie could give me a few hints?" They had been standing in the corridor, speaking quietly, waiting for the mailman to finish slotting letters into the boxes, but Mr. Morales, with his insight into the meanings of body posture and tensed facial muscles, had deduced the subject of their conversation from where he stood at his usual observation post at the doorway. He had known for some time that the Braithwaites had decided to leave, and had taken the news philosophically. He liked the family, especially Charles, and would miss them, but after all, a man with three children and another one coming could not expect to raise them here. Mr. Morales's brother had four children and was raising them in Washington Heights, where some of the public schools weren't too bad.

If the new board had wanted only to make the building fancier, Mr. Morales would have had no objection, especially if salaries rose too. Yes, it would be hard on some people but good for others; that's how it was with money matters. The board, however, also had in mind some changes in how the building should be managed, which he found more objectionable. There had been several meetings at which a committee of three board members had called in Mr. Morales, Willie, and Roberto and told them to stop all the schmoozing and the lounging. The porter was fired, and the new man, who was chosen by Mr. Metzger, was standoffish and always huddling and whispering with that Lyons woman, who was on the board. The mailman was not to be permitted to do his yoga meditations in the armchair, and the cop on the local beat was no longer to eat his lunch in the back of the lobby with the handyman.

Unexpectedly, it had become hard work being the super at this building. The floors were to be polished more frequently, repairs made more quickly, trash removed more often. Equipment and tools were not to leave the premises and were to be inventoried regularly. Even well-known visitors were to be announced, and uniforms were to be worn at all times — and not just the shirt or the pants: the whole uniform, including the cap, *every day*. Even their manners were to be reformed; they should show more respect. This was a business relationship, and Mr. Morales and the other employees were to treat it as such. Mr. Morales looked into the board members' hard faces, and knew they meant it. They were saying to themselves, he saw, that they knew how to be fair, but they expected something for their money and they were going to get it.

When Victor Marx left, Mr. Morales sidled over to Charles and poured all this out. He was aggrieved, wounded. "You know, lots of people here have big problems with this building now — ever since those new people got in here. They have money, and they want to change everything. These people are not . . . comme il faut."

"They're barbarians," Charles said, thinking that these capitalists did not understand the feudal intimacy between superior and inferior. Mr. Morales did. He'd grown up in a house with a half-dozen servants, and, unlike the members of the co-op board, he was an educated man. "I don't know what can be done, unless the other residents can elect a better board. But that won't happen. There's one big group who don't understand anything, another group who don't care so long as they're not affected, and a lot of people who think it's all wonderful."

The elevator door opened and Mary O'Reilly got off, slowly pushing her walker. Lately, she had contrived a basket that hung on the front edge and held an assortment of seedy-looking items: a crumpled, greasy brown paper bag; a large envelope covered with pencil jottings; a ball of knitting; a small, scarred and bruised handbag. She shuffled slowly to the mailboxes and back, and stood reading a letter while awaiting the elevator. But, noticing Charles and Mr. Morales, she turned to talk.

"I told her, you know," she told Mr. Morales. She spoke so loudly that the other residents who had gathered to wait for the elevator showed, by their sudden grave attention to the ceiling and floor, that they had experience with Mary's lobby tirades.

"Roberto has been telling me," Mr. Morales replied, trying, by speaking low, to set her an example. "You do yourself no good. Mr. Braithwaite, she's been yelling and yelling at this woman on the board, Ms. Lyons, and says she'll sue her. Last night, when Roberto was here."

"Mary, you're out of your mind," Charles said. "That's just what they want you to do. They'll write it down in an affidavit and use it against you."

"Can't you speak up? I can hardly hear you. And I don't care what they do. I'm not afraid of them. They'll carry me out of here kicking and screaming. Not like you. You're a coward. That's what you are."

"Coward! Mary, what's the use of courage in a situation like this? No, this is an old story. This is just new money pushing everything out of its way. It's what we ourselves did to others so we could live here."

Morales nodded. He saw things just this way.

"That's nonsense! No one ever got in here before by pushing someone else out. You should've talked to Lizzie Miller. She could've told you. The Millers were here at the beginning, and before them there were open fields here."

"Well, I won't quibble about a particular building or block. You don't have to go back too far, just a generation or two, to find the crime. Where did they get the capital to build all these grand places around here? How many dark-skinned people live in them?"

"You're just making excuses."

Charles laughed. "You think I ought to just refuse to leave?"

"What's so silly about that?"

"Mary, don't get yourself into so much trouble. You're getting cantankerous, you know."

"Who says I am?"

"Here's the elevator. Get in and behave yourself." Charles took her arm and helped maneuver the walker into the elevator, conspicuously forcing the other passengers to make room.

# 27

MERRIT WAS WALKING north on Broadway after a visit to a health club, marking changes in the neighborhood as she passed them. A hideous new Rite-Aid had gone in, and hardly a block away a notice posted in an empty window announced that a Duane Reade, too, was imminent. How she detested these anomic chains, with their uniform offerings, long lines, and sullen, minimum-wage cashiers. How she missed the mom-and-pop stores she had grown up with. These grievances freshly in mind, Merrit was ill prepared, when she arrived at 112th Street, to discover that Mama Joy's was locked up and dark. The owner had retired, and no one could be found to carry on a complicated, old-fashioned business like that. People taped mournful good-bye notes on the door and peered wistfully into the windows, remembering the wedges of Stilton, Brie, and Saga, the fresh mozzarella, crusty breads, salamis, bagels, teas, coffees, and imported chocolates they used to bring home from the shabby deli. When Merrit, in her dark frame of mind, remembered childhood expeditions to Mama Joy's, early adventures in independence, and how the clerks had slipped her candy, tears rolled down her cheeks.

The soup line was getting longer at St. Ursula's, despite the neighborhood's increasing prosperity. Watching the line of hungry people, Merrit began to feel hungry herself. At 116th Street, instead of going home to try to work, she turned right and walked across the Columbia campus, intending to visit the Hungarian Pastry Shop yet again, although this habit had apparently caused her to put on a couple of pounds. No doubt her melancholy moods lately were contributing to this effect as well. Merrit felt depressed, tired, and middle-aged. Even her hair seemed to have changed its ways. It was becoming dry and coarse, and strands of gray had appeared. Too many things had gone irretrievably wrong; perhaps she was succumbing to her misfortunes. Dr. Freilich had not bothered to disguise his concern for her. She had broken off the affair with Jeffrey on the grounds of age difference, but it was only when she told him that she could not conceive children that he had stopped calling altogether. She was surprised at how clearly he seemed to know he wanted children, and at such a young age.

As she walked across the campus, Merrit observed the students curiously. You would never know, looking at this place, she thought, that such a thing as a marriage market exists. Here were hundreds of young women who conscientiously suppressed extraordinary beauty. Great numbers of them were emaciated, and a few, defiantly plump: no makeup, scruffy clothes, harsh hair styles, hard faces. What future did they dream of? she wondered. Did they scorn the idea of marriage? Then what was their emotional capital? What were they going to draw on for sustenance when the parent generation was gone? Were they going to end up like her, probably even without her resources of money, status, and friends? What, the social scientist in her wondered, would be their ultimate marriage rate? She knew that it had declined precipitously, and here, on this archurban campus, you could see the restraints on heterosexual signals. All the young women looked smart; they wanted to be smart the way girls once wanted to be pretty. Just as plain girls used to use tricks to look prettier—clever clothes, hair, and makeup—now girls with ordinary minds used trickery to create the illusion of smartness; they talked smart, dropped smart names, made smart distinctions, wore smart-looking glasses. Average well-raised girls posed as edgy wits. They aspire to be me, Merrit thought—me, at least, as I was until this summer. The female population of the campus was herself universalized—keen, quick, thin, smiling, careerist, independent. The problem was, she thought, that her own life, taken as a model plan, worked only for about ten years at most, and even then only under favorable circumstances. Being pretty was a very favorable circumstance, which Merrit had repeatedly relied on. But they had contempt for prettiness; it was acceptable only as a camp or gay thing. Merrit perceived resentment underlying this attitude, and a little masochism—resentment of beauty in those who lacked it and masochistic suppression, concealment of beauty, in those who had it. Prettiness isn't democratic. Not everyone can be pretty, but everyone can be thin. So they go for thin, which is also meritorious; thin girls earn their status through the suffering of starvation, but prettiness is like inherited wealth. Resentment and masochism, she concluded, on an extraordinarily widespread level, loudly insisting it's something else, something quite opposite. When they get to where I am, they'll be wretched but insist that everything is fine.

Merrit was not simply shattered by the realization that she would never have children. After all, that had become socially unlikely long before it became physically impossible: professional women in their late thirties rarely married and had children. She was also depressed and weighed down with regret because, she now believed, she had lived her life without protecting or even discovering her own real interests. She had not known how much she wanted and needed a family, and a partner to share life with. It was dangerous, she thought, not to know oneself. She could seek medical help. But what was the point of that without a partner? Merrit did not want to be a single mother, and did not want to impose fatherlessness on a child deliberately.

This was another of the intimate subjects that Merrit had submitted for analysis over lunch with Teresa Smith. Teresa had scoffed at this reluctance. "So you'll find a man someday," she had scolded. "In the meantime, if there is any chance at all that you will have a child, it has to be now." This seemed quite rational, but Merrit had suffered in her own life from the absence of a father. She knew the desperate dependence a child felt on a lone parent, the insatiable hunger for the missing one, the way one's feelings got permanently, ruinously, twisted up. All these things would be multiplied when the father had not died but had never even been there. A child might hate a mother who failed to provide a father.

This, too, Merrit knew about from her own life. "You were on the horns of an emotional dilemma. You could either feel psychically orphaned," Dr. Freilich had said the day before, "or, finding this unbearable, you could swallow your anger—preserving love for your desperately needed mother, but at a cost." Merrit had been tallying this cost during her recent sessions. All her life, she had preferred to be ignorant of her mother's evident flaws rather than to let her own rage instruct her about them. "Instead, you raged at everyone else's mother," said Dr. Freilich, "writing books about how children have been badly raised through the centuries."

"Now you're telling me my work is a sham? As though I haven't got enough problems—how can you!" Merrit cried.

"You misunderstood," Dr. Freilich replied patiently. "I haven't read your books—my prejudices are all in favor of what you tell me they say, assuming my prejudices matter. But can you think it quite accidental that you spend your life analyzing cultural cruelties in child-rearing practices, in historic patterns of motherhood, fatherhood, and childhood, calling for great reforms, while—as you yourself insist—you were blind to your own mother's unkindnesses, and rationalized them, to a degree that is almost incomprehensible?"

Merrit not only saw but once more felt humiliated by how oblivious she had been to the clear patterns of her own life. She had thought the motive for these writings was father-hunger.

"That too, possibly," said Dr. Freilich equably.

"I still don't think I want to raise a child alone," Merrit had finally replied, after setting these ideas free in her mind to create whatever havoc they might in her settled habits of thought.

Dr. Freilich had been silent.

Anne, however, had suggested that Merrit should not rule out adopting a child who might otherwise lack any family at all, and Merrit said she would think about this. But Anne was dismayed that Merrit, in her depression, had failed to seek a second medical opinion about her infertility, and urged more strongly that she explore the medical options. If a partner for Merrit were to appear, why not know the score or work to improve it? Merrit agreed, but did nothing. When she thought about trying, she experienced her loneliness with redoubled anguish. Moreover, she knew that seeking medical help would raise her hopes, and she could not endure the loss of these hopes a second time.

Merrit called her mother as soon as she got home and, inwardly steeling herself, told her what the doctor had said at the end of the summer. She had not been able to face this disclosure until now. Mrs. Roth showed little reaction. "Well really, Merrit," she said in her quavering, sarcastic voice. "What difference does that make at this point? That door closed on you a long time ago. You were never cut out for marriage and the family."

But why not? Merrit tearfully asked herself in bed that night. Why not? She fell asleep sobbing for the first time since childhood, and opened her eyes late the following morning with an ominous sense that something was wrong, despite the cheerful electronic burbling of the telephone. To her surprise, it was Lily Freund. Merrit remembered to ask her whether she and Morris had set a date, and Lily responded that they had, with what

Merrit recognized as a psychoanalyst's neutrality. But why does she bother, Merrit wondered. Surely she doesn't think that if she shows her happiness it'll make me feel bad that I'm not engaged. Lily said that she had been deserted by Morris, who was always in his lab in the evenings, and she wanted to go to the movies that night. Merrit was pleased to have Lily's company to look forward to, and wondered whether they would be friends after Lily married. It was doubtful. Merrit and Morris were too uneasy together. That incident on the mountain, which she was often forced to drive from her thoughts, had made things both better and worse. Now he never quarreled with her, but he looked at her with a peculiar, indecipherable expression on his face. Sometimes she thought he was simply suppressing the old urge to correct her faults. Sometimes she thought he felt sorry for her. Worst of all was the occasional feeling that, perhaps, he wouldn't object if it were to happen again.

During the cab ride downtown, Lily began talking about Morris, and continued after the movie, in a café. She explained Morris's feelings about getting married, his epiphany about Sam, and Lily's belief that he was good, compassionate, and warmhearted. Merrit was impressed—with Morris's unsuspected ability to know himself and with Lily's ability to know him. But she could think of nothing to respond that did not hint of secrets, and Lily may have sensed that something had happened between Merrit and Morris. Is she warning me off? Merrit wondered. It didn't feel quite that way. She thinks something happened, but she's not sure what.

"Do you think Morris will make a good father?" she began lamely, and volunteered, on impulse, that she'd been told she probably could not have babies. "So supposing I find someone I want to live with, it has to be someone who could do without children. I'd always thought kids would be nice, but to my surprise, after learning that I couldn't have any, I realized I was quite desperate for them."

"Not me," said Lily, who had heard from Morris about Merrit's problem. "I think I'll love them if they come, but I could be happy without them."

"Are you sure?"

"Absolutely."

"But Morris is very keen on the idea, isn't he?"

"Oh yes. To the extent that I feel I let him down a little. I'm an odd duck. Actually, I feel that way about marriage too. I think it's a good way to live, but it isn't necessary to me the way I see it is to some women. Of course, it's better not to be alone, but something less than marriage would do for me. I really think I'm willing to get married only because I met Morris. He makes it worthwhile. Otherwise, I could take it or leave it. But he says he doesn't understand wanting just the person and not the institution. He says if it's love, you want the whole package."

Merrit had to make an enormous mental adjustment to consider Morris in the light of a man so desirable that he made marriage attractive to the indifferent. Having tried the idea on for size, she decided that Lily was perhaps less neutral on matrimony than she thought. "Well, he's an old-fashioned guy in a lot of ways, and I don't really agree with him. But I have to admit I feel a little skeptical when you tell me you don't care about being married."

Lily smiled without replying, and Merrit saw that her openness had vanished. Merrit had begun to think she would never really understand Lily. Did Morris? Nor did she understand what sort of marriage they had in mind. She remembered how, the last time they were together, Lily had argued in favor of practical marriages built on mutual esteem. Was it possible that she was as good as her word? But even in this case, she wondered, why Morris?

Now Merrit realized why Lily had made such a point of talking about Morris with her. Lily was wondering whether Morris could be happy in the only kind of marriage that she, Lily, was capable of making. That was surely it. She was testing this idea against Merrit's opinion. Merrit, motivated by her own guilt, responded more reassuringly than truthfully. "I have a feeling that you and Morris are going to make a good life together."

"Do you?" Lily asked hopefully. "I worry about that. The longer we're engaged, the more I fear I'm not doing the right thing. About once a week I find myself doubting whether I'm cut out to make Morris happy."

"Only once a week? I know lots of happily married people who had doubts every day, morning, noon, and night, when they were engaged. What does your analyst say?"

"She says that I have enormous resistances against marrying, and the closer I get to doing it, the more loudly they're protesting."

"Sounds about right."

Lily, gratified by this remark, smiled warmly at Merrit and once again they parted with every appearance of goodwill. But at home, alone, Merrit collapsed on her bed, exhausted with the effort of hiding from Lily how aggravating she had found the conversation—no small trick when dealing with someone trained to read meanings in brow twitchings and finger tappings.

The next evening, Morris left Lily standing in her doorway, waving sweetly and watching until he disappeared behind the elevator doors. She had asked Jonathan to join them for dinner, and Jonathan had stayed until ten minutes ago, when Morris was already late returning to the lab. It was very cold when Morris trudged up the block from Lily's apartment toward Broadway. Lily had urged him not to stay too late and to call her first thing in the morning with the news from the lab, but she hadn't much protested Morris's departure, nor had she asked him to come back when his work was finished. Morris knew he wasn't very good company. He never was anymore. Lily had probably been smart to ask Jonathan to join them, as she often did, when Morris was so silent and moody. No doubt this had saved them several unnecessary arguments. On the other hand, it annoyed the hell out of him.

The lab news was bad again. Morris, without much confidence, had hypothesized a means by which the expected results of his tests might simply have been chemically masked, but this too had now been disproved. He and his students spent an hour arguing in circles, then, near midnight, agreed to give it up for the night. Morris scheduled another meeting for tomorrow after lunch, not too early. They'd sleep on things, decide where to go next, and resume work after the Thanksgiving break. Morris arrived back at 635 West 117th at the same time as Charles, who was coming home from a performance. Makeup was still smeared into Charles's hairline and his eyes were startling with their rings of black eyeliner. He insisted Morris stop in for a quick beer, and, with Anne, listened to the bad news. It pained him, Morris's being stymied this way.

"Morris," Anne said. "I'm sure your theory is true. But you haven't been thinking like yourself lately. You're in a rut of some kind. You need to get a really good night's sleep, or two or three, and dream all about it. Is something besides work bothering you?"

"I just can't help wondering *why* you feel so sure my theory is true."

"Because I know you."

Morris snorted. "I do have something on my mind, but it's not exactly something that's bothering me. I'm engaged. I'm going to get married to Lily Freund—that psychoanalyst I met at Jonathan Riesbeck's when I was here in the spring, the one I visited in Maine. She's kind of a friend of Merrit's. We've been engaged for a few weeks."

"You mean you were already engaged the other night when I was over at your place?" Charles exclaimed. "Why didn't you say anything?"

"I didn't have the energy to go into it."

"You didn't have . . . Morris, what the hell kind of attitude is that? Why haven't you brought her over yet? Anne's prepared to be crazy about her." Charles's annoyance was real, not politely feigned. Indeed, he felt more than he dared show. When it came to his love life, Morris always went weird on you.

"I'm so glad for you, Morris," said Anne, leaning over to kiss his cheek. "Merrit speaks very highly of her."

"Really?"

"Of course! And I'm glad you've had someone to talk to through all this."

Morris was apparently too depressed even to be jovial with the Braithwaites about his engagement, but he promised to bring Lily to dinner that weekend. She'd been urging him to set something up with the four of them. When Morris rose to leave, Anne pulled him aside.

"Don't forget what I said. You're not solving the problem because you're not even tackling it. You're not like yourself. You're not thinking. You're boring."

At home, Morris found a new e-mail from Joey Delano. "Sam is pressuring Schmidt to leave his wife," it said. "She wants to move in with him, probably wants to marry him, but I don't think he's gonna go for it." Morris, knowing Sam's good qualities (most of which were apparent only in bed), thought Schmidt might go for it. Sam's bad points would never dawn on a guy like him, since he had a lot of the same ones. Morris had never been tempted to marry Sam. Despite her absurdities, Anne was still his idea of the perfect wife, even now that he was engaged to Lily.

Morris always felt intense gratification when Anne got his number—understood something about him that he hadn't understood himself—and found words for whatever it was. It didn't work that way with Lily somehow, yet Lily was probably even more perceptive than Anne. He had sought that feeling of being known ever since he'd met Anne and discovered it existed. No one who hadn't grown up in Indiana with fundamentalist parents, who never once managed to perceive that their children had insides, could know how badly Morris had hoped to find it. Everything his parents had ever said to him was a lie on one level or another. He had run away from his parents' world, a society that believed only in the outsides of things. It's why I became a scientist, he thought. I wanted to understand what was behind all the appearances. How lonely he had always been, having all those sisters yet none of them really knowing anything about anybody else. But he loved his sisters, and was glad that two of them were coming for Thanksgiving.

Morris went to bed and fell asleep almost immediately. When he began to awaken at nearly eleven the following morning, his thoughts were a jumble of Lily, Sam, Schmidt, marriage, his parents and sisters, chromatin and walls, barriers that moved around, and the H19 and Igf2 genes. Then he came to, with a delicious feeling of sleep satiety and fragments of dreams hovering near consciousness. He dressed and walked through the cold wind to the shuttle bus. Forgot to call Lily, he realized as he climbed on.

Riding uptown, he outlined first in his mind, then in his pocket notebook, an addition to his original hypothesis that would explain the mysterious results they'd been getting these past weeks. This was it, he thought, vainly trying to restrain a rush of confidence in the new approach until he could carry out the work that would confirm it. It would take some careful procedures to prove it, and even if they did, there was still the Duckworth problem. But now they would at least be able to move forward.

Morris found it odd both that he hadn't thought of this solution before and that he had thought of it at all. He had had a mental block of some sort, which had prevented him from perceiving an obvious answer to the problem. Under normal circumstances, he would have seen it quickly, easily, but he had been blinded somehow. He didn't understand in the slightest why it should be this morning instead of next year or last week that he regained his capacity to think, but it didn't really matter now. He should have gotten Anne's advice to begin with, he thought, smiling to himself. Once more he compared Lily's painstaking, doubting, rational approach to his problems with Anne's sweeping, uninformed confidence. Although he disliked admitting it, he wasn't so sure that talking these things over with Lily didn't somehow tie him into knots—a thought that tempered his excitement over the morning's insight. But he quickly rejected it. He was not going to hold Lily to impossible standards, as he had done with so many others. What, was he going to insist on having a wife who could solve his scientific problems for him?

# 28

ANNE AND HER BROTHER, Paul, made Thanksgiving dinner in alternate years. This year was the Braithwaites' turn, and, as usual, they invited a crowd. Besides Helen, and Paul and Greta with their two children, they also invited Merrit, to avoid leaving her to the mercies of her mother, Mrs. Roth, whom they also invited, because Merrit was not willing to leave her alone at Thanksgiving. Two couples from the city, one with children, were coming—old friends whom they tended to see, Anne said, only on state occasions. For the first time, they invited Victor Marx and his friend, Bart Stevens, an elderly semi-invalid they scarcely knew, a writer of travel books before his health problems precluded his going anywhere. Anne was surprised but agreeable when Charles suggested having them. He was impressed with Vic, and was always quoting his lobby conversations. At the last minute, they had also asked Father Merriweather, who seemed to have nowhere else to go. Morris and Lily, along with two of Morris's sisters, who were visiting, couldn't come because they had already accepted an invitation from Jonathan Riesbeck, whose Thanksgiving dinner was always, and famously, a gourmet feast. Even so, it took all the leaves of the Braithwaites' table, and two card tables and several borrowed folding chairs, before they were confident that they could seat everyone.

This year the holiday mood was dominated by the gloomy anticipation that it would be their last Thanksgiving in this home. After months of excursions to hamlets farther and farther distant from New York City, to visit smaller and smaller houses, the Braithwaites had finally found an affordable place in southern Putnam County, near schools reputed to be good, about an hour and a half north of the city by train—an old frame house, painted white, with a rickety porch, but pleasant and, they were assured, sound in the pipes and plumbing. Some rewiring and roof repairs would be necessary. The owner was a lively, chatty eighty-year-old named Irene Schaffner, who said that she intended to move into a retirement place where you had your own apartment but there were doctors on call and all the housekeeping was done for you. This idea wasn't much to her taste, but she felt that she had little choice.

Mrs. Schaffner had held on as long as she could, she said, but it was too much work for an elderly widow. So many of the people whose help she had relied on in the past were gone now. It was too hard to find new grass cutters, appliance repairers, tree trimmers, window washers, house cleaners, and, lately, car drivers when she wanted to go anywhere at night, now that she didn't trust herself behind the wheel after dark. None of these helpers seemed to be available more than once or twice, and then you started all over with new faces. Her children had grown up in this house, but they were all over the country now. It made no sense to go live near any of her children. They didn't stay put, none of them, long enough.

Mrs. Schaffner had taken to Anne within five minutes of the Braith-waites' arrival, and wanted them to buy the house. The price she asked was, they knew by then, low. Charles and Anne looked at each other, defeated, unable to find any excuse to turn it down. The yard was shady, with old-fashioned roses, a cherry tree, and a playhouse with fascinating old toys kept for her grandchildren's visits. The rooms of the house were small, but there were well-made cabinets, a generous pantry, and an attic where the children could play. Even Jane found consolation, looking out the window of what would be the girls' room into the branches of the cherry tree. They found a place for the piano, and there was room for a small studio for Charles. The low price would make it possible for them to afford some repairs. Mrs. Schaffner even took an interest in these, and made a half-dozen good suggestions. She hoped they would be friends. They shook hands, and agreed to have the lawyers draw up papers.

But, despite the presence of the children and the hired driver from Manhattan, Anne began lamenting as soon as they got into the car: "That's just horribly sad. As if getting old weren't bad enough, you should be separated from all your children and have to give up your home and all your ways and your belongings." Charles, too, found the woman's situation disturbing. But he had seen worse lately, and he supposed that his and Anne's grief was the result of the sundering of their own connections, not Mrs. Schaffner's.

"Anne, this is an incredible piece of luck. It's remarkable, your effect on elderly women."

"Do you think that's what it was?"

"Of course! She wanted you to have that house. She must have thought that if you were there, it wouldn't change. It would still be all about raising babies and pruning the rose bushes."

"I think it was different. At the end of life, people want their mothers. When they die, they call out for their mothers. In her eyes, I'm a mother, and she's making sure she has one in her house. Poor lonely woman. I almost feel we're robbing her children."

"If any of them want to come back here to take care of her and it, I'll gladly opt out of the deal. In the meantime, we're probably going to do her as much good as the money."

"Oh please, Charles. None of this feels right."

"You wouldn't feel right unless we were paying through the nose for it."

"I'm going to call Lily to see what she says," said Anne. She and Lily had hit it off instantly when Morris had brought her to dinner, and had had a deep and useful discussion of attachments to mother figures. "Lily will understand how psychologically delicate this is going to be."

"Satisfy your curiosity by all means, but we're taking the house at the price we've just agreed on. We've got to protect our own children." The idea that Anne would even consider walking away from the best situation they had found made Charles flare up.

"Yes. But I'll just talk things over with Lily. You know, this won't be just a business relationship. We'll be talking to that woman for the rest of her life."

"If we enjoy talking to her, and not otherwise."

"I thought she was lovely to talk to."

They announced this decision at Thanksgiving dinner, where it made their guests no happier than it had made them. Victor Marx and Bart Stevens wanted to know if Charles and Anne could drive, and thought they should reconsider staying in the city. They'd heard there were some good schools in Washington Heights. Or what about Park Slope? Helen sighed disconsolately. Merrit, in particular, looked distraught at the idea that Anne and Charles would soon be gone from the neighborhood. In fact, Merrit wasn't looking at all well, Anne noticed with a pang.

"Well, Anne," interjected Mrs. Roth. "How are you feeling? You look a little worn-out, but I know you feel the way I did. I loved being pregnant."

Anne stole a worried look at Merrit.

"You never said so before," Merrit said to her mother, irritably.

"Why would I? I loved being pregnant, but I never did like babies. I still can't see why people make such a fuss over them. I liked older children— found you far more likable when you were out of diapers and could talk. Before that, as far as I was concerned, babies are for their nurses. Nurses get paid to put up with them."

Anne, at a loss to say anything on this touchy subject that might not be wounding to someone, brought the conversation back to real estate. "And we close with our buyers next month. They want to renovate and move in here by summer."

"I can't bear to hear about it," Helen moaned. "Anne, I will never be reconciled to this. I won't be able to pick up the kids after school, and you won't be able to run over with them for a quick visit. And what about their lessons? Charles will have to rent a studio in Manhattan for teaching; you'll never see him. You can't expect students to go up to Putnam County. You're not really going to save money doing this, you know." Anne glanced at Paul and Greta, making sure that they were not taking offense at being overlooked, somehow, in this conversation. Helen had not protested their move to Berkeley with anything near the energy with which she fought Anne and Charles's to nearby Putnam County. But Paul and Greta merely appeared resigned to hearing again what they had heard often enough already. The fact was, as Anne knew, that although they may have felt a little jealousy, they were much more worried that once the Braithwaites had moved, Helen might lean on them and their children more than Greta could easily tolerate. That fear was only natural, Anne thought. Things were so different with your own mother; Charles had always been remarkably content to have Helen be an important part of his family life.

"We most certainly will save money," said Anne, frowning at her mother for bringing up such things in front of the children and the company. "Everything is arranged. We'll be back every Saturday for music school, so we'll see you every week, and the kids can stay over sometimes on Saturday night."

"Of course!" said Frieda Ellis, a cellist who had married a lawyer and lived in a large, modern co-op near Lincoln Center. She and her husband saw, with painful sympathy, just how things were for the Braithwaites, as did the other guests. All of them were trying to appear cheerful and encouraging, but Helen could not restrain herself.

"It won't be the same," she said.

"Regards from Melanie Malcolm," Charles said to Merriweather, with such unconvincing heartiness that everyone knew he was trying to change the subject.

"Melanie's in town again?"

"With another sister," Charles said, "Bonnie, who's next youngest. Melanie's just finished her prelims. She's going to start writing her thesis next semester, assuming she passes, which of course she'll do with flying colors, being a Malcolm."

"Have you met the Malcolm sisters?" Merriweather asked Merrit in his third effort to draw her into conversation.

"No, but I hear they look just like Morris. It's hard to imagine," said Merrit.

"They look like him and talk like him—at least Melanie does," said Merriweather.

"And think like him," added Anne.

"Yes," Merriweather agreed. "Very logical. They're quick, straight thinkers, no nonsense. Ask questions, find answers."

"Not me," said Merrit. "My thought processes go in loop-the-loops and they're all either unconscious or nonverbal—right-brain stuff. First I know what I think. Then it takes me months to figure out why I think it."

There, Anne thought, glancing at Charles to see if he noticed. That's twelve-year-old Merrit. No defenses, all out there.

"Does it ever happen that when you find out why you think it, you decide that you don't think it anymore?" asked Merriweather.

"No. The right brain is smarter," said Merrit.

"I'm glad Morris isn't here," Jane said scathingly.

"Just kidding," Merrit said, but her laugh lacked sufficient energy to convince anyone.

"Of course, the right brain does think and gather evidence, doesn't it?" said Merriweather, "And it doesn't talk. So that doesn't sound crazy to me."

"Well . . ." But Merrit wasn't interested enough to catch the ball and throw it back.

Merriweather was discouraged for a full five minutes before he tried again. He considered asking her about her book, but decided this would appear ingratiating. He ruled out the election primaries, novels, Seamus Heaney, tonality in music, and the future of organized religion. By this time, the bravery and persistence of his efforts had caught Anne's attention. It struck her, moreover, that he wasn't merely being nice to someone who was feeling low. ("My right brain had known it for weeks," Anne told Charles later, "but consciously I didn't know why I thought it, and I ignored it.")

"Merrit," Merriweather began finally, indulging in his first use of her name, after observing that Merrit seemed most interested in her dinner and ate with a hearty appetite. "How about some more stuffing?"

"Merrit, for someone who is putting on weight," said her svelte mother, coolly, "you are certainly making free with second servings."

Merrit glared at her but blushed.

Bart, who was modestly paunchy, objected. "My goodness, most women would love to look like Merrit when they put on weight."

"Thanksgiving dinner is not an occasion for weight control," Helen announced severely, and patted Merrit's hand.

"Why isn't there a good Italian restaurant in this neighborhood?" Merriweather asked, with seemingly indefatigable goodwill, more in Merrit's direction than in anyone else's. But Merrit had been put off food by her mother's rudeness and once more refused the bait.

"The best pizza is at V and T's," Ellen volunteered sweetly.

The rest of the meal passed off pleasantly enough, but, despite the perfectly browned bird with chestnut stuffing, spirits were not high and the conversation lacked zest. Merriweather couldn't help noticing that no one said anything, or felt anything as far as he could tell, about being thankful. On the contrary, most of them seemed to feel deprived. Even he himself had forgotten to offer a thanksgiving prayer—a strange and unprecedented lapse.

This time, thought Charles, looking around the table, we can't overcome. Anne is down and tired, and can't hide it. Getting up this dinner was too much for her, but she had to do it. Helen doesn't help things at all. There is poor Merriweather trying to get a conversation going with Merrit, who reeks misery—and there's Merrit's smug little mother, completely pleased with herself and indifferent to anyone else.

The doorbell rang just as they rose to go into the living room. Charles and Anne were surprised to see Morris with Lily and his two sisters, who smilingly offered a pie they had baked. They were going to visit Morris's lab, which Lily had never seen, and in the evening they were off to Jonathan Riesbeck's dinner, an all-grown-up affair. They were persuaded to stay for a few minutes before heading out into the chill November air, and Charles and Anne hoped the infusion of new blood would give the party a little energy. Lily and Merrit kissed affectionately, while Morris looked at them sternly. He had an odd way with Lily: respectful, smiling, warm—but slightly detached. Actually, Lily was the same way with him. They don't act like they own each other, Charles thought. But maybe this is what each of them needed, someone who would allow emotional distance. This thought was heartening. At least someone was going to be happy. While he listened to Morris talk about new plans for his work at the lab, his eye rested momentarily on Merrit. Morris dropped his voice for a moment and nodded her direction. "What's wrong there? She looks like someone punched her." Charles could only shake his head.

Morris, who knew that Charles and Anne always had music on occasions like this, asked Anne if they would begin now so that his sisters could hear. Anne encouraged Charles to sing, but she begged off playing for him. She was too worn-out. "You do it, Mother," she said to Helen, but Helen declined in favor of Morris, and a general cry for Morris made it impossible for him to refuse. While Charles burrowed for music in an untidy stack on the floor, they conferred briefly and somewhat discordantly. It was several minutes before they stopped bickering and settled on three Schubert lieder, which they performed so passionately that Anne's wan face went pink, and Lily, who had never heard Morris at the piano, lost her habitual air of knowing placidity. "Why didn't you tell me you could play like that?" she asked Morris afterward, and he coolly answered, "I told you I played." Schubert was too much for Merrit in her despondent mood; but she managed to conceal her tears from everyone but Merriweather, who felt a kind of desperation on seeing them. He couldn't help her; she was too immersed in her misery to be interested enough. Surprisingly, however, when she had brushed the tears away she begged the performers for more, somewhat abashedly, and for a few minutes seemed more like herself than she had for the entire evening.

The music seemed to arouse the listeners, and for a while the gathering felt almost like a real party. Then Paul asked Jane to play, and she refused. "I thought I was supposed to be having a good time," she said to her parents, ignoring her uncle. She was so rude that even the doting Helen noticed that everyone present took her for an appalling brat. The four new-comers soon had to leave, and a certain dispiritedness returned. Nonethe-less all the guests stayed for hours, and the children, at least, played happily, until Merrit said she had to go. Then Merriweather stood up and said he'd walk her home, the others seemed to overcome their own inertia, and all were gone within a quarter of an hour.

"It was the worst dinner party we've ever had. Neither you nor I had a thing to say for ourselves," Anne said matter-of-factly when the guests had all gone. "Yet none of them would leave."

"That's the last time we ask Mrs. Roth."

"I wish it were all over with and we were out there in Putnam County. It's this in-between stage I can't stand."

The two of them stood surveying the chaos of the dining room table, the disarranged furniture, and the wild dispersal of Pokémon cards, Monopoly money, and Legos.

"Let's just get through it. Complaining doesn't help," said Charles, eye-ing the dishes stacked in the kitchen and thinking as much of the chores to be done as of the impending move.

"I know we're lucky, Charles. I know that most people in the world would feel fortunate to have our kind of problems. But it's still sad, giving up our home and a life we love. How do you think the kids will do, with you gone all the time?"

Charles, however, turned away. Anne infuriated him when she whined about the move. Besides, it was over already, this life she was clinging to, as this miserable Thanksgiving dinner had proved. It didn't work anymore, and they had to see what they could build somewhere else.

# 29

IN EARLY DECEMBER, the Braithwaites signed a contract agreeing to sell their co-op to the young couple, the Nicholson-Kahns, whose bid they had informally accepted before Thanksgiving. They rode the bus back from the midtown lawyer's office; Anne was too hugely pregnant to feel comfortable in a cab. When they returned, Mary O'Reilly was in the lobby showing a paper to Willie. It was a letter from the board, she told the Braithwaites, holding it out to them with trembling hands. They were going to try to evict her. This came after she left the water running in her bathtub one night and flooded three apartments—the latest in a series of events that the board intended to cite in court, the letter said.

"You go right to Legal Aid," Charles told her, "in Harlem. They'll help. You get on the bus and go up there. I don't think they can really do this to you, but you've got to have a lawyer."

Mary, however, seemed dim, stunned, not at all herself, and Charles feared she lacked initiative enough to find the address and get herself uptown.

While she and Charles stood in the lobby talking to Mary, Anne's water broke, gushing down her legs and spreading across the floor. "We've got to get to Mt. Sinai, but I tell you, I'm not having contractions. Oh, I hope they won't have to induce. I'll just go upstairs and clean up and get my bag. My God, I hate this elevator! The girls probably picked up Stuart already. They'll be home any minute. Will you call Mother? What should we do with the kids until she gets here? It won't take her ten minutes to get here. Could we leave Janie in charge? No, let's just wait for her." Anne chattered on as they waited for the elevator, flustered and giddy, while Willie, calm and experienced, was on the spot with a mop and bucket, waving away Anne's apologies.

"Never mind. That's all right," he said. "Go up and get your things. I'll call a cab. The kids can sit in the lobby with me until your mother comes. You go on to the hospital."

"There it is. There's the first one," Anne whispered to Charles. "God, it's a killer. We'll have to hurry."

The Lyonses had walked in midway through the scene, unnoticed by Charles or Anne until, at this moment, they heard Ms. Lyons mutter to her husband, "I have lived in a half-dozen different buildings, and I have never before seen a disgusting thing like that happen in a lobby. Why these things always happen in *our* lobby—the doorman baby-sitting people's loud kids in the lobby and this . . . this slimy mess—I'll never understand it."

Charles and Anne stared at her incredulously. Mary, regaining energy, said to Anne, "Never mind her. That's the one I was telling you about, Lyons, on the board." And she tapped her finger against the side of her head significantly. Distracted though she was, Anne was struck by this. It dawned on her that it was most likely true. It was probably Ms. Lyons, and not Mary O'Reilly, who had tendencies that way. Mary was just cantankerous and whiny; Lyons was bizarre—profoundly narcissistic, with a hint of paranoia.

"I'll be a witness for you on that, Mary," Charles said pointedly as they entered the elevator. He was so angry that for a moment he had imagined hitting Mr. Lyons—in lieu of hitting Ms. Lyons, which was not feasible even in fantasy. "I heard it with my own ears." Ms. Lyons, continuing to her own floor, was not sure that she understand what they meant, but they scared her a little. They were saying *she* was crazy? "Calm down," her husband said gloomily.

The baby was born less than an hour after Charles and Anne arrived at the hospital. They named him Gilbert, after Charles's father. He was a strong, healthy boy who looked like Charles, and he sucked expertly on the first try. Telephone calls to and from the hospital described everything to the little ones at home, and provided instructions on dinner. Anne encouraged Jane in her practicing; of course she was to play in the competition, coming up in three days; Grandma and Daddy would be there and would videotape it if Anne wasn't able to come, but maybe she would.

Anne thought she'd be home in the morning and was having a tender conversation with Stuart, who most needed reassurance, when something went wrong. "Now Daddy wants to talk to you, Stuey. He's been waiting his turn a long time." Anne, looking white, handed the telephone to Charles and began vomiting violently. He rang frantically for the nurse while talking affectionately to Stuey.

Anne grew sicker by the hour. The doctors diagnosed pre-eclampsia, and said it was very dangerous. Rarely, as in this case, it appeared after a birth rather than before. Charles's eyes were locked on Anne's dead-white face as she lay surrounded by doctors and nurses, and bottles and tubes. "I'll be all right," she said, but then her face collapsed. "Charles, just promise me you'll keep the baby here, with us. Don't let them take him away to the nursery. Swear to me or I can't bear it." Charles promised very firmly and picked up the baby, who was sleeping in his bassinet, and held him so that Anne could see. But, he thought, she was impossible.

Looking out the doorway of her cubicle in the intensive care unit that night, Charles saw death lounging in the gleaming hallway just outside; he was about Charles's age, rather handsome, casually dressed, and stared quizzically back when Charles stared at him. And he was there again in the morning and throughout the day and the next day, shrugging or smiling mildly or pacing patiently, depending on the latest turn of events. He smoked cigarettes, and Charles, who had smoked years ago, yearned for one but wouldn't take it when he offered the pack in a friendly way. Charles wouldn't let him see the baby, either, and was frightened at how he kept trying to come nearer and nearer the bassinet, almost as though he were more interested in the baby than in Anne. Yet he seemed a gentle, humorous figure, not wholly without ordinary decency. He actually avoided eye contact when Anne began to convulse.

"What have you told the kids?" Charles asked Helen on the telephone, holding Gilbert. The figure of death was leaning against the wall right outside, listening in, which Charles resented. As though reading Charles's thoughts, he put his hands in his pockets and strolled a few yards down the corridor. Charles was too tired to fight against believing in him anymore.

"Nothing. I said the doctor said she had to stay because she was too tired. It's only been three days."

"We have to tell them something now. You tell them . . . let's see . . . she's very sick and sleeping all the time, and we're all really worried, but the doctors here are trying hard to help, and, uh, trying to make her feel better. Just tell them the doctors don't know yet what's making her sick. They don't need to know a diagnosis at this point. Helen, she woke up once this afternoon and asked how the kids and Gilbert were, and she said the kids should see Gilbert. So tell them you'll bring them to the lobby to-morrow and they can see Gilbert, but the doctors won't let them come up here."

"What do you think, Charles?" Helen asked, her voice shaking, and Charles remembered abruptly that Helen was Anne's mother. But she had to be told.

"It's bad, Helen. Very bad. I'm scared."

Charles sat by Anne's side for hours and sometimes sang softly to the baby. Her eyelids fluttered, and she could hear, he knew. She also heard the baby crying, but reacted to little else. The death figure, unfortunately, loved the singing and always drew close to listen.

Visitors, of course, came and hovered in the lobby. Charles would whis-per to Anne to tell her who was there, and, carrying the baby, would go out for a moment to talk to Merrit, Morris and Lily, and many more. Merrit had broken down and wept hopelessly in the lobby, but Morris put his hand on her shoulder and said, "Look, Merrit, this is no good. Take a walk around the block and pull yourself together. The kids are coming, and Charles will be down here any second. You don't want them to see you so upset, do you?" Merrit had shaken her head and walked out, not return-ing for twenty minutes. The girls were rapturous over the baby. Stuart, des-perately hungry for his parents, darted into Charles's arms and clung to him. He smiled shyly from Charles's lap when Helen brought out Gilbert, who was sucking a bottle, but got upset when the baby cried. "He misses Mommy," he said, looking worried. Charles said he probably did but that Daddy was taking care of him just fine.

That evening, when everyone else had gone, Father Merriweather showed up, looking anxious and sad. He'd come as soon as he heard, he said, and thought he'd sit with Charles, see if he needed anything. He showed no inclination to talk. Charles, who was surprised by his visit, was also surprised to find that it felt good having him around. Merriweather was a comforting presence, undemanding and reassuring, quite nontheo-logical. They even let him come with Charles into Anne's cubicle and stay after visiting hours ended; and after a while Charles, sitting with Merri-weather at the window across from Anne's bed, unburdened himself of his worries about the figure of death standing in the hallway.

"I can't tell anyone else. They'd think I'm crazy. Am I crazy?" He spoke in a low voice, almost a whisper, for sometimes it appeared that Anne was not entirely unconscious. They both looked at her, but there was no sign that she heard. She was still, except for the slight rise and fall of her chest when she breathed.

Merriweather, disconcerted by Charles's story, replied awkwardly, in an equally soft voice. "Of course not. I mean, there isn't anyone there, you know. You do realize . . . ? But it doesn't mean you're crazy. This happens commonly. Well, no . . . that's not quite . . . But people have, er, reactions under stress, you see. You're just a sensitive man."

"Can you do something about him? He terrifies me. I'm afraid Anne will see him."

"There's no one to see, Charles. I'll get your doctor for you. Maybe he can prescribe something to settle your nerves."

"Absolutely not. You hear me, Greg? I absolutely forbid you to tell any-one what I've just told you."

"Of course, Charles, I won't tell anyone. Actually, I'm supposed to be able to deal with this myself." Merriweather looked apologetic. "You wouldn't like it, though."

"What?"

"I should pray for Anne. Would that offend you?"

"Offend me? Good God, Greg. I'd feel ridiculous myself. But it's okay with me if you do it."

"Fine, then. But you know, Charles, you're like a lot of people who reject religion because it's so irrational and then end up buying into worse irrationality. 'When people stop believing in God, they'll believe in anything'—I read that somewhere, but I can't remember who said it."

Charles had no answer to this. He could see Greg's point—here he was with all his rational objections to prayer on the one hand, and, on the other, believing in something as crazy as the idea that death was a guy hanging around in the hallway just outside Anne's cubicle. The shoe fit, but it just wasn't Charles's style. Merriweather went to the window and leaned on the sill, looking out silently for a long time and, so Charles as-sumed at least, praying. Gilbert emitted treble snores in his little bassinet. Charles held Anne's hand. Then Merriweather patted Charles's shoulder tentatively. "I'll check in on you both tomorrow," he said. He squeezed Anne's hand for a moment, murmured something to her, and left.

Charles slept for a few hours on his cot, and when he woke up, the death figure was gone. He knew that he had had a brief psychotic episode and had chosen to seek help from a priest, not a psychiatrist. He was glad at least that they hadn't had to lead him away, ranting about the grim reaper, and drug him into acquiescent rationality. He felt unembarrassed about having told Merriweather. He wasn't quite sure just what Merriweather thought was happening, but knew he had a broad tolerance for the primitive and dark parts of the human soul—more than tolerance, he had respect for them.

The night nurse was there, doing her last check before she left. "I like these readings," she said neutrally. "Nothing's getting worse. Pulse is a tiny bit better. I'll see you next shift, Mr. Braithwaite. You continue resting. I'll take that baby to the nursery now. Your wife's not conscious. She won't know, and you can rest."

"Absolutely not! Do you hear me? The baby stays here. I'll have Anne's mother here to spell me. We're fine."

Anne's doctor, too, expressed cautious optimism when he examined her later that morning. She showed no further change by that evening, which, he said, was good news under the circumstances. Merriweather came again, and was touchingly happy when informed of Anne's progress. Nor, Charles was glad to see, did he appear to think his prayers had anything to do with it. He didn't bring up the death figure, but Charles thought it only decent to tell him that it had disappeared. On this subject, too, Merriweather appeared to think his own contributions were irrelevant. The two of them stayed by Anne's side for a while, then sat again beside the window and talked softly.

Merriweather, avoiding Charles's eye, talked about how the loss of religion had entailed the loss of a common moral ground based on a shared moral vocabulary and morally orienting stories that everyone knew. Religion was the only remaining reservoir of such things. Without them, he thought, people could sometimes go wildly off course without even knowing it; they got mixed up and could not see what was good and why good was better, and stronger, than evil. They put these issues on the same level as inconsequential matters of private taste, and had no idea how much thought and strength the moral life needed. Charles had only a confused notion of what Merriweather was driving at. He suspected that Merriweather had decided that he needed a lesson about something, which made him feel a bit resentful, but he made up his mind to listen politely; after all, he had asked the man for help.

"Those are things that people have lost their grip on," Merriweather said. "They're equally ignorant of Moses and of Gyges's ring, by the way. It's not as if they have some secular or classical tradition that helps. And then there are people," he continued with a timid smile, "who have lost half of it. They continue to think in moral terms derived from religion but treat their own moral sensibility as a kind of . . . attractive illusion, or I should really say *delusion*, shouldn't I? This puts them in all sorts of paradoxical positions—undermines what's best in them, undercuts their defense of the things and people that are most important to them, which leaves them frightened, really scared. And the thing that is most terrifying of all, of course, is their own capacity for evil."

Charles himself thought privately that the idea that goodness is better and stronger than evil was sort of silly, and so was the idea that people are terrified by their own capacity for evil. He'd never known anyone—other than Greg—who indulged in that kind of thinking who wasn't up to no good on some level. And did Greg mean to imply that there was any moral significance to Anne's dangerous illness? The idea that it was punishment, for example, was itself immoral. But Merriweather, when Charles confronted him with this thought, agreed and said he didn't mean that at all, simply that there were other moral dimensions involved in all of life's troubles. Charles smiled and would not argue further. Critical objectivity was unbecoming in him at the moment, in light of his debt to Merriweather; he kept his further thoughts to himself.

The conversation returned to Anne's condition, and the two men went and hovered over her, watching her diaphragm move up and down as she breathed and studying the pasty-white of her skin. "Her lips have more color, don't they?" Merriweather whispered. "I thought so too," Charles whispered back. They sat down and were silent for a while, and Charles noticed again how he felt better when Merriweather was around. Still, he hoped that Merriweather was not praying again, as he felt foolish participating even indirectly.

The next day, Anne's eyes opened briefly and she spoke; in the following twenty-four hours it became evident that she was rapidly mending. The doctor, baffled, said that he had not expected her to recover at all and that it was almost miraculous that she seemed to have suffered no damage to her health that time and rest wouldn't cure. The whole thing was peculiar and Anne-like, oddly Anne-ish, Charles thought, as though the course of the illness had taken the imprint of her personality and implausible optimism. Only Anne herself could have expected things to turn out as they had.

Remarkably soon, she managed to breast-feed Gilbert, who by this time had grown used to the plastic nipple and had to be coaxed. But his mother was an experienced and affectionate coaxer; and, she speculated, perhaps he remembered those first two or three times. Why not? That evening the other children, big-eyed and resentful of their days of loneliness and fear, came to visit and showered Anne with equal parts of affection and anger. She was not surprised that after the initial kisses, Stuart cried, Ellen sulked, and Jane was sarcastic. But they looked a bit more themselves when they left; they all kissed Gilbert good-bye and cooed at him. Charles refused to go home that night, because Anne still insisted on having the baby in the room, even though she was not strong enough to get out of bed to pick him up.

By the following evening, they had hired a private nurse to stay with Anne at night and help with the baby—this was no time to worry about spending money. Charles was sleeping at home; the danger had passed. It was strange, however, to return to ordinary existence when Charles had, in his mind, given it up and prepared himself for something darkly different. It made everything feel exaggerated and extreme, urgent. He wept over his morning coffee and choked on tears every time he tried to sing.

# 30

"I'VE COME TO the point," Anne said, "where I actually want that house. I'd be sad to think we'd never live there, and I would never have believed that I could feel this way." On a lazy Saturday morning, she was propped up on the living room sofa with pillows, comfortably disheveled, nursing Gilbert, with her feet nestled against Charles, who was reading a newspaper and absently caressing her ankle. She looked wan and haggard, but energy was returning to her voice and the fullness of pregnancy had already begun to recede from her face. Stuart was intent on building with Duplos on the floor near her. Ellen was reading the latest Harry Potter, curled up in an armchair. Jane was playing desultory scales. She had not practiced much since the day Gilbert was born. She had refused to play in the competition while her mother was so ill and now, where her music was concerned, felt aimless and lost. It wouldn't be the same next year, when she was fourteen; Anne had won when she was thirteen.

"Me too, Mommy," said Ellen. "I can't wait to have that room with little cupboards with doors." Ellen, like all of them, felt chastened by Anne's illness and was trying hard to be a good sport about the move, setting things right, as children do, by making a moral bargain with past events. She thinks that by being a good girl she's erasing danger that existed two weeks ago, Anne thought.

"And you'll have a new desk and bed, won't you. Janie, how do you feel about the move these days?"

"The house is okay, especially my room and the cherry tree. But I like it better in the city, and I don't want to go to a school with thousands of kids."

"I know, but the school has excellent teachers. I wish it was smaller, but eventually you find your niche in a place like that. It's like living in New York with seven million people. You don't have to deal with all seven million—just a few of them."

"Janie will be fine there," Charles said breezily. "It's Ellen who tends to go quiet in a crowd. But she'll do fine too. I'm just sorry you'll both have to start in the middle of the winter term. It'll all work out, though."

"Mom, I've been learning a part for this year's Gilbert and Sullivan at school. I'm going to try out," said Jane, obviously making an effort to appear casual.

"But, sweetheart," said Anne. "Isn't that in late February? We'll have moved. Better not." Anne realized that some bomb had just been dropped, and cast about vainly for clues to the size and nature of the explosion she should be expecting. How opaque Janie had become in just two weeks!

"I'll come back for the performances. I'll come in on the train for the final rehearsals."

This intensity about singing in a school production surprised Charles and Anne. Perhaps it was a way to hang on at her old school as long as possible, or perhaps she wanted compensation for her lost chance in the concerto competition. Anne suspected there was more going on. Eventually they would find out, but it would be futile to ask directly.

"If you explain your circumstances to Ms. Roselli and she agrees, we'll do our best to get you there," Charles decided, after he and Anne stared at each other for cues. Of course, it would be impossible, but neither of them could dredge up a no. Jane ran out of the room and was soon heard talking excitedly into the telephone. It rang a moment after she hung up.

It was the Nicholson-Kahns, calling to see where things stood. They were delighted to hear that Anne was back from the hospital and getting well. Naturally, they were anxious to get on with the closing. Unfortunately, Charles told them, Anne was under doctors' orders to delay moving, as she had had a very bad time and was still exceedingly weak. She shouldn't travel or do anything strenuous, like packing, and should stay near her doctors for the time being. It seemed likely that she would be on her feet by the end of January or thereabouts, but the original plan to move in the early part of January would have to be scuttled. If they wanted to close on schedule, perhaps they would like to buy the apartment, then rent it back to the Braithwaites until Anne got well enough to move.

These developments greatly upset the Nicholson-Kahns. They didn't know about any of this. They reminded Charles that he had agreed to be out by the first week in January, and they didn't want to get into being landlords. Charles concealed this conversation from Anne, and was not surprised when Nicholson called back within a half hour. It was very important to them, he said, to close earlier rather than later. Anything else would be a major inconvenience, and, as far as he was concerned, constituted a breach of their contract, which listed a closing date of December 28, and stated that "TIME IS OF THE ESSENCE." Did Charles really expect them to believe that in this day and age a woman needed weeks and weeks to recover from childbirth? They didn't know what he was up to, but they would be speaking to their lawyer on Monday morning, and no way were they going to forfeit their deposit.

Charles hung up on him, but this did little to relieve his feelings. At least their obligation to buy Mrs. Schaffner's house was conditional on the Braithwaites' closing on a sale of their own apartment. Now he had to tell Anne, who was at first chagrined, but soon felt optimistic about finding another buyer. They had to move fast, however. Anne called Mrs. Schaffner, who was greatly concerned about Anne's health and unconcerned about any delay. On Monday evening, Charles called the Nicholson-Kahns and said he would release them from their contract, and advised them to have their lawyers do what was necessary. The real estate agent promised to bring new prospective buyers the next day.

Charles went off to rehearsals the following morning. Merrit came by, darted around making the apartment neat, and then helped Anne bathe Gilbert. She got the older children ready to go off for a few hours with their grandmother, and bundled them up and put them on the elevator when Helen rang for them from the lobby. Anne put on the stylish robe Helen had brought her for the hospital and dabbed on a little lipstick.

"It makes me look more yellow," she complained, peering into a mirror Merrit held up to her face.

"Rub it off," Merrit ordered, digging in her bag for another color. "This'll do it." Anne tried it, and agreed. Then impulsively she reached up and took Merrit's face between her hands.

"Merrit, you don't look right. You're worrying everyone more than I am. Are you completely well?"

"I'm just tired lately. Actually, I've thought I might be anemic, or maybe I have a little thyroid problem. I canceled my Berkeley lecture. I just don't have the energy."

"But why not try to reschedule it? Promise me you'll see a doctor, right away. Or maybe you're just depressed. Is it all about babies? Must you see this as such a tragic absolute, black and white? There are so many ways in which that is just not true."

"I know. It's taking me some time to digest things. I'll pull out of it. But this is one adorable little boy you've got here. What a darling! Yes you are. You are so sweet . . . Anne, he smiled! He did!"

"The experts say they don't this young, but mine all did—I thought."

Merrit continued smiling and whispering nonsense in a high-pitched voice to the tiny, intent face. "See! Again!"

"Yes, that was a smile. He likes his aunt Merrit. You like pretty girls, darling, don't you."

The doorbell rang and Anne took Gilbert while Merrit greeted the first visitors, who arrived without the broker. She walked them through the apartment, pointing out several advantages in the layout and stressing how quiet the bedrooms were, how airy and well planned the kitchen. Anne was impressed both with Merrit's demeanor and her sensible comments.

"You're even better than the broker—more believable," she said when they had gone.

"But they won't take it," Merrit said. "It's too much for them. If they make an offer, it'll be too low. Anne, how do you like Lily Freund? She's wonderful, isn't she?" This last, intended to be enthusiastic, fell slightly flat.

"She is," Anne said, without conviction. "But they make an odd couple—at least so far. He hasn't figured out how to be himself with her or something. I don't quite get it."

"That's strange, seeing as how she thinks he's a god among men. The thought went through my mind that she's seeing not a false Morris but a highly . . . restrained one?"

"I think that's too suspicious. I think he's a god among men too—we'll never agree on that, I know—but he seems to lose his light side, his boyish mischief, around her."

"Maybe we're not saying anything different," Merrit said, looking sour.

"He may simply be overwhelmed with the seriousness of marriage," Anne reflected, "rather than responding to anything in Lily. And it's not as though he doesn't have other problems to deal with. His experiments didn't work out, and he's had to do some over and revise parts of his thinking."

Merrit had expected as much. Morris should have been content to work at backing up other people's research. He didn't have what it takes to go out on his own. "And what was the outcome of that quarrel he had in the summer with his ex-girlfriend about the cribbed data?"

"The essay was published, but he decided not to make any more fuss. He'll respond in print when he finishes this last series of experiments—if they work out."

"That's very strange, a combative man like Morris just letting it drop. Doesn't that suggest to you that there could be something a little fishy about his claim that they had no right to publish it?"

"Merrit! How could they possibly have a right to publish it?"

"If, in fact, it was produced in a collaboration, or if the idea was dreamed up by someone else, or if they had agreed to exchange results."

"No doubt they dreamed up some rationalization for publishing it, but that's all it amounts to. Merrit, as long as you've known Morris, have you ever known him to do anything downright dishonest?"

Merrit hesitated, then answered, "I'm not sure. It's possible."

"Whatever you think he did, I would be very sure that there's some explanation."

"And I'll bet that any ex-girlfriend of Morris would disagree with you."

"You don't know any of them, but you know me and you know Lily. Whatever his flaws, he is honest, Merrit, in all parts of his life. I can't imagine what lapse of integrity you accuse him of. I think you're being terribly unfair."

Merrit said nothing for a few moments. She was intimidated by Anne's unusual heat and thought of chalking it up to convalescent irritability, but began to feel unsure of herself and then remorseful. She shouldn't have made insinuations without being prepared to say what he had done wrong; she shouldn't have attempted to persuade his friends that he was a wrongdoer rather than a wronged party in his professional woes. Merrit recognized that she had said it vengefully, without considering why. The lapse of integrity she was thinking about was the incident with her, Merrit, on the mountain. But that might have happened before he was involved with Lily; and, even if it had happened afterward, she herself was as much to blame as Morris, maybe more. Moreover, aside from the questionable evidence of this one incident, nothing that Merrit knew about Morris suggested that he had any tendency to infidelity—whatever his other flaws. Merrit, finally, so regretted what she had said that she struggled to find words to rehabilitate herself in Anne's eyes.

"What you said is all true. I'm sorry I said what I did. It's unforgivable, but I hope you'll forgive me. I'm sort of going to pieces lately. I shouldn't burden you, but my . . . my physical problems. It's so unexpected. The doctor said that at thirty-eight—actually closer to thirty-nine now—it's not so premature, that this is quite common. But my mother was fifty-three, so that's what I counted on and I'm just not ready. I'm not ready to face the losses and all the physical changes. I dread the tests and . . ."

Anne conveyed her forgiveness with a squeeze of Merrit's hand. At the end of Merrit's awkward speech, however, a puzzled frown came over Anne's face and she began in a determined voice, "Wait a minute, Merrit . . ." But the doorbell rang, with more people to see the apartment.

"Wait for what?" Merrit asked, walking to the door. "It doesn't help me to pretend I don't know what's happening when it's so obvious. What's going to help is learning to face the music. But I haven't yet."

The conversation was cut short by the entry of the visitors, and, a short time later, Charles. "Well?" he asked hopefully when they had all left. Merrit and Anne both shook their heads pessimistically.

When Merrit had gone, Anne reported their conversations to Charles. "Good God," he said. "Well, I suppose it's a big divide in life. She didn't need this, did she? Five years ago, I couldn't imagine ever having to feel sorry for Merrit. That was foolish, wasn't it?"

# 31

MERRIWEATHER VISITED CHARLES and Anne with news about Lizzie's will. Morris, who had dropped by, as he often did on his way back to the lab in the evening, stayed to listen. With help from the church's lawyers, Merriweather had filed papers in Justice Jacobs's court contesting the 1998 will on behalf of Anne, Monique, and Claire, and Becker had filed answering papers. Justice Jacobs, in an unusual move, had retained jurisdiction of the will contest, which would ordinarily have gone to the surrogate's court. Her inquiry into Becker's fraudulent use of his mother's appointment as guardian for Elizabeth Miller, she had said, put her in charge of most of the relevant factual inquiries in both proceedings. The court papers made accusations and brought new facts to light. For one, the original guardianship documents, filed in court years ago, established that Lizzie Miller had cash and investments worth at least several millions when Mrs. Becker became her guardian; but all that remained in Eugene Becker's hands were investment accounts and bonds that had not yet matured, together worth perhaps ten thousand dollars. Becker maintained that everything was used for her support and maintenance or for charitable gifts according to her instructions. But his credibility was undermined by his prior suspension and questionable practices, by the absence of key records, and by the fact that he had not only failed to inform the Social Security Administration and her annuity fund of her death but had received and spent the monthly payments that arrived after she had died. Merriweather and the new court-appointed conservator were studying the documents separately, trying to determine whether Becker could conceivably have dispersed the assets solely for Lizzie's upkeep and her charitable giving, as he maintained. For the ordinary expectation would have been that with so much capital back in 1984, Lizzie would have had many millions when she died. The explanation Becker offered in his court papers was that there had been inflation, enormous cost of living increases, high medical expenses, Lizzie's insistence on making charitable gifts (including some to Becker himself), some unfortunate investments, and, in later years, yes, he had spent capital for her to live on. After all, she wasn't immortal, and, besides, only he himself was the ultimate loser. In the last couple of years, for lack of ready cash in her accounts, he had paid many of her expenses out of his own pocket. It was outrageous that after taking care of that woman for all those years, and freely spending down anything he could have hoped to inherit, even supporting her with his own money, he was to be accused of robbing her. It was outrageous and baseless. In fact, he maintained, the debts of the estate, owed largely to him, exceeded its assets.

Depositions submitted by Lizzie's caretakers, however, told a different story. They alleged that the Beckers were stingy and had provided minimal care, depriving Miss Miller of anything but the bare basics. They wouldn't pay to let her see her own doctors, but found cheaper ones. Back at the beginning, Miss Miller used to go on drives in hired cars, shop for little things for herself and her apartment, go to a concert or a play, but soon they were telling her she couldn't afford those things anymore. One former caretaker reported that Lizzie had fought with both the Beckers, mother and son, not long after Mrs. Becker's health began to decline. When the Beckers pushed hard, at one point, to have Lizzie move into a nursing home, she threatened to have Mrs. Becker replaced as guardian; they backed off and tried to calm her down. Lizzie told the caretaker then, "I have so little time left, it seems hardly worth it to fight them. It'd probably kill me." By the time Mrs. Becker died, Lizzie had not spoken to her for over a year. By the time Lizzie died, Becker was giving them barely money enough to buy her food.

The depositions mentioned only two occasions on which Becker had come to Lizzie's apartment. The first visit was in 1995, when Lizzie was ninety-nine years old. He had sent Josefa out of the room, but she could hear him talking angrily, although she was unable to make out the words. When he left, Lizzie was frightened and upset. The second time was the night before she died. Becker had called earlier that evening and spoken to

Lizzie, as he did three or four times a year. When he showed up later that night, he went into Lizzie's bedroom, where she was lying in bed listening to the radio. Monique hadn't heard any of their conversation, but Becker came out and went around the apartment feeling all the walls. Then he went in to talk to Lizzie again and finally left, saying she'd fallen asleep.

The news that Becker had visited Lizzie on the night she died startled and puzzled them. Had Becker been looking for the will? Had she finally told him he'd been disinherited? Perhaps he believed there was a wall safe. And could it have been—surely it was—the shock of seeing Becker, whom she hated and feared, that had actually killed her?

Claire's deposition for the most part laid out the story they already knew, with one disconcerting new fact: Lizzie had instructed Claire never to tell Becker about her 1995 will but to go to Willie, the doorman, after her death, and tell him where it was. Claire had done this, but Willie had told her that she should shut up about it and not get involved. Willie had scared her, so she did nothing. But she hadn't felt right about it, and was relieved to be able to set things straight when she was contacted by Merriweather. When Merriweather had tried to talk to Willie, he had answered only, "I'm not saying nothin'."

Becker had plausible explanations for everything. Lizzie's dislike, he chalked up to her age and her incomprehension of her circumstances. She was used to things being easy; she couldn't accept change. As for feeling the walls, he said he was checking to make sure things were clean and well cared for and that there was no dampness. He was concerned about Lizzie's lungs. There had been leaks in the past, and they had to worry about mold. Her death right after his visit was a bizarre coincidence. It had really shaken him up.

According to Merriweather, however, Monique said he was feeling the walls in rooms and closets where there had never been any leaks. Anyway, nine in the evening was an odd time to be checking for leaks, and why not call the handyman and have him check? So far, however, unless and until the accountants turned in their report with hard evidence that Becker had robbed Lizzie, nothing had been unearthed that was likely to prevent him from inheriting anything that remained of her property. Even incontrovertible evidence of thievery most likely would not affect his rights as heir. Charles was convinced that Becker had been stealing. Anne was not sure, except that she didn't doubt the validity of the 1998 will. Merriweather, however, thought the truth was probably quite close to what

Becker claimed. He'd helped himself to a little, perhaps, but by and large it was a case of a woman who had outlived her income and ended in dependency on someone whose care was grudging but not wholly indecent. Becker could have walked off, but he didn't. He kept hiring reliable caretakers and probably did, finally, reach into his own pocket, knowing he'd picked hers a little.

"This visit on the night before she died," Anne said. "Did he think she had some more money somewhere that she was holding back from him? I'll bet he needed money and maybe he thought she had some, or maybe he was trying to find valuables. I know she had some nice jewelry."

"There's certainly no secret wall safe," Morris said. "I had the wallpaper stripped. No wall safe. Wonder if there could be a floor safe."

"I wondered about that, too," Merriweather said. "Suppose Lizzie got mad and told him she had a will disinheriting him tucked away in a safe. So he starts looking for one, not realizing it's in the bank. Claire says Lizzie never had a safe or hiding place at home. Wouldn't she know if Lizzie had been secreting things somewhere in the apartment?"

"Probably," Anne said, "but not necessarily. They didn't stay with her every minute. She slept alone in her room, and she'd sit at the kitchen table alone with her tea or watch TV in the living room while they were cooking or cleaning. They'd leave her for an hour to run errands. After all, she wasn't really sick, just old and frail. When she was feeling well, she could walk around her apartment, and Claire said that even in her last week she'd still write checks and notes at her desk or at the kitchen table."

"What I don't understand," Charles said, "is why he continued to support her at all at the end, paying for all those women to work there. I don't think he has a conscience, so why didn't he just abandon her? He must have had a reason."

"I think he tripped over his own feet," Morris said. "If he just abandoned her, he would probably have gotten in all kinds of trouble. The caretakers might have gone to the police and said he robbed her. He needed to preserve appearances, show that he was taking good care of her, keeping her reasonably happy. Look, even as things are, the weakest point in any argument that he robbed her is the fact that he kept her in her apartment with around-the-clock care. He understood that. Greg, you obviously don't think that in the end he'll be accused of any serious wrongdoing. You don't really think he's guilty of anything, do you?"

"I'm sure that he robbed her a little," Merriweather replied. "But I think that if you keep digging into this, all you'll find is mitigation. Becker is greedy and crass, but those aren't crimes. And feeling the walls and hoping to find valuables aren't crimes, either. He's done his best. He really thinks he did right by her, and by his lights he did."

"It's also no crime to be suspicious when things look really fishy," Charles said.

# 32

"HAVE YOU HAD the tests yet?" asked Dr. Freilich, and Merrit heard his chair creak in the way that meant he was leaning forward. So this had gotten his attention.

"Not yet."

"Then you don't really know. Yet you announce this with great certainty, and begin your grieving in advance." He did not bother to conceal his exasperation.

"Let's not be silly. It's the hypothesis that is ninety-nine percent likely given the evidence we already have. Of course I'll have the tests done, but it's not like there's a rush. Dr. Crowley says she is fairly confident that this is what's going on."

"It may be the case, for all you or I know yet, but there are medically many possible causes of your disturbed menstrual cycle in the past six or eight months other than that you are menopausal at a relatively early age. You went through the strain of a major breakup, for example, and there are a dozen potential physical causes. I wonder about any doctor who would say such a thing before ordering tests and evaluating them, or looking seriously for other problems. It's surely a case that calls for a second opinion."

Merrit did not respond. They both considered.

"Have you had a pregnancy test?"

"What would be the point? My periods stopped months and months ago — long before . . ."

"Before you met Jeffrey Mayhew? So pregnancy may be quite unlikely, yet I would bet that most women in your circumstances would take a test, just to be sure. After all, it's perfectly easy to do, and you have only one doctor's opinion as to your infertility."

"I'm not going to put myself through the upset of a futile pregnancy test. At this point, being pregnant would be about as bad as being infertile, anyway."

"Why's that?" Merrit heard real curiosity in his voice.

"I don't know. I'd be a single mother."

"You could perhaps marry the father."

"No, I couldn't. It would be a terrible problem."

"You've said you're not in love with him, but are you sure that if you were pregnant . . ."

"I don't want to talk about it. Every time you say 'if you were pregnant' I want to scream. Can't you see this is painful to me?"

"Of course I can," said Dr. Freilich gently.

After her session, Merrit walked to Madison Avenue, where she stopped in a drugstore and bought a pregnancy test. She rode the M4 to 116th Street and went straight home and into her bathroom to take the test. The test showed bright pink. So that meant yes—positive. Pregnant. She read the paragraphs of tiny type on false positives, and called the 800 number. Yes, said the voice, some pathological conditions produce hormonal situations that mimic pregnancy. She should definitely check immediately with her doctor. Merrit ran to the drugstore and bought two more pregnancy tests by different manufacturers. Both showed positive. Yet they might all be false positives. She called Dr. Crowley, who was skeptical. "You'd better come in," she said. "We may as well start running some blood tests anyway. We should've done that long ago."

Dr. Crowley felt her uterus, and frowned. She took blood and urine samples and sent her to a lab that would give same-day results. Merrit paced the floor of her apartment, waiting until it was time to call for the results. They were unquestionably positive. Moreover, her hormone levels indicated that she was in her second trimester of pregnancy. Merrit understood that theoretically, none of this was possible for her, and she felt that Dr. Crowley, whom she called immediately, disapproved somehow. "You're sure then?"

"Yes, I was convinced from the physical exam. But I wanted double confirmation." Dr. Crowley sounded cool. "You need to think through your options."

"An abortion?" asked Merrit, horrified.

"A second-trimester abortion is a serious matter. I could help you with arrangements, if it's what you want, but . . . I don't know your circumstances."

Merrit called Anne as soon as she got home, and tried to run the block to her building, but stopped with a stitch in her side.

Anne was propped up on the sofa, nursing the baby while reading to Stuart. She was looking much better. Her skin was taut with a healthy color, and the bags under her eyes were almost gone. She had some trouble getting Stuart out of the room so that they could talk, but finally Ellen agreed to play with him in the bedroom, as a favor to Merrit.

"Prepare yourself for something strange, Anne. Just after the doctor told me I was infertile, I had unprotected intercourse. I wouldn't normally do that, but under the circumstances . . . I thought afterward I should have gotten a second opinion before I did something like that. But I just never dreamed . . . I should never, never, have . . . I'm pregnant. I just want to die."

"Are you out of your mind? Merrit, what are you saying? Yesterday you were ready to die because you couldn't have children."

"Anne, you don't understand. I can't raise a child without a father. Not me. I suppose I could have an abortion. I don't want to, but . . . my doctor said it was still a possibility. I just can't imagine it—a second-trimester abortion. But having a child without a father—I can't imagine that, either. I have no right. How could I ever explain to her? It's so wrong. I wanted children, but not like this. This is like one of those horrible fairy tales where you're granted your wish but you don't phrase it properly and you get it in a distorted form that makes you wretched. I might have to have an abortion, Anne, or lose my mind."

"But the child has a father. You'll just go tell Jeffrey that doctors are not infallible, and both of you should have known that. What's the problem? He'll be happy."

"I don't love Jeffrey. He doesn't love me."

"I don't know that I believe that. At all events, he'll love his child. Give it a try. If it doesn't work, you can separate down the road, but the child will have two parents at the start, and that will be vastly better for all of you. And maybe it'll work. And maybe it'll be a boy."

"Charles! Charles!" Anne had heard his key in the door. "Charles, Merrit is pregnant and she keeps saying she can't have the baby and she should have an abortion." Charles took several seconds to digest this extraordinary information, then turned on Merrit, outraged.

"Merrit, if you were thirteen, an abortion would be essential, but you're thirty-eight and desperate to have a child. This is some kind of insanity. You're not going to do this. I won't permit it." Charles realized, after announcing this, that he had no particular authority in the case, but neither Anne nor Merrit seemed to notice.

"You've got to call Jeffrey immediately," he continued.

"Jeffrey is not the father," Merrit confessed in a small voice, creating another round of silent shock. She seemed less agitated, however, having admitted this. "The father will not marry me."

"Who *is* the father?" Charles said, looking immensely tall from where Merrit and Anne sat on the sofa. "I'll kill him."

"I can't say."

"You can't say? You're not Hester Prynne, you know. We live in tolerant times. It's not—who? Not Brendan Whatsit? Oh my God!"

Merrit said, "I can't say who it is. He won't marry me. Believe me, I know what I'm talking about. I'm calming down now. I'll talk to him. I'll see whether he'll take any responsibility for the baby."

Anne was glad to see that Merrit had begun to talk in terms of the baby's actually being born, but Charles was offended again.

"What do you mean you'll see whether he'll take any responsibility? There's no choice, Merrit. He has no choice. You know that. You have to think straight on all this. What kind of jerk is he anyway?"

"I don't mean money. I suppose he'll contribute, but that isn't my problem. I mean raising it—being the baby's father. It would be a serious problem for him. You don't understand, Charles. You don't understand."

"Anne, do something with her. Where does she get these ideas? She means it was a married man, I suppose, and he'll have to face the music at home. Probably has six kids already. Great guy you picked to have fun with, Merrit."

Merrit sat staring now. "Charles, stop. I'm glad that my doctor at least tries to be neutral, or I'd lose my mind."

"Merrit," Anne said tenderly. "We can see how hard this is for you, and we don't want to make it worse. Charles is just upset—on your behalf. He thinks you're Janie or something. You know that. And I'm not so sure about that doctor of yours. Don't forget she also told you that you couldn't have any babies, without doing the kind of examination and tests that would give her any real basis for saying so. She's got an attitude. It seems to me, talking to Dr. Freilich is more important than talking to Dr. Crowley, seeing how far you've let this doctor—forgive me, Merrit, but you've let her mislead you for obviously neurotic reasons. How far along are you, anyway?"

Merrit ignored the question and got up to leave, saying she couldn't bear to discuss it anymore. But she insisted she was not angry, and promised to talk to the father and not to make any drastic decisions until she had also discussed things with Dr. Freilich. "I feel like your worst kid or something," she said. Both Charles and Anne kissed her when she left, and said she shouldn't worry.

"But she's better," Anne said. "She was wild when she came in. It is shocking, isn't it? I'll call her later and make sure she's all right."

Merrit went across the hallway and knocked on Morris's door, but he was out. She went home and called him at his lab.

"What is it?" he asked guardedly after a graduate student called him to the telephone saying it was someone named Merrit.

"I need to talk to you," she said.

"You do?" he asked, curious, slightly mollified.

"Right away."

"Well, okay . . . Naturally, I'm wondering why you would need to talk to me of all people right away. Is this something about Anne, maybe? Is she all right?"

"No. I'd rather wait to tell you in person. I'll meet you somewhere if that would be easier."

"Uh, sure. You wanna get dinner?"

"I have to see you alone."

"Lily's at a meeting in Boston."

"Okay. Any place quiet."

"Uh, the Symposium? Or 107 West or the Indian Café?"

"Symposium in half an hour?"

"Symposium, half an hour," said Morris.

# 33

IN A LIGHT snow that muffled traffic noises and slowly covered over the ordinary drab of the neighborhood, Merrit walked toward Broadway. She observed the twinkling lights on the cherry trees that lined the entrance to Columbia at 116th Street and looked at the students sitting near the windows in Ollie's, books and papers spread out on their tables, cramming mind and body simultaneously. How innocent it all was and how innocent they were, quietly pursuing knowledge, as Merrit used to. Merrit used to be innocent herself, but she could not help feeling that she had done something terribly wrong. She was pregnant with a child to whom she could not give the ordinary comforts and securities of an ordinary home and family. Lines from that Yeats poem she had always hated so—with its inveighing against anything in women that makes men uncomfortable, like too much beauty, brains, or strength of character—went accusingly through her mind: "And may her bridegroom bring her to a house / Where all's accustomed, ceremonious; / . . . / How but in custom and in ceremony / Are innocence and beauty born?" Her rational mind noted and feebly protested such crazy thinking, but the thoughts ducked or fled when she tried to pin them down and confront them. Broadway was nearly empty, although it was not quite eight. At least half the students had finished their exams and gone home, and the rest, like those in Ollie's, were cooped up somewhere warm, studying.

She turned left on 113th Street and walked down the steps into the Symposium. It was dark, cavelike, and quiet. How innocent were all the people in here too, how blameless the food and the waiters and the lumpy tables. Nothing in the menu, from the tzatziki to the spanakotiropita, nothing in the dark-wood decor, had changed in twenty years—probably longer, Merrit thought. Even the aged mints in the bowl next to the cash register were the same. For once unconcerned about arriving at an appointment early and looking over-eager, Merrit sat down and waited impatiently. She ordered a glass of wine, then, remembering, changed her order to bubbling water. Chagrined, she counted up the number of glasses of wine she had drunk during her pregnancy; well, they all had a glass of wine in France and no one had fetal alcohol syndrome. Her thoughts raced from this to other, increasingly inane, subjects, although she had hoped to collect herself and talk sense to Morris.

After fifteen minutes, the door opened and Morris entered, his nose reddened, a dusting of snow on his hair, and with fogged glasses. He blew his nose noisily, and, sitting down opposite Merrit, in his flat, Midwestern twang, with its insistent r's, remarked on how the snow was getting heavier. He seemed calm, imperturbable.

"Things tough at the lab, I heard," said Merrit, unable to plunge into things.

"We've had a few rough spots," Morris said with a stoical nod.

Merrit nodded, implying a grasp of what must be his feelings.

"I think you should . . ." she began, then stopped. She had been about to say "prepare yourself for something serious" when it occurred to her that he might not regard it as serious, might even regard it as her problem. Maybe he would sneer, or attack her. She felt suddenly small and unimportant, and sat silent for a minute, reining in a half-dozen inner demons who were screaming out these and other unpleasant hypotheses. After she had locked them away somewhere in the back of her mind, she began again. Morris watched all this play across her face with fascination. He had never before seen Merrit as unguarded and transparent as she was now.

"I'm pregnant," she said. "I just found out I'm fourteen weeks pregnant."

Morris's eyebrows lifted but he said nothing, thinking about this for several moments before he replied, with a curious mixture of delicacy and aggression. "Um, I don't want to jump to conclusions or anything, but you're telling me this, *me* you're telling, for a reason. I mean, I simply . . ."

"You're the father."

He was still, then nodded slowly, over and over again. "You're sure you're pregnant? I mean, I heard . . ."

"The doctor made a mistake about that."

"Look, I'm not accusing or anything, but naturally I'm wondering, under the circumstances—don't take this wrong, Merrit—can you really be sure *I* . . ."

"It's absolutely certainly that you are the father. There's no one else it could be."

"That guy Jeffrey?"

"Impossible. The timing would be way off." It was odd, she thought, that Morris knew his name, but it was not the time to bring this up.

They spent another half-hour laying out the facts in this fashion: statement; silence; delicately worded inquiry; statement; silence. At the end, Morris agreed that the facts must be as Merrit had stated them. They thought, and stared self-consciously at the table.

"What a mess," Morris finally said, and rubbed his face with his hands, reddening it. "I don't know what to say, what to think."

He thought it was very serious, Merrit noted, and slumped in relief. Then she tasted her food, and found she was ravenous. Morris watched her dig in, and after a few minutes tasted his own food.

"I'm sorry, Merrit. It's my fault, isn't it?"

"Why your fault?"

"I, uh, I mean, it was mostly my idea, wasn't it? You didn't jump on me, exactly. You were all cold and wet and hurt, with a sprained foot."

"I was open to suggestion."

"You really surprised me."

"I'll bet."

"I've never seen you eat so much."

"I've been this way for weeks."

"Did you ever think about it afterward?"

"What? You mean up on the mountain?" This, for a moment, stopped Merrit from eating. "I tried not to. I was embarrassed. And then you got engaged to someone else, whom I liked and didn't want to hurt."

"Yeah."

Morris began again. "I didn't have any ideas when I went looking for you, you know. I just felt bad that I didn't warn you when you set out."

Merrit waved her hand vaguely. She knew that, and surely there was no need to go into it.

"—And I got ideas only because you were glad to see me for once, and helping you change your wet shirt and sharing my coat with you was . . . cuddly."

Merrit remembered this, and how Morris had smelled close up, and her stomach fluttered. She put down the piece of pita with which she had been wiping her plate.

"It's okay," said Merrit. "We both got ideas. Morris, do you think I should have an abortion? I've always been against second-trimester abortions."

"Are you out of your mind?"

Morris, Merrit saw, looked positively appalled, which made her feel exceedingly uncomfortable, even though she did not understand why he had reacted this way. Not for a minute did she believe that Morris, the super-rationalist scientist, was morally shocked at the idea of an abortion. Moreover, being engaged to Lily, he would seem to have every reason to favor one.

"The baby won't have a real family, a father," Merrit said, and her sadness moved Morris.

"What am I, the fairy godmother?"

"You'll have another family, and that would make this child miserable. She'd think, Why does my father live with them and not me? And your other children would be harmed by knowing this child existed. Oh yes, I know we could survive all this, deal with it all, but wouldn't it be better just to make sure it doesn't happen?"

Morris grew indignant listening to this line of reasoning, and responded irritably. "No, that wouldn't be better."

"There's more. I'm not sure I can bear the life we're talking about. I couldn't bear feeling for the rest of my life that I'd let her down. And she'd be mad at me, and I'd be guilty as charged. And she'd have only me, really. There'd be no father in our home."

"It's a girl? How do you know?"

"No, I mean, whatever. Whichever it is, it's the same."

"Merrit, you mean you couldn't bear not having a guy yourself."

She nodded, and her eyes filled with tears, which softened Morris's anger.

"Of course you feel that way. That's nothing to be ashamed of, you know. If a woman is going to have a baby, she wants a guy. I'd feel the same way."

Merrit was not so far gone in despair to fail to register what Morris said as ridiculous, as well as disagreeable and, overall, false—however true it was in her own case. But guilt toward Lily was the stronger force in her mind. "You'll have to tell Lily. I'll do whatever you tell me to do to make it easier on her. Just tell me what you think is best."

This elicited a deep sigh from Morris. He did not object to the demand that he offer direction, but he did not know what to tell her. "I've never had a problem like this before," he said. "Never been in this type of jam . . . but . . . I'll talk to her when she gets back, and I'll let you know . . . how things are." He waited for Merrit to respond, but she could come up with no answer but a sigh of her own.

"Seeing how things have turned out," he continued, "I want you to know that I've thought about that night over and over again. I never told Lily, but she has some kind of sixth sense about it. It's like being engaged to a Jedi princess or Santa Claus or something. She gets feelings about things, and they're right. She just knows. Anyway, on the one hand I felt bad about how it happened, but on the other I really . . ."

"Stop!" Merrit said. "This is no good. This is making it worse."

The open expression on Morris's face disappeared with this rebuff. "Merrit, what do you want me to do?" he asked, reverting to the snide tone of voice he ordinarily used with her. He waited, but she didn't answer. "You called me up and said you had to talk to me. So what do you want from me? Just be straight."

"Well, I'm not sure but . . . at least don't marry Lily. Not yet, anyway."

"Hm?"

"That gives us some time."

"For what? Come on, Merrit. What do you need time for?"

"I need time to think. Maybe you and I could, for example . . . I don't know, make some arrangement. Maybe we could share rearing this child somehow. If we both live in this neighborhood, we could cooperate easily and . . ."

"Merrit, I don't know what you want, but my plans in life are to get married and have a family. Besides, you just said it was bad for the baby if the father didn't live in the same house."

"Yes, I know, but it may be the best we can do. Unless, well, maybe this is crazy, but I suppose we could live together."

"I want a wife. I'm not going to live with anyone but my wife."

"Why do you care so much about a flimsy legalism? Let's talk about how we should live."

"Merrit, you were making sense before, but that's garbage. I've been straight with you. I'm going to get married, but I'll be a father to this child. It's that simple."

"Then marry me."

"Hm?"

"Then marry me, not Lily."

Morris, looking stupefied, considered this proposition for what seemed to Merrit a very long time. She was hardly less surprised than Morris by what she had said. Yet, having said it, she began to think it was a good idea, in fact, the only possible solution; and when Morris, having finally gathered his wits, began to speak, his response was a mixture of satisfaction and circumspection. "Now you're making sense," said Morris. "Of course that's what you want. That's good. That's really good. Now, I'm not sure I can . . ."

Merrit started.

"That's right. I'm not sure I can. I'm engaged to Lily, and I have to talk to her. And I'm not sure you and I should be married, because there is a lot more to straighten out here. But it's good you're clear on what you want, and I am too. You want me to marry you. Good. Very good! That's a start at setting things straight."

Merrit started snickering.

"What's so funny?"

"If you won't marry me, Charles is going to kill you."

"You told them . . . ?"

"No! I told Anne I was pregnant, but I wouldn't say who it was. I told Charles that the father wouldn't marry me, and he said, 'Tell me who it is. I'll kill him.' "

Morris sniggered, and Merrit giggled uncontrollably.

"Why were you so sure I wouldn't marry you?"

"Only because you've always hated me, and you're engaged to someone else." Merrit's giggling fit subsided, and she saddened again.

"This conversation is not over, you understand," Morris said. "But I've got to talk to Lily now, before we go any further."

Merrit nodded.

"I have to say one more thing." Morris's voice had a foreboding, dissonant note in it, and Merrit, having received so many blows lately, braced herself for one more.

"You know, I love you. Ever since the beginning—remember that summer when I was staying with Charles and Anne—you made sure I knew it was no-go. Remember?"

Merrit nodded.

"You knew it, didn't you?"

Merrit, hesitated, then nodded again.

"It used to irk the hell out of me that you knew I was in love with you and pretended you didn't. You pretended you didn't even like me—when on some level I got the message that actually you did. Walk you home?"

Merrit nodded.

"You got enough food at home to last you till morning?"

# 34

AFTER THE INITIAL flurry of papers, phone calls, and cagey conversations, the participants in the Becker case were coming to the conclusion Merriweather had pointed to weeks ago—that there could be no clear proof that during Elizabeth Miller's lifetime Becker had robbed her of significant sums. Or, rather, the people involved could not afford to pay the accountants, investigators, and lawyers whose work would be necessary to provide clear proof. Becker had undeniably defrauded the Social Security Administration and the annuity fund. But had he really made such stupid investments, or had he faked the records? Was it Lizzie or someone else who had received costly medical treatments or spent large amounts for furnishings or on charities years ago? It would have taken tens of thousands of dollars to answer these questions. Moreover, if Becker was her heir, as Lizzie aged and her wants and capacities diminished, any thievery of his actually deprived her of very little, and it all would have been his in the end anyway—which must have affected his thinking.

Not only was there very little left in the estate, but Becker himself would make large claims against it, for he could easily establish that he had at times paid her expenses with his own money. Charles and Anne suggested to Merriweather that they offer to settle with Becker if Becker would agree to give the cash in the bank account at 113th Street to Claire and Monique. Although Becker had loudly protested this idea, Merriweather thought he intended to agree to it later, when he wouldn't seem overanxious.

A few days before Christmas, Father Merriweather came to have dinner with the Braithwaites and give them the latest legal report. When he arrived, seeing Willie on duty at the doorman's desk, he stopped to chat about the snow and how quiet the neighborhood was when the students had all gone home for the holidays. Turning the conversation to Lizzie Miller, he induced Willie to go so far as to opine that Becker cared nothing about her welfare. Becker had showed up soon after she died—to go through her things, Willie guessed. Merriweather again tried, as delicately as possible, to find out why Willie had told Claire not to tell anyone where Lizzie's will was. But on this subject Willie was still mum.

"I don't know nothin' about that," said Willie, eyes fixed on a point ten feet behind Merriweather and slightly to his right.

Merriweather continued to look hopefully at Willie.

"I don't know nothin'," said Willie.

Merriweather then wondered aloud whether Becker and Willie had ever talked about Lizzie or about anything else, but Willie knew nothing about this, either.

Having duly admired Gilbert, distributed Christmas candies to the other children, and exclaimed appreciatively that something smelled delicious, Merriweather told Charles and Anne that Becker had actually provided an inventory of Lizzie's household goods, which he had put in storage and had appraised. He had been about to sell them off when he was stopped by Justice Jacobs, after Merriweather's visit to the court. Lizzie appeared to have had some valuable things—silver, paintings, rugs, crystal, and china, and all of it would have been Anne's under the 1995 will.

"No jewelry?" asked Anne. "I know she had a couple of nice pieces, but of course Becker probably just put anything like that right in his pocket."

Merriweather agreed, and turned to the mystery of Willie's conduct. He found it hard to understand why Lizzie had wanted Claire to inform Willie, of all people, about the will, but it made perfect sense to the Braithwaites.

"He's the old people's lifeline," Anne said. "He keeps tabs on all of them—he's the one who got Mary O'Reilly a social worker, and he makes sure Al Bernstein eats breakfast."

The only puzzling thing was that Willie had fallen down on the job. They were all sure that there must be some reason why.

"I've got an idea," Charles said. He walked to the telephone and called Mr. Morales, who knew everything that went on in the building.

"I have to talk to you, Mr. Morales," Charles said. "Would it be okay if I come down for a minute?"

Charles went to the basement and was met at the door by Mr. Morales, who led him to his living room, which was half-dark and filled with respectable overstuffed furniture. Framed photographs of well-dressed relatives, carefully posed in groups, crowded the walls and tabletops. Mr. Morales poured a cup of strong, dark coffee for Charles, without asking whether he would like any, and Charles drank it with pleasure. He told Mr. Morales about the discovery of Elizabeth Miller's 1995 will in the bank deposit box, the court case with Becker, and Willie's silence about the existence of the will.

"Why didn't Willie tell someone about the will?" Charles asked at the conclusion of his recital, which had elicited a pained frown from Mr. Morales.

"Your wife was the heir under that will?" Mr. Morales asked. "Then she would own Ms. Miller's apartment, if that will was valid."

"No. Lizzie rented her apartment. She didn't own it."

"Of course she owned it."

"What?"

"Becker almost sold it months ago, but the deal fell through, and then he said things were tied up in the estate."

"Good God. You're sure she owned it? He's never listed it among her assets."

"Most certainly she did."

"If she owned it, then Becker has kept it a secret from the court and he's in big trouble. Why didn't you tell me?"

"You never asked me. I never knew you wanted to know."

"So Becker was paying the maintenance and mortgage every month?"

"Sure. I hear he was complaining about the assessment and the increases. He says she can't pay."

"But Lizzie didn't know she owned the apartment. She thought she rented it."

"She was old. She got mixed-up."

"Morales, come on. She wasn't mixed-up. He never told her. Did he buy when we did? When the building went co-op?"

"Sure. Him, his mother, I don't know, someone signed everything back then."

"Did you ever discuss this with Miss Miller?"

"Why would I? I never talked to the old lady. She couldn't talk. I could never hear what she said. If we did talk, we said nothing more than good morning. I talked to her women up there if there were repairs or leaks."

"But now things make sense. As her guardian, Becker got his hands on everything she had—except the apartment. He couldn't take that, because she was living in it, and, anyway, people get lawyers who ask lots of questions when they're buying real estate. It would have been very tricky to sell it while she was alive. So instead, he just sat tight and watched it appreciate and made sure he'd inherit it when she died. That new will, from 1998, has got to be a forgery."

"Braithwaite, I don't believe what you're saying. Look, maybe the newer will is real. And why shouldn't he have the place? He had the trouble of seeing about her all those years. That's no small thing. Who else should have it?"

"Look, Morales, he stole from her. It's beginning to look like he stole a lot from her. He spent her money on himself, and he didn't treat her so well. She was afraid of him. He took everything but her food and the roof over her head."

"It can't be true."

Here both of them were quiet for a moment while Mr. Morales poured a brandy for Charles. The weak winter sun had set, and they sat in darkness relieved only by a small, dim table lamp while Morales thought, sighing and clasping his hands. Charles was familiar with his style of thinking. The idea had to be filtered through his entire character, so that its full meaning could be parsed in a leisurely and thorough way and its implications plotted by means of some complex inner compass. Otherwise, Mr. Morales might be guilty of something that could later feel like a misstep. He was a man whose calmness reflected his confidence that he meant whatever he did—which is different, Charles thought, from confidence that whatever he did was right.

"Well," Mr. Morales finally said agreeably. "It's a mess, eh? But let it be a little while, and we'll see. I'll talk to Willie. Let things fall into place, and then we'll see."

Charles nodded and sipped, as relaxed as Mr. Morales. He always liked talking to Morales, and on this occasion stayed as long as possible to hear his reflections on these strange developments. Almost an hour had passed when Anne telephoned to hurry him. "The kids are starving, and this is so rude, Charles." Only then did he depart, shaking Morales's hand and offering warm thanks for the hospitality. Everyone at home was annoyed until they heard what Morales had said, and then the talk at dinner grew hectic as they imagined the possibilities. Of course, this changed everything.

"We were within an inch of settling with that S.O.B.," said Charles, "and never finding out what he was up to. Still, you wonder how he thought he was going to get away with this."

"From the beginning, he knew we didn't know that she owned the apartment," Anne pointed out, "because you were talking to him about her rent when you set things up for Morris. So why were we going to find out now? And if we did find out, we would also have figured out that he was deceiving her, because we knew that *she* thought she was a renter. So he had to just keep his fingers crossed."

Of the three adults, Merriweather was most surprised, having from the beginning, in his own mind, circumscribed the arena of Becker's misconduct. He had always insisted that the man would go only so far. Confronted with such gross deception and greed, Merriweather grew more and more uneasy. When they had known nothing, he was confident that they knew everything; and now that they were learning the truth, he was filled with dark and growing doubts.

# 35

BECKER WAS IN his office telling Josephine Slevinski not to talk to any lawyers or to any of those people from the church, and Josephine was forming an uncomfortable idea that she knew things that could get him in trouble.

But just what she knew, and what kind of trouble, she was not certain, except that she had signed things, often without really knowing what they were. The more she understood how stupid that had been, the more upset she got. One of the papers she had signed was a will, despite having been told in class that a will had to be witnessed in the presence of the testator or testatrix, among other requisites, all very technical. She had signed because Becker had told her, "In the real world, witnesses sign wherever and whenever it's convenient. Who would ever know otherwise? Nobody follows all those ridiculous rules they teach in law school." She was not sure that it was the will that was worrying Becker, but it seemed possible.

Judging from Becker's intensity, Josephine guessed that whatever trouble he was in might be serious. That she herself might also be involved made her feel ashamed and uneasy. She would have felt better if Becker had allowed a little team solidarity to develop in the face of these troubles. Josephine had always felt a subterranean attraction to him, and so, instead of being angry with him, was disposed to feel sorry for him—if only he would accept a little human feeling between them. The man didn't seem to have a friend in the world, despite his middle-aged good looks and Ivy credentials, which had always both beguiled her and intimidated her. Tonight, he seemed weak and vulnerable, and on impulse Josephine spoke as an equal, rather than up to him, for the first time.

"You need to take it easy," she said with a comradely sympathy. "Why not meet me after class for a drink or something?"

Becker had been expecting something like this, and half smiled. He had noticed how Josephine always came in all got-up and perfumed. But, he thought, openly appraising her, she wasn't pretty enough to get him to jump over the class line for her—or smart enough, either.

"I don't drink with the help," he said, still wearing the little smile.

Josephine, painfully humiliated, muttered something and walked out, slightly awkward in new stacked mules, which drew attention to her legs. Becker had always noticed that she had nice legs. But legs are not enough, he said to himself, reconsidering as he watched her exit.

Josephine did not appear in the office the next day, and did not answer when he called her at home. Her mother, on Long Island, was wary, and insisted that she didn't know where Josephine was. Becker had already begun to think that he would see no more of Josephine, which would be a serious inconvenience, when, opening a file cabinet, he discovered that things were missing. She had been back here last night and taken things. She had fled.

But that was good! No one could depose her now, which was a great relief. She had taken some things she had signed, he noticed. She was afraid he'd get her in trouble—that was it—and she was trying to destroy any evidence of her own wrongdoing, the little twit. She was truly simpleminded.

It was hard to know what all she had taken. He began to sort through the files, and soon came to a large empty place in the drawer. It looked as though she'd taken all the court papers from the Miller case. Every damn document that had been filed in court, from every party, along with his personal working file. She had cleaned him out. Now how was he supposed to . . . This was a problem. It would look funny going to the court for copies of everything. Could he go to Merriweather?

He tried to remember what was in the file that might present a problem or give Josephine ideas. But after a little thought he was reassured; she wasn't bright, and she wasn't going to come up with ideas the other side didn't already have. The answer to everything was just to make sure she stayed away long enough so that it didn't matter. This could be accomplished by making a few angry telephone calls to her answering machine and her mother. When she lifted those files, she gave him good reason to be furious. Anyone would be.

Becker had resigned himself to the likelihood of another disciplinary suspension of his right to practice law. He could live through that. The thing now was to keep his hands on what remained of Lizzie's money and, more important, her apartment, which he reckoned would bring seven figures in this market. No one had figured out that it was part of her estate. Only an unlucky accident could disclose it, and Becker was the lucky type. The worrisome thought that Josephine would find something in the files about Lizzie's apartment crossed his mind, but he went through them mentally and reassured himself that they contained nothing about it.

Having thought things through, Becker was prepared to stop worrying about Josephine, if he could just be sure that Merriweather or one of the accountants had not put her up to this, and he thought he could be. He knew her. She had done this by herself, for one reason: she feared that something might endanger her brilliant legal career. It had been shrewd, having her sign things and telling her that she too was in trouble. It meant that she would stay out of the way, and she wouldn't be anxious to cooperate with the other side.

# 36

MORRIS HAD CALLED Lily in Boston to forewarn her. There were serious issues to be discussed when she got home. This caused her no alarm. Tackling emotional issues was what she lived for. Sitting in her living room the next day, she listened to Morris's recital with fascination and an utter lack of hostility, nodding slowly at the conclusion. The silence that followed was unnerving to Morris, but Lily was concentrating so hard that she noticed neither the pause nor Morris's discomfort.

"This won't work," Lily said finally. "Neither of you is really interested in being married to the other. You're interested in the baby."

Morris found himself wishing to protest this interpretation, but he stopped himself because it felt ungallant.

"Of course, it's important to do right by the baby. It won't work, but it might be better for the baby if you tried. That is certainly possible. But," Lily continued, "what about us? I understand what you're trying to do, and it makes sense. But are you really obliged to tear up your whole life?"

Morris tried to find kind words for the facts, and, failing, remained silent. The truth was that he'd rather marry Merrit. He'd fallen in love with Merrit years ago, back when she had been too interested in eminent older men and too contemptuous of him to give him the time of day. Lily resumed speaking before he could decide what he should and should not say.

"This incident that left her pregnant," Lily said. "What was that all about? It sounds as though you were feeling sorry for her, or you just wanted to be nice. Under the circumstances, of course, you had no thought or fear of pregnancy." This time Lily waited for Morris to speak.

"Actually, I can't really say it was pure generosity on my part."

"And what about her? She's not exactly a fan of yours. Why would she do this out of the blue?"

"I don't know." This sounded rude, but Morris really did not know, and he was beginning to feel interrogated.

"Are you telling me," asked Lily, finally grasping the situation, "that you'll marry me if I insist but that otherwise you'll marry Merrit?" Morris could not dissent.

Lily was incredulous and outraged now. He was saying, more or less, that he didn't want to marry her but that he felt duty-bound to do so. What a strange man he was—duty-bound to fulfill an engagement at the end of the twentieth century!

Morris knew that this wasn't much of an offer, but then again, he thought, what was she offering him? She wasn't in love with him—he could swear it. She was sexually friendly, but without any real passion. She was lukewarm on the subject of children, although she'd accommodate his wishes. Yet she did seem very much to want to marry Morris. This, he couldn't understand. A woman doesn't really want to be married or a mother, but she wants to marry *me*, *really* wants to marry me, and will have my kids if I insist. Morris, at length, said all this to Lily, and then demanded, in a nasty voice she had once heard him use to Merrit, "So what kind of marriage do you have in mind, anyway?"

Lily was shocked by his incivility. Until now, all their conversation had been warm and kind. Morris watched her cheeks redden, and realized that for the first time he had made her angry and she had made him angry. This was unexpectedly gratifying.

"Now things are a little more realistic at least," he said in the same rough way. It infuriated her, but she was not altogether sure of her ground. She did not want to give Morris up, but she couldn't see how to avoid it.

"This is off the pale! You act as though I should just congratulate both of you!" Lily cried, in an attempt at sarcasm that momentarily mystified Morris. "How do you expect me to feel?"

These words, being so garbled, were not as moving as they might otherwise have been to the guilt-ridden Morris. "I don't know," he replied. "What does a woman feel who claims a right to go around engaging in mock marriages?" Off the wall—or off the charts? Beyond the pale? he wondered. Surely she had some brain disorder.

"What about you? You're saying you were doing the same thing."

"I was wrong," said Morris, thinking how often, lately, he had said those words. "And this sounds bad, but the fact is that at first I was following your lead. I was actually relying on your judgment that we were doing something that made sense, because I had my doubts. That wasn't right, and I'm not blaming you for it. But as we got closer and closer, the whole idea was getting to be a strain. I was beginning to think we should postpone it or call it off, which you knew as well as I did. That's why you were taking all those trips and hanging out with Jonathan, or bringing him along all the time. You knew, but you were going to try to coax me into it, because it suited you for reasons I don't get. You tried to tell yourself you were marrying me for my sake, didn't you? You thought I was some kind of cripple, so what you had to offer was good enough. Isn't that it?"

"Weeks before we're supposed to get married, you announce that you've gotten another woman pregnant," Lily said bitterly, "and somehow in your mind it ends up that I have wronged you. Maybe Merrit was right about you all along."

"Does this mean you're breaking our engagement?"

"*You've* broken our engagement."

"Whatever. It's broken, and we agree on that?"

"You couldn't marry anyone else unless I *agreed* to break the engagement? You're reasoning on the moral level of a seven-year-old."

"I try to keep my promises."

"You're kidding yourself. This is inhuman and mechanical. I wouldn't have believed it. Merrit doesn't know you. Even she would not believe this."

"I'll tell her, don't worry," Morris said, and left.

Now it was Merrit's turn to hear a recital by Morris in her living room. She found it distressing, and cringed guiltily in her mind before Lily's righteous fury. As he had promised, Morris told Merrit what Lily had said about his making Lily out to be the wrongdoer even though he was the one who got someone else pregnant and broke their engagement; how he had said he would feel obligated to marry her if she insisted; and, further, how Lily had remarked that Merrit had been right about Morris all along.

Merrit, however, had spent the intervening twenty-four hours pondering the revelations they had made to each other at their last meeting—that Morris loved her, and that she was pregnant with his child. These two circumstances, it became increasingly clear, were not so terribly painful as she might have expected. In fact, although for hours she tried to conceal it from herself, she was soon forced to recognize that she was having some remarkably sweet feelings about the whole thing. Her face, reflected in the mirror, was no longer drained and sunken. She remembered that summer, years ago, when she had met Morris and treated him almost with disdain. She was ashamed of it now, but knew that she had been trying to forestall his getting ideas, because, of course, she had recognized that he already had some. But Morris had implied that Merrit, too, had had some ideas back then, and Merrit was newly able to recognize how that might be true, how those ideas might have been stored in a corner of her mind that she had refused to look into until the past few months. If so—and Merrit was almost willing to admit it—then perhaps her cruelty years ago was aimed as much at her own tender feelings as at Morris's. There could be no doubt, however, that her misconduct, and possibly her blindness, had inspired Morris to reciprocate.

The more they understood the peculiar history of their relations, the more they found themselves forgiving each other. Now, in fact, Merrit discovered that she didn't mind Morris's loving her—not a bit. Didn't think him presumptuous at all, didn't object to his feeling sorry for her, didn't worry that when they had been together at the Symposium he perceived how very hungry she was in every way. The truth was, Merrit admitted to herself, that all her cold, hard feelings about Morris were melting away since she had heard his confession there. She replayed the entire scene again and again in her mind, from its start with her own humiliating sense of exposure and need, to its conclusion with Morris's confessing, in effect, that he had spent most of his adult life avoiding the same feelings—by convincing himself and her that he disliked and disapproved of her.

In the end, therefore, Merrit bore up nicely. Despite her guilty sense of having betrayed Lily, she began to feel a sneaking delight in the thought of marrying Morris; and Morris, once he had settled things with Lily, took it quite for granted that this is what they should do. Part of her took pleasure in his absurd straight-arrow approach to resolving the predicament in which they were all entangled. That was his style, and she could not altogether object to it. Once she might have called it simpleminded. Now it struck her as being direct; perhaps it had a kind of strength. In fact, many qualities in him that used to madden her acquired a sudden appeal. Having Morris's anger and critical judgment deployed on her side, instead of against her, was rather agreeable. His once-odious grin had a new boyish charm. Morris, reading a good deal of this on her face, was encouraged to lean over and kiss her, and she didn't mind that, either.

# 37

ONE OVERCAST MORNING in December, just before the school holidays, Anne's brother, Paul, drove her, Charles, and the baby to Putnam County to visit the children's new schools. They arrived early enough to look around Putnamville, a shabby, elderly cluster of shops and houses, which in its prime had served the farmers who used to populate the surrounding countryside. Anne, still weak but unwilling to stay at home, sat in the car while Paul and Charles, taking turns carrying Gilbert, walked up and down the main street, peering into shop windows. There were few pedestrians, and gusts of chill wind took Gilbert's breath and made him cry.

Putnamville seemed to be denatured, in the manner of hundreds of other small upstate towns that had lost their purpose. Three streets intersected at the town center, which included a dry cleaner, a medical office, a hair salon that still thought it necessary to advertise its services as "unisex," a hardware store, a used-furniture store, a women's clothing store filled with the sort of matronly garments that had not been seen in Manhattan for two decades. The drugstore was part of a chain. The shopkeepers and almost everyone else whom they saw were astonishingly overweight by city standards.

"No movie," Charles noted, looking around him. "No greengrocer. No supermarket, newsstand, library, bookstore, shoe repair."

"You go to the mall," Paul said, "and into bigger towns, or the city, for fancier stuff. The chain stores for clothes are at the mall, too."

There was a small WPA-built post office, which they admired, with its rows of ornate cast-metal mailboxes, labor-worshiping murals, and sturdy redbrick walls.

Watching from the car, Anne thought that Charles looked needlessly dramatic in these surroundings. Repressed indignation stiffened his posture and hardened his face. His excessive good looks—at least to Anne they seemed a bit over the top here in Putnamville—gave a foolish emphasis to these signs of his emotions. She watched as Paul and Charles entered a deli/grocery/diner for coffee and bagels, which they carried back to share with her. "Sugar in the bagels," Anne said.

They left Putnamville and drove through sundry stands of houses that, to their city-trained eyes, appeared to have haphazard and pointless locations; and they drove slowly past their own future house, just to let Paul see it, but hadn't the will to knock on the door and respond to Mrs. Schaffner's stream of hungry chatter. Wherever they went, the streets were empty.

"It's chilly," Anne said.

"The adults are at work," said Charles, "and the kids are in school and day care. There's no one here except a few old folks."

"No sidewalks," said Paul. "People don't go out walking where there're no sidewalks."

"And no place to walk to," Anne said.

They were scheduled to visit Stuart's nursery school first, then Ellen and Jane's school. At the nursery school, the classrooms felt, they thought, flat. The preschool teachers they had known in Morningside Heights had a mission, a spark. They had gone to Columbia Teachers College and Bank Street and had a devotional intensity about tiny children, which was backed up by graduate work in child psychology and reading readiness. Here, however, Charles and Anne thought the children were simply coaxed, doggedly, into orderliness and phonics. Not only did they fail to interest their teachers, but the teachers appeared to categorize everything the children did and said as either expected, and thus uninteresting, or as unexpected, and therefore an annoying disruption of the days' plans. "I've been taking so much for granted," Anne said, thinking of what might happen to Stuart's enchanting ways if they were met with mere tolerance instead of the animated responsiveness he had been used to. The new teachers looked kind enough, however, and perhaps that was the main thing.

Ellen and Jane's school was a sprawling modern place, low-built and surrounded by acres of treeless grass campus. Inside, there were large tiles in bright colors on the walls and floors, upbeat messages on bulletin boards, and mazes of hallways that thousands of children navigated with loud voices and quiet, sneakered feet. In the classroom that Ellen would join, the atmosphere was calm and friendly, and the teacher and the curriculum seemed almost as good as those in her Manhattan school. Told that Ellen and Jane were musical, the principal encouraged Anne and Charles to have Jane sign up for band. But Charles snapped that she would not be taking band, and Anne had to squeeze his arm warningly. The principal was a nondescript man, whose bland looks and manners belied a will of iron. He refused to enter Jane in advanced English and Composition. After all, her grades were something short of mediocre, and Charles and Anne's urgency that she be offered a sophisticated education in literature only increased his determination. A girl like Jane would be more comfortable with students on her own level, he told them as they left.

Outside the principal's office, Charles and Anne examined posters for a student production of *Annie Get Your Gun* while waiting for Paul, who had been wandering the building. Paul, like most lawyers, made snap decisions about what facts portended. He began to envisage the Braithwaites in Putnam County, wearing social masks and concealing their tastes and opinions; he imagined the children, like immigrants' children, negotiating between their foreign parents and this new society, which would be their only escape from childhood. They'd have to join. Charles and Anne would lose one or two of them for a good while, maybe permanently. Paul decided, in two or three minutes, that he opposed the move.

"That was really depressing," said Anne. "That man thinks Janie will be more comfortable with the less-bright kids of southern Putnam County. A man who thinks our daughter doesn't need to read Shakespeare or William Blake is in charge of educating her."

"I don't know, you guys," Paul said, choosing his words carefully. "It's not too late to back out of this. I mean, Scarsdale would be one thing. With this place, you're really out there. And after school your kids are going to have no place to go but that mall over there."

"We can't afford places like Scarsdale," said Charles. "No place is going to be like Manhattan, but I didn't see this one coming. I never thought they could have all those good programs at the school but keep Janie out of them. I assumed that she would be entitled to whatever good things the school offered."

"She'd have to study hard," Paul said. "It's public school. Before, you bought her access to things. Now she has to compete for the goodies or she won't get them. Charles, you know Janie won't do that. You can't bring her here. Anne, you have time to rethink." He stopped, however, when he saw Charles glowering. He was aware that Charles was cold to his sister lately. While not without sympathy for what he imagined were Charles's complaints, it was Anne he felt sorry for. But she would have to find her own way out of this one.

They timed the drive home: one and a half hours. At rush hour it would be much more, and it would take still longer to Lincoln Center on the train. Paul drove them to their door, but wouldn't come up.

"We're back," Anne called from the foyer. "Oh no. Is this Janie's backpack? Did she forget it?"

Helen met them in the hall, looking worried.

"She's in her room. Something happened at school, and she came home early, but I can't get her to tell me anything. She says she's got a bad bellyache."

"When . . ."

"About ten minutes ago, she just showed up, crying, and went into her room. We'd better call the school," Helen said. "I'm not sure she told anyone she was leaving."

Anne put Gilbert in his bassinet while Charles went to Jane.

"As far as I can figure out," he said, after ten minutes in her room, "it was those same girls again, the ones she tangled with last spring—at least three of them were from last spring. There were five or six this time, she thinks."

"They travel in packs—feral brats," Anne said. She was slumped in a kitchen chair, exhausted from the trip, her face lined with what had become habitual anxiety.

"It sounds like all they did was tell her in a singsong voice that they loved her nails and her hair and her cool sweater. I told you not to let her go to school looking like that."

"Don't blame me, Charles."

"Anyway, why can't she handle that? They only do it because they see she's so fragile."

"She insists on chewing her nails down to the quick and tying her hair in a knot and wearing my old black sweater. That's why they do it."

"Have you noticed that she's stopped practicing?"

"Of course."

"She was using music as a defense against a lot of that stuff."

"Yes, she let go of her music and started worrying about what they think. Charles, she'll be out of this school in a month or two, but she'll have the same thing to cope with up there. The kids there will think she smells different, too, and that's what it's about."

"We should've sent her to some progressive school, like Bank Street."

"We've been over that a thousand times."

"Anyhow, Ellen doesn't smell like them either, but she never has troubles like this."

"Ellen's troubles are worse. She isn't forward enough to attract the teasing, but she doesn't make many friends at school and Jane does."

Helen interrupted in a sharp voice full of maternal authority. "Both girls are fine. Their clothes are fine. They're not lonely."

Anne felt a sudden warm release from her anxiety and found herself going teary. Surely her mother was right and things weren't so bad after all. But Charles, in breach of longstanding familial conventions that tolerated — even courted — Helen's occasional intervention in matters concerning the children, responded with princely ire. "Don't interfere, Helen. Leave the children to us."

Charles had never entirely forgiven Helen for spoiling Jane with clothes and expensive pens and notebooks when Jane had wanted to drop out of school a few months before, even though Helen had taken Charles's side entirely. In his own cutting words, however, Charles recognized the sound of his father's voice berating his mother, and wished he had not spoken them. Yet he did not apologize, and stalked out.

After he had gone, Anne said, "I don't know what it is — it isn't you, Mother — but I'm beginning to close in on it." Helen merely looked stoic. Charles had married Anne and therefore had become her son, sometimes annoying but beloved no matter what he did. She had been through worse, she told Paul that night on the telephone, and Paul told Greta the story. Greta, a freelance editor who worked regular hours in a tiny office off their living room, thought Anne should never have had that baby, or Stuart either for that matter, and should earn more money. Paul and Greta were good with money. They could afford just two children, and had no more.

In the wake of this sour incident, Anne realized that Charles worried about Janie but not about the others. He thought of Ellen as a second, perfect Anne — Anne without the excessive sense of entitlement and confidence, or the annoying perceptions of Charles himself. Stuart he worshiped, and never thought Stuart had any problems. Janie is the problem child for both of us, Anne thought, and she's the one Helen thinks is perfect.

"Who worries me is you two, not the kids," Helen said, prompting Anne to the disquieting thought that perhaps Janie's difficulty was precisely the fact that her parents experienced her as a problem child. But she was not prepared to arm her mother with such an idea, not with Charles having acted the way he had, and, indeed, she felt that her mother should not have remarked on whatever marital tensions she had picked up. Any need to sidestep the subject, however, was obviated by a shriek from the hallway—"Mom! Mommy!"—so alarming that it gave Anne strength to fly to Jane while Helen ran to Gilbert, who was wakened by the noise and screamed irritably. Stuart, laid for a nap on Charles and Anne's bed, slept on despite Anne's bustling mysteriously in and out of the room.

A half-hour later, Anne reappeared in the kitchen, and Charles, who was too worried about Jane to stay away, came to hear the report. Even in his resentment and trepidation, he saw that Anne was drained, and had an impulse to carry her in to bed.

"She got her period. Her first period."

"My God," said Charles.

Helen laughed triumphantly. "Can I tell her Mazel Tov?"

"By all means. She's in there feeling proud of herself," said Anne, and, turning to Charles, told him, all smiles, "That must be why she was so emotional, with a bellyache."

Charles was quiet for several minutes, dumbstruck, Anne thought, and she herself sat silent with exhaustion. "What does a father say to a daughter under these circumstances?" he asked.

"I was just remembering. My father told me, 'Now you're a woman,' and the next day he gave me my pretty jeweled watch. Not too original but it sent the right message."

"I doubt my father knew anything about it when my sister got hers," Charles said. "Seems like the wrong thing for the occasion though— a watch—doesn't it?"

"Maybe his mind was on time flying."

After thinking it over, Charles announced, "I guess I'll get her a dressy watch. Nothing else seems serious enough."

Anne found this funny but was too tired to laugh. At least, she thought, they had a bit of a truce to get them through dinner with the children. She wouldn't let Charles carry her, but went to nap on their bed beside Stuart, who, when he awoke, was enraptured to find her fast asleep beside him.

That evening, after the children were in bed, Anne tapped softly on the door of Charles's studio, where he had spent several hours studying a new part he had been offered—a leading part in the world premiere at the Met of a new opera. "We don't think anyone in the world could handle this the way you could," they had said.

"The problem is," he told Anne, "I just don't like the thing. It's junk. I can't do myself any good with this part, and it would be easy to do myself harm, vocally and otherwise. This idiot knows nothing about singing. The vocal demands are insane. And it's for nothing. Musically, it's worth nothing. No matter how well I sing it, I will be criticized."

"Why on earth are they doing it?"

"Half politics, half idiocy. I keep thinking I just won't do it, but then I think about the money. And then more politics—what the fallout will be if I turn it down. Gus says it would be just short of suicidal. I know agents never like you to turn big things down, but this time I'm sure he's right."

"Who cares? Since when do you listen to your agent? They should let Risono do it. He'd stand up there and sing random noises for three hours if they asked him to. Why did they have to ask *you*?"

"Risono couldn't do this. It's very, very difficult."

"Charles, it's fine with me if you just don't do it. If you hate it and it's such a physical strain, you shouldn't do it, sweetheart." Both of them knew that not long ago, Charles would not have hesitated to turn down a part like this, and he would have been indifferent to the consequences. What did this new hesitation mean? They sat on the lumpy sofa in the studio, enervated. Anne's pallor and thinness frightened Charles and for a moment he felt tender, as he had when she first returned from the hospital. He put his arm around her and resolved to pay more attention to whether she was eating enough, yet could not help feeling annoyed that she added to his anxieties—no matter that this was, he knew, unkind and unfair.

They sat as they were for another five minutes, both aware of darkening, stormy feelings that their feeble mutual offers of affection did nothing to relieve.

Charles's annoyance broke first. "I find it maddening that you say, 'Just don't do it,'" he began, and Anne knew immediately what he meant, "when both of us know perfectly well that I don't have that option. It's just a way for you to avoid facing how much responsibility you have for putting me in the position I'm in. We need money so desperately that I'm going to have to abandon my standards and risk damaging my voice."

"That's not fair, and it isn't why you're mad at me, either. You've been in a rage with me for months and months, and it's affecting the kids. My mother is watching us like a hawk."

"I don't know why you decide, in all this chaos and stress, that it's me that's upsetting the kids."

"Because it is." But she regretted saying this when she saw the fury in his face. She had rarely seen him so angry.

"What do you want me to do?" she asked. "Tell me what you want."

"There's nothing you can do now, but it might help if you could be honest about things. If you hadn't had the baby, you could have started making some money. We could've had one less tuition bill, one less mouth to feed. We could've slept nights and had some time for each other. Maybe we could've made a go of it here in the city—sell this place and buy something else. Now we're in for another three years of night feedings and croup and all that. We lose our home. We stop living in a society and instead live in . . . a yard. I can't teach at home. I'm spending three hours a day on the train. I could make this list indefinitely long. But you had to have another baby."

"You know what I think? I think it was you, Charles, not me. I did nothing to get pregnant. You know that."

The discussion was old, but this idea was new; and it left Charles briefly mute, then livid with cold fury. "I know nothing of the kind. You'll say anything, won't you? I know, on the contrary, you always get pregnant exactly when you want to—not a month sooner or later. It's incredible, your control over it all."

"I have no more control over this process than any other woman. But even though I didn't purposely get myself pregnant, Charles, I did want another baby very badly. You're right that I was longing for another baby."

"I had no doubts on the subject."

"You have a hard time telling me no. Sometimes I think you're pathologically generous to me. You give me things, but not because you want me to have them."

"Sometimes I think you're pathologically spoiled and selfish."

"Which is fine with you as long as you can be the same way. But I think you couldn't bear that I should not have another baby when I wanted it so much. Let me point out again that the means of avoiding pregnancy were at the time in your hands, not mine."

"Just what are you getting at? I never took any chances—not that it would make any difference if I had. You're the one who makes it all happen."

"Charles! That's lunatic. I don't know what you did, exactly. But we both knew, from February on, that I had no birth control, and from then on it was up to you. This little family joke about me being able to control it all is just that."

Charles stood up and paced the tiny room, as though restraining angry words, but, Anne perceived after a few moments, his irritation was feigned; and in a few more minutes, Charles made a noise that was something between a snort and a laugh. He continued pacing, but there was a hint of a spring in his step.

"You did it on purpose, didn't you?" Anne said, seeing that he was no longer disposed to deny it. She had not been sure, when she proposed the idea, that it was true, but this reaction was more or less an admission that he had gotten her pregnant and then furiously blamed her for it—for months. Now Anne felt that she had a right to be angry. She was not angry about his getting her pregnant. That was mere psychological mishap, for which she had perfect tolerance; that the unconscious should take over for a split second or two was something that could happen to anybody. But that he had so abused her for it, and subjected her to months of cold rage—and now felt free to find it so amusing . . . Her sudden sense of release from guilt gave her energy, and, exhausted as she was, she got to her feet and glared at him.

"Anne, it could just be true, you know. Maybe it was me. I'm kind of remembering this one night when . . ." Charles began, his voice tight with latent mirth.

"What are you so cheery about? Why aren't you ashamed of putting me through all that? You can stand there and laugh?"

"It just strikes me as funny—if I really did it after all. And maybe I did. I knew that it would be a major disappointment in life for you if you had only three children, and I had a kind of superstition about that—something like an idea that if even Anne could suffer and be denied, then all hell might break loose."

"I'm so glad you made sure we were all safe," Anne said. Charles noticed, however, that her sarcasm had no bite.

"It was the least I could do. Don't pretend you're so mad, Anne. It's a *folie à deux*. It took two to bring this one off. You were perfectly willing to take the rap for nine months, if that was the price for getting a baby, and I was willing to give you a baby as long as you were willing to take the rap. I wasn't going to be so irresponsible as to have a baby when we were in such money trouble. We'll have to make the best of it. Anyway, he's a cute little guy."

"I love him so," Anne burst out, weeping, and Charles knew that what he had said was true and that she knew it. "He's so patient and good-humored about everything, and so trusting. It was unbearable to think I had no right to have him, and that you saw him as our ruin."

"Oh, I imagine we'll be all right," Charles said. And with this, Anne thought, they had succeeded in transforming their neurotic misery into or-dinary unhappiness. She had always known they would, but it had been a long time coming. In her relief, she collapsed onto Charles's sofa and told him that she was so exhausted she thought she'd sleep there, but this time he did carry her to bed.

"Imagine being Merrit or Morris, Charles, trying to grow up in their cir-cumstances, trying to get into the game and join the parent generation at this point in life," Anne said before falling asleep.

"I can't."

"Janie's grown-up now, isn't she? She's getting into the game."

"Well, Anne, that's not . . ." But Charles was too tired to finish the thought.

# 38

JOSEPHINE SLEVINSKI RODE the No. 2 train from Borough Hall in Brooklyn to Chambers Street in Manhattan. From there, leaning into a bitter wind, she walked to the county courthouse, where she found the clerk and handed him an envelope. She had intended to say that it was urgent and the judge should read it immediately, but was overcome with misgivings. What if she was wrong about everything? Why didn't she have someone read this first? But having begun, she couldn't back out now. The clerk asked what it was about. "The Elizabeth Miller case," she said in a faint voice. "You'll see when you read it." Josephine was intimidated by the grandeur of the court and the severity of the clerk, and was alarmed by her own temerity. She suppressed tears of self-pity. It was almost Christmas, and she intended to leave the court and take the Long Island Rail Road to visit her mother, who would offer love, safety, and moral clarity.

"The letter tells how to reach me," she said, turning to go. "Just don't tell Mr. Becker about this please."

The clerk knew Becker's name.

"Young lady, you'd better stick around a minute," said the clerk. He pointed to a chair, and Josephine sat, not daring to disobey, despite her desperate longing for home. "Did you know we have a lawyers' conference in this case this afternoon?" he asked her. "All the parties are going to convene to discuss a calendar, and it's possible some claims are going to be withdrawn. There may not be much of a case left, in fact, after today."

"Then maybe—" Josephine began, rising and reaching for the letter, but the clerk said he would have the judge read it right away.

Three hours later, Father Merriweather and others involved in the Miller case convened in Justice Jacobs's courtroom. Merriweather was curious to see Josephine, whom he recognized from Becker's office, sitting in a front row, off to the side. An accountant arrived next, quickly followed by two lawyers from the church and the new court-appointed conservator of the Miller estate. Becker arrived late, a full minute after Justice Jacobs had taken her seat at the bench. He walked up the center aisle confidently until he saw Josephine; then he hesitated, turned, and walked casually back to the door. Justice Jacobs, however, called out to Becker to be seated, and the bailiff, at a nod from her, shut the door and stood before it. When Becker muttered that he wanted to visit the men's room, the bailiff stood with his arms crossed, impassive, and pointed to the chairs at the front of the courtroom. Becker sat down to the right of the church lawyers. Two men, whom Merriweather did not recognize, arrived last and sat on a bench near the door. Becker stared at them also, trying to figure out whom they might represent: the bank, presumably, although he was surprised they'd send one lawyer, let alone two, for the chicken feed involved here, unless they thought they had some liability exposure or unless somebody had been holding out on him about Lizzie's assets—a thought that made him bristle.

"All right, I'll hear statements from two of the parties before we get down to business," Justice Jacobs began. "Mr. Becker, why don't you begin?"

"Thank you, Your Honor," Becker said, coming to his feet. "I want to provide some context for this whole discussion. I'm in an awkward situation, as I'm sure you appreciate. I acted informally as guardian for Elizabeth Miller for many, many years. She was my mother's best friend and a second mother to me when I was growing up. She took care of us when times were hard. We took care of her when she got too old to take care of herself. Now you're looking at the records in the case, and what you see is a lot of very sloppy stuff. I won't argue about that. I didn't pay much attention to formalities, because the understanding between us was too good. Yes, I should have gotten myself appointed guardian. I didn't bother. Miss Miller wanted me to take care of her affairs. I didn't want to, but my mother was sick and they both begged, so I did it. That was it. I did what they wanted. In fact, most of the time I did whatever I did with her property because she told me to. Can I prove that today? Not always so easy. And sometimes I didn't really agree, or think it was best. But she was the boss, and she was like my mother. So I'd argue with her and then do what she wanted—for a long time, anyway."

Merriweather had to give Becker credit for a very smooth, plausible delivery, with that crunchy-peanut-butter voice, the respectful dignity of that suit, of his whole manner, and the appeal for help and understanding in his handsome face. Good heavens, Merriweather thought, his courage ebbing as he listened to Becker's statement and observed, doubtfully, the wizened little woman on the bench. It was discouraging to think that this poor old soul, who had been assigned to review guardians' reports, had stumbled into responsibility for an increasingly troubling and complex case. Merriweather was unsure whether she was up to something like this, and feared that Becker would prevail despite the evidence of his wrongdoing that would be introduced in court today.

"Eventually, money started to get tight," Becker was saying. "She got poor, but she was used to having plenty of money and she never really believed she didn't anymore. It made her mad when I tried to tell her. She started to have bad days, when she seemed senile, paranoid, and was very unfriendly. I looked past that. I tried to keep things as much the same as possible for her, but I couldn't do everything she wanted, because the money just wasn't there. At first, I wasn't too worried, because, let's face it, she wasn't getting any younger. I assumed she'd have enough to make it to the end, even though I was spending down her capital—which I did for one reason: to keep her in her home. That's what she wanted more than anything. I knew the money was going to run out, but when she hit a hundred, the doctors were saying she had only months, days maybe, left. By the time she hit a hundred and three, I was paying to keep her at home out of my own pocket. I'm not complaining. I wanted to do it. But it would be extremely unjust, unfair, Your Honor, if the informality of our arrangement—which was highly consensual—were to be regarded as evidence of wrongdoing. And this would also be contrary to the purpose of the guardianship statute. So I'd like to ask the ladies and gentlemen representing the various parties here if we could avoid spending a lot of time showing where I didn't cross t's and dot i's, because I'm not going to argue about that. I admit it. But Miss Miller lived to one hundred and three, with around-the-clock care in her own home, and died in her own bed. As the saying goes, where's the beef? I only hope someday I'm as lucky as she was. I get nothing out of this, which doesn't matter to me, but if I could break even that would be nice. Thank you, Your Honor."

"All right, Mr. Becker. That's an interesting approach to the mess you're in here. Now, the gentleman from . . . the Episcopal archdiocese? . . . Mr. Merriweather, representing Claire Cooke, Monique Javelle, and Anne Braithwaite, tells me they have some news for the court."

Merriweather was startled, and heartened, by the justice's irritable comment, and his confidence began to rise again. She did seem to have been listening, taking it all in. And her remark was certainly not friendly to Becker. "Your Honor," Merriweather said, "we had originally expected to be able to withdraw our motion and settle the case at this conference, but we have just learned that Mr. Becker has concealed from the court the Miller estate's most valuable asset. In 1988, when the building at 117th Street went co-op, Mr. Becker, or his mother—it's not clear which— appears to have purchased Miss Miller's apartment in an insider sale, in her name, purportedly acting for her but in actuality acting against her wishes, and never told her about it. Indeed, we don't see how we can avoid concluding that this was done with the intention of defrauding and robbing her. We suggest that although Mr. Becker's original plan was to acquire the apartment under the so-called 1998 will, inheriting it, he concealed from us and from the court the fact that it was part of Miss Miller's estate for a variety of reasons. He was trying to make sure that my clients believed there was next to nothing in her estate so that they would have no motive to contest the will, or, if they did, would settle without demanding much. And he was also trying to make sure that he would be able to gain ownership of it fraudulently even if he lost a will contest or never bothered with probate. I would suppose that he was using her income to pay the maintenance and mortgage on this place, without her knowledge, of course, and that's one reason why she was so poor in her last years. We'll submit these documents establishing ownership, with some appraisals attached. We also submit affidavits from Claire Cooke, Anne Braithwaite, and Victor Marx and Mary O'Reilly, two other residents of this building, who knew Miss Miller, stating that Lizzie Miller always believed that she lived in her apartment under a rental lease and refused to buy it."

"Were there any other holdouts in that insider sale of co-op shares?" asked Justice Jacobs.

"Yes indeed, Your Honor. Quite a few, from what I've been told. In fact, another of them is Mary O'Reilly, whose deposition you have in front of you."

"So these are people with fixed incomes who have stabilized low rents, presumably, and they fear they won't be able to afford owning their apartments."

"Yes, Your Honor. The Braithwaites, in fact, are at this moment trying to sell, because they can't afford the greatly increased monthly costs of their co-op. If you're advanced in years, with a fixed income, and what matters most to you is just staying in your home, you might be wise not to buy—and that, apparently, is the decision Miss Miller arrived at."

"Well, Mr. Becker," said Justice Jacobs nonchalantly, looking at the depositions. "This is quite a sizable oversight on your part. Is this one of the *t*'s or *i*'s you were referring to just now?"

"Your Honor, she intended me to have it. She knew I was buying it. Naturally, the people who would inherit under the 1995 will, and their friends, are going to say Miss Miller didn't know about it. But she most certainly did."

"But you see, Mr. Becker," said Justice Jacobs, "we have no reason to believe you. There is strong testimony against you on this point, plus the self-evident intent to deceive the court as to a matter of assets worth sizable amounts of money. The more we see of these deceits, the less reason we have to believe in the validity of this will dated 1998 or in anything else you may have to say. Now, ladies and gentlemen, I'm going to ask you to be patient while I read to you parts of a letter I've just received today from Josephine M. Slevinski."

Becker frowned but looked calm. "You know, Your Honor, you're making a big mistake here. This young lady has stolen documents from my office. She—"

"It states here," Justice Jacobs continued, holding up her hand to silence Becker, "that Ms. Slevinski is a law student who worked part-time as a legal intern in Mr. Becker's office from February of this year through this past week. Is that correct, Ms. Slevinski?"

Josephine answered, "Yes, Your Honor," in a barely audible voice. In response to a whispered communication, Justice Jacobs announced, "And Mr. Mahoney further informs me that he was able to confirm that much with some telephone calls. I'll read here a portion of the letter that particularly addresses what we've heard this morning. It says, 'Sometime before 9:45 A.M. on April 17, 1999, Mr. Becker asked me to fill in the witness signature on a will for an old lady who had died. He said that it was accidentally omitted, and that it would be perfectly all right for me to do this. I should have known better, but I didn't, and I signed my name as a witness there in Mr. Becker's office without reading the will. Later, when I read it and saw that it named Mr. Becker sole heir, I began to be worried about what I had done, but Mr. Becker said that the will was a mere formality as there was no property involved. According to Mr. Becker, Ms. Miller had been his mother's best friend and, since she had no family, wished Mr. Becker to have her personal effects, which had only sentimental value, after her death.

" 'This week,' Ms. Slevinski goes on to say, 'I discovered in Mr. Becker's files a death certificate for Ms. Miller, and learned that she had died sometime on the evening of April 16, 1999. I vividly remembered signing her will months ago, and remembered that Mr. Becker had asked me to do so the minute I arrived at work, before I had even removed my coat or sat down at my desk. I know that it was the morning of the 17th, because Mr. Becker required me to keep a diary in which everything I did was recorded. My first entry on the 17th is "sign will, E. Miller." In addition, I checked the file manager of the computer I work on in the office and learned that I first saved a document at 9:45 that morning, showing that I signed the will before 9:45 A.M. (I enclose a Xerox of the time diary page and a printout of the computer file manager with that entry highlighted.)

" 'This week, reading the court files for this case, I also learned that Ms. Claire Cooke, caretaker for Ms. Miller, had called Mr. Becker on the morning I signed the will to inform him that Ms. Miller had died. I confirmed this by Mr. Becker's office telephone log, which showed a call from Claire Cooke for Mr. Becker at 10:25 A.M. I also learned from the court files that Mr. Becker had visited Ms. Miller on the night that she died. I concluded, therefore, based on Mr. Becker's statements to me, that Mr. Becker must have known that Ms. Miller was dead before Claire Cooke called and that he must have known she was dead, or dying, before he left her.

" 'I removed this log, along with other files, from Mr. Becker's office. I realize that this was probably wrong, but I wasn't sure how else the evidence could be preserved.'

"Skipping now to the end of the letter, where Ms. Slevinski states:

" 'I am sorry for any wrong I have done, and hope to make it right somehow.' You stick by all that, do you, Ms. Slevinski?"

"I do, Your Honor," Josephine murmured.

"We have present in the courtroom two police officers. Officers," Justice Jacobs continued, addressing the two strangers at the back of the court,

"Mr. Becker here, it appears likely, stole from the deceased, Miss Miller, and made no effort to get help for a dying woman, to call a doctor, to report the death, or anything like that, and her death was not discovered for many hours. I think you should arrest Mr. Becker, and we'll turn this case over to the district attorney. I would expect the D.A. will want to bring charges related to the stealing, and maybe charges related to Miss Miller's death. Criminally negligent homicide is a possibility that's crossed my mind—they used to call it 'depraved heart' murder, Ms. Slevinski—but it's up to the D.A. Mr. Becker, you know how it all works. The officers will fill you in on the particulars, and you will be arraigned and bail will be set in the proper court. Officers, this man's credibility with this Court is very low, and my opinion is that he would be likely to skip bail and tamper with evidence and testimony. So the district attorney has to find out what's been going on over here right away. But, officers, if you don't mind hanging around for a minute, I want Mr. Becker present until we adjourn."

"We'll hang, Your Honor," said one of the detectives as they walked toward Becker.

"Your Honor," Becker cried. "You're doing this all on the word of a totally dishonest, disgruntled employee. She's stolen documents out of my office. Why aren't you arresting *her*? She was the false witness. She's lied endlessly . . . and, and . . . Your Honor, I mean, if you'd seen Lizzie Miller, you'd know—this woman was a hundred and three. I just kind of expected her to die momentarily, that was all. I just misspoke because she was so obviously on her last legs. This is crazy." Becker sounded so convincingly like an outraged and injured innocent that Merriweather wondered about the man's grip on reality. Surely this could not be acting.

"There will be time for all that later, Mr. Becker," said Justice Jacobs, not unkindly, with an air of speaking to someone she knew well.

"But, Your Honor, none of these charges make any sense. And as for negligent homicide, this is lunatic. This woman didn't have one foot in the grave; she was in there up to her neck. How can you murder someone who's almost a corpse, whose life expectancy is minus a few years? Failure to render aid to a hundred-and-three-year-old woman who might be dying? That's doing her a favor! Her life is worthless, over. No hospital in the city would resuscitate her. Besides, it wasn't like that at all—not a thing like that. This is lunatic. Totally lunatic."

"This Court has no jurisdiction over those issues, Mr. Becker. Right now it's in the hands of the police and the district attorney."

The officers sat on either side of Becker while Justice Jacobs spoke to the tense courtroom. "Mr. Becker seems to be under the impression that there is no right to life beyond our statistical life expectancies. But this is untrue. We have a right to every day of life our bodies can support, no matter if other people are not so lucky as to live so long, and even if we are silent, weak, alone, expensive, uninteresting to our neighbors, and in the way. And no human being has the right to decide that any of our days are so low in value or pointless that he can take them from us. Likewise, we never grow so old that other people have a right to make free with our property because they think they would enjoy it more than we do.

"We're going to have to hold a hearing to determine the credibility of Ms. Slevinski's testimony and rule on Mr. Becker's petition to probate the 1998 will. If Ms. Slevinski's testimony holds up, the 1995 will is the valid will and the 1998 one is fraudulent. This 1995 will would make Claire Cooke, Monique Javelle, and Anne Braithwaite the heirs of Elizabeth Miller, entitled to her bank account, bonds, personalty, and apartment, and if it's proven that Mr. Becker plundered the estate, these persons would be entitled to recoup from him, to the extent he has any assets to go against. I want everyone to cooperate with the district attorney's office so that any facts relating to criminal proceedings can be established expeditiously. I'm going to ask the conservator especially to help us learn what property there is. I understand he's already made great progress in looking into any possible debts of the estate so he can pay them up and see to the distribution of the property as Ms. Miller intended. Ms. Slevinski, it's no disgrace to make a mistake, and we are grateful to you for having come forward. It took some courage. Happy holidays to all. Let's come back rested and ready to resume in January. Court is adjourned."

# 39

OUTSIDE THE COURTHOUSE, snow was falling in the twilight, and the gray court district, covered over with white that was iridescent under the streetlamps, lost its forbidding aspect and looked kindly and humane. Father Merriweather walked to the subway station and rode north. By the time he arrived at the 116th Street station, the snow was heavy; he longed for his boots and muffler as he plodded through the slush to 635 West 117th Street. Minutes before Merriweather arrived, Charles had gone down to the lobby for the mail and found Mr. Morales and Willie in serious consultation at the doorman's station, their faces at right angles, their voices low. Clearly, a major communication had been made, and something was being decided. Charles stepped over to them, looking through a fistful of bills and letters. "Morales, I thought you'd like to know that Becker is going to be in big trouble in court today. When the lawyers and the conservator found out what you told me about Miss Miller's apartment, they went crazy. The judge is not going to like it."

Both Morales and Willie gave Charles a sidelong look, followed by a direct glance at each other. Morales nodded almost imperceptibly, and Willie turned confidentially to Charles.

"You know, that night before she died, he was here."

"I knew that. Monique told everyone he was here."

"Right, but this is what happened. He come down out of there about nine o'clock, and his face was all funny-white and sweaty. I'm telling you, he looked like—like that wall. But I didn't act like anything's strange, because that's this job, right? And he says to me, 'I checked for the leaks up there.' And I says, like everything's normal you know, 'Oh yeah. You checked for leaks, huh?' And he says, 'Yeah, I killed her—I mean, *called* her, and she says there's leaks, so I come to check.' And I'm like, that's weird, and he left and the next morning Claire tells me she's dead."

Charles and Willie stared at each other.

"And you know," Willie continued. "He come back over after she died, when there's nobody there, and he's up there for hours, and when he leaves, he comes up close to me here and he says, 'Be careful what you say to anybody. You don't say nothin' about her apartment, or me, or anything I ever said to you. Otherwise, someday you might be working night shift all alone and something bad might happen to you.' "

In the silence that followed, Merriweather arrived in the lobby, too full of his courtroom news to wait. He announced to all three that Becker had been arrested, and Willie, who was delighted to hear it, repeated his story for Merriweather. But before any of them had a chance to digest these mutually startling disclosures, the broker appeared, leading an unctuously smiling young couple with two small children in tow, followed shortly by Morris and Merrit, who—strangest of all—were holding hands. Charles led the group to the Braithwaites' door.

Their noisy entry magnified the domestic disorder inside to chaotic levels. Ellen and Jane were decorating the Christmas tree, their faces sullen. Stuart and the baby were both screaming. Anne looked worn-out. While the broker discussed with the strangers the possibility of enlarging the living room, Merriweather paced, to the extent that the small room permitted pacing, crammed as it was with people, the piano, and the Christmas tree. Merrit and Morris settled as unobtrusively as possible on the sofa to wait for the apartment seekers to finish their business, while the Braithwaites and Merriweather suppressed their intense curiosity about the two of them—painful curiosity, in Merriweather's case. He could not resist looking at them whenever he thought they would not notice. Charles and Anne, however, masters of polite oversight, ignored them and turned their attention to the broker's couple, who continued to smile without cause and assured Charles and Anne that it was completely normal, entirely expectable, that their two little ones were crying.

"Why," Charles asked Morris innocently, while the couple examined the bedrooms, "do people nowadays keep trying to convince each other that things are normal? That's what happens on those chat rooms where someone confesses to murder. They all tell each other how normal and understandable it is."

The couple and their children circled the apartment only once before making up their minds on the spot. They would buy at the asking price.

"You could probably close mid-January," said the broker.

"As long as we agree that Anne can't move for another month after that," Charles added.

"No problem!" the man said. "But you don't mind if we send in an architect and a couple of contractors to start looking around, taking a few measurements, right?"

"No problem," Anne and Charles said.

"When did it happen," Charles said, pulling brandy and glasses from a cabinet after the visitors had left, "that buying an apartment came to mean, inevitably, architects and contractors instead of a couple of coats of paint or maybe, if the place was really dilapidated, a few tiles. All these people are planning to spend another hundred thousand or so."

"Much more," said Anne, handing drinks around. "And they buy everything new to go in it, too. Imagine having all that money at their age. Let's call the lawyer and see about the contract."

"No, wait," Merriweather burst out, after a fortifying sip. "Things happened in court today." He told the tale from beginning to end, stopping only to permit punctuating exclamations. Charles followed up with Willie's odd new revelation. There was long discussion of the evidentiary value of a Freudian slip, with Anne—who was near tears—arguing that anyone who heard the story would conclude, correctly, that Becker had murdered Lizzie. Merriweather, however, thought that Becker's later threat against Willie promised to carry more weight in court; the Freudian slip could at most establish guilty feelings, not actual guilt, and Becker may have felt guilty without actually having murdered her. For example, perhaps he felt that she died because he had upset her greatly. Even if that were true, it wouldn't make him a real murderer. In any event, Willie's story supported Josephine Slevinski's. Becker had surely known that Lizzie was dead, or dying, when he left her that last night.

"And as to the will," Merriweather wound up, "Josephine Slevinski's statement that she signed the will in Lizzie's absence, in fact when Lizzie was already dead, just about settles things—unless anyone comes up with a devastating attack on her credibility, which seems improbable at this point. So Anne definitely inherits Lizzie's apartment."

"That's why he killed her, I suppose," Anne said. "He was in a hurry to sell it. He was like us: he couldn't pay to keep it any longer." Anne could not yet rejoice at being an heiress, knowing that her benefactress had probably been murdered. Such a source of riches undermined her most fundamental prejudice—that she was fully entitled to all the good things life offered her and that her possession of them was always innocent.

"It's not clear that he did kill her, and so far no one has even accused him of intentional homicide," Merriweather said. "But even if he did, that isn't why you're getting the apartment. You would have gotten it anyway."

"Of course he murdered her," Anne said, "and that's why I'm getting the apartment. She might have lived years longer, you know. I feel so strange, so bad. Willie must have known it all along, but he was too scared to say anything. And, anyway, she never intended me to have her apartment. She didn't even know she owned it. Becker robbed her to get it for himself, and it's an accident that I get the stolen property instead of him."

Ellen, who had read about longevity in the *Guinness Book of Records*, agreed that Lizzie might have lived much longer.

"Becker didn't see why he had to make a big sacrifice just so she could have a little more time," said Charles. "In his mind, she'd overstayed her lease."

"We knew weeks ago that Becker was here, for the first time in years, on the night she died," said Anne. "Wasn't that a tip-off? But the thought never crossed my mind that he'd harmed her, even after we knew he'd robbed another old woman. We knew he was squeezing her. We knew she hated him and was afraid of him. But I never stopped thinking that she had it good. I thought she was so lucky, to be at home with caretakers instead of sent off to a nursing home, to live so long. But she was deprived, impoverished, and forced into total dependence on someone who finally murdered her to take what she had. And here we were, seeing every terrible thing that happened to her as just what's to be expected when you're a hundred and three, as though she had no rights at all, because she'd gotten so old."

"That's exactly what the judge said," Merriweather put in.

"What bothers me," said Charles, "is that if someone had bothered to slap Becker's hand years ago, maybe things wouldn't have escalated."

"Charles, we don't have a right to any of this. It makes me feel guilty and ashamed. I barely gave her the time of day. I hardly ever visited her. She asked me over and over to come, and I went twice, maybe three times, in fifteen years. If I'd been more . . . neighborly . . ."

"Well, but strictly speaking," Merriweather interjected, somewhat irrelevantly in Anne's opinion, "no one ever deserves the good things they get—health or love or money, whatever. They're always gifts. They're always unmerited."

Now it was Merrit's turn to agree, thinking of her own undeserved good fortune. "It's all right if you didn't deserve it, Anne," she said.

"It isn't," said Anne. "I stood by for years while she was pinched, starved, terrorized, then murdered—and was never even curious enough to ask how things were going. It never occurred to me that there could be anything to tell. I actually complained to her about my problems."

"True," said Morris. "But the one who understood all that best was Lizzie Miller."

"Right," Charles said.

"Exactly," said Merriweather.

"Besides, Anne," Charles said. "You were neighborly. You took over candles in the blackout. You got groceries for her during the big blizzard, and went over and sat with her one day when Claire got stuck in the subway. It was only two or three times, but it was enough to let her know that you were there for her in case she needed something."

"That's it," said Merrit. "She just needed to know that someone was there. She knew you would know what her wishes were, and no one else would. She was actually being practical, I think, under the circumstances, in leaving this gift-giving to your judgment."

But Anne was not to be comforted. Merriweather thought about trying again, but was uncertain whether he should. He could see Anne's point, and, besides, the rector had recently been telling him how convincing guilty people not to feel that way doesn't help them. Unless they face up to being guilty, how can they feel forgiven? How can they resolve to change? And even if you talk them out of feeling guilty for the moment, they're going to wake up alone at night and face it then. He began a somewhat confused explanation of this, but no one was interested except Merrit, and she was too distracted to listen for long.

"I don't understand anything, Mommy," Ellen said.

"We probably don't have to move," said Anne, "because Lizzie seems to have left us her apartment in her will. We feel bad that we never found out about her troubles and never tried to help her, since she has been so good to us."

"Are we going to live in her apartment?"

"No, sweetie," Anne replied. She and Charles would discuss it later, but he'd certainly think it best to sell the place.

"I wonder how long this will all drag on in court," said Charles.

"The estate business won't take so terribly long," Merriweather said. "This judge is known for moving things along, and now that the 1998 will is going to be thrown out, the estate is actually not complicated, except that some of the property is missing. They won't need to establish where it all is for you to have what they know about. The criminal case is another matter, but it won't affect you."

"Where shall *we* live?" Merrit asked Morris privately, but Jane heard.

"Together?" she asked skeptically.

The grown-ups were as embarrassed as they were curious.

Merrit said, "You tell." And Morris announced, his unwonted embarrassment leavened by a hint of smugness: "That's what we came to tell you before Greg upstaged us. We're going to get married." Ellen giggled, and the others responded only with noncommittal muttering. "Don't fall all over yourselves congratulating us," Morris said. He put an arm around Merrit's shoulder and patted it, which at least had the effect of convincing everyone that they were not joking.

Anne looked puzzled, and then as though she would like to laugh, but Charles gave Morris a baleful look. "Are you telling me—mind the children, Morris—you mean? . . ."

Merrit nodded. "Yes, that's what he's telling you. That's right, Charles. So you see, everything's all right. We're going to get married in a few weeks." And she and Morris couldn't help breaking into smiles.

"But what about Lily?"

"In view of the circumstances," Morris replied, "she has broken our engagement, although she insists that I did."

Unconvincing congratulations from Merriweather ("Excellent news"), who looked wistful, and Anne ("You're both lucky, only I think neither of you knows it") resolved the conversational impasse. The talk turned casual, although somewhat stilted, and then quickly resolved into good-byes. Merriweather announced that he had better be going, and Merrit and Morris stood up to go when he did.

For the first time, Anne gave Merriweather a good-bye kiss, which he received clumsily. She and Merrit embraced, but Merrit had not looked Anne in the eye since telling the news. Charles held Morris back while Merrit went across the hall into his apartment.

"What are you doing, Morris? Is this for the child? I couldn't quarrel with you on that, but I don't find any of it as funny as you seem to. You surprise me a little."

"Charles, you don't understand. I love Merrit. I always have—for years—and I shudder to think how close I came to marrying Lily, which would have been a marriage right out of a Henry James novel."

"But this sounds crazy. There's no lead-up to this."

"There is a lead-up. I just never talked about it. I couldn't, because I was going to marry Madame Merle."

"Madame Merle didn't marry anybody."

"That's not the point. The point is that there were deep plots going on in Lily's head that I wasn't in on. I'm still not. Anyway, I was already trying to talk to Lily about canceling, but she turned out to be slippery. I couldn't ever pin her down to the subject. Then I heard the news from Merrit about the baby—best news I ever had."

"And what about Merrit?"

"Well, I can't say she fell in love with me fifteen years ago, but there was always something going on between us. And recently she . . . she had an open mind. Actually, she says, what made it possible was the whole combination of events. the breakup of one more unworkable affair, seeing her shrink, and being forced to be around me so often that she got to know me in spite of herself. The strangest part of it is that she got friendly with Lily, who apparently talked about me so much that it affected her attitude. She keeps saying that Anne's sickness changed her, too. Anyway, she changed. I think, well, I don't want to sound immodest, but I think she really . . ."

"Loves you?"

"Yeah."

"Does she say she does?"

"Yeah."

"Then she does. You're awfully lucky, Morris. Do you know how lucky you are?"

"Oh yeah. She's everything. She's gorgeous, she laughs, she's more than smart—she really thinks, really digs into a subject. She doesn't settle for what's on the surface. I mean, she's really not a conventional mind. And she's got a good heart."

"You don't need to convince me. I'm glad for you, that you finally figured it out, but I'm having a little bit of a hard time with this—remembering how you used to talk about her. I hope Lily is okay."

"She's pretty upset. But Lily never was in love with me. I don't really understand what she was up to. She's angry, but she's not heartbroken. So I don't feel as guilty as she thinks I should."

After Morris returned home, he and Merrit sat at his kitchen table to talk things over. They had been immersed in talk for days, spending long hours together or on the telephone between Morris's lab and Merrit's desk. There was still so much to be planned and understood that a prodigious amount of talk, they felt, was necessary. They had to cover everything from the number of bedrooms they would need to the compatibility of their political opinions. They had to learn their depths and shallows, and adjust to the weight of someone leaning on them, which, it turned out, was easier than adjusting to the ease of being able to rely on another person's strengths. The discovery that someone else's life had become as full of intimate and urgent interest as their own was gratifying, even exciting.

In a pause, Morris stared at the ceiling, contemplating, and Merrit gazed around the shabby old kitchen, looking at all the cabinet doors, with their fresh paint and their promise of intimate and satisfying contents.

"The sexual frustration of that poor woman's life is hard to imagine," Merrit said, "especially added to all the other frustrations. Imagine—she had no one from the 1940s on. Sixty years of abstinence." She stood and began opening cabinet doors randomly, discovering, to her surprise, that most were empty.

Her eye lit on the knob of a little door, or panel, in the wall next to the table, under the window, and she began pulling at it.

"What's this?" she said. "I think it's painted shut."

Morris looked at it thoughtfully, and took his own turn tugging at the knob ineffectively. Then he sliced at the seams of the panel with a table knife.

"Anne said this is some kind of potato-storage thing," he said.

"Let's get it open then. We'll put potatoes in it."

Morris, energized by the prospect of sharing potato storage with Merrit, pulled more vigorously on the knob.

"I'm afraid I'll pull it right off," he said, ceasing his efforts and staring at it.

Merrit got another table knife, and they attempted to ease the door open from both sides simultaneously, failed, then pulled again on the knob, but nothing moved. Morris then turned the knob, which did nothing. Finally, he absentmindedly turned the knob in a full circle, and felt a catch being released. The door then opened easily, like a tiny oven.

"It stays cold in here, I guess. And here're some really shriveled nine-month-old potatoes. Smells nasty. Nothing else in here. Wait. Here's some kind of hole in the wall . . ."

Morris pulled out two small wooden boxes and a long, bulging envelope. One box held wadded-up flannel pockets and glassine envelopes that contained jewelry, along with yellowed appraisal slips from the diamond district dating from the 1950s to the 1970s. The other held letters, papers, and scribbled-over scraps of paper. The envelope was crammed with old brokerage and bank statements, canceled checks, and receipts, along with a small blue envelope, marked BANK DEPOSIT BOX in pencil. It contained a little key. They gathered up these treasures and rushed back to the Braith-waites', where they poured it all out on the table.

The jewelry was valuable, even according to the 1970s appraisals. It would be worth much more now, Anne thought. Some seemed gaudy; some Anne thought lovely. The most modern piece was from the 1920s and some were considerably older. Slips of paper tucked in with each piece established that most had come to Lizzie from her mother and aunts, who had had them from their mothers, aunts, and grandmothers. There were diamonds, rubies, sapphires, pearls that had peeled from the humidity—all set in brooches, rings and earrings, necklaces, a tiara, hat pins, and a few strange pieces whose use Anne could not guess: the collected finery of Lizzie's female ancestors, which had ended in the hands of their only sur-viving heir. The canceled checks were made out to the church, neigh-borhood merchants, and an insurance company. The letters, at a hasty glance, seemed prosaic—none from lovers, none from soldiers off at war. They were from girlfriends in the country or long-dead relatives upstate. The brokerage-house statements showed that Lizzie had retained control of some investments, which had swelled greatly in value over the years. There was a life insurance policy, which named Anne Braithwaite as bene-ficiary.

"Are we rich?" Jane asked her stunned parents.

"Why didn't any of the caretakers ever get curious and open that drawer?" Morris wondered. "Or maybe they did and just didn't see any-thing but potatoes. They'd have no reason to stick their hand up in a hole in the side of the wall. But you could easily do that from a wheelchair. You'd be at exactly the right height, just sitting at the kitchen table. What really puzzles me is why she'd put all this in the potato bin and not tell anybody where it was. She had no reason to think anyone would ever find it. Notice, she was very careful to make sure someone knew where her will was."

Charles added, after they had carefully examined each scrap and slip of paper, "I'll bet Becker figured she had some jewelry, and wondered what had happened to it. This must be what he was looking for, feeling the walls that night."

"His mother would have known about the jewelry," said Anne. "Even I knew she had some. Women notice what jewelry other women have, and they tell each other things like that. Maybe his mother told him that some-day they'd inherit some valuable jewelry, and finally he desperately needs cash and goes looking for something he can hock fast. It's remarkable, really, that Lizzie managed to keep it from him."

"Oh! Look!" Merrit cried, holding up the large manila envelope that had held most of the papers. "The postmark is April 15—this year!"

"Ah, what a shame. The poor old lady," said Morris. "She put it all in the potato bin the day she died. This envelope came in the mail that day and was lying out, so she used it to carry things. Remember, he called and said he was coming over, and something he said made her guess he wanted money. So she took all this stuff and stuck it in the potato bin, and then she died. She never had a chance to tell anyone what she'd done. He ransacked the place after she was dead, but he never found anything. I wonder if he tried to open the potato bin. If you thought it was stuck, you'd figure the old lady was too weak to open it."

The first thing to do, they agreed, was to tell Merriweather, and while Charles and Morris went off to call him, Anne took Merrit aside.

"Maybe you'll think I have no right to ask, but I have to, Merrit. You *want* to marry Morris? This isn't just getting a father for the baby, is it?"

"I want to marry Morris and no one but Morris. I don't know why I didn't feel this way all along," said Merrit. "Why didn't this ever happen to me before? You know, he says he never wanted to marry anyone but me. I wasn't very nice, was I? I have a lot to make up to him."

"You amaze me. But don't worry. Before long, you're going to remember that he has flaws, you'll have a baby, and you'll start thinking you don't have anything to make up to him. Oh, but I'm suddenly so happy—in spite of all of Lizzie's miseries. I can't help it. You and Morris are getting married and having a baby. I'm not dead. We don't have to move. Of course you have to live in the neighborhood, you know."

"Oh yes! That was our first decision—that we had to live in Morning-side Heights."

When the jewels and papers were delivered to the court, Becker's lawyer protested vigorously that the Braithwaites had had them all along and had concealed them. It was just too coincidental, he protested, that all this had been discovered only after Josephine Slevinski gave testimony strongly supporting Anne's right to inherit. But today Merriweather had brought along Charles and Anne, who came into court leaning on Charles's arm, and Morris and Merrit; and all four testified to the manner in which these riches had been discovered, hidden in what was formerly Lizzie's kitchen and then brought to Charles and Anne. Justice Jacobs did not pretend to suspend judgment as to whether they were telling the truth. She thought all these witnesses were reliable and that there had been no concealment of the riches, and noticed, as no one else had, that the Braithwaites, and not Becker, would eventually, most probably, be entitled to Morris's rent payments. "Do we have any record of any such amounts being paid in or out of Miss Miller's accounts?" she asked Becker's lawyers. "We'll have to make sure the district attorney is informed of all these developments. Now, who is Mr. Martinez, Mr. Merriweather? He has something to tell me too?"

Willie arose, and, after throwing a nervous glance at Merriweather, went and sat in the witness stand. "Well, it's a little bit weird, Judge," Willie began, weighed down by a sense that his story would sound silly in this stately setting. But after initially stumbling, he proceeded to describe his interchange with Becker on the night Lizzie died, fluently, in precisely the terms in which he had told the story to Charles. Justice Jacobs, like everyone else who had heard the story, did not react immediately, but sat silent, looking baffled. The same vague, perplexed expression that Justice Jacobs wore, Anne noticed, appeared on the faces of Becker's lawyer, the clerk, and others present who were hearing the story for the first time.

"What did *you* make of that strange slip of the tongue, Mr. Martinez?" Justice Jacobs asked at length.

Willie shrugged, half embarrassed. "I thought he musta killed her."

"You go to the D.A. and tell him all this, please. The clerk will tell you where to go and who to ask for."

"Okay, Judge."

But Willie's story was not the last shock that Lizzie Miller's friends and neighbors were to experience on her account. The records that Josephine Slevinski had removed from Becker's office established that Becker had managed, illegally, to arrange a pauper's burial for Lizzie Miller and that her remains were interred in Potter's Field. Made suspicious of the worst by Willie, the D.A. quickly moved to have them disinterred so that an autopsy could be performed. Based on the autopsy results, which left no doubt that her death, through suffocation, had been brought about by unnatural causes, Becker was indicted for intentional homicide.

# 40

THE SMITH-SMYTHES heard from Jeffrey Mayhew that Merrit was pregnant and intended to marry Morris Malcolm. Jeffrey Mayhew had heard it from Merrit, who wrote him a letter begging him to understand and not feel injured. But he did feel injured. At first, he even suspected Merrit of having lied to him about her infertility. Teresa, however, dissuaded Jeffrey on that point. She knew that for months Merrit had really believed herself to be infertile. This cooled him off by a few degrees but did little to diminish his overall sense that Merrit had pulled a bait-and-switch on him. Had she done it just for some fun, or was it possible that she simply could not face the inevitable strains in a marriage to a younger man? Whichever, she had acted contemptibly, and he was furious. Merrit's letter had alluded vaguely to what might have happened had he not backed off when she told him she was infertile. But Jeffrey was not to be pacified by being told that he himself had contributed half, or maybe even more than half, to the breakup of their affair—not yet, anyway. And it seemed undeniable that Merrit preferred Morris to Jeffrey, which Teresa found incomprehensible.

"I'm going to talk to her," she told Chalmers, pulling on a long black coat and black leather gloves. "She needs to hear sense from someone. Besides, Brendan is so concerned. He begged me to talk to her. This situation is a lot more complicated than we've realized."

"I wouldn't let him put you in the middle of this. Anyway, what kind of sense can you talk to her? She's pregnant with Malcolm's baby."

"That doesn't mean she has to saddle herself with a charade of a marriage to one of the most unpleasant men I've ever met."

"What are you doing?" Teresa asked Merrit a few minutes later, sitting on the antique sofa in the living room of Merrit's small, tasteful apartment.

Merrit responded, stricken, "You mean with my book? It's terrible, I know. I haven't written a word for months."

"No, no! I mean your marriage. Why are you marrying a man like this?"

Merrit blushed deep scarlet. She hadn't known Teresa had heard the news. She and Teresa had traded negative opinions of Morris not so many weeks ago, and just now Merrit had no wish to try to disabuse Teresa of her misimpressions; the story was too long and too hard to explain. Instead, she attempted to sidetrack her with the obvious practicalities.

"You may not realize—I'm pregnant."

"I know that. But that doesn't mean you have to marry some second-rate mouse scientist no one has ever heard of, without even a permanent job, whom you don't even like. You could raise the child without him. You can do it yourself, and the whole world will be on your side. You should talk to women who've had experiences similar to yours—women who've been through this. You'll get more confidence in yourself."

"I don't think I want to talk to women who've had similar experiences," Merrit said irritably. Teresa angered her by saying such things about Morris, but, still, she would rather not have to explain her change of heart.

"Oh, Merrit! Really! Or if you insist on marrying someone, why didn't you go to Jeffrey? I know he was angry, but he'd have come around if you played it right. I'm sure of it."

"I don't want to marry Jeffrey, and anyway you're wrong. Jeffrey would never marry a woman who's pregnant with another man's child. You don't know him if you think otherwise."

"All right—whatever. Forget Jeffrey. He's not what I came here to talk to you about. Anyway, he's not your only option."

"Teresa, please. You don't understand. Look, I . . ."

"Listen to me, Merrit. I have something to tell you—something you won't want to hear but really *must know.*" Teresa stood and folded her arms across her chest, fixing on Merrit the kind of penetrating look that, in films, reduces its object to intimidated, wondering silence. Merrit was mystified and aghast at Teresa's air of melodrama, but could not help feeling curious.

"What?" she asked.

"Brendan McGarry is an extraordinary man. I've spent a lot of time talking with him in the past week."

"Really? I thought you hardly knew him."

"We've grown close very quickly. We're very much alike, and he needs a strong woman in his life."

"I guess you are very much alike, aren't you?" Merrit wondered why she had never before questioned her intimacy with Teresa, when at the moment she found herself almost regretting it wholeheartedly.

"Did you hear what I said?"

"Oh. Oh no. You can't be serious." Merrit was so embarrassed by Teresa's affected manner that she could not look her in the eye or devise any response that would cut off what she began to realize, with a sense of nausea, was coming.

"I've hesitated to say this to you."

"I'm expecting Morris in twenty minutes. Perhaps we'd better end this conversation," said Merrit.

"He wants you back—I'm sure of it. Sybilla is simply too young, too weak. He married her on the rebound. You don't realize how your breakup devastated him."

"It didn't."

"Merrit, you always underestimate yourself. Look, Brendan says right out that he's realized he'd rather live with you and Malcolm's child than with Sybilla and his own. He never wanted to be a father, you know. He was honest with you about that. If he has to live with a child, he'd rather it was a child some other man is responsible for. Don't you see? This would solve all the problems."

"Poor Sybilla."

"She's young. She has time to recoup. Be honest with yourself, Merrit. This is what you want. How could you not? At least talk to Brendan. His feelings for you haven't changed."

"Teresa, you can tell Brendan I think he's a joke. No, don't say that. Just tell him I'm happy with the choices I've made."

"But that's not true, and no one will believe it," said Teresa. "Do you have any idea what a laughingstock you'll make of yourself if you go ahead with this marriage? Howard Kappell said to me last night, 'Now that I realize how desperate she is, *I'm* going to propose to her.'"

"And what did you say to him," Merrit asked, "when he said that?" She had an idea that Teresa hadn't exactly rushed to her defense, which irked her, but Howard's nonsense didn't.

"Look, Merrit, your friends cannot watch you destroy your life and say nothing. Morris Malcolm is a bad-tempered, bad-mannered nobody. He's unsophisticated. He's not on your level. Not only is he not an intellectual, but it's not like marrying some lawyer or banker, who might at least have personality or money. People would understand that. No one will understand this. Think!"

Merrit declined to think, however, and, trembling from a combination of suppressed laughter and outrage, told Teresa that, actually, she cared a great deal for Morris and thought that things had turned out fortunately for her and for the child. "And I'm sorry," she said, rising, "but I won't hear or say anything more on the subject." It was odd, thought Merrit, how cool people, people whose usual modes were affectless sarcasm or political puritanism, descended into fake, goopy sentiment when they tried to deal with matters of the heart.

Later, Teresa and Chalmers said to each other, "She's sacrificing herself for the baby," and wrote her off.

Morris appeared at Merrit's door an hour after Teresa left, and so enjoyed the story of her visit that he looked forward to an opportunity to greet the Smith-Smythes as a couple. Merrit had changed lately, but not enough to contemplate such an encounter without inward shudders. She was glad to be able to assure him that the Smith-Smythes would soon be leaving the country to lead a year-long seminar in Prague that would be attended by international stars in political theory from all over the globe. The subject was Text and Terrorism.

Morris brought news from the lab that they had been waiting for, although they had been so confident of the outcome, for nearly a week, that today's success inspired mere smiles rather than cheers. Not only was the Duckworth theory all but dead, but it had been disproved in a manner that Duckworth had not anticipated in the *Biologica* article that had used Morris's data. Morris's independence and originality were no longer in question, and his solid work was sure to bring him recognition and the kind of tenured position he had been aiming at.

An e-mail from Joey Delano later that evening confirmed what Morris had suspected for some time: that Joey had a contact in Morris's Columbia lab who sent Joey up-to-the-minute bulletins. Thus, this final outcome had long been knowledgeably anticipated by his former colleagues at the Leland Center. Meanwhile, Joey had been amusing himself by terrorizing Sam with hints that Morris's paper was going to be so different from what Duckworth had anticipated, and so differently reasoned, that Duckworth would be exposed for what he was, and so would the people who had put him up to this. Sam had kept her nerve through all that. Now, however, the final news from Morris's lab was having extraordinary repercussions at the Leland Center.

"Strange developments!" Joey's e-mail began. "You remember when you warned Sam that she might get burned in the end instead of you?"

Morris, reading a printout of the e-mail to Merrit, scowled. "He only knows all that because Barbara, the secretary there, listened in on the phone call. Listen to the rest:

'She never forgot, and I reminded her periodically just as a kind of favor to you, so when she heard about this nice new idea of yours (hey— congrats!) she really flipped. So you're not going to believe this, but she has publicly accused Schmidt of having stolen your data and given it to Duckworth. He did it out of jealousy, she says. Do you believe it?

But really what happened is that when she kept pressuring him to marry her and really kind of harassing him and calling his wife and all that, he started hinting around that if she didn't lay off he'd tell everyone that *she* had done it. Then she got scared and decided that she could both get revenge and get herself off the hook if she blamed him. She's going around blowing your horn, and saying how wonderful your work was. Now Schmidt is starting to blame her, but it's too late. Everyone believes her. They think he was sexually exploiting her. It is all so, so terminally weird.

Pasternak says he's going write a letter on your behalf to the editors at *Biologica*. And everyone wants you to please come home as soon as possible.'

"I don't know about this," Morris continued. "That guy is always trouble from the word go. People might think I put him up to this."

"I don't think so," Merrit said. "And if Pasternak writes that letter, then you're entirely clear. *Biologica* will have to run their own explanation letter. They'll have to do something. If they hadn't been such fools, none of this would have happened."

"You're probably right," said Morris. "Not even Joey is going to derail things at this point. And now that I've got all that under control, we've got a lot of decisions to make—where to live, who gets the side by the window. All that."

"I've been thinking about nothing but those things," Merrit said.

"What happened to your book?" he asked. "Shouldn't you think about that sometimes?"

"I've decided to do a different book, something more psychological, less historical—but I'm still not sure how it's going to work. I simply can't go on with fornication and bastardy."

"Been there, done that?" said Morris, and Merrit looked at him out of the corner of her eye, not sure whether he was making fun. Although she was often unsure of Morris's meanings and intentions, she felt confident that she knew him. He knew her, too, and she now understood that this was why they had so readily developed a sexual affinity. Dr. Freilich had pooh-poohed the hypothesis she had initially proposed—that she felt sexually released because she regarded Morris as her inferior. "But you feel no sexual release with a man whom you regard as your inferior," he had said in a rare expansive moment. "The opposite is true for you, as for many women. And in any case, you don't really believe that he is your inferior. You're tempted to depreciate him defensively, but your heart isn't in it anymore. No, I think the real story is that you feel exposed to him, uncovered emotionally, and this excites you."

Merrit was all but convinced that this was right. In her twenties, when she first met Morris, she had found direct emotional contact with men impossible and had constructed a social persona that she hid behind even in love affairs. Morris, who had a vocation of looking for hidden realities as well as a Midwesterner's impatience with social façades, immediately penetrated Merrit's. Finding that unendurable, she had scorned him and set in motion the cycle of vituperation that had continued until so recently. How obvious it all was, she thought.

Now Merrit was learning to accept what she knew about Morris, which was a great deal, if not everything. He wasn't as hard to get along with as she had expected. His bad tempers turned out to be, for the most part, traceable to specific grievances, which were easily resolvable. He was remorseful about past unkindnesses; he no longer attacked and criticized her. He was musical, as she had seen long ago and ignored. His thinking was cultivated—and she had used his lack of pretension as a means of concealing that from herself! He had more thoughtful things to say about the transformation of science in the past fifty years than anyone she had ever met.

"I have a lot of important things on my mind just now," Merrit continued, resisting an impulse to defend herself against an accusation that she was abandoning her work. "I'm too preoccupied to give enough attention to writing. When I begin again, I intend to be sure that I'm doing the work I really want to do."

But Morris was not accusing her. Far from it: he thought it quite natural that she should be distracted by their upcoming marriage, a baby on the way, and the practicalities of setting up a new, shared household. He liked her thoughtfulness about it all. It was very satisfying—even better than Anne, Morris told himself. Merrit was more rational. With Anne, you sometimes got flashes of insight, but just as often you got intellectual and emotional gobbledygook. Merrit was just right for him, even when it had come to discussing the Duckworth rigmarole. Unlike Anne, she understood a great deal of it. She's really smarter than Anne, he thought with a sense of revelation—and she was so sympathetic, really sweet about it all.

"Anyway," Morris said, "it looks like this whole miserable Duckworth episode is about over."

"How awful it was," Merrit said. "And it could have ended so differently."

"Yes and no," said Morris. "The scientific process lends itself badly to his kind of shenanigans. That's why I love it—it keeps people straight, and people who aren't straight don't usually find it very attractive. You get a bad egg or two, of course. But even competitive nastiness can't do much damage in science, as long as it's scientific competitiveness. It's when money and patents and selling drugs and calls from the TV networks get mixed up in everything that you have trouble."

"Then there's trouble, you know."

"That's what I'm saying. There's trouble for a while—until people make some fixes, which inevitably they will in the long run. But this Duckworth sleaze was definitely going to be exposed in the short term—a year, ten years at the most. Of course, if it had taken ten years, or even five, it could have tanked my career, but that was unlikely. There're too many curious people out there who just want to know what the truth is." And Morris smiled with satisfaction at the way the world worked.

"You wouldn't still be so optimistic about science if things had gone the other way and your career had really tanked." Merrit could share his smile but not his attitude.

"Oh yes I would! I don't understand why some people would rather think the world is a bad place than admit that they had a bit of personal bad luck or that they screwed up."

"That's an essentially religious outlook, Morris. You're just insisting that the world is good. There's nothing particularly scientific or rational about that attitude."

"I can see that you and I have to have some long talks," said Morris, who always liked a good argument about where rational belief ended and arbitrary faith began.

# 41

LILY, STILL GREATLY perturbed several days after her confrontation with Morris, visited Jonathan and told him the whole story of the end of her engagement. He listened with eager attention.

"Extraordinary!" he exclaimed, and Lily was angry that he showed so little sympathy.

"I'll tell you, Lil," he said. "I know this is hard on you, but I have a bit of an idea about where Morris was coming from. I never really understood this engagement. I could see he wanted out long ago, and I didn't understand why you were ignoring that."

They sat in silence in Jonathan's living room, and Lily remembered watching Morris and Merrit recognize each other at dinner and then talk tensely in this very room, each bending slightly toward the other so that they might quarrel privately. With a sudden enlightenment, she recalled that she, like Howard Kappell, had grasped instantly that the two had a connection of some sort. She had known it, of course, from the beginning—before they did. She had always known that Morris was preengaged, and to whom; that, perhaps, had been part of the attraction. Marriage without the marital emotions had been her object.

"You know, dear," Jonathan said, patting her knee, "not everyone is cut out for matrimony."

"It's better not to be alone, I think."

"In the abstract, maybe, but when you look around at the real options—for me or for you—maybe marriage isn't the way to find company. It could happen that way, but it probably won't."

Lily nodded. "But I don't like being alone all the time."

"I tell you what," said Jonathan. "Why don't you move in here? We're good company; we're really family. You'd have a nice room of your own. We'd both be better off. Sooner or later, you'll forgive Morris and Merrit, and they'll come over to dinner."

Lily, strangely, found her heart soaring, but she restrained her feelings and said only, "It's not a bad idea. I'll think it over. You're not saying this just to be nice, are you?"

"Oh no. I've often thought about something like this, being older than you and more settled. I'd rather not live alone, and you're the person I feel closest to. And if you move in, whenever you want to go out on dates, fly the coop, or get hitched—why, you'll just do it, because we're not going to be married. But if it doesn't happen, you'll still have a home to share with someone and so will I, and that's what we both need."

Lily's feelings told her, unmistakably, that she would rather live with Jonathan than marry Morris. No wonder Morris was angry, she thought, and she was filled with remorse. Perhaps she had been behaving badly, madly even. But what was the nature of this attachment to Jonathan? She recalled her silly high school crush on him. There would be plenty of time to parse this. She needn't say anything to Jonathan about it, not just yet anyhow.

Unlike Lily, Father Merriweather had been afflicted with a real injury to his heart when Merrit and Morris announced their engagement at the Braithwaites' apartment. In solitary misery, he had plodded through the snow back to St. Ursula's. Merrit going to marry Morris, and Morris and Lily breaking it off! Merriweather loved Merrit, and even though he had always known she would never return his feelings, he felt a shock on learning that she loved someone else. He was surprised to see just how wretched this news made him, and, accustomed though he was to his loneliness, he now felt ground down by it. He saw that there was a little gathering at St. Ursula's and remembered with chagrin that it was the evening of the Christmas party in the rectory. He hadn't brought any presents. But he had something to tell that would excuse his thoughtlessness. He was glad to see all the people gathered there. They would listen attentively to the story about Elizabeth Miller, who was, after all, one of their own, whom they had abandoned to age and death but who had reached out and reclaimed them. They'd have to have a memorial service for her. Maybe Charles would sing.

A memorial service was indeed held in the spring, when St. Ursula's re-buried Miss Miller in its own graveyard with a portion of the money it received from Anne Braithwaite, given in accordance with the instructions in Miss Miller's will. Mr. Morales, Willie, Roberto, Claire, Monique, and the other caretakers, who were also recipients of gifts from Anne out of Lizzie's legacy, all attended, as did Victor Marx and several other elderly tenants of 635 West 117th Street, and a large contingent of St. Ursula's parishioners. Charles sang Bach, poignantly, and Merriweather wept from the first note to the last.

Merriweather had attended another Braithwaite performance just a month earlier, when Jane had played Josephine in her school's production of *H.M.S. Pinafore*. What a singer she was! And how could that little sour-puss be such a skilled comic actress? Her parents, Merriweather observed, sat through the performance open-mouthed, as surprised and impressed as he was. "I didn't know she sang and acted too," he had said to them at intermission, and they had replied that they didn't, either. How two sensitive parents, who were both musicians, could be so unaware of their own child's talents and interests, Merriweather could not comprehend.

The Braithwaites moved into Lizzie's apartment that summer, and for the first time, Ellen and Stuart had rooms of their own. The Braithwaites also bought Mrs. Schaffner's house in Putnam County. Anne did not see how they could back out after Mrs. Schaffner had trusted them for so long, and, besides, Anne argued, it would be wonderful for the children to have a country house to visit in the summer—and what better investment than real estate? Anne also insisted to Mrs. Schaffner that she need not be in a hurry to move out. They liked knowing that someone was there looking out for the place, Anne said, and Mrs. Schaffner did not mind staying after Charles took on responsibility for the nuisances of taxes and assessments and found reliable help for the repairs, maintenance, mowing, and snow shoveling. The Braithwaites have never yet stayed in the house—the subject has become something of a marital sore spot—although Anne speaks glowingly, and often, of summering there before long. Morris drives Charles upstate to tend to the place every couple of months.

Within the year, Mary O'Reilly was evicted, her furniture carried off by two burly men, who gently pushed past her at the door, ignoring her terrified cries, and she herself was last seen screaming at her social worker in the street, with an ambulance standing by. They had a place for her, said Willie, some place where there would be supervision, but she didn't want to go. After this horrifying scene, the pace of change in the building and in Morningside Heights seemed to slow. Vic and Bart began to think that, after all, the way things were going, they could afford to stay. "Nothing like a murder in the building to keep out the gentry," Charles commented. The new people in the building appeared to back off from their efforts at reform. Two members of the board, in fact, had resigned after Mary O'Reilly was evicted, and Mr. Morales hinted that harsh words had been spoken at a board meeting. Until they saw it, they didn't know, those silly people, how terrible it was when people lost their homes. When they had to watch it happen, they learned they had no stomach for it. Some of them moved out before the year was over. The young businessman on the seventh floor, for one, seemed to have vanished.

In fact, it was possible that the building and neighborhood were remaking the newcomers, molding them to their own ways rather than the other way around. What would the neighborhood be like when the kids were big? Not much different from now, Anne predicted, or from thirty years ago, when they had been kids. "You watch," she said.

# MORNINGSIDE

## HEIGHTS

### A Reader's Guide

Cheryl Mendelson

# A Conversation with Cheryl Mendelson

Q: Although *Morningside Heights* is your first novel, you've written a previous nonfiction book—*Home Comforts: The Art and Science of Keeping House*—that was a nonfiction bestseller. What prompted you to switch genres, especially after having been so successful with nonfiction?

A: Actually, *Home Comforts* was the detour. I had been writing fiction, both short stories and novels, most of my adult life, but had never tried to publish any of it. My publications before *Home Comforts* were all essays in scholarly journals that only a few specialists read. When I wrote *Home Comforts*, I didn't think of it as establishing a new career pattern or choice. It was just fun and interesting, and although I had serious intentions of trying to publish it from the outset, I never dreamed it would become as popular as it did. I always pictured it on some dusty out-of-the-way shelf in the back of the bookstore where a few aficionados would find it and think, *Aha! Just what I wanted!*

The experience of succeeding with the reading public, I think, emboldened me to try to publish some of my fiction, and it did so in two ways. First, I got over what you might call the "stage fright" that had always prevented my trying before. My printed words were already out there circulating in public, and I was surviving it. Second, many, many people told me that they liked my writing and liked the way I told the "story" in the first chapter of *Home Comforts*.

People have always told me they like my stories. When I write fiction, I try to combine a plain, clear writing style with story-shaping instincts I learned at home, along with a sense of connection with the listener. In the rural place where I grew up (until age thirteen), television reception was hit-or-miss. Entertainment meant reading or social gatherings that were always amazing storytelling sessions. You grew up listening to adults you knew well shaping stories in front of you for their friends—fascinating, hilarious, moving, and frightening stories created with a variety of techniques. You figured out that a great deal that was offered as truth was really fiction, which was fine as long as the story was good enough and the people in them interesting enough.

Q: Is there any connection between the content of *Home Comforts* and that of *Morningside Heights?*

A: I sat down one afternoon at the end of the publicity period for *Home Comforts* and, without knowing I was going to do it, wrote the first page of *Morningside Heights.* The story just poured out, and only later did I understand the connection between this new novel and *Home Comforts*, which, I should explain, was an attempt to write a twentieth-century housekeeping book modeled after the popular housekeeping books of the nineteenth century, a genre that had died out.

Both books deal with threats to the survival of some part of ordinary middle-class lives and aspirations. *Home Comforts* is really about the middle-class mentality that roots itself in domestic life, home life, a cast of mind that is under great stress in the contemporary world. *Morningside Heights* is about trying to maintain the patterns of middle-class life—with its solid marriages, well-raised children, stable communities, and work aspirations that frequently include a prominent strain of idealism—in the face of all but irresistible social and economic forces that weaken such things. How do you pay the rent, raise your kids right, hold together your marriage, and live meaningfully in a world like the one ours has become?

Q: Tell us a little about Morningside Heights, the New York City neighborhood where the novel is set. Why did you choose to write about it?

A: Morningside Heights (I live there) is a real neighborhood, whose special history presents the dilemmas of the contemporary American middle-class with poignant clarity. It houses a number of extraordinary institutions of religion, art, and learning: Columbia University, one Christian and one Jewish seminary, a huge cathedral, the astonishing Riverside Church, a school of music, and many more. Thus it attracts a large population of ide-alistic and learned people who are economically middle-class—academics, scientists, librarians, editors, artists, musicians, writers, and seminarians and students, plus many more people with all sorts of professions and skills who cherish the atmosphere and the street life of a place where the insti-tutions that define and support the middle class and its values are so promi-nent and powerful. Morningside Heights is a place where many people still think the world makes sense, still experience their own lives as meaningful, and still trust the values and institutions they were raised with to uphold them through life's trials, even as economic and social pressures are un-dermining these faiths.

*Morningside Heights*, therefore, is very much about a particular real place, but the dilemmas of that particular place are simply a crystal-clear instance of problems most middle-class Americans face today. The Braith-waites, musicians who are the emotional center of the book, want to do something with their lives that matters—something besides earn money and work—but they feel their ability to do so contracting; they find their lives constrained more and more by compromises they dislike. They are like us.

Q: Random House has contracted with you to write two more novels set in this neighborhood. Can you tell us how they'll relate to this first novel, or anything else about them to pique our interest?

A: The next two novels pursue love stories through a set of social and eco-nomic circumstances that draw on the themes of the first one. The Braith-waites and other characters from *Morningside Heights* will appear in minor roles in the second, which looks at love across the generations, again from the point of view of social changes in attitudes toward love and marriage and money. This book also explores the morality of divorce in a forty-year marriage, in a tale that crisscrosses two stories of young love. Class and status, barriers to life in the middle-class mold of Morningside Heights, are also barriers to love in a world in which young people are in-creasingly concerned with success.

The third novel returns the Braithwaite family to the center of attention, focusing this time on its younger generation, and in many respects it will read like a coming-of-age story. Each of the three books, however, can be read independently.

# Questions for Discussion

1. Anne Braithwaite is extravagant and feels so entitled to her customary luxuries and privileges that it wouldn't be far wrong to call her spoiled. Is it consistent, then, to describe her also as generous, warm, and empathic? Why or why not?

2. Is Anne's optimism a flaw or a virtue? Is she a likable character?

3. Anne refuses to get a job, insists on staying home to care for her children, and thinks day care is wrong. Both Charles and Anne dislike abortion and divorce. Moreover, despite their politics, both feel entitled to the high status that they are losing as the world changes. Would it be fair to describe them as cultural conservatives? Are the values that guide their private lives consistent or inconsistent with their political left-liberalism? Do you agree or disagree with these values? Do you think your own values are consistent with your political beliefs? Do you identify with Charles and Anne?

4. Merrit thinks her psychotherapy had little or nothing to do with her finally being able to let herself love Morris. Is she right or wrong? Despite her psychotherapy, or at times even because of it, she grows more and more unhappy, until the events described near the end of the book. Would she have been better off if Dr. Freilich had prescribed antidepressants instead of pushing for insights? What's your own view on the effectiveness of psychotherapy as opposed to antidepressants?

5. Morris Malcolm, an atheist who hates religion, worships science, and accepts Darwinian evolution as a scientific given, is a Republican who thinks of himself as a social liberal. Although he very much wants his baby with Merrit, he does not disapprove of abortion per se. And unlike the Braithwaites, he has had many girlfriends and for years lived with someone he refused to marry. Given these significant differences in values and style, what accounts for the depth of friendship that exists among the three of them? Would you find the terms "conservative" or "liberal" helpful in understanding their differences?

6. Is the friendship between the atheistic Braithwaites and Greg Merriweather, an Episcopalian priest, realistic? Is Greg's friendship with Morris realistic?

7. Greg seems to have a number of serious religious doubts, an obviously nonliteral way of reading the Bible, and questions about his vocation. Should he give up the priesthood? What explains why such a gentle, accommodating, sweet-natured, and just plain *good* man would be prone to such aggressive religious doubt? Do you think Greg is a believable character? Have you ever met anyone he reminds you of?

8. Greg thinks, sadly and with compassion, that the Braithwaites and their friends have never really faced up to the fact that someday they have to die. What does he see in them that makes him think so? What connection is the author making between Lizzie's death and the Braithwaites' blindness?

9. In some peculiar way, Becker responds emotionally to Anne when she goes with Charles and the priests to his law office. She gets his attention, and he aims a good deal of his persuasive lying at her—even though she mistrusts him and conceals her real attitude toward him. Why does Becker react to her this way? Father Quincy detests Becker. How would you describe Anne's attitude to Becker? Although the author tells us little of Greg's response to Becker, do you think it would be more like Father Quincy's or like Anne's? Justice Jacobs is patient and calm with Becker. She speaks to him "not unkindly," even though she sees through him completely and, obviously, understands the enormity of his crimes. Given the terrible nature of those crimes, would you prefer that the judge be angrier and more critical—more of a "hanging judge"?

10. Do you blame Lily for agreeing to marry Morris while knowing that she cannot offer him the kind of love and marriage he wants? Do you think she understands her own motives? What is the nature of her feelings for Jonathan Riesbeck? Is their decision to live together, apparently platonically, tragic or happy or something in between?

11. The Braithwaites are saved from being forced out of Morningside Heights by some fairly unlikely events—from Greg's willingness and ability to jump in to help legally and the peculiarity of Lizzie's singling them out as her heirs to the accidental way that they discover what's in the potato bin, and even the strangeness of relying on something like a potato bin. What point is the author making with such obvious insistence on being unrealistic?

12. The author shows, at various points, that her protagonists rely on religion, the insights of psychoanalysis, science, the classical arts, the liberal arts, the ultimate humanity of our legal system, and progressive humanitarian politics—but without realizing it, and without realizing how precarious is the survival of all these institutions and cultural artifacts. With these facts in mind, as well those listed in question 11, what do you make of the suggestion, on the book's last page, that Morningside Heights might be as likely to remake its newcomers as to be remade by them? Of Anne's optimistic confidence that in thirty years Morningside Heights won't be much different, in essentials, from what it is today? Do you know any places in your own life that have changed this way? Have similar changes ever profoundly affected your own life or the life of anyone you know?

PHOTO: © JERRY BAUER

CHERYL MENDELSON received her Ph.D. in philosophy from the University of Rochester and her J.D. from Harvard Law School. She has practiced law in New York City and taught philosophy at Purdue and Columbia universities. She is the author of *Home Comforts: The Art and Science of Keeping House* and the novel *Love, Work, Children.* She lives in New York City with her husband and son.

ABOUT THE TYPE

This book was set in Electra, a typeface designed for
Linotype by W. A. Dwiggins, the renowned type designer
(1880–1956). Electra is a fluid typeface, avoiding the
contrasts of thick and thin strokes that are prevalent in
most modern typefaces.